PATRIOT'S ABOUND

D1519739

Patriot's Abound

A Novel By

John M. Bede III

Rev. date: 06/23/2014

To order additional copies of this book, contact:
Xlibris LLC
1-888-795-4274
www.Xlibris.com
Orders@Xlibris.com
623231

DEDICATED TO

Marine Lance Corporal James T. Reddington, Marine Rifleman
E-Company Third Platoon Second Battalion Fifth Marines
First Marine Division
Fatally wounded, March 23, 1967, Operation
Newcastle, Dai Khuong, South Vietnam

Marine Corporal Joseph J. Bede
Ninth Engineer Battalion Second Marine Division
Nonfatal wounds, August 1967, near Tam Ky,
south of Da Nang, South Vietnam
Joseph, age sixty-six, is retired from the building and
construction industry and is living in upstate New York.

This pair of good friends enlisted in the Marine Corps together.
They were two of the bravest men ever to wear the Eagle, Globe,
and Anchor. Semper Fidelis. When freedom called, they answered,
they were there, and they gave up a lot of their yesterdays so
we could live in peace. Some gave up all of their tomorrows.

CHAPTER ONE

First Lieutenant John M. Braz slowly gazed out the window of the old French taxi. He suddenly realized where he was and became fully aware of his surroundings. The letdown from the previous six months of the last field operation, where constant vigilance becomes second nature in order to stay alive, surely can tire out the best of the young men and women that the CIA uses in its clandestine war on communism and terrorism.

Bangkok, Thailand (French Indochina)
20 December 1959
Office of the Station Chief CIA (Military Attaché)

John hated his last assignment. The CO of his logistical intel group was a major who was a freaking idiot. The only reason John happened to be in this group was his background in architecture and structural engineering. The JOC brass back in the Pentagon were of the mind that they and they alone, with help and with urging *from* the White House, would run these missions because of their superior intellect and influence, thrown in with a good bit of arrogance. Even though John was in the army, his immediate boss was the CIA, and John's loyalty and love of country meant that he obeyed any and all orders of his superiors. His mantra was, above all, "Duty, Honor, Country," and he lived by that saying each day.

First Lieutenant John M. Braz was commissioned an officer after five years in ROTC at the Pennsylvania State University and OCS at Fort Benning, Georgia, US Army Infantry school. Lieutenant Braz became a paratrooper with the Eighty-Second Airborne Division and eventually an army ranger. His ambition was to attain the highest rank possible for as long as his army career would last.

John was something of an enigma to his teachers and higher-ranking and junior officers, the NCO staff, and almost everyone who came to make his acquaintance, for John had an IQ rating of almost genius. Most people he knew or just met him took an instant liking to him. At six foot four inches tall, with bluish-green intelligent eyes, 185 pounds and not an ounce of fat on him, all solid muscle, meat and bone, and handsome to a fault, he honestly didn't realize how good-looking he was, so unobtrusively, it added to his good fortune more often than not. Plus, and a big plus it is, he is wealthy.

John got out of the old wrought iron and wood cage elevator, looked both ways up and down the corridor, determined everything was okay, and proceeded to Andy Lord's office. Andy was the station chief for the CIA and also known as the military attaché, but that title fooled no one in the political stew known as Southeast Asia.

Lt. Col. Andy Lord, about forty-five years old, was an old warrior from the days of Merrill's Marauders (circa 1941). These were the guerrilla fighters that kicked the hell out of the murdering Jap bastards all over the Indonesian peninsula. The accolades for Andy came from the US Army, the Brits, the French, the Australians, and the Chinese.

Pressing the buzzer to the outer office door, John was filled with trepidation, not knowing why Lieutenant Colonel Lord brought him back from Laos.

In his mind, a whirlwind of recent events culminating with the unauthorized killing of two known Vietcong sappers has John a little concerned. But the second Ms. Laura Diskin buzzed him into the outer office, he forgot all that other crap. Laura, of the Chicago Diskins meatpackers and producers of rations for the military, is breathtakingly beautiful, with long dancer's legs, flaming red hair. And a figure that would make a movie star jealous and seriously rich. Needless to say, John was instantly in love or in lust, probably the latter. He had not smelled perfume with such an exciting and sexy bouquet in a long time, He could not help being aroused and started searching frantically for a place to sit down. Greeting Miss Laura with an embarrassed grin and a pink face, he started sweating some.

Laura, laughing as usual, being used to her countenance, offered John to sit in one of the rattan chairs with the overstuffed pillows. He was so grateful he forgot about the arousal in his pants.

"So, Laura, how is he today?" (He and Laura go back a number of years.)

"Is he in a foul mood or fair?"

"No, he's okay but a little bit detached with something on his mind. Gen. Shorty Wells is with him, and the both of them want to speak with you."

"Oh shit, now I really got my ass in a crack."

"No, I don't think so. They both seemed pleased with your 201 file. I'll let him know you're here. You're on time as usual, and that always makes the colonel and the general happy."

Just as Laura was getting out of her chair, *ka-blam,* the loudest explosion with that unmistakable smell of gunpowder, cordite, semtex smoke, and a shock wave that blew open the door to Andy's office and knocked both John and Laura to the floor. John, having recently been in combat over in Laos, wasn't too shook up, but Laura was hiding under her desk with a frightful and very terrified pale face.

John rushed over, picked her up, and hustled them both into the secure room that every CIA station has. *This girl is tough and strong as five-day-old coffee,* thought John. "Do you have a weapon?" he asked.

"Of course, I do. It's in my purse, a Walther PPK 9 mm. My father insisted I take it when he knew I was coming here."

"You're going to be all right in the secure room with the rest of the team. I am going to check on Andy and Shorty."

Only fifteen seconds had passed since the explosion. John rushed into Andy's office and was met with glass all over the floor, desks and chairs and file cabinets overturned, but Andy and the general were very lucky. They were standing next to an outside wall between two windows and weren't hurt at all, just very pissed off. John slowly peeked around the window jamb so as not to give any assassin a clear shot into the room. "It looks like you're going to need a new car, sir. They just shredded your old Chevy like coleslaw. Looks like you might have been their objective, sir."

At this news, Shorty turned pale, and John got a chair upright for him before he collapsed. Colonel Andy went to his closet and brought out a bottle of Jack Daniels and some coffee cups and told John to get some in the general. He had to check on the rest of the office personnel. In the meantime, John got his ass back in gear and went into the reception office where minutes before he was having lusty thoughts while ogling Laura. He yelled into the secure office for somebody to help him bar the outside door in case the bombers realized they failed in their attempt to kill the general. After a few minutes, the smoke and dust settled down, and there were running footsteps in the corridor and hammering on the door to the reception area. It was security from the first floor checking up on this office and giving a report on what happened.

The sergeant of the security detail reported that a pedicab loaded with explosives pulled alongside the general's car. The young Thai driving the pedicab jumped off the bike and ran to the far corner of the street and, using a homemade handheld detonator, demolished the car and anyone in it. Fortunately, the general's driver, a master sergeant, went into the hotel bar in the same building as the agency's offices and was far enough away that he received no injuries. To add to the intrigue of this scenario, the interpreter assigned to the general was nowhere to be found. After the Bangkok police forensics people cordoned off the site, they found no evidence of a human body, blood hair, clothing, nothing. "It looks pretty fishy to me, General," said Andy. "I'll bet my entire pension that your so-called interpreter was part of this bombing."

The CO of the army contingent garrisoned at Udorn, the air force base near the American embassy, sent two companies of soldiers to stand guard and help clean up the mess and put the office back together.

"General Wells here" (on the phone). "Yes, Shorty Wells. Ambassador, get me a secure link to Washington ASAP. No, not the Pentagon, the White House. Yes, goddammit, I mean right now. You know what just happened over here? So get me that secure link, and I mean right now. Them sons o' bitches will hear about it in the *Washington Post* before I can tell them what really transpired."

"Hello, Chief of Staff Walter Bedell Smith here."

"Beetle, this is General Wells calling from Thailand."

Beetle thinking, *Oh nuts, some one-star about to give me a hard time.* "What can we do for you, Shorty?"

"Walter, get me Ike right now. This is very important."

"Sorry, Shorty, the president is indisposed at the moment."

"Goddammit, Beetle, I need to talk to Ike, so don't give me a load of bullshit. If I have to come back to DC and kick your ass up and down Pennsylvania Avenue, you know I will. So get me Ike on the phone now, you brownnosing ass-kissing sumbitch. We have been attacked and my car had blown up and the CIA offices have been firebombed. That ought to get me some action." Walter Bedell Smith had been General Eisenhower's chief of staff all through the Second World War, and he was nicknamed Beetle by everyone in the army. He was a lieutenant general (three stars) when the war ended, so he mitigated to Ike's staff, and he was not about to let a lowly one-star brigadier general intimidate him, but he was also a practical man and sized up a bad situation in a hurry. Better get Ike was Walter's decision.

"General Wells, how are you? Are you okay? What happened?"

"Well, Mr. President, my car was firebombed, and the CIA office was almost destroyed from the blast. I was very fortunate not to have been late for my meeting with Colonel Lord in his offices. Sir, we are in the wrong part of town. It's a slum out here. We belong in the embassy, but that narrow-minded liberal-thinking ambassador of ours won't let us in even though the whole third floor of the embassy building is vacant. Sir, this is a travesty. We need the CIA chiefs' offices to have the protection that the US ambassador gets.

"The small wars are increasingly getting larger. Each week that goes by, the Commies are getting bolder by using guerrilla tactics and unconventional warfare. Our people are at a complete disadvantage in where we conduct business. I know when you sent me out here I was to be an overseer to the behind-the-scenes people. Well, sir, I am reporting to you directly and not the people at Fort Meade, Maryland. Sir, the bottom line is Colonel Lord and his people need to be in the embassy. Thank you for listening to me."

"Okay, General. It was good talking to you. It seems that some people around here don't want to disturb me with trivial things. Your call was and is very important. Is Colonel Lord handy? I wish to speak with him. So long, Shorty, and keep up the great work and be careful."

"Colonel Lord here, sir."

"Colonel, good to talk to you. Are you okay? You're not hurt or anything, are you?"

"No, sir, just a little shaken up. Everything the general iterated to you is what's really happening all over Southeast Asia today, including Cambodia, Laos, Vietnam, Indonesia, and the Malay Peninsula. They are all getting armed by Red China and the Soviets. It's like the Nazis when they were trying to take over Europe."

"Okay, Colonel. Send me your after-action report by secured wireless from the embassy. I will talk to the ambassador as soon as I hang up with you, and you can rest assured that you can start moving into the embassy tomorrow. Oh, and, Colonel, you will probably have to move into the second floor. The highest floor is usually reserved for the ambassador and his family."

"Thank you, sir. General Wells can be right persuasive, can't he?"

"Yes, he can, Andy. Don't tell him, but his second star has been approved by myself and the Congress. Next month he will be a major general."

Lieutenant Braz was helping with the cleanup and securing the mess in the offices when Shorty and Andy called him in Andy's office. "John, don't bother with trying to put things back together here. We are moving into the embassy tomorrow. Call—thank god the phones are working, the dirty bastards didn't cut the lines, frigging amateurs—the CO over at the army base. His name is Col. James Newcomb. His aide is a major Evans, or something or other, a real self-important asshole, but the colonel is a real soldier and a good Joe. Tell him what transpired in the last few hours and ask him (don't tell him) that we need all the trucks he can spare and as many men to help with our move. We have to make the move as quickly as possible. This colonel is a logistics expert. He probably will have some good ideas about how to get this done. If he wants to be in charge and command the whole operation, relinquish all power to him. Like I said, he is a good leader.

"In the meantime, see to it that Laura and all the female staff are secure and see to any of their needs personally. I know that is a shitty job, but somebody has to do it. Oh, and, John, don't try to take advantage of their vulnerability right now. I know I can trust you."

John is thinking, *Well, it's getting on toward lunchtime. Time to see what these people normally do for chow. Why did the colonel have to put a guilt trip on me about fraternization with the women? Dammit, I've been in the freaking jungle for almost six months now and haven't seen a white female all that time. Anyway, there is a lot to do to get all the secret files and furniture ready for transportation tomorrow. You know, I still wonder what Andy and Shorty wanted with me. I guess it will just have to wait. Maybe if I ask Laura to have a drink with me tonight, she might give an insight as to what's up. A guy can dream, can't he?*

CHAPTER TWO

Saigon Republic of South Vietnam
26 December 1959
Cam Lo Hotel, Tu Dou Street

In room number 10, first floor, sitting in old beat-up chairs and in a ratty vermin-laden couch, near a wrought iron and wood top table, were one of the world's most detested and feared assassins and his partner in crime and murder, Charro Lequesta, and NVA Major Than Vo Luc. The major was the political and clandestine leader of the local Viet Minh sapper cell. After several drinks of local homemade rice beer, the major was getting impatient. For one thing, if someone from the local White Mice, nickname of the Diem's regime secret and not-so-secret police, should recognize him, he would be killed instantly. Lequesta had a lot of patience. He sat in waiting for many hours for just the right moments to kill someone and/or receive stolen goods.

"Where the hell is he?" Vo Luc shouted at Lequesta.

"Don't yell at me, you little yellow bastard, or I'll cut your ears off and send them to your wife."

"Well, how long do we have sit in this shithouse waiting for this Irish pig?"

"He will be here. He is just as greedy as you, so you better have the relics."

"I got the gold. He better have my money."

"Our money, Vo Luc, or did you forget who set this meeting up? Listen up, he's walking down the hallway. I can hear his sloshing on

---
16

the tiles like the pig he is. He will have at least two bodyguards, so don't make any moves to the guns, or we will be a bloody mess. This crooked senator is very powerful back in the States. He employs only ex-Green Berets as his bodyguards, and those soldiers are trigger-happy and very mean to Vietnamese. If they find out you're an NVA soldier, they won't think twice about wasting you. These guys don't care all that much about money. They are like you—they get their rocks off killing Orientals."

Omalley says, "Now where are the goods, Vo? We have to get as much artwork and relics fenced, along with the pot that has to be sent to our friends in Mexico. Why is this stuff rolled up in this orange silk?"

"That's the robe of the monk I got relics from."

"You mean the monk you killed, along with your own VC soldier?"

"How do you know what I did?"

"Listen, you amateur, I know everything about you and Lequesta. I know where you were born, the names of your wives and kids, the name of the daughter of Gen. Van Duc whom you have been screwing, and when you went to Russia to study at the Lenin Academy. So don't try to put one over on me, Vo, or you, Lequesta."

"Now tomorrow we are all going up to the A team camp 105. So everybody has a job to do. Charro, you get in touch with that crooked ARVN quartermaster sergeant and set up the delivery of the weed. Van Duc, you talk to your agent in the ARVN contingent as to any patrols going out on recon. I would really like to burn that Green Beret major who squealed to the CIA about an illegal operation going on in his sector.

"This is my cover story. I am in his camp sent by the Senate to investigate any irregularities by our troops. The warmongering bastards hate me already, so they are not going to welcome me with open arms. And don't steal anything so as not to bring any undue suspicion to us now."

The next morning, Sen. Sean Thomas Omalley and his little band of cutthroats drove north from Saigon to Bien Hoa and on to A team camp 105 at Lai Khe. They were not concerned about being killed or captured. The word was out to the VC that these sons of bitches were on the Communist payroll.

Bangkok International Airport
2 January 1960

Colonel Lord and General Wells were with Lieutenant Braz and his new command of intel and recon soldiers in the secure waiting room offered to them by the courtesy of the Thailand military government. Colonel Lord was iterating to John not to underestimate the sycophant and duplicitous nature of Omalley and his thugs. Having briefed John and his troops to get as many convincing and provable facts about the smuggling and dope dealing going into the United States without getting anybody killed or captured was of utmost importance. Having heard enough, John called his men to attention, saluted, and marched his men out on the tarmac to the waiting Douglas DC-3 Skytrain operated and flown by Air America, the airline of the CIA. The 385 klicks (kilometers) was a nice slow ride for this group of rangers (i.e., undercover intelligence operatives). The DC-3, sometimes known as the Gooney Bird to the fliers who piloted them, was an honor. This plane has been around since the first one built in July 1933. Having twin 1,200-horsepower Pratt and Whitney Wasp SIC3 air-cooled power plants, she moved along at 230 mph with an operational ceiling of 23,200 feet and carrying a load of 5,180 pounds. The first leg was to Phnom Penh, Cambodia, where she unloaded mail and supplies to the station chief. The last leg was to Saigon's Tan Son Nhat Airport taken over by ARVN forces of the South Vietnamese. When the Dakota touched down and followed the follow-me truck, Lieutenant Braz was the first off the plane and was escorted to the headquarters of US Lt. Gen. John Desmond, the commander of the assistance and advisory group known as MACV.

General Desmond welcomed John back to Vietnam and called him by the most infamous nickname he ever earned, Mad Dog, which was the title given to him by his old ranger group.

Lieutenant Braz was not too happy with this honorific, but first lieutenants don't go around telling three-star generals to clam up.

Lieutenant Braz and his squad of counterinsurgency troopers boarded a CH-21 Sikorsky helicopter, the first of four that were on the route to Lai Khe, the Green Beret camp 105.

It was a very short hop, thirty klicks or thereabouts. Not too much was said on the chopper this morning. All the men knew they were going back in combat, and that was just fine with this bunch of professionals. To a man, they relished the upcoming skirmishes.

Every single trooper was highly trained and possessed great courage and mental stability. They would have each other's back (or six, as most professional soldiers say it). The thought would never enter a mind of one of these guys to ever leave a comrade in the field. All of them would rather fight and die together than give up on anything especially in a firefight (or over a beer or a girl).

Every man was cross-trained in weapons, commo, medical, tactics languages, and light artillery. Also every man had a specialty. For a starter, Yorkie was the medic, and Hun was the communications expert. Lieutenant Braz himself was a tactical genius possessing an uncanny ability to analyze a situation as fast as it took place. There wasn't a soldier anywhere who had situational awareness instincts as sharp as John does.

Green Beret
Special Forces Camp 105
Lai Khe, South Vietnam

The Sikorsky helicopter set down at the forward end of the dirt and rocks, mud, grass, and sometimes level landing strip. John is thinking, *I am sure glad I don't have to fly my Piper Super Cub or our old Luscombe single-seater onto this piece of shit real estate airstrip.*

The rear door of the chopper opened, and the squad, weary from all the flying, tumbled out. Lieutenant Braz was last out the door. "Mad Dog," Captain Jenkins yelled at Braz.

"Shush," John said close to a whisper. They grabbed a hold of each other's arms and embraced in a big welcome hug. "Don't say that out loud," John beseeched the captain. "No one other than you is supposed to know who we are and what our primary mission is."

"I see that slimy bastard in the seersucker suit is already here planning his dirty work. Have you lost any troops lately or any KIAs?"

"No, John. We have been quietly and slowly building up our resources, you know, ammo, food, medical supplies, more men, etc. Omalley and his crew just got here yesterday, so there has been nothing out of the ordinary going on. We know we're going to get hit pretty hard real soon. That's what those three other choppers are unloading. We requested four more heavy machine guns and eight more 81 mm mortars and their respective crews. Headquarters supply said they could only give us two machine guns and only four mortars. The pricks cut my order in half. I also requested two hundred thousand rounds of 7.62 mm rounds for the machine guns, but they said I could only have half again. Johnny boy, if I don't get more ammo, this camp could easily be overrun by the NVA."

"Well, Jerry (Capt. Jerimiah Jenkins is the Green Beret CO of camp 105), yesterday when we got to Bien Hoa, General Odanials and I had a heart-to-heart talk about your and other SF camps in this sector. I told him I had read your req, along with the refusal. He blew a fucking fuse, and we walked over to the new warehouses the Seabees are building. He asked me what special requirements I needed. I said we will send a req to his chief of staff and not to this quartermaster whom we have reason to believe is selling equipment to the guys that need it. I know that your guys will take care of our needs—can't fight a war with no guns.

"To make a long story short, all you requested is on those Sikorskys, and you are getting the extra men to man those mortars and machine guns. The only difference in men is they are all not Special Forces troopers. Some of them are rangers, and there is a small team of only four navy SEALs. The carrier analysts (photographer types) have spotted some ground-to-air missile sites along the Song Lily River and want their own boys to take them out. Also the general added two thousand of the new shaped plastic claymore mines.

Captain Jenkins is thinking, *The call I got this morning from headquarters wondering mostly why General Desmond asked me to tell Mad Dog job well done.* "Johnny boy, thanks for interfering in my behalf. Now let those fucking VC bastards try to overrun us. We will be waiting with every able-bodied trooper behind a weapon—they won't stand a chance, especially with enough claymores to ring the defensive perimeter with four overlapping fields of fire. John, we have a briefing every morning at 0600. Be there with both your squad leaders. I am going to ask you to go on a recon mission up the river to Long Ghy Point. The purpose is to see if the NVA have a secret tunnel system from the trail, Ho Chi Minh, a main supply route from Laos and north all the way back to China.

"Great, Jerry. My guys are up for a little walk in your park, and we may get to wax some of the little brothers off the Russians."

"John, you have to be extra vigilant. Omalley, Than Vo, and their hired assassin Lequesta watch everything we do around here. The rat bastard says he has the authority to go wherever he cares to. I don't believe an ounce of the bullshit that flows from his fat pig face. When he was here before and over at SF camps 103 and 106, the Tenth SF group lost eight troopers in an ambush a half a klick from their wire. It was so well set up it could only have had inside intel to fuck up the normal way we operate. At the morning briefing only let your squad leaders know where you're going. The local ARVN troops can't be trusted. They are all afraid of Than Vo. He intimidates the dog shit out of them. I suspected he is NVA a long time ago, but now we have to prove it. And that prick from the Senate keeps waving the justice department statuette in our face. Boy, you talk about trying to fight a war with one arm tied behind you and only partial ammo and resources?"

At 0530, the morning mist is so thick you could almost swim in it. That does not deter Lieutenant Braz and Sergeants Yorkie and Hun from the usual run of at least five miles every chance they get. Several laps around the interior perimeter adds up to about six and a half miles. This is what paratroopers live for—to get the woozies out and the juices flowing.

The morning briefing started on time and started to get to the very secretive and sensitive operations, for the eyes and ears only of the recon groups are going out.

Yorkie and Hun were getting antsy. "Something isn't copacetic," Hun said. "I feel that this operation is fucked from the start." Hun nudged Yorkie and whispered, "I bet this hooch is bugged, that's what I feel." Yorkie looked at him and nodded; he too has good instincts, honed to a fine edge from years of jungle fighting, Operation Snake River.

The briefing ended. Captain Jenkins told all the men involved in the operation to make the last checks. Equipment, ammo, commo gear, smoke, water, grenades, explosives, and the new radio signals and call signs. The teams started out thinking, *This is my job, and I hope to do it as good or better than I ever did.* Some guys said the usual prayer; others bantered about with friendly insults. Everyone was a little scared (it's normal), but every trooper to a man was very confident. Mostly in the leadership qualities of Lieutenant Braz and the squad leaders, older noncoms who had seen a lot of combat all around the world, these older sergeants were involved in every kind of warfare there was, and they had the scars and wounds to prove it. The more experienced guys recognized the courage and talent to sum up a bad situation in a hurry that the lieutenant possessed, and that gave them the confidence to bring the fight to the enemy in their own backyard.

Lieutenant Braz and his two squads of rangers began boarding the CH-21 Sikorsky helicopter with its twin rotors and double rudders aft. The banana-shaped chopper was a very stable aircraft that had to operate in the steaming hot jungles and torrential downpours in sector two of South Vietnam.

Every man had on his bullet-retardant vest with all the extra pockets for extra magazines of .30-caliber NATO rounds, grenades, morphine pack, and assault knife, and some carried extra batteries for the radios.

All the men carried the M1 Garand .30 cal semiautomatic rifle, except two men who carried .60 cal machine guns. Their buddies carried extra bandoliers of rounds for these heavy guns. The M14 and M16 rifles had not been introduced in this theater of operations yet.

Lieutenant Braz carried a M1 carbine and his .45 cal 1911 ACP pistol, and a Fairbairn–Sykes dagger strapped to the underside of his left forearm. This was a very special gift from a marine who later in the war was killed in a Vietcong ambush.

As they were getting on the chopper, Yorkie says to Lieutenant Braz, "Look over by the visitors' hooch. Omalley and Than Vo Luc are scoping us out. Lieutenant, Hun and I both got that heebie-jeebies feeling about this mission."

"Yeah, I don't feel so hot about it myself. Don't pass it on to the rest of the squads. We need as much confidence as the men can muster. We just have to be extra vigilant. Now that we are on the helo, tell Hun to alert the men what the mission is about. I've been hearing them grumble all the way up near the flight deck."

The navigator hit the switch for the red light on the forward bulkhead, letting the men know it's ten minutes away from touchdown and they are in Indian country. Normally these rangers would parachute into the area, but there was no safe LZ to jump into. So they just go in as the regular troops do. The green light came on—time for any last-minute checks on the men and their equipment.

The change of pitch in the rotors and the winding down of the jet turbine engines mean the ground is coming up fast and embarking time is right on schedule. The eastern sky is getting a little pink glow. The morning mist is pretty heavy, so the rangers will just set up a defensive perimeter. They will wait till they can see a little better before they shove off.

The Sikorsky CH-21 lifts off fast, and turns right and then south on a heading back to camp 105. Command pilot WO1 Jeff Lightfoot radios back to Lieutenant Braz to call back if they need an emergency liftoff or help with directional fire, as there are no FACs (forward air controllers) in this sector. Jeff signs off, thinking to himself and relating to his two other crew members, "Guys, before we left the skull session last night with our boss (squadron air commander), he told me to take on as much gas as the bird will hold. We are going to hang around up here at twenty thousand feet out of missile range and kind of watch over Mad Dog and his boys. In case they need air support, I don't know where it would come from. This mission is a black ops and not on the books, so the other services don't know about it."

On the ground, Lieutenant Braz wishes he could rely on some backup air power. The problem being no one knows about this mission, so he and his men have only themselves to count on. There is a lot of scuttlebutt that the army is going to get an air wing like the Marine Corps has, with assault and attack helicopters, but that is just a dream as far as Lieutenant Braz is concerned.

CHAPTER THREE

The morning mist started to disappear fast. The order was given to move out. The well-trained rangers put the men in a skirmish line about five yards apart. "No bunching up. If Charlie has a well-sighted machine gun aimed at us, he could kill a couple of guys in a heartbeat." The two squads came upon a small villa, with a French-style farmhouse, a garden plot, and about four acres of rice paddies.

The old fisherman wearing the traditional conical straw hat, black short pants, and shirt came out of the house and started talking in pidgin English. "What do you want? Why you are here? No VC here. This only very poor farm and fishing village. No VC here. Go away. We no like Americans. Go away."

Yorkie sidled up to Lieutenant Braz. "This is as VC as you can get. See the antenna on the back side of the roof? Why would a poor fisherman need a tall antenna such as this one?"

Lieutenant Braz said, "Listen, what don't you hear? No monkeys or birds or any of the tree-living animals traditionally normal to this environment. Squad leaders, alert the men. We are going to get hit as soon as we cross that second paddy dike."

No sooner were the words said than all hell broke loose. Crump whoof four times quickly signaled mortars leaving the tubes. "Incoming," yelled everybody, and all the rangers dove for the ground near the nearest berm. Kaboom four times in a row; the mortars all fell short. "Looks like these guys need a lesson in aiming those Russian pieces of shit. Lucky for us these little bastards can't shoot straight. They must be VC and not NVA, or else we might have our ass in a crack." Then the real shooting started. Most of the outfit were pinned down by heavy machine gun fire. Everybody was returning fire. The two .60 cal machine guns were tearing up the Charlies along the front line. The VC started to try to outflank the first squad on the left perimeter, but the troopers cut them down as soon as they came out of elephant grass. This end of the line was the up hillside, and the rangers picked off the Charlies with really good shooting.

Lieutenant Braz sized up the situation and started yelling orders to the men to shoot some grenades from the grenade launchers as close to that heavy machine gun. No sooner had he ordered than the crew served gun along with three bad guys who were eliminated, never to pull a trigger again. Braz was thinking, *Good, we opened the center of the ambush. Now we can outflank them from the uphill side.*

When Sergeant Washinski came half running, half crawling, out of breath, he's trying to tell Braz, "Three guys are down. Billy's hit. An AK-47 round through and through his shoulder."

Braz yells, "Get Yorkie on it."

"Can't, says Wash, "there is a bad situation near the river. That's where Billy got shot."

"Well, where the fuck are Yorkie and Hun?" says Braz.

"Here comes Staff Sergeant Caporelli running like a son of a bitch."

"Lieutenant, Lieutenant, they got Yorkie and Hun."

"Are they hit bad?" asks Braz.

"No, Lieutenant. The VC got both of our guys captured."

"What? Are you fucking kidding me? They would never let themselves be caught like that," says Braz.

"They got down as soon as the mortars went off. They leaped over the dike, and six or seven NVA soldiers were right on them with AK-47s right in their faces. The bad guys had ropes and duct tape. Billy was closest to them. He killed one guy, but you're never gonna believe this—the guy that shot Billy was that Lequesta prick, the one hanging around with the senator."

"Okay, Billy, which way did they take off to?"

"Sorry, sir, but they dragged Yorkie and Hun to the river and were kicking them and hitting them with the rifle butts to get them in a small boat. The boat has a big outboard motor, and Lequesta is driving it."

"Goddammit, and, shit, we could never catch up with that boat even if we had a boat powerful enough. Where is Hun's radio?"

"Billy shot it up so the VC could not use it."

"Good thinking, Billy, but we are screwed without a radio. We need help, and fast. Sergeant Wash, get the staff sergeant up here. He has a handheld Hallicrafters unit. I hope the batteries are fresh."

While all this was happening—it was only about ten minutes— more small arms fire started pouring in on the rangers. Lieutenant Braz is glassing the area with the only pair of binoculars. "Sergeant Wash, can you get that helo or anybody in this area on that frequency?"

"Already got him, sir."

"Hand me the radio please, Wash. Army Helicopter 1, this is Cochise (call sign of the leader; the name of the operation is Snake River). Do you read me?"

"Cochise, I read you five by five."

"Good boy, warrant officer. Can you get me some air support? We seemed to have walked into a hornet's nest here."

"Yes, sir. I am in contact with a pair of A-1D Skyraiders. US Army guys are the guys driving them. Putting you right through to A-1."

"Lieutenant Mad Dog, this is Army Skyraider 1. My ETA is four minutes to your position. Lay me some smoke down in your lines so we don't hurt you guys. I will tell you the color so Charlie doesn't screw with you."

"Skyraider 1, thanks for coming to join our party. The smoke is out. Tell me what it is?"

"Skyraider 1 to Cochise, it looks like St. Patrick's Day down there."

"You got it, baby. We are tossing different-color smoke at the Charlies. We're using the grenade launchers to get it out as far as we can."

"Cochise, we see yellow and red smoke. I will be coming in from your starboard side at about three o'clock. Keep your heads down. I got two two-hundred-pound iron frag bombs. The concussive shock wave will blow your eardrums out, so cover up."

The Douglas Skyraider A-1D is a perfect dive and torpedo bomber that first flew in 1945. The power plant is one 2,500 hp Wright R-3350-24W air-cooled radial engine, 321 miles per hour speed, with an operational ceiling of twenty-six thousand feet, sporting two 20 mm cannon and capable of carrying eight thousand pounds of weapons and ordnance (rockets).

Pilot Tony Ameratto in Skyraider 1 dives down from two thousand feet to seven hundred feet as low as he dares before pulling back on the stick, pressing the release button. "Let's loose both iron bombs." They arch up with momentum of the plane, reaching the apogee of their arc quickly, and fall to earth, and a whole lot of VC are on their way to nirvana.

Quickly, Leslie Franks, pilot in Skyraider 2, lines up a half mile further back from where Tony made his first dive run and proceeds to make a strafing run to keep the dazed enemy from getting too coordinated. Helo 1 comes on the radio and tells the pilots that from his advantage point at ten thousand feet, he can see more NVA trucks nearing the battlefield. The Russian trucks are canvas-covered troop carriers. As the trucks get closer, they start spewing more NVA troops.

The rangers on the ground are keeping up the fire at the enemy, picking at the target-rich foreground. Lieutenant Braz knows he doesn't have enough ammo to keep the skirmish going for any length of time, plus he has to get his men out of there so he can get after the VC/NVA who grabbed Yorkie and Hun and get Billy to the field hospital.

"Cochise to A-1 Skyraider, come in, Tony."

"Army 1 to Cochise, I read you loud and clear. Go ahead, Cochise."

"Tony, can you guys stick around long enough till we get the helo down here for an extraction? We are getting low on ammo. Do you have enough fuel for at least twenty minutes? That's how long I need to leapfrog my guys back far enough so the helo isn't coming into a hot LZ."

"Army 1 to Cochise, yeah, Mad Dog, we have the go juice, and we each have twenty-four two-and-a-half-inch diameter rockets, about one thousand rounds of 20 mm cannon bullets, and Leslie still has his bombs."

"Cochise, this is Army 2. Talk to me, Mad Dog."

"Army 2, this is Cochise. I wish you guys would call me Lieutenant Braz instead of Mad Dog. I don't deserve the moniker."

"Mad Dog, stop pissing and moaning. We're up here saving your ground-pounding asses. So get on with your retreating."

"We are not retreating, you son of a bitch. We're staging a tactical advance to a better position," Lt. Braz screams into the radio. "Wait till I see you on the ground. We will see who's going to retreat. Now get those bombs on the enemy so I can take my men home to a hot shower and a cold beer."

"Cochise to Army Helo, come in, Helo."

"Helo to Cochise, standing by."

"Helo, can you set it down back off the first rice paddy? With the Skyraiders covering, we should have a cool LZ."

"Yes, sir Lieutenant. Give me five minutes to spill some air out of my rotors and will line up so the port door is facing your men so we can lift off quick."

Once in the air, everybody made sure all weapons are clear—sure would not want a hot round going off in the helo. Lieutenant Braz puts on the helmet reserved for the leader. "Can you connect me with Skyraider?" Braz asks the pilot.

"Sure thing, sir," answers the warrant officer.

"Army 1, this Army Helo. How do you read me?"

"Five by five, rotor guy, go ahead."

"Tony, this is Cochise. Can you put some ordnance and/or rockets in that old farmhouse so the VC can't use it anymore?"

"Yes, sir Lieutenant."

"We are going back to Bien Hoa for some chow and fuel and going to load up on some hi-test and scoot right back."

"We think we may be able to get an eyeball on the river traffic and locate where the VC are taking your boys."

"Thanks, Tony. I really appreciate your efforts, but be careful. The NVA may be trying to suck you into where they have SAMs or smaller ground-to-air missiles."

"Good thinking, sir. We haven't seen any missiles in this sector yet. Our intel says the only missiles other units have spotted are a little bit further up north, but we will be careful. We now have a new radar intercept directional finder in both these planes. So far we haven't picked up any noise. These little bastards are like ants—they can carry pieces of missiles and big guns for days. Then they bring the Russian techs down to put it all together."

"We are getting out of range now, so I will sign off, and I hope your ranger is okay. They will take good care of him at Bien Hoa."

CHAPTER FOUR

Army Helo 1 puts in at the MASH Hospital landing area 2 in the Bien Hoa compound. Lieutenant Braz and Sergeant Wash accompany Billy to the triage area. There they are met by a large in-charge nurse who happens to hold the rank of lieutenant colonel. "My buddy is hurt bad. Please do the best for him?"

"Lieutenant, we treat everybody with the very best the United States has to offer. Now get the hell out of my way and go back to your unit. We will send him back when he's ready, and don't try to go over my head and get special treatment, Mad Dog, or your ass will be mine. I know you are pretty tight with General Desmond. So I am telling you again, get the hell out of here and let me do my job."

Damn, if she wasn't so stacked and dripping with sex (well, that's another story). "Wash, we got to get these men back to camp so that I can plan my mission to go after Hun and Yorkie."

"I will go with you," says Sergeant Wash.

"Me too," says Staff Sergeant Abrams.

"No, you aren't. This is a one-man excursion. I can travel a lot faster alone and do a more thorough search on my own."

"Captain Jenks won't let you go alone."

"Fuck Jenks. He has no authority over me. Remember we are on loan to the CIA. Wash, when land, I want you to help me get my special rucksack ready."

"You mean the one with the crossbow?"

"Yes, my son. I need all the stealth I possess to crawl through their lines. I have a real good idea where this interim POW camp is located. I got some good intel from those two good Montagnards we gave the new carbines to last time we were upriver."

Army Helo 1 leaves Bien Hoa with Lieutenant Braz and his men for SF camp 105. On the way, Braz is so pissed off over the way they were fucked over by the senator. He is muttering to himself how many ways he can inflict enough pain before he kills Omalley. Braz is actually pacing up and down (much to the dismay of the pilots and his men; he is rocking the aircraft because he is not sitting down and strapped in). Now the new guys understand why he is called Mad Dog.

Back at camp 105, the helo lands, and the men disembark. Lieutenant Braz goes up the flight deck and commends WO Lightfoot for the great job getting his men away safely. When the copilot leaves to talk to the crew chief, Braz whispers to Jeff Lightfoot if he can scrounge up a Little Bird helicopter later when it gets to be dusk. WO Jeff says he can't, but he knows a pilot over at the security revetments where the choppers are secured from mortar and artillery attacks. "Can we go talk to him now?"

"Sure, Lieutenant. I will introduce you, but I don't want to be a part of anything illegal."

"No worries, Jeff, you won't be compromised at all."

Braz knew that the senator could not be found anytime soon, so he will have to put off doing him in till another time. In his hooch, Braz met up with Sergeant Wash. "All your kit is laid out on the bunk for your inspection, sir."

"Wash, when we're away from everybody, call me John, okay? Leave the saluting and other protocol for the parade ground."

"Sir, okay, sir—I mean, John—but I like to call you Mad Dog like the rest of the guys."

"Don't even go there, Wash, you know better."

"Now listen, Sergeant Washinski, this is official business. I am making you the interim commander of this unit as of right now. You can tell Captain Jenkins I had a little business to settle with the Vietcong and the North Vietnamese. Other than that, you don't know where, why, or how I'm going, just that I am gone.

"Now you and I know that Jenks is gonna bitch and moan and call you a fucking idiot for letting me go on off by myself. He will get on your ass for not coming right to him and letting him in on my plans. This doesn't concern him. Those guys are my men and my brothers just as you are. I have to try to get them back safely—I owe it to them. Are there any of our guys outside now? Get them all in here please? Oh, and, Sergeant, get your duffel.

"Men, listen, I have to make this short. Sergeant Washinski, get the master sergeant's chevrons you have been carrying around for the last six months. Men, on behalf of the United States Army and with the power as an officer in such, I, 1st Lt. John Braz, as the commanding officer of this unit, promote Sergeant First Class Stanley Washinski to master sergeant. Now, men, I don't know how much booze Captain Jenkins allows on this post, but under my bunk, there are three bottles of Black Jack, so get your canteens and any ice you can find and toast the sergeant." The uproar and clapping and congratulations were pretty loud for a few minutes, but the noise settled, and Lieutenant Braz spoke, Sergeant Washinski, as your first official duty in that rank, you are to write up the after-action report. I will do mine as soon as I come back with the prodigal sons. Men, I want to say you are some of the best soldiers, rangers, and gentlemen I have ever known. God forbid I don't return, don't come looking for me, for I will be dead. I will never let those bastards take me prisoner or alive.

"Adios. My chariot awaits. Remember, men, *duty, honor, country.*"

John sneaks out of the hooch and makes a beeline for the Bell Ranger helicopter waiting for him at the far end of the flight line. WO-1 Tim Malone is waiting for him with a big grin on his face. Tim loves doing things on the edge of legal, or all the way illegal; it doesn't matter to him as long as he can fly his Little Bird, a Bell Ranger.

The Bell Ranger is a very quiet helicopter and can navigate small rivers and canyons that bigger birds can't. "Tim, do you have any of those new starlight scopes?" (early version of night vision goggles).

"Affirmative, sir. We have two pair of the scopes made into goggles. I know they are a little crude, but they work real good. Everything looks green at first. They get their power from ambient light, heat, the moon's reflection on objects, or light from a fire in a hooch. Don't look right at a lighted object after removing the goggles—you will be temporarily blinded for a couple of seconds.

So just close your eyes and slowly open them, and all of your vision will return."

"Tim, I like the fact that you can keep this little jaunt a secret. I know that, for Jeff Lightfoot filled me in on your sordid past. What the fuck did you do to piss off the general's chief of staff? For the general to bust you from a captain down to WO?"

"Well, sir, I did some shit like we're doing now, only I got caught. Lieutenant, what are you going to do if you get your guys?"

"I hope to steal a boat with an engine and run like hell down the river back to where the good guys are."

"Okay, sir, we're very near your jumping-off position. In fact, there's my reference point by those taller trees."

"Set me down, Tim, and get the hell out of here as fast as this Little Bird can go."

"So long, sir, and good luck."

Yeah, Johnny boy, you got yourself in some deep shit now. I will need all the luck I ever had to pull off this trick. Shit, Johnny, now is not the time to second-guess your abilities. Get that crap out of your head. You are one of the very best of the best warriors in the world today. So, you NVA and VC, say your fucking prayers—Mad Dog is coming to put all you bastards away.

In order not to alert any sentries in an OP (observation post), I can't travel any of the paths that lead up to the camp, so it will be slow going through the jungle, but I've been there before, so no sweat. Let me hide the glow from the radium dial on this watch and see how much time I have left tonight. Good, it's only 2200 hours. By the time I reach this shit hole of a camp, most of the VC will be sleeping, and the NVA troops will most likely have passed out from the cheap booze.

Boy, I'm glad I run five or six miles every day. I feel good even after not eating evening chow. While I think about it, a slug of water and this candy bar will get me through. Whoops, slow down, goddammit, you almost walked into their camp. Shit, I hope that sentry in the first guard tower didn't see me or smell me.

After sitting for at least forty-five minutes, observing everything he could see, Lieutenant Braz slowly crawled around the perimeter of the camp and located the bamboo huts of the prisoners and the living quarters of the enemy. No one except the four guards in the towers seemed to be awake or moving around, not even to use the latrine.

This is a good thing, Braz thinks to himself.

Setting up his crossbow, Braz sets the first bolt in the firing position and aims the crosshairs right at the neck of the VC sentry. A very slight tap, and the guard feels the bolt made out of hardened teak go through his windpipe and right out back of the medulla, which kills him instantly.

He didn't have time to utter a cry. The blood started to run down the posts holding the tower in place, and the best part was the VC had set his AK-47 in the corner, so no noise was made. *So much for Charlie number 1,* thinks Braz. Slowly he low crawls to his left toward the next tower. The guard is alert and smoking. *What an asshole,* Braz thinks. He can see the glow from the cigarette a hundred yards away. *He has got to be VC. An NVA soldier would never smoke on guard duty, especially at night.* Braz crawls around to the back of the VC and loads up the crossbow again. Another nice shot, right in the back of the head where the bones of the head knit together. The bolt goes right through and comes out the eyehole. This guy made a little yelp, but not loud enough for the other guards to be concerned. The AK-47 rifle fell off the tower, but the jungle ground is so soft from the torrential rains that no sound was made.

Gotta get closer this time, Braz ponders. If I could get almost under the tower, I could sucker him to look over the side. He can't see me anyway—the shadows are so black from the jungle canopy, and the moon is behind the clouds for at least another five minutes. I can hopefully catch his weapon if it falls. Boy, John, you got a big ego. Ah, fuck it, it's worth a try. Anything to try and save my brothers, Now what's the word for asshole in VC lingo? Just whisper "asshole," he will look over—it's only human nature to look. Another great shot right in the center of his face. Yep, here it comes, a bucket of blood and the rifle. Shit, I almost missed the gun, but the blood got me. Okay, three down, one to go.

What the hell is that? Snoring—this fuck is sleeping. Now my job gets harder. I am going to have to crawl up that bamboo ladder and kill that fucker with my hands. Can't risk a shot and wake up the whole camp, although there are only about twenty enemies here that I make out. The POW hut can't hold but maybe five or six people, and the sleeping hut can only hold about twelve to fifteen men. Okay, here we go, slowly step near the rung part that's tied to the vertical stringer and alternate your steps so the weight gets distributed evenly. There're twelve steps, and my boots are bloody. Shit, I have to go extra slow so the slimy blood doesn't tip my ass over tin cups. Unclasping the strap from the Fairbairn-Sykes commando knife, John slowly leans over the floor to the find the sentry sleeping. *Asshole,* John thinks, and plunges the knife in the larynx and cuts from left to right and right to left (ear to ear; the blood from both carotid arteries spews out like the fountain at Trevi). After wiping the knife on the dead soldier's shirt, John slowly returns the blade to the sheath and grabs the AK-47, puts it around his shoulders, and slowly climbs down the ladder.

Reconnoitering the area near the POW hut, John slowly and silently makes his way to the back of the prisoners' hut. The hut's floor is about three feet above ground level, with a crude ladder leading to the only door in front, which is latched with a crude wooden latchkey system. The hut is made of bamboo all tied together with leather lacing cut from the hides of water buffalos. The prisoners are all tied up with parachute cord and duct tape, courtesy of Uncle Sam. It's hard for them to move around, so they just lie there and ponder their fate.

John creeps up and with his mouth close to the openings in the bamboo rods and whispers, "Yorkie, Hun, are you there? Yorkie, Hun, are you there?"

"Oh my god," Hun says, "is that you, Mad Dog?"

"Yes, it's me. Who were you expecting—Santa?"

"Don't fuck around, Mad Dog. these motherfuckers are going to execute us in the morning."

"Okay, listen to me, how many are you in there? There's me and Yorkie and three flyboys who were shot down a couple of days ago."

"Is there a guard in there with you?"

"No, thank god, or we wouldn't be able to talk with you."

"Now I'm cutting these leather ties so I can reach in and cut your bindings." Braz cuts Hun free and passes to him his little old Barlow knife, which of course is razor sharp. "Now cut everybody free. How bad is anybody hurt?"

"Yorkie and I are okay, just a little sore from where the bastards hit us. The marine pilot is okay. He just got beat up by the VC. The navy guy is okay, but he's shit scared, not of the VC or NVA, but his father is a vice admiral at the Pentagon, and is a real ballbuster. He said his old man will kick his ass if he screws up. Looks like he is in for an ass kicking. The air force pilot is a lieutenant colonel, and he is in real bad shape. If he lives another day without medical help, he won't make it. Yorkie helped him as much as he could, but without his medical bag, he wasn't much help." All the time this was going on was only a few seconds.

"Hun, I am going to cut the bamboo rods away from the back of this hut so we can get everybody out the rear side, so if any VC comes out of the command hut, they hopefully won't see us. So get to work cutting the shackles off everybody. We have four AK-47s I took from the VC and my pistol, two grenades, and one claymore mine.

"Now that everybody is out, this is the plan of action. I will tie the claymore to the front door. When it blows the door in, it should kill a lot of Charlies. As soon as the door goes, you and Hun lob those frags in, and you, major guy and navy guy, start shooting short bursts at anything that moves. Only shoot three round bursts. We may have to conserve what ammo we can scrounge up in case more Charlies show up. Yorkie, let us take a minute to digest what I just said. Is everybody clear on the plan?" There were yeahs all around. "Hun, did you guys notice any more boats at the pier where they landed you?"

"Yes, sir, there were several fishing boats with small outboard motors, but nothing big enough for all of us."

"We may have to make do with what's down there. Set the air force colonel down away from harm's way, and the rest of us slowly crawl about ten yards in front of the hut. I will hang the claymore on the door and hope I don't wake up anybody inside. I have the electronic blaster in my left hand and my .45 in my right. If they get me, try to kill 'em all and hotfoot it for the river, and don't leave the colonel.

"Wait, wait, son of a bitch, looky there, it's a Russian helicopter. I wonder where Ivan is? Don't shoot anybody that's six foot tall or is wearing a flight suit, or is blond and hefty. I can fly us out of here if there is enough fuel in that big ugly Russian cargo piece of shit.

"Okay, guys, close your eyes so the initial blast and fireball don't screw up your night vision." Braz presses the electronic blaster, and the noise of the claymore is deafening. The claymore mine is a curved-shaped explosive with C-4 plastic explosive shaped in an arc and has steel ball bearings shrapnel as the killing pieces. It can tear a person or persons to a bloody and mushy mess in a heartbeat.

As soon as the initial explosion went off, Hun, Yorkie, and the marine major rushed the front of what was left of the hut. They were blasting away with the AKs when out of the corner of his eye, the marine saw the side loading door of the helo open, and a great big bear of a fellow in a blue Russian flight suit waving a small pistol (Russian Makorov 9 mm) jumped down to the deck. The marine turned, and Braz yelled, "Don't shoot," but it was too late. The marine let loose with a shot that caught the Russian in his lower leg. The marines are schooled in marksmanship and taught to shoot first before the enemy gets a chance to kill you first. Fortunately, the bullet went through and through the calf muscle and was not life threatening. It hardly bled enough to fill half a beer can.

Braz ran over to the pilot and motioned the marine (who had a gun right in the Russian's face) to lower the weapon and he would take care of this situation. "*Tovarishch*, comrade," Braz says, "we really mean you no harm (as Braz is waving his arms in front of him). Do you speak English? My Russian is not too good."

CHAPTER FIVE

"*Da*, Lieutenant, I speak the English some very guut."

"Oh, that's great, sir. I see you are a colonel in the Russian Air Force. Who did you piss off in the politburo to get a crappy assignment like this?"

"Meester Lieutenant, it is a very long and sad story inwolving a commissar who is a liar and a thief. Colonel, what's your name?"

"I am 1st Lt. John M. Braz, US Army."

"Yes, I see that from the way you order the men to do your bidding. I saw it from the little slot below the pilot's seat before I came out and the marine shot me."

"Well, Colonel, I am sorry. The marine major is a little trigger-happy, but the Charlies treated him very rough. He might have thought you were a VC piece of crap. Colonel, let's get down to business. We are going to borrow your aircraft to get us all out of here, and we got to do it quickly."

"Dat is goot, Lieutenant. I hate these peoples. They are barbarians, and they make wery bad soldiers."

"How much fuel do you have on board?"

"Plenty of petrol enough to get us to your camp at Bien Hoa, or to the coast at Nha Trang."

"You still did not identify yourself."

"Sorry, Lieutenant. My name is Col. Sergi Ivanovitch Prokodnov, Russian Air Force." The two men shook hands.

Lieutenant Braz asked Sergi. "How do we get this bird started?" I don't see a mule or an external power system to fire this helo up."

"There is no mule, as you call it (portable generator). We start the engines with compressed air from the tanks on top. I will explain the system once we are ready to go."

"All right, men, start loading the air force colonel on board."

"Mad Dog, how are we going to carry him without hurting him anymore?" asks Yorkie.

"Sergi, do you have any body bags on board strong enough to carry a man?"

"Da, Lieutenant. They are stored in the last locker in the right bulkhead behind the copilot's seat."

"Colonel, where is your first aid kit?"

"On this wall right here, Lieutenant."

"You heard the man, Yorkie. Hop to it and be careful—he is in a lot of pain. The poor bastard, I hope we can get him to some professional medical attention before it's too late. Everybody get on board. Hun, get a head count. I know there are only seven of us, including Sergi, but we can't leave anybody behind."

"We are all on board, sir."

"Good. Secure the door. Colonel, show me how the compressed air function starts the turbines."

"Okay, Lieutenant. Engage this lock to open and throw the switches. You hear the air rushing noise? As soon as this gauge (as he was tapping on a dial) reaches the green pie piece, the turbines can be started. You now flip the master switches number 1 and 2, and the turbines will rotate."

A great whoopee, whistling, and cheering came up from the cheap seats. "Okay, Johnny, the bird, she is in your hands." Lieutenant Braz turns his head to look back in the cargo area and motions for Hun and Yorkie to don the flight helmets like the ones Sergi and Braz are wearing. Flipping the switch to talk to the crew, Braz reminds everybody to strap in on the canvas and pipe seating.

The H-1D Hind helicopter is a very large cargo chopper that can be configured to a bomber, a fighter (for strafing), or troop support aircraft. The Russian Air Force is using them in a place called Afghanistan against the Muslims.

Once Lieutenant Braz was satisfied the oil pressure and temperature and hydraulic pressure were optimal, he lifted the big bird off and turned south to a heading that would place them on a line with the base at Bien Hoa. Lieutenant Braz is thinking, *It normally takes two people to fly this kind aircraft,* and his ego and confidence level is at an all-time high. He was still scared and a little bit wary that he and Sergi would be able to pull this off in spite of this ambiguous thinking. He can't let the guys know that he has never flown a helicopter as big or complicated like this one, so every move he makes to adjust for movement (yaw and pitch, skid or slip), it has to look as coordinated as possible because he can feel ten pairs of eyes boring into the back of the pilot's seat.

I know just what to do to throw these guys off of my skills—Sergi and I will speak Russian. I need to know what radio frequencies to get on to alert the Americans who we are, and I can't let everybody look askance when I need to know what this or that instrument gauge is doing.

"Col. Sergi Ivanovitch Prokodnov, is it okay if we converse in Russian?"

"Da, Lieutenant, is okay. I think I understand reason for this."

"Da[1] yashu prah chee yahy eh tah sloh vah, vastohk a vah syeh veer, Oh cheen khah rah shoh vi znaht eekt yashu.

Khah roh shiy ti znaht vahsh yoohk."

(Yes, John, read this word? "East," and this word "north." Very good yashu)"

"Dahs tuh vaht Bien Hoa bis triy" (Good you know your way south).

"Shtaht nah eekh gah lah vah seet ee ah mi" (Stay on this heading and we get to Bien Hoa quickly).

"Mayday, Mayday, Mayday. This is United States Army first lieutenant John M. Braz flying a Russian Hind H-1 helicopter in sector B South Vietnam. We are trying to reach any friendly Allied or US aircraft. We are in need of assistance in the way of escorting us to the army base at Bien Hoa. I am not declaring an emergency. The helo we are flying is a good aircraft. Please don't shoot us down.

"We have on board three US pilots that were shot down and captured by North Vietnamese troops. We liberated them from a small temporary POW camp along the Song Lily River, north of Lai Khe and the Special Forces camp 105. Also on board with me are

---

1   The Russian words are written in a phonetic style, as we have no Cyrillic alphabet to reference to.

two US Army Rangers and the Russian pilot whom we persuaded to be repatriated to the land of the big PX.

"Any friendly aircraft, please call us. We don't want to be mistaken for the enemy."

"Russian Hind, this is F-105 Thunderchief. I have you on my radar, so don't do anything you will regret. I am carrying a full load of ordnance. Identify everyone on board your aircraft so we know who you really are."

"American 105 Thunderchief, I read you loud and clear. I don't really know the protocol for a situation like this, so we will let you talk to all the people here."

First is the marine pilot. "F-105, boy, am I glad to speak with you. I am United States Marine Corps captain Micheal S. Williams. I flew with the Marine Corps VMF 250 Squadron on the USS carrier *Harry Truman*. I was shot down by a ground-to-air missile three days ago. I was captured very quickly as my chute got entangled in a tree as I was just about to hit the deck. The VC wanted to shoot me right then and there, but an NVA officer, who apparently was the boss, made them take me to the little camp and put me in a bamboo cage."

"F-105 to Russian helo, that's a good sob story, Mike, but how do we know you guys are not just a bunch of English-speaking assholes? Who would fly a chopper loaded with explosives onto the base at Bien Hoa?"

"Listen, you air force dickhead, call the carrier and verify my departure and no return. If you glammer boys in those brand-new planes shoot us down, you have to answer to the United States, and my call sign is Tiger. VMF Squadron 250 knows my plight."

"This is US Army lieutenant Braz. Is there anybody else who can help us and run interference? I know you guys monitor all the frequencies."

"Navy F-4 Phantom to Army Hind—boy, that feels strange saying that. This is US Navy F-4D Phantom. Tell me some more about this mission. Who else is with you?"

"Navy Phantom, this is US Navy lieutenant commodore Billy Joe Evans, call sign BUBBA."

"Bubba, is that you? We looked all over when we heard you got hit. This is Leslie Wilkes."

"Les, oh my god, please don't let the air force guy put a missile up our ass. The Vietcong were going to execute us today. Thank god this crazy fucking army lieutenant came to our rescue. The son of a bitch is a one-man frigging army."

"Navy guy, this is the crazy lieutenant Braz. Do you have the new sophisticated commo equipment on board your plane?"

"Navy to Army guy, yes, I do. What can I help you with?"

"Can you connect me with Andy Lord, CIA station chief, Bangkok?"

"Yeah, hold on a sec." The secure radio phone rings in Andy Lord's reception area.

"Andy Lord's office of the military attaché, this is Laura."

"Andy please. Laura, this is John Braz."

"Johnny, is it really you? At camp 105, they figured you were dead or captured."

"Nah, those bastards can't shoot straight. I would rather talk to you any day, sweetheart, but I really need Andy now."

"John, what's up?"

"Colonel, I got a really good deal for you. I am driving a Russian Hind H-1 helo with some of my boys and a couple of former POWs. The Russian pilot and I became fast asshole buddies. He wants to defect to the United States. You and the CIA can take the helo and reverse engineer it. Please talk to him. He needs to get his wife and daughter out of the Soviet Union. They are in Kiev. We have assets close by, don't we? Your Russian is very good, so you two can converse. He will tell you addresses and phone numbers. I was thinking, if you get a black chopper to Bien Hoa with a pilot that can fly this bird, within the hour, we will be setting down at the far end of their east-west Runway 91R. You can transfer Sergi Ivanovitch Prokodnov (my new best buddy) to your bird and whisk him away from the army and, worst, the State Department—they will try to make an international incident out of this.

"I know my ass is in a real bad crack right now, and I will either get an attaboy or get tossed out on my ass and may even see the inside of Fort Leavenworth from a prisoner's perspective. But it is all worth it. We got three of our flyboys back that took the federal government millions of dollars to train, and their mothers many months of worry.

"So, old buddy, if you can get the Hind and Sergi off of Bien Hoa in a hurry, it will solve a lot of problems because you know how General Desmond hates the Russians. He was with Patton and General White when Ike wouldn't let them cross the Elbe River and take out the Stalinists and the last remnants of Red Army. Desmond figured he would have made lieutenant general and come home a bona fide hero."

"Sounds like a workable plan to me, Mad Dog. Laura is listening in. She can contact our people in Kiev. There is a little burg about twenty-five miles south of Kiev called Khmelnytskyi. That's where we have a safe house, and our assets work in Kiev every day. Put the colonel on this frequency, and we will get this snatch and grab and put it in the history books. John, one more thing, I am glad you had enough sense to refer to the colonel with his full name. It is a big insult right off the bat to introduce someone of his rank by a first name only."

"So when you talk to him again, say Sergi Ivanovitch Prokodnov."

"Okay, put him on." John switched to a different frequency in order to talk to the local air traffic.

"Army Hind Helo, this is US Army Sikorsky Helo H-1. How do you read me? Helo H-1, I read you six by six, is this WO-5 Lightfoot?"

"You got me, Mad Dog. We are on your six back about three hundred yards and five hundred feet above you. We heard the nasty exchange you had with that F-105 jockey. I wouldn't put it past him to buzz your aircraft. If that would happen, it could dispel the air over your rotors and you would sink like a rock. So that's why I am riding rear shotgun for you."

"Thanks, Lightfoot. I knew you were one of the good guys. Just don't get yourself in some trouble 'cause I am in enough of a shit storm for a whole regiment."

"Don't worry about it, Mad Dog. My squadron CO told me to get up here and render assistance."

"Army Base Bien Hoa Control Tower, this is US Army first lieutenant John Braz requesting landing permission. Come in, Bien Hoa."

"Army Hind, we have you at twenty-five miles out. Turn left and start descending to angels two for seven minutes. Call me when you have reached altitude."

"Bien Hoa, acknowledge turn left, drop to two thousand, seven minutes, call. Bien Hoa, we have reached altitude. Further instructions please? We have the runway in sight."

"Army Hind, turn left and line up with the center stripe. Complete your descent till your glide slope aligns with actual descent. We put you on final because of the wounded airman. You are nosing out a C-130 Hercules cargo coming from Nha Trang with supplies for the marines, and he is not a happy camper. He was on final way out, and I made him go around."

"Army Hind to Ground Control, we are over the numbers now, wheels on the ground. I am moving over to the navy ambulance chopper to off-load the wounded and ambulatory pilots. Thanks for your assistance."

"Colonel Prokodnov, I hope your conversation with Colonel Lord was worthwhile?"

"Da, Lieutenant, it was hopeful. He said they would be out of Khmelnytskyi before morning, their time. Good, my friend. It is already 3:00 a.m., Russian time now."

"Okay, Colonel. The CIA chopper is next to the navy helo. Why don't you sneak over and get on board? The crew chief is waving at me and giving me the heads-up sign. They want to get all three choppers in the air as fast as possible.

"I will be able to keep in touch with you through Andy's office. I wish you a good life, and we all hope you like it living in America."

"Thank you, yashu. I will give you Russian bear hug then I go get on the other chopper."

Lieutenant Braz, Yorkie, and Hun are making their way over to the H-1 Sikorsky that landed right after Braz set the Hind on the ground. "The rotors are idling," says Yorkie. "We better get on board and get back to camp before the brass gets here."

"Uh-oh, too late. Here comes Captain Jenkins and General Desmond."

"Hold up there, Lieutenant Braz," yells Captain Jenkins. "The general and I want a word with you guys."

"Yes, sir," says Braz, as the higher-ranking officers approach Braz and his men snap to attention and present a hand salute.

The general salutes back and says, "Stand at ease, men." General Desmond is perspiring not from the heat but from how irritated he is.

"Braz, what the hell do you think you are—a fucking whole army by yourself? I know you are not trying to get a shitload of medals ('cause you won't wear them anyway no matter who issues them). If the news boys get a hold of you stealing a Russian helicopter, them socialist bastards will try to make an international incident out of this.

"I know you rescued your guys and three flyboys, and I commend you heartily for that. I might recommend you for a commendation myself (yeah, when pigs fly)."

"General, if I may say a word, I did not steal the helo—we borrowed it. We got to be buddies with the Russian colonel Sergi Ivanovitch Prokodnov who was the pilot, and he expressed an interest of repatriating to the United States, so he let me fly the helo back to Bien Hoa."

"Wait, wait, wait a damn minute. Who the hell taught you to fly a chopper like that?"

"No one, sir. I always flew the Little Birds and some of the Sikorskys around, and once you know how to pilot one chopper, they all are the same in theory."

"Braz, is there no end to your so-called autonomy in this man's army?"

"Sir, I just feel that I am doing my job the best way I know how."

"Okay, Lieutenant. You are going back to Colonel Lord, and he can put up with your shenanigans. Oh, and another thing, how did you do away the sentries at that POW camp without shooting them and making a lot of noise?"

"Well, sir, I—"

"Don't lie to me. I know you killed them with a crossbow, and you know that crossbows are outlawed by the Geneva Convention. That's why this could lead to an international incident."

"If you would only let me explain, sir, there were four sentries and twenty other NVA soldiers and Vietcong sappers in that hut. If I made a lot of shooting noise when I wasted those sentries, we all would have been captured and executed. And I didn't kill all the sentries with the crossbow. I knifed the last bastard 'cause he was sleeping on guard duty."

"I suppose you used your Fairbairn-Sykes commando dagger on that guy?"

"Yes, I did, sir. He lost a lot of blood fast."

"Spare me the details, Braz. Now get on back to 105 camp and teach those SF soldiers how to use a knife."

"I don't need to teach them, sir—they taught me."

"Captain Jenkins, are you riding with us?"

"No, Braz, I have my own Little Bird. I will be close behind you all. And, Braz, you and Sergeants Yorkie and Hun, report to my hooch as soon as you land. Do not, I repeat, do not go anywhere else until I see all of you. Do I make myself clear?"

"Yes, sir's" all around.

Army helo H-1 comes into camp 105, and there is a pretty big group of Special Forces and other army types waiting for Braz and his men to off-load on the dusty strip. A big and incredibly loud cheer goes up welcoming back these guys. Braz tells Yorkie and Hun to disembark the bird. He waits for WO-5 Lightfoot to shut down the helo so he can talk to him and his copilot.

"Jeff, and you too, WO David (WO-2 David 1. Storm), I really can't thank you guys enough for watching my six back there and for coming and getting us out of the ambush site upriver. Both of you men are good pilots, and I will so note it in my after-battle reports and in today's action. If any of you ever find out who the 105 Thud pilot was, please pass on that info. That SOB was just a little bit over the top in his zeal to interrogate us. I am sure no Oriental can mimic a southern drawl like the marine pilot. That should have been clue enough as to who we were. Thanks again. I have to get to Captain Jenks's hooch for another ass chewing.

CHAPTER SIX

1600 hours, Captain Jenkins's command hooch

Captain Jenks enters, and the three rangers stand at attention. "At ease, men. Sit wherever you can. Lieutenant Braz, before we get into a fistfight, I would like to welcome the two sergeants back to the land of the living. I hope you men realize what Braz has done to get himself inasmuch trouble as he is in now. I know you are only here because of his uncanny skill and love for his men. And I know you will be forever grateful because you're good American soldiers.

"But he could have gotten all of you killed, and himself. That rescue mission called for a whole platoon, or even a company-size unit to make it work."

Braz, Yorkie, and Hun all are thinking the same thing, *Bullshit. This go-by-the-book Special Forces captain can't even comprehend the difficulty it would be for that many troops to get there fast enough to save anybody.*

Braz speaks, "May I say something, sir?"

"Go ahead, Braz, it's your ass on the fire."

"Well, sir, I realize you are West Point trained and have been in the army more years than me. Your by-the-book regulations and small and large group tactics just don't fit into a guerrilla style of warfare.

"By the time a larger fighting unit got to that camp, the prisoners would have been killed, and the enemy long gone. Sir, I realize I have been in the army for only sixteen years, yet I've been fighting in the jungles for over twelve years of that time."

"Braz, I know you are right on most of what you profess to be fact. I have to look at the bigger picture. I have to answer to the higher brass, and most of these colonels and generals are World War Two veterans used to fighting more conventional style of warfare.

"General Desmond said to me he knows why people call you Mad Dog. Your CO in Thailand before Andy Lord referred to you as a loose cannon. The vice admiral of MACV said you were an unguided missile. Why do you think you haven't been rotated? And I know you turned down *twice* the promotion board's recommendation for you to be a captain. With your time in grade, you should be on the list for major at this time.

"I know why—you don't want the responsibility of a large command, you hate politics, you abhor red tape and bureaucracy, and you don't like to take orders and do things the army way. I am correct, aren't I?

"Now, men, I am sending you all back to Col. Andy Lord. Sgt. Hansl Von Stead, you and Sgt. Dean Vincent Young (a.k.a. Hun and Yorkie; Yorkie was called Yorkie because the first time Braz met him and found out they were both from Pennsylvania—Yorkie was from York, Pennsylvania—he just had to refer to him as Yorkie), the both of you are going on thirty days R & R (rest and recuperation)."

"Oh no, sir," they both said in unison, "we have a lot of work to do here."

"Like what—keeping Braz out of trouble? Believe me, you both will be better off with some time away from Lieutenant Braz."

"Oh, please, sir, we had leave less than six months ago."

"Sorry, guys, it's out of my hands. Army regulations states anyone captured and made a prisoner of war, when he or she is released, is required to go on leave, unless a medical condition prevents it. And you can't go over my head, for the COS (army chief of staff) approved the orders himself.

"And you, my young lieutenant, along with these two, will be on the C-47 Air America due in here at 0400 dark time, taking you back to Bangkok and the waiting arms of Colonel Lord." Braz is fantasizing about the perfume-enrapt arms of Laura Diskin. But at this time, his mind is not on the flight to Thailand; he is jumping out of his skivvies wanting to get his hands on the throat of that bastard senator Omalley.

When they were getting off the helo about an hour ago, Hun spied the senator over by the hooch he used when in camp. He nudged the lieutenant. "I see him," said Braz. "My yards are keeping watch on him. When we get through with Jenks, we are all going to make like we're going to get some chow. There I can rendezvous with my yards and snatch Omalley and get him out of camp where we can dispose of the treasonous son of a bitch."

Captain Jenkins strolls out of his hooch. "Hey, Lieutenant Braz, give me another minute?"

Oh, fuck, what does he want now?

"John, I know that you want to kill the senator, but be very careful. See those guys he's drinking with? The short guy in the civvies is CID (Criminal Investigation Division) for the army. He helped write some of the new laws in the Army Uniform Code of Justice Manual. The taller guy is Congressman Owen Spurling from the great state of Colorado, you know, the bastion of liberalism. The three of them together make a nasty headache for the good senators and congressmen trying to get the appropriations we need to end this war. That congressman along with that no-good socialist movie star who was seen sitting atop an NVA tank in Hanoi, waving a Vietcong flag are good friends. It was all over the news reels back in the States. The antiwar draft card burners loved it.

"Now, Johnny, I am not telling you your business, but please stay away from that unholy duo. And I want all you and the sergeants on that C-47 at 0400 dark time."

"Yes, sir, we will make the plane. Now I need some chow and a cold beer if anybody has one."

"John, in your hooch, is an old Styrofoam cooler with a six-pack of Budweiser and some clean ice that just came in today, and your half of a quart of Black Jack is still in your locker. When the word came out that you slipped out, most of my guys figured you were not coming back. So they wanted to get your booze, but I blew a fuse and said I would cut the balls off anyone going near your area. Anyway, I knew you would be coming back. I didn't know how or in what venue, just that my intuition and my faith in knowing Mad Dog told me so." John went to his hooch first before he hit the mess tent. The cooler with the beer was just as Captain Jenks said it was. That first cold beer tasted so good he wanted another, but he knew he needed to share with Yorkie and Hun. Plus in his footlocker were two envelopes he needed to retrieve, the envelopes he got from Andy Lord before they left Bangkok. In each packet was an amalgamation of bills, American, Thai, Laotian, Cambodian, and Vietnamese.

This money was for the yards John was to meet at or behind the mess tent. It depended who was at chow and if they were spying on John and the sergeants. There were only a few Special Forces troops lingering around, having a last cup of coffee. John invited the yards to sit with him, Yorkie, and Hun. Yorkie conveniently laid an old map on the table, and everybody crowded around to look and listen to what John was whispering. Very slow and cool, John slipped the packets of money under the map, and when the yards were ready to leave, Meong Hua, the leader of the group, folded the map around the packets, and nobody was the wiser.

It was not uncommon for commanders to go over maps and other intel while sitting in the chow tent. So no interest was taken in this meeting of warriors. "Meong, where is the girl?"

"Back in my family hut, Lieutenant."

"And where is the VC soldier that is going to give his all for the cause?"

"Lieutenant, you make it seem like this is a game. There are very high and important doings here. I have to get my family out of this district to a safer place to live before the Cong realizes they are not responsible for what we are to do this night."

"Meong, and you too, Song La, don't worry. This will be an easy mission. I saw that the fat senator and his friends are well on their way to getting plastered. What time is the girl going to proposition Omalley?"

"Lieutenant, she is coming to the bar at nine o'clock. By that time the lawyer and the CID man will be pretty drunk, my sister and her girlfriend will escort them back to the senator's hut. They know how to act very friendly and let the pigs think they might score a little bit of sex. But my sister Nguyen and Thanh have some whiskey laced with sleeping powders we got in Laos. One drink of this, and the Americans will be asleep for hours, if not for a whole day.

"When the decoy girl gets the senator back to my hut, he will be pretty sloppy drunk and, as you Americans say, growing big horns."

"Ha-ha-ha." Everybody got a jolt out of the yard's joke, even though Meong didn't catch it. He was just happy John was pleased with the plan.

"Okay, Sir John, we will wait for you at about 9:05 at my hut. If you don't see my red neck cloth on the door, the girl and the senator are not there yet. So hide in the shadows till you see this going down.

"Meong, I know how to do surveillance. Just inject the pig with the syringe like I showed you in the Green Beret camp over in Cambodia. Then all we have to do is get him across the river and finish the job."

Ming Liu, a Vietnamese girl with Chinese ancestry, is a beautiful woman, tall for an Oriental, with typical long black hair and almond-shaped eyes with dark piercing centers that just beckon to anyone staring into them. *You will do my bidding and fall in love with me. You have no choice but to come with me and service my every desire.* This is how Omalley saw this goddess as she came into the bar with Nguyen and Thanh. Ming and the girls were dressed in the typical Vietnamese ao dai and cheongsam that was slit all the way up to their thighs. The very filmy and clingy material showed off the shapes of these lush torsos and legs against the drab background of a hastily made den of relaxation. This bar was only open one or two nights a week for visiting brass, newshounds, and other self-appointed VIPs, and that was only if beer could be had this early in the war. And it was not for the regular troops, only on a special occasions. For the warriors who did the heavy lifting (fighting), this place was off limits.

When Omalley saw Ming, he almost had a heart failure. He made a drunken beeline for her (as he was the most important person in the room in his own mind). Ming Liu in typical B-girl fashion made a great big smile and very coyly introduced herself, letting the cheongsam fall away from her leg. Omalley was hooked like a trout on a royal coachman fly. She offered to sit down at a makeshift table made of wooden pallets and mortar containers. "You will buy me a drink sir please?"

"Oh, you betcha." He was falling all over himself, trying to get another chair.

Meanwhile, Thanh and Nguyen had the lawyer and the CID man hooked and reeled in. Ming leaned closer to Omalley and said, "I know you will want to come down to my house, where we can have some privacy." Omalley's eyes were glazed over with lust. Her perfume was all encompassing and acted like the aphrodisiac it was. Omalley would have followed her to hell right now; he was the horniest guy in all of Southeast Asia.

The lawyer and the CID man went with Thanh and Nguyen back to their hut, where the biggest headache in the world waited for these guys who thought for sure they were going to get laid.

Ming Liu and Omalley walked, stumbled, and crawled to the Meong family hut. It was just five minutes to nine. Meong opened the door and let both of them in. In a flash, he had the syringe jabbed in the carotid artery of the fat neck. In a few hours' time. he won't ever need a carotid artery or any other kind of artery again.

Meong handed over to Ming one of the envelopes with cash for her part in the snatch and grab. Lieutenant Braz walked in the door and was very pleased at what he saw. He being the gentleman and officer had an old French automobile waiting to take her back to Saigon. She could not show her face or body in these parts in case someone recognized her from the bar at the camp.

There will be a wholesale investigation when this gets out that Omalley is missing. And Braz thanked her with a hug and kiss that rocked him to his boots. Omalley wasn't the only one filled with longing and lust. Braz is thinking, *Another time, another place, and maybe I will take up that offer from Andy to do intel work in Saigon. No, not now, Johnny boy. Get on with the program. We only have few hours to do the dirty deed and get back to the 0400 flight.* Meong had his water buffalo cart loaded with what small amount of belongings his family brought from the Montagnard village of Sui Thong. They all helped load the carcass of the senator on the cart. Meong's wife, Laht Ygongh, helped to guide the cart over river on the hidden underwater bridge (built by the Vietcong to harass the Americans).

The small group was making its way toward the rendezvous point when Lieutenant Braz suddenly held up his right hand with a closed fist, in the universal sign to stop and be very still. He whispered to Meong, "There is a Vietcong patrol ahead of us and to our right. We will sit here for a while. I will go ahead and scout out the safest way to proceed. Don't move a muscle and stay right here. Pass on to everybody what the situation is."

Finally, the small cadre of men and women reached the small clearing. Lieutenant Braz asked the men to unload Omalley from the water buffalo cart and tie him to a large tree right next to the Vietcong soldier who was captured earlier. About this time, the rotten senator was awake and started to realize what was happening. "Meong, I am glad you and your people wore the rubber gloves we stole from the medical supply tent. We can't afford to leave any fingerprints. When the army finds the bodies, the CID (Criminal Investigation Division) will do a very thorough search and autopsy 'cause the US Senate will be up in arms over losing one of their own, even though a lot of them know what a scoundrel he is."

Now comes the nasty part. Braz tears the duct tape from Omalley's mouth. "What the fuck is the meaning of this, Braz? I will have your ass in Leavenworth for the rest of your life. Release me immediately, you army asshole."

"Now, Senator (Braz has a big smile on his face), we know you and Than Vo Luc and Lequesta set up me and my guys for the ambush at the Song Lily River. We—meaning the CIA—know all about the money laundering, the stolen Buddhist relics, the gold South African coins, and the drugs and cocaine you are smuggling into the United States. If you were just a plain ole thief, life would be different."

"What are you going to do with me? Let me go, and I will make you a very wealthy man."

"No, Sean Thomas Omalley. We have closed down most of your overseas bank accounts, and contents of your safe deposit boxes are in the coffers of the CIA. As we speak, your wife has taken most of the assets from your US accounts, and she has filed for divorce in your home state of Colorado. She has known for years about the cheating you thought you were getting away with. But when the brother of the president who was banging Marilyn Monroe found the four of you in the White House having a sex orgy—he with the movie star, and you with a sixteen-year-old Catholic school girl—the brother was so jealous, he let a rumor get started through the liberal press about the whorehouse the White House is turning into."

"Meong, we have the senator's gun, don't we?"

"Yes, Lieutenant, It's over there next to the wad of cash and keys and a notepad."

"Where's the wallet, Meong?"

"Thanh and Nguyen are looking at the pictures."

"Okay, as long as they don't leave any prints on it. Did you count the money?"

"Yes, sir, it's USD 8,000 and VND 2,000."

I have to make a silencer for the senator's gun, a Tokarev TT-33 7.62 x 25 mm Soviet pistol, and a silencer for the Vietcong pistol. Bring it here to me please, Meong? This is an old Belgium weapon, a Nagant model 1895 7.62 x 38 mm. It will be harder to craft a silencer for this pistol, but I can make it.

"Those two plastic water bottles will do nicely. First, I cut a hole about an inch in diameter in the bottoms. Then, Meong, let me have one of the stuffed pillows from the cart. Now we stuff some of the spongy stuffing in the bottle then we insert the barrel of the pistol in the small hole at the top of the bottle. With duct tape securing the pistol to the bottle, we have a good makeshift silencer.

"Mr. Sean Thomas Omalley, I am going to try and hurt you as much as I can in the time I have left." With that statement, Braz grabbed the arm of the Vietcong (the Cong prisoner was all trussed up and sedated) and pressed the Tokarev 33 into his hand, pushed the trigger finger in the trigger safety, and aimed the gun right at the left kneecap of the senator. The only sound was the cowardly senator screaming beneath the duct tape mask. The pain of a shot-up kneecap is one of the most excruciating in the world. The blowback from the shot was all over the Vietcong's hand. Braz shot the senator in his shoulder, trying to not hit a major artery, for when the army found the bodies, forensics would tell the approximate time of death. And Braz needed it to be as near 4:00 a.m. as possible; the time now was 3:15 a.m. Braz figured the senator would take at least one hour to bleed out if the bullets didn't hit any major arteries, or if he didn't go into shock and have a heart attack.

So to lessen the chance of something going wrong, Braz had another part of the plan, which included giving fatso a shot of something like Demerol in a spot the best forensic investigator would not find. They untied the senator from the tree and took down his pants and underwear, which he had pissed in several times. Braz took the syringe, rolled back the foreskin on the senator's dick, and inserted the needle up the pee tube and pushed it till he felt the needle go into the flesh. Then he pushed the plunger all the way till all the medicine was gone, therefore leaving no marks for the pathologist to find. At this time, they redressed the senator and rolled him over near the dead VC, so as to look like they shot each other. Braz put the gun in the senator's hand and shot the VC in the chest again.

Braz shared the wad of cash with Meong and all his family. He said, "I am hoping to have a date with a pretty lady when I get to Bangkok. I haven't gotten a paycheck in a while, and some of the senator's money would be well spent if things work out." The poor boy still has lust in the forefront of his skull and places further south.

He wished them all well and asked Meong to dispose of the silencer makings and all the ropes and duct tape used to tie up the bad guys.

"You can put the trash in a pillowcase, weigh it down with a rock, and throw it in the tributary of the Song Lily just over the ridge from where we are. The small river is called Song Due Toa and is only a few klicks west."

CHAPTER SEVEN

4 January 1961
Green Beret camp 105
Near Lai Khe, South Vietnam

Braz hightailed it out of there, crossed the river, and made it to the camp at quarter till four just in the nick of time. He made sure no one saw him. Braz went into his hooch and fell asleep almost instantly. At five to four, the droning noise of the DC-3 Dakota 1200 hp Wasp engines startled Braz, Yorkie, and Hun just as Captain Jenkins came into their hooch. "Well, I am glad you juvenile delinquents are all bright eyed and bushy tailed. Your ride is here, so get your boots on, grab your gear, and go back from whence you came."

"And a wonderful good morning to you too, Captain Jenkins," says Hun.

"We were just leaving but did not want to go without saying a fond fare thee well."

Captain Jenkins and his second in command escorted the guys to the Dakota. Coming off the plane were two more sticks of paratroopers (all Green Berets) with all their gear, weapons, mortar tubes, M60 machine guns, Browning Automatic Rifles, .45-caliber tommy guns, two Springfield model 1903 sniper rifles, .30-caliber M1903 outfitted with Redfield scopes.

The pilot of the Dakota shuts down the inboard engine, gets out of his seat, and walks down to the port-side door. Captain Jenkins asks, "Is there trouble with the motor?"

"Sir, it's nothing I can't handle. The inboard engine has been running a little hot all night. We had this trouble on this engine before. My crew chief needs to replace an old oil line that clogs up every now and then. I can disconnect it and, with a can of compressed air, blow it out and add a quart or two of lighter-weight oil And run it up to get the oil pressure at the correct PSF, and then we can take off."

"Well, Braz, thanks for making the camp a lot of fun again. I hope you don't take my remarks as gospel. You are really a good soldier and the most dedicated man I ever had the experience working with. Andy Lord is lucky to be getting you back. I held my breath through most of the night wondering if you went and killed the senator. Now that you are going, I will bet he goes somewhere else in this sector to justify his reason for being in Southeast Asia. Keep your nose clean and tell your sergeants that they both can qualify to the recruiter at Fort Bragg to take the exam for qualification to the Special Forces of the United States Army. I know that will make their day. When the both of them bitched and moaned about not staying in a combat zone, I knew they would make good SF troopers. All the CO at Bragg has to do is call me, and I will surely give Hun and Yorkie a good recommendation."

0500 hours
4 January 1961
Somewhere over Laos, Southeast Asia

The DC-3 carrying the three soldiers of the ASA (Army Security Agency) who were attached to the CIA on a somewhat permanent/ temporary basis was on a west-southwest heading to Bangkok, Thailand. Sergeants Hansl Von Stead and Dean Young were somewhat pissed off that they were being sent Stateside for thirty days' leave, as required for any ex-POW. They knew that Lieutenant Braz was getting some new assignments that would be a lot of hard and dangerous work. *This is what we trained for and what we know best.*

Their pleas fell on deaf ears. Army regulations called for the R & R, so Yorkie and Hun were going home for their thirty days' leave.

Lieutenant Braz had held on to the news about the Green Beret qualification course until now. He figured, *If I tell them now, they will quit pestering me, and I can get some much-needed sleep.* All the seats were removed from the plane to make room for the two sticks of paratroopers and their gear. The only seating was the canvas and pipe row seating along the inside walls of the fuselage. That's where Braz stretched out to catch some z's.

Yorkie and Hun were ecstatic about going back to Fort Bragg. The qualification course would be a snap, for these guys could teach the whole curriculum in their sleep. The only problem they faced was to not go to the fort before their accrued leave was over, or they might seem to eager and be disqualified right off the bat.

So Braz put the fear of God and General Patton in them. He said, "If I find out either one of, or both of you, was seen hanging the local bars in Fayetteville, North Carolina, trying to pump information from any of the young soldiers, I will come after you and have you thrown in jail till it is time to report to the recruit depot."

"Yes, sir."

"Yes, sir. We understand and acknowledge your orders, sir."

0800 hours
4 January 1961
The airport at Bangkok, Thailand

The Air America DC-3 lands, and ground control sends it to the Air America ramp. The three soldiers deplane and were met by Col. Andy Lord and his deputy, the breathtakingly lovely Ms. Laura Diskin. At the bottom of the stairs, the guys snap to attention and salute the colonel with a hand salute so crisp and professional that only a paratrooper could perform. Braz and the colonel greet each other with a quick handshake. Yorkie and Hun do the same. Miss Laura greets Braz with a very warm embrace and a kiss on the cheek, which makes everybody green with envy.

"Come on, Sergeants, you can ride with me," says the colonel. "Lieutenant Braz will ride with Ms. Diskin. I am sure they need to catch up on the intel and the latest poop from our assets."

Yorkie and Hun are both thinking the same thing, *The lucky SOB. I will bet his pants are wet by the time we get to the embassy.*

At the Embassy gate, the colonel's car is halted. The marine sentry comes over to the driver's side and salutes. "Good morning, Colonel Lord. May I see your ID?"

"Here you are, Sergeant."

"Would your two passengers mind stepping out of the car? And would you please open the trunk?"

"No problem again, Sergeant. The marine sentry is all business, guys. After we got firebombed, all the US facilities are under a concentrated terrorist alert."

Yorkie says, "We understand, sir. Maybe we can help round up some of these bad guys?"

"Nice try Sergeant. It won't work, though. I have your orders, airline tickets, back pay, and some of the marine guards to escort you both tomorrow evening to the Bangkok International Airport where they will accompany you to your seats. You will be watched all the way to Chicago and Pittsburgh."

"Goddammit," says Hun. "I bet Braz had a hand in this."

"No, Sergeant, Ms. Diskin made all the arrangements."

"That's what I meant—Braz had a hot little hand in this."

Yorkie popped up and said, "It wasn't his hand that was hot."

"Oh yeah, I get it now," as Hun made a face that would freeze a clock.

As Ms. Diskin's car (a 1957 Cadillac DeVille) rolled up to the embassy gate, the gate was swung back, and the sentry just waved her right on through. She raised her white-gloved hand and made a little finger wave to the marine sergeant. He was thinking, *Who is that lucky bastard riding in the front seat with her?*

When they parked, Braz ran around to the driver's door to open it for Laura and hopefully get a glimpse of those million-dollar legs. "Thanks for picking me up, Laura. It sure is wonderful seeing you again."

"John, it's going to be great working with you again, and General Wells has a surprise for you."

"*Groan*, oh no, what is it this time? I wish he would stick to soldiering instead of trying to play the spy game."

"Oh, don't worry, Johnny, it's a good thing."

"Laura, I . . . I . . . I . . . um . . . am having a devil of a time trying to ask you this."

"Johnny, I know what you want to ask me."

"You do?"

"Of course, I do, And the answer is yes, I will go out to dinner with you."

"Oh my goodness, Laura, this has been building up for quite a while."

"And for me too, John. You are such a badass when it comes to your job, but such a pussycat when you are around women."

"Oh, I don't think I am what you describe."

"Like hell, Johnny, your manners are impeccable, you hold open doors for women, you stutter and stammer around me like as if we were in the sixth grade, and you wanted to ask me to be your girlfriend."

"Holy crap, is that how I come across all the time?"

"Now, John, before we go upstairs to the office, here is your key to the new apartment in the Marriott Bangkok on Nong Chok Avenue. The embassy staff has taken all your duffel and weapons over there. It's only two blocks from here in a very safe area."

"What about Hun and Yorkie? Where are they staying?"

"Right here in the embassy. We need to keep an eye on them so they don't run off and try to get on board with you. They have to be on that plane tomorrow, John. Those guys are loyal to you—they will do anything to please you, including take a bullet for you."

"Yes, we trained them well, but they are going to the Green Berets after their leave, so I know they are very happy."

"Well, here we are—suite 210. The reception area is very large and comfy. This is my office now. You are here in the center office, next to General Wells, and the bull pen and secure room are over there in the center of the whole complex, and Andy is on the other side of your office."

"Who the hell set this arrangement up—Andy? What a fucking dork. First of all, your office should have an anteroom with bulletproof glass. The secure room should have access to a secure rear stairway. I don't want to be between Andy and Shorty Wells. The general and Andy will be passing through my space a thousand times a day. And my door will always be open as I sit and gaze and daydream about—"

"So is that a bad thing?"

"Of course not, but I won't ever get any work done."

"Darling, you are just going to have to reel it in now that you're back in the spook game again. When we go to dinner tonight, we are going to have a heart-to-heart long talk. We will go over our history with each other and just have a wonderful session getting to know the truth about you."

"Wait, wait a freaking minute, that crap goes both ways, ya know. I am not the—"

"Shush, John, here comes the boss and your guys, and look who popped in from the other door?"

"General Wells, good morning, sir."

"Morning, all. Johnny boy, it's good to have you back among the living."

"Oh heck, sir. You know the old Mark Twain saying (The rumors of my death and all that horseshit)."

"Well, son, you beat the Grim Reaper again. Let's get down to business. Laura, where are the tracks?"

"In my purse, sir."

"What the hell are they doing there?"

"I didn't want to lose them, so I kept them where I knew I could lay my fingers on them in a minute."

"Okay, good girl. Go over to the lieutenant and take off the old insignia. Lt. John M. Braz, you are promoted to captain in the United States Army. And don't let him give you a hard time, Laura. If he does, kick him or knee him where it will really hurt. You know he turned down a promotion twice. He can't do it now. We have him right by the short and curly hairs. Laura, give him a kiss—that way he will know it's for real this time."

"Yes, sir General. When I kiss 'em, they know they have been kissed."

Congratulations went around the room, and a bottle of Crown Royal was brought forth. "Now, John, Ms. Diskin set up your billet at the Bangkok Marriott. You will have a suite there in case we have to set up more space for our operations. This war is growing bigger every day, and the intel is coming from everywhere."

"Please let me cut in, General," says Col. Andy Lord. "John, if you stay with us for at least one more year, you can retire from the army and work for us full time. You will have all the army benefits, and you can still do the things you like without the oversight from the Congress and Senate—oh, and the White House."

"Oh sure, I can still be your hit man, and you have all plausible deniability that everybody I take out was in the venue of national security. And I would still have to secure the okay from you even when my ass is in a crack. That's a bunch of fucking horseshit. If some dumb fucker is pointing a gun at me or has a knife ready to fillet my nuts, I am going to kill him or her before they can get the thought out of their pea brain. So when do I start work, right now or what?"

"No, Captain, you got the day off to familiarize yourself again with the city. So go to your apartment and do your personal stuff. We will see you at 0500 hours."

Captain Braz left and walked the two blocks to his apartment building. Walking down the main boulevard, he noticed a black Mercedes with blacked-out windows parked near the far corner of the embassy compound. *I don't like the looks of that deal,* he is thinking.

In the lobby with the checkout counter, he gets his card key and parking slot number. Asking the desk clerk for the concierge, John casually turns around to check out the lobby. Again his sense of danger kind of tingles but does not turn into a full-scale alert. The concierge comes out of the office and greets John, "What can I do for you, Captain?"

In a low voice, John says, "That man sitting by the window, is he a guest?"

The concierge named Theadore answers, "No, I never saw him before." John slips a C-note to Theadore and asks him to keep an eye out and report to John any untoward behavior of this guy.

John takes the steps two and three at a time; he needs to get to a secure phone and fast. John calls the office half out of breath. "Laura, get me Andy ASAP."

"What's up, John?"

"Just get me Andy now please."

"Hey, you don't be such a demanding bastard, or I will take back everything I said earlier."

"John, this is Andy. What's up?"

"Do we have any assets in the hotel?"

"Yes, as a matter of fact, the concierge and the desk clerks are all on our payroll."

"Good, because there is a surveillance dude sitting in the lobby doing a bad job of hiding behind a newspaper. Also on the far east corner of the embassy, a blacked-out Mercedes with three guys in it is sitting there idling. It isn't one of ours, is it?"

"No, it's not. Johnny, please don't go after these guys alone. Let me send two of our big boys to help you."

"Don't worry about me. I am just going to put a bug (transponder) on the Mercedes. I will call in the license plate number. I got to go now. Don't allow Laura to go home without an escort or at least a tail. I am going to put my play clothes on and see if I can avoid getting in too much trouble."

Captain Braz changed to all-black pants and long-sleeve shirt, stuck a balaclava in his back pocket, and topped off the outfit with a Pittsburgh Steelers ball cap. Down the back stairs, he practically flew and knocked on the rear door in the service corridor that led to the private offices of the hotelier. Theadore opened the door, let him in, and said he just got off the phone with Andy. Braz asked if the dude was still in the lobby, and if there was an easy way to creep up on the dude. Theadore took him on a roundabout route on the other side of the lobby. John said thanks and told him to get lost, for he had some questions for the sloppy dude.

John slowly got in the back of the chair and took out the Fairbairn-Sykes, his favorite tool. With his left hand, grabbing the neck and windpipe, he set the dagger's point right under the jaw of the shit-scared bad guy, whispering in the guy's right ear, "Put both hands on the armrests, or I will slice you right here in this chair." John asked, "Do you have a gun on you? And don't lie, or it will be the last word you will ever speak." John eased up on the grip on the bad guy's neck so he could speak. John moved the tip of the razor-sharp knife and cut the flab under the jaw to draw a little blood. Blood always keeps them afraid and wondering if they are going to die.

"Who are you working for? Tell me the truth, your miserable life depends on it."

"I don't know who the man is, senor, only that he contacted me at the sailor's home where I stay when my ship is in port."

"How does he contact you?"

"He leaves a phone number for me to call to get instructions."

"How do you get paid?"

"An envelope is at the bar next to the sailor's home, with my name on it."

"Now tell me his name, you miserable sack of yak shit."

"Please, senor, I only know he is a Corsican. He speaks several languages. I overheard him talking to someone else when he was talking to me. I heard the other man call him Karol in Portuguese."

That lit up John's fire. "Talk to me and tell me the truth. Is this man's name Charro Lequesta?"

"I don't know for sure, it might be, I mean maybe it is. Please, senor, this man is a bloodthirsty killer, and he will kill me and my family if word should get out I said anything."

"Get up slowly. You and I are going for a little walk." The idiot sighed a little, thinking he could get the drop on John with the knife in a sheath in his left coat pocket. John felt the knife when he grabbed the asshole's neck. He felt it with his left elbow and forearm. As soon as he got out of the chair, John had him pinned to the wall with his forearm up against the dude's neck, almost breaking the larynx. A mighty punch to the gut almost made him vomit. He dropped to his knees and laid over on his side. John reached in and relieved him of the knife then patted the dude down, searching for other weapons. "Get up, you lying piece of trash." They went outside in the back of the hotel near the trash bins and close to the kitchen doors. One of the clerks who worked for Andy was sitting on a piece of concrete wall. He asked John if he needed any help. "No, I have this situation well in hand, but I need a car. Does the company let you have a vehicle?"

"Yes, that Ford Fairlane is the one I use."

"Good, get me the keys. I need to borrow it for a few hours."

"Okay, Captain, but please bring it back in one piece, or Colonel Lord will string me from the nearest light pole."

"Don't worry, son, I was driving when your daddy was a teenager." Braz clocked the dude with the side of his fist so hard he might have killed him. But all he wanted to do was put him out for a couple of hours.

John drove the Ford down to the waterfront. There he went in the chandler's shop, bought some line, and tied the dude up, threw him in the trunk, and shut it, hoping the dude wouldn't die before John had another go at him. He had stuffed a pair of dirty underpants in the dude's mouth so if he woke up, he would not cause a noisy ruckus.

Wandering around the waterfronts seedy bars, looking for anybody looking remotely like Lequesta, proved to be fruitless. It was getting dark now, and John had a date tonight. *Time to get back to the nicer part of the city.* Opening the trunk, staring at him with eyes as wide as trash can lids and full of the inevitable, the dude had pissed himself in abject fear. John pulled him out and sat him up against the rear tire, pulled the soiled underpants from the dude's mouth, and said one word, "Talk." Then he added, "Or you die." John did not like to kill someone in cold blood unless he had a reason. "Why were you surveilling the hotel?"

"The man who pays me had me watching the beautiful lady with the CIA."

"What? Are you shitting me?"

"No, senor, he told me if we could kidnap her, we could get to the army lieutenant he failed to kill in Vietnam." John's fury and rage went over the top; this is when he was at his best. He could not imagine anybody ever touching Laura. Now he had a reason to dispatch the dude. The Fairbairn-Sykes went in the left side of the dude's under jaw and cut the neck from left to right in one easy motion. It was only thirty or so paces from the car to the little quay at the water. John being as strong as a small gorilla and the alcoholic and dope-using dude weighed only 110 pounds made it an easy task to throw the body in the outgoing tide in the Chao Phraya River. John carefully backed the Ford out of the little space he parked in so as not to get any blood on the tires and leave a bloody trail. That could get the clerk in trouble with the local police.

As professional as John was, the killing of just another human piece of trash would not even make him think twice about it, for some people just needed to be done away with as much expedient as possible, for it makes the world a safer and better place to live. And tonight he was going to live as happy as he had ever been. Driving back to the hotel, he had to stop at a pay phone and call Laura. He had not been issued a standard secure satphone yet. When she answered the phone on the first ring, he let out a sigh of relief. She said to him, "What's the big deal having me escorted? I can take care of myself, big boy, so don't be having me followed around like I was ten years old, or I will kick your ass around the fucking block. And you know I can do it." Laura was a four times black belt in Israeli jujitsu (Krav Maga) and an instructor in knife fighting. Plus she shot at the embassy range almost every day with a variety of pistols, rifles, assault rifles, shotguns. She won national champion marksman medals in all these weapon categories, where she shot expert in nine out of ten times.

John hung up the phone, got back in the Ford, and took a different route back to the embassy area. He wanted to see if the Mercedes was still at the same corner. It was gone, and John was pissed off. He wasn't all too happy about getting his ass chewed by a woman, even if it was Laura. Second, he wanted to get into the Mercedes and rough up the occupants and get some answers why they were at that location.

He was used to making his own plans, and thinking the way this new job is starting out, there are too many restrictions going to be put on his modus operandi. Andy, Laura, and Gen. Shorty Wells are going to have too much control over him. *Shit, now that dammed car is gone, how can I get the intel we need to find that no-good bastard Lequesta?*

I better return this Ford to the clerk at the hotel and get my mind on tonight's engagement. I really am out at sea thinking of any commitment I might make in the throes of passion, or any other foolish gibberish that would come out of my mouth because of eagerness to please her. Boy, she has a vise-grip-like hold on me, like no other girl ever did since Barbra, and it has taken me almost twenty years to get her out of my tormented soul.

CHAPTER EIGHT

In his room, John has shaved, showered, dressed, and was just ready to pour himself a Grey Goose whiskey with ice. A knock on the door in the living/entertainment area has John wondering, *Where the fuck does that door lead to?* He grabs his HK .357, sidles up to the door, and says in a barely audible voice, "What?"

A woman's voice says, "Let me in, you big goof."

With a scrunched-up face and a puzzled look, John unlocks the door and quickly steps to the hinge side to let whoever it is enter. He looks through the slot between the door and jamb. "Laura, where did you come from?"

"Next door, silly, it's my apartment."

"What? We have connecting suites?"

"Of course, I felt it necessary to keep you as handy as possible in light of the trouble you always seem to gather around you."

"Oh, bullshit. Andy put you up to this, didn't he?"

"No, he doesn't even know what suite I put you in."

"Well, if you're happy, I am okay with this arrangement."

"We are going to the Samut Prakan Bang Po District lebua State Tower Breeze Restaurant for dinner and dancing."

"Great, I know how much you love to dance."

"There are several hotels with small musical combos and trios that play American music in that area, and we can try as many as we like.

"What are we driving tonight, one of the company's armored vans or your Caddy?"

"I am driving my Cadillac. It's nice and clean. The boys at the embassy take good care of it for me. It's always washed and polished, and the oil and other fluids checked weekly. The boys I am talking about are mostly ex-American servicemen. They fall all over each other to see my car in excellent condition."

Braz's jealousy is bouncing around in his skull, thinking, *Yeah, I bet they do, the sneaky peeking bastards.*

"From the look on your face, Johnny, I think you are a bit jealous?"

"Yeah, just a bit. I think I am overreaching, somewhat thinking we might just be a couple when we are just having our first official date."

"Well, Johnny, dreams do come true for a lot of people."

"Sweetie pie, that only happens in the movies, and only to good people."

"I am a good person, aren't I?"

"Laura darling, you are the very best of all the good people in this screwed-up world. And you know that I am bad to the bone, at least that's what most people say are my good points."

"Johnny, you egotistical freaking maniac, it's true, you are a professional killer and all-around mayhem expert. You do have a lot of wonderful compassionate attributes that completes you as a human being."

"Holy Christ, sugar, can you lay it on a little thicker? My head is too big for my cover now."

Getting to the restaurant, the valet parking was a nice touch. John, ever the alert one, looked 360 degrees to make sure the coast was clear and no one was lurking in the shadows of the potted tropical plant. Dinner for John was a rare treat. He had not had a real American steak done medium rare in ages. Laura feasted on traditional Thai food. They shared before-dinner cocktails and no less than two bottles of New York State prime red wine, plus a small bottle of champagne. Dancing to a very nice combo helped to lessen the effects of the alcohol. As the night wore on, the closeness of their bodies put this star-crossed couple in trance that only happens once in a millennium. With his face pressed close to hers and drinking in the aroma of the perfume she had the perfumery in Paris brew for her personal chemistry, John had a hard time not saying "I love you" a dozen times or more. Laura and John were falling in love as fast as a dive bomber zeroing in on a Vietcong missile site. There was no pulling back from this nonstop trip.

They had been with each other longer tonight than at any other time since they first met twelve years ago. Neither one wanted this night to end. It's like the beginnings of a puppy love to two teenagers who had never kissed before. The longings built up in each other were coming to an awakening that could only be described as a volcano getting ready to erupt.

"John, we have to get out of here and go home," Laura said breathlessly.

"Yes, darling, I know. It's almost one o'clock, and we have work tomorrow."

"Oh, you sad paratrooper, don't you have any romance left in your soul?"

"Yes, darling, I know what's happening here, and I am so looking to later when we get home. Shall it be my place or yours?"

"Johnny, *good, good, good.* You do realize how much we need each other, and I mean now. Get our waiter and let me sign the bill."

"No, Laura, it's on me."

"No, it isn't. The company's paying this one."

Out on the entrance porch, the valet brought the Caddy around, handed John the keys, and opened the passenger door for Laura. "Hey, no, uh-uh, this is my car, and I drive."

"Not tonight, sweetie, you have had too much to drink. I'm doing the chauffeuring home."

"Okay, lover, you get to drive this time, but only this time."

Back at the apartment, they fell into each other's arms. There was no frantic disrobing or tearing off of clothes. Laura maneuvered him to her settee, sat down with her legs tucked under her, and proceeded to slowly unbutton her dress in front. John, never taking his eyes away from what he considered the most angelic face in the world, took off his dinner jacket and tie, slipped out of his shoes, and knelt down facing her. In a millisecond, John had her long legs out from under the skirt part of the dress and was undoing the garters from her stockings, all the while thinking, *I better be careful I don't put a snag in these.* Standing up, he pulled her up and pulled the dress over her head and did the same with the beautiful black lace slip. Then in another second, he was undressed, except for his tighty-whities, and back into another embrace and deep kiss. They shuffled into her bed, which the covers were already folded back in anticipation of a trip to paradise. The bedroom was dimly lit, and they both were thankful for that. Although neither of the lovers had ever seen each other naked, there was no embarrassment; instead, it seemed like they did this every day. Laura sat with her back to the headboard. John just crawled up to her, kissing every part of her face and neck, and reaching around unsnapped her bra (black to match her slip and panties), and the panties slid off next. Pulling her over to the bed's edge and kissing her lips, neck, breasts, belly, and navel, and inhaling the dabs of her perfume she put in the strategic bikini area, John was so worked up and hard as a titanium rod he had to taste her and use his tongue to bring her to the same level of passion as he was. After a few seconds, the orgasmic rush was the most passionate she ever thought possible. She had almost passed out from the pulsating way his mouth and lips kept the movement nonstop. Then he couldn't stand it a second longer. Getting on the bed, John moved Laura to a position where he slowly slid into her.

Gasping with pleasure, she cried out, "Johnny, I love you."

He reciprocated with "I have always loved you."

It was past three in the morning, when after multiple orgasms, their bodies covered with sweat, and both of them exhausted, they finally went off to sleep, only to be awakened by both of their phones ringing at 0530 hours. John, naked as a newborn baby, leaped out of bed and ran to his bedroom to answer his landline phone. Laura, a little bent out of shape (she knew it was Andy calling), said into her satphone, "What the fuck are you busting my chops for this early?" It wasn't Andy; it was Shorty Wells.

Shorty said, "Oh, I am so sorry for it being so early. But I do love to hear a lady swear in the morning."

"Sorry, General Wells, for that shout-out. But I am not due in till 0630 hours. No sweat, my dear lady. I am looking for Captain Braz. I understood you had a date with him last evening."

"Yes, sir, I did. We had dinner and danced, and he dropped me off at my door at 0100 hours."

"I see, Laura. See you later at the office."

"Is there anything I should know, sir?"

"No, I don't think so. Andy has everything under control. Bye now."

John answered his phone, "Good morning, John here."

"Mad Dog, I am going to ask you a question, and you better come up with the correct answer."

"Can it wait till I get to the office? This is not a secure phone, you know."

"No, goddammit, I need to know right now. Okay, since you're not on a secure phone, get here ASAP." Starting to run in the shower, he almost bowled Laura over.

"What in hell is going on? Was that Andy on your phone? General Wells was on mine. There is something happening, or those bastards are fucking with us. I don't like this, John. I really don't care to have other people screwing around with my private life. And that means you too, unless I want you to, and I do want you to, but only you."

"Get a shower while I get mine? And we had better skedaddle over to the office before Andy has a shit fit. Will you give me a ride over so I don't have to run all the way?"

"I thought you troopers ran every day and everywhere?"

"I do run at least five miles every day. I could never have kept up with you last night if I wasn't in shape." Then he bent over from the waist, curled his arms in a body builder's pose, and let out a gorilla yell like Tarzan.

Laura started laughing and said, "You egomaniac. All you guys are like little boys trying to outdo each other, bragging who has a bigger dick."

John said, "Oh no, not me, I don't compete in that arena. I know what I have and how to use it."

Laura just walked away and smiled, thinking to herself, *Thank god he does know how to use it and his wonderful mouth.*

John was dressed and waiting for Laura. He would not consider her driving alone to the office even though it was only a short ways away. He kept going over in his mind what the little guy in the hotel said about kidnapping Laura. *It was all about getting to me,* John realized. *Well, I will get those bastards before they have a chance to do any harm to any of us. Those assholes don't know whom they are messing with. They don't call me Mad Dog for nothing, and I am more than mad. I am fucking pissed off, and that is when I plan my best moves. So you fucking amateurs are in for a real good ass kicking.*

When they got to the office, Andy was there and in not too good a mood. "About time you two showed up. Have a nice time last night?" Braz was too shrewd to answer right off the bat. He caught Laura out of the corner of his eye and ever so slightly nodded his head so as to say, "Keep your mouth shut and don't fall in any verbal sparring." But Laura was way ahead of John; she knew when to keep it on an even keel.

"Okay, Captain Braz, I want the truth—did you slice a guy up last night?"

"Me? Hell no, all I did was ask the guy in the hotel lobby if he knew where Lequesta was. Oh yeah, and I put a bug on the Mercedes that was surveilling the embassy."

"You know something, Mad Dog, for the first time ever, I don't believe you."

John is thinking, *This may be the end of my career in the agency, and I don't really give a flying fuck because now it's my turn to get pissed off.*

Shorty Wells came in the room at this time and added his displeasure to the scenario. "Captain Braz, before you start, and I can see the wheels grinding in that skull of yours, let us tell you what's happening this morning. The police chief of this district (who, by the way, is an old friend of mine, a Brit who stayed here after the war) is due here in a few minutes, and he wants to talk to you.

CHAPTER NINE

"So let him talk. I have nothing to hide."

Laura speaks, "John, don't let your arrogance get the best of you. The chief is a good Joe and a better friend of this office. I can vouch for you all night. He will believe me. He and his wife are good friends, and we don't want to screw that up."

General Wells cuts in and says, "The army CID (Criminal Investigation Division) also called for an appointment with you and Colonel Lord. Do you know what that is all about?"

Very flip and ready to fly off the handle, John answers, "Nope, I don't, and again, I really could give shit. Those army cops hate us guys who do all the heavy lifting, shooting, killing, and anything else the cowards in the Pentagon, the Senate, and the White House want us to do so they don't get their hands dirty, or bloody, I should say. But those hypocrites get all the credit and accolades. They all say, '*We* fought the Japs at Mount Suribachi' or '*We* repulsed the Nazis at the Battle of the Bulge,' and only a few of those guys were even there. I will be as helpful as I can to the police chief, but this poor CID cop is in for a whole can of patented Braz *whoopass.*"

"Now, John, please settle yourself down and get a shot of the general's cold remedy in the Black Jack bottle.

"We also have the good news. Laura, the president has chosen you to replace the deputy director of the CIA. Of course, you knew it all along—your daddy can't keep a secret when it pertains to his little girl."

"Yes, sir, I knew back six months ago of the secret meetings at the White House and Langley."

Captain Braz is really pissed now. "Well, holy fucking horseshit, did you ever think I might like to know? I am so fed up with this spook crap. It's about time I hit the fucking road."

"Hey, Johnny boy (he hates when she calls him that), settle down. There is a lot going on here that you need to get up to date on. After the cops leave, we have a general meeting with the whole office staff, and you and I have a lunch date to discuss other things."

Just then the phone rings. "I've got it," says Laura. "Yes, he's here. Speak slower, Mr. Meong. Oh, I am so sorry. Here's Captain John."

"Lieutenant John, oh, Lieutenant John, I am so sorry to tell you this very terrible news." Meong is crying.

"What's the matter, my brother?"

"My family, Lieutenant, they are all killed by that Lequesta beast."

"*What?* Oh my *god*, Meong, I am so sorry. What happened?"

"Lieutenant John, I was hunting. When I come back to village is everybody at my house. My brother say, 'Don't go in, everyone is dead.' I push him away, and there is my lovely wife all bloody, my daughter Nguyen and Thanh, all cut to pieces.

"That one Lequesta fella tell villagers if I don't tell him where you are, he will kill whole village. All my friends are on lookout for this one crazy devil. You be careful, my soldier brother? We will make offering to our Buddha for your health and safety. Village never forget how much good you have done for us Montagnard people."

"Meong, I swear to you on my father's grave, I will kill Lequesta and bring to you his head. Then you can cut off his face, and he will never be allowed to enter his nirvana. Peace be with you. I will always love you and your family."

"John, John, sit down. You're shaking like a fish out of water," says Laura. "You have got to compose yourself. The brigadier will be here soon as well as the CID investigator."

John looks at Shorty and says, "I know it is 1700 hours somewhere in the world, so if you don't mind, I would like to take you up on that cold remedy. Maybe two doses if it pleases you."

"Johnny, remember the army CID guy will be here, and you don't want alcohol on your breath."

"There is mouthwash in my cabinet in the ladies' bathroom."

"Wait, wait, wait a damn minute! You are starting to sound like my mother, and she hates my fucking guts. So lay off the mother hen shit, okay?"

The look Laura gave John was colder than the cryogenic canisters they freeze body parts in. John caught the look and is thinking, *I really fucked up that deal. Now it's going to be a long time before we repeat last night's dream.*

Two long raps on the outside door and enters the brigadier. "Jolly good morning to all, and especially to the lovely Ms. Diskin," says the tall distinguished gentleman with a handlebar mustache, wearing an English tweed suit, an Austrian hunting hat with a green feather, and Mario Andretti soft leather gloves, even though the temperatures would reach into the eighties today. General Wells, a brigadier general himself, is the first to offer a salutation to "our English friend."

"May I offer some coffee and Danish?" says Shorty.

"Thank you, General, just coffee please. I seem to know all you chaps, except this handsome captain. My dear captain, you must be the Mad Dog chap everyone seems to be talking about."

"Sir, my name is United States Army captain John Michael Braz, late of the Eighty-Second Airborne Division, sir."

"Then you are the fellow I need to ask a question of."

"Ask away, sir. If I can be of assistance, I will surely try." A great big gasp and a warming feeling came over Laura at this time. She knew her guy had the brigadier right where he wanted him.

"Captain, I will be very straightforward with this, as one soldier to another. Where were you last night from 1900 hours till 0100 hours?"

"That, sir, is an easy one. Ms. Diskin and I were at the Samut Prakan Bang Po District lebua State Tower Breeze Restaurant. We had a most wonderful dinner followed by dancing, till I brought Ms. Diskin home to her apartment at 1:00 a.m., whereas I went to my apartment and fell into a deep sleep, of course dreaming about Ms. Diskin."

"Sir, I can vouch for the captain's whereabouts last night," says Laura.

"That won't be necessary. No one could make up a story about the wonderful evening that you had. Captain, you are a bloody lucky chap. And my investigation shall be terminated right now. I see that you are wearing one of our Fairbairn–Sykes. We are very proud of that knife—it saved my bacon a few times. Take good care of it. And yes, I do know that you can kill wharf rats with it as easily as we killed the Japs on the Malay Peninsula," as he winked at Laura. "Well, cheers to all and thank you for the good coffee, and, Mr. Mad Dog, be a good fellow and stay out of the waterfront area."

"Thank you, John. You handled that very well."

John's thinking out loud, "He-he-he, he had to believe we were together last night because his spies already checked out the restaurant. And that wink he shot at you was meant for all of us. He had to make the remark about my Fairbairn 'cause he truly thinks I did away with that waterfront scum. He knows my modus operandi (i.e., the knife), and in a way, he just chalks it up to one crook killing another—case closed."

John is still a little hot under the collar and wants to talk more about Laura's appointment to Langley when there is another rap on the outside door. John says, "I've got the door," and locked the door to this office. "We don't know who might be throwing a homemade bomb in the reception room."

John goes in the reception area and slowly reaches around his back and withdraws the 9 mm pistol stuck in the small of his back in the waistband.

He goes over to the bulletproof glass doors, presses the switch for the intercom, and asks the three uniformed soldiers to identify themselves. The first soldier, a major, says, "I am US Army major Robert Kent, and he is—"

"Whoa, hold up a second," says Braz. "Did the army take away his right to speak along with any common sense he may have had? Who are you, Captain?"

"I am US Army captain Donnell McNabb,"

"And, sir, I am US Army second lieutenant Joseph L. Bacon."

"Okay, men, show me your IDs. Hold them up to the glass. Thank you. Now, soldiers, place all weapons, wallets, intercoms, radios, pocketknives, change, and pictures of your wives and girlfriends, yes, even the naked ones, in the revolving lazy Susan. And I will lock it from in here.

"After I unlock the outer entrance, you will proceed through that door one at a time then I will lock the outer door and unlock my door and let you into our holy inner sanctum sanctorum."

The door to Andy's office opens, and the rest of the crew comes into the reception area. Before anyone has a chance to speak, the self-important major says to John, "Do you know who I am?"

"No, Major, and I don't give a rat's ass who you are. I can see you're wearing the insignia of the CID. And in my book, you might as well be KGB or GRU for all I care."

"Well, you will care if you are Capt. John M. Braz, the loose cannon referred to as Mad Dog."

John, taking on an air of self-confidence and flippancy, says, "And just why are you and the keystone cops here? Don't you guys have enough bad shit to hurt innocent GIs in the States?"

"I resent that slur. Colonel Lord, can you rein in this so-called criminal?"

Shorty Wells speaks up and says, "Maybe, Major, if you speak to Captain Braz in a more civilized tone, you won't get your words shoved right back up your nose."

"Sir, we came here all the way from Washington DC to try and find out who killed the powerful and well-liked senator from Colorado."

At that statement, everybody almost gagged, and Shorty blew coffee through his nose from trying not to laugh too hard.

Major Kent, looking at Colonel Lord, pleads, "It was my understanding that we were to interview Colonel Lord and Captain Braz in a confidential setting. Meaning no disrespect to the general, I don't know what your part in this investigation is."

"Major Kent, please do not insult this body of United States soldiers and CIA operatives by calling this kangaroo court an investigation. I am Brig. Gen. Sherman Wells, a.k.a. Shorty, the liaison between the Defense Department US Army and oversight for MACV and the CIA covering all of what was French Indochina (Thailand, Laos, Cambodia, and South Vietnam, and the Malay Peninsula. That, sir, is my part in this crock of rotten fish sauce."

Laura asked everyone to retire to the secure conference room so the proceedings can begin. As everyone was picking out a place to sit, Laura collared John and whispered, "Please behave and do what you do best. You have these guys so rattled they don't even know where to begin. Let me run this meeting, and they will be recommending you for a silver star before they go back to the States."

Laura sat at the head of the conference table, introduced herself, and said, "I will be the moderator of this meeting. The *Robert's Rules of Order* will prevail. You raise your hand when you have something to say. Is that understood, gentlemen? There is no pecking order because of higher rank. This will be, and I mean *will be*, a civilized discussion.

"Now, Major Kent, I believe you have questions for Captain Braz."

"Thank you, Ms. Diskin. Captain Braz, where were you on the evening and night of 3 January 1960?"

"Well, Major, you read my after-action report and the one of my master sergeant. They all say the same thing. After we got a ride from Bien Hoa to the Special Forces camp 105 at Lai Khe, it was close to chow time. Myself, Hun, and Yorkie went to the mess tent, ate, had made small talk about going back to Thailand, got my ass chewed out by Major Jenkins, and was told we had to make the C-47 flight at 0400 hours the next a.m. So we all were pretty tired and went to sleep. We were woken up at about 0345 hours by Major Jenkins, plus we heard the Gooney Bird's engines as it was landing.

"We waited right at the plane, while the pilot and crew chief replaced an oil line, which took about fifteen minutes. And right at 0410 hours (by my watch), we were taking off from camp 105. We flew all the way nonstop to the international airport at Bangkok. It was 0800 hours and very bright outside when we landed."

"So, Captain Braz, you could not have killed the senator?"

"Sir, I didn't know he was missing until yesterday. And, sir, if I may ask, when was he supposed to be killed?"

"The CID forensic pathologist put the time of death at 0425 hours."

"I see. I guess that exonerates me?"

"Yes, Captain Braz, you have an airtight alibi and a lot of people swearing as to your whereabouts at the time in question."

"People are usually swearing at me, not for me."

Laura chimed in and said, "If you haven't any more questions, Major, can we declare this meeting history? "General Wells, are you satisfied with these proceedings?"

"Yes, Ms. Diskin. If Major Kent is done with us, I suggest we adjourn for an early lunch."

"Ms. Diskin, may I confer with my staff for a minute?" asks Major Kent. "And I am sure we are all done here. Thank you," expressed Major Kent.

The second lieutenant Baker, who was so enamored with the beautiful Ms. Diskin, raised his hand to be allowed to speak. In a voice that was punctuated with a lot of stammering and stuttering, he asked her if she was the lady in the newspapers that was slated to become the deputy director of the CIA.

She answered that she had not given her answer to the president yet. The lieutenant voiced that the *Chicago Tribune* said it was a done deal. Laura said that "Chicago was my hometown, and they are cashing in on a hot story," all the while thinking, *My dad is up to his old tricks again.*

The sad sack young lieutenant, who was sitting a little too close to Laura, was almost totally overcome with her deadly perfume. When they all got up to leave, he had to hold his briefcase in front of his torso because the obvious bulge would just not recede. The poor bastard was embarrassed, and John was almost wetting his pants laughing at the predicament. John's thinking, *I have been in your shoes, you poor son of a bitch.*

This incident did not go unnoticed by Laura. She had an almost smirky smile on her face when she turned to talk to Captain Braz.

Braz is thinking, *She is going to knock them on their ass when she gets to the White House and Congress. She is so confident and brilliant. I know that in less than five years, the directorship of the CIA will be hers. Where the hell does that leave me? I am head over heels in love with this goddess, but can I stand having her as my boss?*

That does it. I can turn in my retirement papers now—the army can do without me. Sixteen years as a ranger, paratrooper, and army security agency spook is enough excitement for one man. I know right off the bat that Shorty and Colonel Lord will want to promote me to major (pro tem), but I need to get on with my private life.

I have to get back to Pennsylvania and confer with Uncle Joe about setting up the company we have been talking about these last ten years. But first of all, I got to catch that Lequesta bastard. I can't let him get anywhere near Laura. I know she is tough and she thinks she is Wonder Woman, but that Corsican/ Portuguese has a lifetime of killing and murdering in his repertoire, and he is as slick as the shit of a baby's first summer. And the bastard smells the same.

At lunch in the embassy cafeteria, John announced he is putting in his retirement papers. Both Colonel Lord and General Wells were nonplussed at this revelation. And Laura was pleased.

General Wells, getting all red in the face, says, "The hell you are, Captain—I am going to make you a major. And you are staying right here with us. And don't try to go over my head to General Desmond because it won't work."

"Sir, I know we have been friends and comrades a long time, and I have been surely in your debt a dozen times or more. But I am getting a little long in the tooth for this badass-type fun. And I knew you and Colonel Lord would hinder my retirement process at every juncture, so I sent my papers, my 201 file, and all my bad press, good press, after-action reports (ones I could get my hands on) to the army's member on the Joint Chiefs of Staff four-star general Donald T. Ward. With his recommendation, I should be out of this chicken shit outfit in a matter of days."

"Goddammit, John, don't you posses any loyalty to this organization?" General Wells screamed at John.

"Yeah, I do, but you guys won't let me go after that freaking Corsican who is trying to kill everybody I am acquainted with including all three of you. I am tired of all the oversight connected with the army, the CIA, and me personally."

Laura stated that "while you guys were having a pissing contest," she was on the phone with the White House and accepted the position. She leaves in one week for Washington DC. General Wells and Colonel Lord congratulated her and with the usual tears and well-wishes and "I am going to miss you" coming from the rest of the staff.

John slowly went into his office and stood by the window. For the first time in a long time, he had nothing to say. He just felt as if his whole life was tossed into a garbage can. *I am totally empty and void of all feeling right now. I am feeling as sorry for myself as I ever had since I was a youngster. And as much as I am in love with her, I am jealous of her, and what's going to happen to us?*

She is the smart one. I better follow her lead, for who knows what self-destructive crap I would do? As far as Andy and Shorty are concerned, they can replace me in a minute. The army has lots of young egotistical soldiers wanting to better themselves. And thinking this job is a great adventure, boy, are they in for a surprise.

CHAPTER TEN

One week later, the diplomatic pouch from Washington DC arrives at the embassy. A courier delivers the mail to CIA station chief's office. In the mail destined for the CIA is the official letter naming Laura to the position of deputy chief of the Central Intelligence Agency, Langley, Virginia.

Also in the mail are orders for Capt. John Michael Braz, US Army, to report to Fort Bragg, North Carolina, for a retirement ceremony. John's thinking, *What the hell did I do? I can't ever remember not being a soldier and having someone telling me what to do, where to go, when to eat, what to wear, etc.* A feeling of panic engulfed him for a short while then his confidence came back little by little, and he crossed from his office to Laura's where he showed her his orders.

She was thrilled and happy that her devious plans were starting to come together. "Oh, good, Johnny, we can go back on the same plane together, I will take care of all the arrangements."

John is thinking again, *Oh shit, she has wedding bells on her mind. And if that happens, her old man will plan the biggest shindig since Queen Elizabeth married Prince Charles. And that will blow my cover and endanger my plans for the company Uncle Joe and I are planning to start up. I have to be as invisible as possible, or the clientele that I will be serving won't come any closer to us than an imam to a rabbi.*

John asked for a sit-down with General Wells and Colonel Lord for that afternoon. He felt he had to leave both men with a more positive attitude and to ask a favor. After a heart-to-heart talk with both men he considered brothers, they both gave him their blessings and looked forward to working with him and Laura in the future.

Then he hit them with a bombshell. John said he knows where Omalley and Than Vo Luc hid a large sum of money south of Bangkok on the Malay Peninsula near the town of Kaing, about five klicks north of Kuala Lumpur. "I have a good contact who will lead me to the place where the money is stashed."

General Wells asked, "How much are we talking about?"

"I know that there is at least 1.5 or 2.5 million in US dollars. And we can get it and use it for CIA purposes without any oversight from our government. You both know how much cash I have brought to this office that belonged to our side and our allies. Please let me use one of the small twin-engine aircraft with no markings, and I could be back here in less than three days with the goods."

"Okay, John, but we still want you to take one of our best shooters with you. Like you said earlier, you're not getting any younger, and we want you to have good backup."

At the CIA secure hangar at the far southwest end of Bangkok International Airport, John and CIA agent, twenty-four-year-old James Dwyer, loaded up two small rucksacks with their personal gear. They carried two pistols each, hoping they would never have to use them on this operation. The aircraft was fueled and ready for John and Jim to make the final walk-around check. Both men had over three hundred hours' time in this plane, a Cessna 310 twin-engine turbocharged. This particular airplane was built in 1956 and was owned by a gang of drug dealers. The CIA broke up the drug dealers, killed most of them, and took all their assets, including this airplane and an old C-47, the old Dakota (a.k.a. DC-3 C-47), which was given to Air America, where it still flies today.

Calling the tower and asking takeoff instructions, John and Jim went through the takeoff checklist. The tower radioed back Cessna 310, "Proceed to taxiway 4s and hold at the threshold, as you are number five in line for takeoff." Four planes (airliners) all took their turn on the numbers for takeoff. (The big guys had to start way back at the numbers because this airport doesn't have long runways, and they need all the runway to get off the ground safely.) "Cessna 310, you are next for takeoff after the Qantas DC-3. Hold your position. We have a Nippon C-46 cargo on final, and he asked permission to land ahead of your takeoff. They have a very sick person on board and need to get to the waiting ambulance ASAP."

"Cessna 310 to Tower, no sweat here. Just give us the green light when you are ready."

Bangkok tower points the green light at the Cessna. John turns the plane to the centerline, holds the brakes, and runs up both engines. All the instruments are in sync and in the green zones. With the nose of the bird pointed toward the centerline and headed due west, John moved the throttles forward, and very smoothly, the little Cessna lifted off. "Cessna 310 to Bangkok Ground Control, wheels are up, and we thank you for the assistance. Hope to be back in a few days."

"Cessna 310, climb to five thousand, make a left turn south, and you are out of our control."

Over the Gulf of Thailand at twenty thousand feet altitude, Jim says, "We have gone almost three hundred nautical air miles and are nearing our first fuel stop at Hat Yai, Thailand. These twin turbocharged motorcycle motors eat a lot of that high-octane jungle juice."

"Yeah, I noticed that, but Uncle Sam has a lot of money to spend on national security," John retorts. "So when we land at this gas station, you gas her up, and I will take care of the paperwork."

"Sounds good to me," Jim says. Jim, who is as big a quipster as John, adds, "If the attendant is a girl, I will ask her to check the oil and wash the windshield and don't forget to put air in the tires."

"Jimmy boy, try to get her phone number for future reference. Jim, you want to land this black beauty? I have been in this strip before, and it always has a crosswind coming from west to east."

John gives up the yoke and says to Jim, "She's all yours, or do you want to put her on autopilot?"

Jim answers, "Okay, freaking wise guy, this plane has no autopilot—it's an older model, Mr. Sky Fucking King."

"Gol. Dang it, Jimmy boy, don't get your knickers in a twit. If we can't get along with each other, who is going to watch your back when I send you in to sweet-talk the three pirates that are holding the money to please let us take it home to the convent so the poor little orphans will have something to eat?"

"Hat Yai Airport, this is American Cessna 310 asking landing permission and instructions. We are fifteen kilometers from your airport from the northeast."

"American Cessna 310, we have you on the scope at fifteen thousand feet and descending."

"Thank you, Hat Yai. We are waiting landing instructions."

"American Cessna 310, you are the only aircraft in the pattern. Make a slow five-minute turn to the right, and that will line you up with Runway 90. You should see us in a few minutes."

"Hat Yai, we have a visual now. Please give a ground elevation so I can set my glide slope."

"American Cessna 310, ground elevation is zero niner four."

"I acknowledge zero niner four. Thank you, Hat Yai. My glide slope is on target, my wheels are coming down, and will call ground control when we are on the deck."

"American Cessna 310, be advised wind gusts are coming from your starboard at 25 to 35 kmh at runway elevation."

"Hat Yai, American Cessna here. We have wheels on the deck. Please advise ground control for directions."

"Cessna 310, turn left on taxiway 9 left, proceed to fuel storage area. Then come to the private aircraft FBO to take care of your paperwork. No customs check required—you are still in Thailand."

"Jimmy, don't stop at the fuel dump. See those three ugly washouts from a California drug commune leaning on the fender of the fuel truck? The one with the long dirty beard looks like a refugee from the *Deliverance* movie.

"Hat Yai Ground Control, this is Cessna 310. Can you talk to us on a secure line that you don't have to record the conversation?"

"Yeah, sure, 310, now I know who you guys are. Mad Dog, this is you, right?"

"Maybe. Who is asking?"

"You old infantry dog, I am the guy you beat the hell out of for questioning the virtue of the girl named Barbara when we were at Fort Benning, Georgia."

"Oh, now I recognize that Irish brogue. It's Tom Macomb. Listen, Lieutenant Macomb—it's still lieutenant now, or did the army tell you, '*Adieu,* and don't let the door hit you in the ass on the way out'?"

"No, Johnny, I quit after two tours and twenty-six months of Vietnam. Why do we need the secure line?"

"Tom, you are in the tower, correct?"

"Yes, I'm up here."

"Can you see the fuel depot from your advantage point?"

"Yeah, I see those bozos by the truck. Those guys are bad news. I am glad you noticed them before you pulled up to get gas. Let me call the local police to roust that bunch. We don't have a security force here."

"*No, no, no,* Tommy, don't do that. We are kind of cruising below the radar here, if you know what I mean."

"Oh, I see. This is a black ops."

"Yes. We don't need any undue attention from any source that could screw up our plan. We are not on the books."

"John, two of my best friends are in the second hangar from where you are now. I got them on a short wave set. They will escort you to the fuel depot. They each are carrying a Remington 870 pump 12 gauge. When the dopers see my guys, they will run like a scared rabbit. You may know these guys—both are ex-Green Berets. They are going out the side door and coming up behind the three stooges."

"Ha-ha, look at those fuckers run. Thanks, Tommy. Let me get some fuel, and I will be out of your hair shortly."

John came out of the FBO office (fixed base operator), came to the starboard side of the plane, and said, "Jimmy, get in the left-hand seat and get some more airtime in this bird. I noticed you didn't grease that landing as good as I would have."

"Okay, Mr. Sky Fucking King. I was flying twin-engine birds when you were still screwing around with Piper Cubs and such."

"Like I said before, don't get your underpanties all wet and stinky. Just fly the damn airplane like it was your own."

"It is mine, asshole. My taxes paid for it, and if I want to crash it, I will."

"American Cessna 310, this Hat Yai FBO. Come in please."

"Hat Yai, this is Cessna 310, I read you five by five."

"John, just to let you know, my boys with the shotguns apprehended those dopers, and one of them was talking on a mobile phone. The guy knew your name and was talking in guttural Spanish to someone unknown. The guy stopped talking as soon as my boys grabbed them. He did not get any useful intel out of any of them. So they let them go."

"Jimmy, it looks like someone is tracking us."

"Okay, John, then are we changing plans?"

"Hell no. We go into Kuala Lumpur Airport and stash the plane in the CIA hangar. Then we wait till dark, wheel out the bird, and take off again, making a lot of radio air traffic. But we just get as high as this bird can get, about twenty-two thousand feet. Remember, this airplane is pressurized, so we can cruise around and see who takes off in a small plane right after we do. We ought to be able to lose whoever is tailing us with no problem at all."

Right at sunset, John and Jim are airborne again, making a wide circle around Kuala Lumpur. "There he is, John, that Mooney Mark 12 just getting wheels up. Let's get on his six and see which way he goes."

"Bad idea, Jim. He has a lot of canopy and can see 360 degrees. We are just going to get back to the CIA hangar as quick as you can put us on the deck. Call the airport and get landing info. And hope this guy is not monitoring the ground control channel. In the meantime, I can call Tommy at Hat Yai and find out if he knows anything about a Mooney 12. I just had another thought—maybe this guy is one of Andy's assets? And Andy and the general are tailing us? Don't ever underestimate Andy—he is as slick as they come. That's why he is the station chief. Tell me, Mr. Dwyer, and don't lie too, for your life and mine might be in more jeopardy than we know. Does Andy have more people on our tail?"

"I don't know, Johnny. Miss Laura contacted me and told me to report to you at the CIA hangar."

"Shit, I figured she got her fingers in this pie. She wants to make sure I don't go after Lequesta."

"Who's Lequesta?"

"You will find out soon enough. If he is around, he has a crap load of bodyguards, and everyone of them gets a big bonus if they kill me, and anybody with me."

"Is it his money we are going to repop?"

"Yes, the cash is in his hiding place, but it mostly belongs to the United States Treasury."

"All right, now that we have the plane in the hangar, let's saunter out the back gate and hail us a taxi."

"Or steal a car might be a better idea—that way, a taxi driver can't ID us or squeal to one of Lequesta's spies."

Jimmy and John hopped the low chain-link fence in the long-term parking lot, looking for a car with keys left in it. "John, I can hot-wire a ride faster than looking for keys. We might get spotted if we screw around too long."

"You're right, James. I knew there might be a modicum of a brain in that Green Beret skull of yours."

"I even got a coat hanger wire in my bag. It's GI standard issue."

"Okay. Let's take this older Toyota. It won't be noticed as much as a more expensive car. I'll drive. I know the way to the bar where my guy hangs out." It took ten minutes to drive the five klicks to Kaing and the Soong Wat bar, where they met Rung Satiha, a questionable dealer in intelligence, stolen goods, drugs, and money handling.

Entering the bar, John and Jim did the usual survey of the patrons seated at tables and at the bar, and checked out another egress in case of trouble.

Over in a far corner with his back to the wall and a girl on either side at the table sat Rung Satiha. John spotted him after his eyes got used to the dim lighting and thick smoke. "There's our man," says John. "Let me do the talking, and one or both of those young ladies are for sure going to proposition you to come and see the beautiful lounge out back. And it will only cost you twenty dollars American. And if you want to play in her private playpen, it will only cost you one hundred dollars American. (You bring the booze and condoms.)"

"Ah, Rung, I see you are not without the companionship of beautiful young ladies. Yes, Lieutenant John, and you have a bodyguard, which is unusual."

"It's not lieutenant anymore—it's captain, and he is not my bodyguard. Let's get right to the business part of my visit?"

"Captain, you do have my fee? Of course, half now and half when the product is in my hands."

"No, no, my friend, all up front, or the deal is off."

"That's not what we agreed on, my fair-weather friend."

"Well, things have changed, and it is a lot more dangerous since we spoke last."

"Get off your ass and let's go? I don't have a lot of time to waste in this shit hole you call paradise."

"You don't have time to be sociable and have a drink? They have your kind of American whiskey."

"No, goddammit. Get rid of the Japanese broads, and we travel."

"John, we take Akira Mai with us."

"Why, Rung? She could be in danger and screw up this whole deal."

"Because this girl's mother is part owner of the cannery where the product is stashed. And Akira is the key to our entry and exit."

"All right, we take the little Jap girl. My truck is right outside. I will follow you to this cannery."

"My money please, Captain?"

"When we get to the place and are inside, you will get your money."

Turning into a very dark street alongside the wharf, both vehicles park against the back side of the cannery. John and Jim follow Rung and Akira into the front office of the cannery. The smell is unbearable, and the place is a mess of papers, empty teacups, half-eaten Chinese food containers, and several telephones. John and Jim both carry their rucksacks with them.

Akira grabs a phone and says something in Japanese. The electric lock on the metal door to the work area buzzed, and the door opens. All four of the group walk in the large room filled with boxes of fresh fish, where at long steel tables mostly Japanese and Chinese women are dissecting and filleting the fish and other sea-living creatures. They repack the product in ice-filled containers to be shipped to another packing facility.

The four interlopers to this grisly scene parade to the rear of the room and wind up at a large cooler/freezer. They stop by the huge insulated door, and Rung again asks John for his money. "Open up and show me where my stuff is located, and you get your take." At this jointure, both John and Jim wrap their fingers around the grips of their primary pistols.

Akira opens the door, and Rung, Jim, and John enter the freezing room. Rung shines a light on an ice bin and starts moving ice chips and cubes with a shovel. There wrapped in plastic in a plastic commercial fish container is the package of money. John hands Rung the envelope with the payoff cash. Jim picks up another shovel, shoves his weapon back in his side holster, and commences to start moving ice.

Rung says to John, "I will get us a dolly with wheels to move your package," and goes out of the freezer. He and Akira slam the door shut and engages an electric lock. They are stuck in the freezer. The thermometer reads twenty degrees below freezing. The guys have only light summer clothing on; after all, this area is right on the equator. They have about an hour to live if they don't get out of this freezer.

In a rage, John throws a shovel at the door. "Am I a dumb bastard or what?" he screams. "I should have known better than to have trusted that son of a bitch. When we get out of here, that fucker goes on my growing list of people I have to waste. No, we're not gonna die. In my bag is at least a pound and a half of C-4 and some ignition caps and Primacord. We are going to make like a miner and blow us out of here. Now we got to make a big-enough square out of the C-4 and Primacord to blow a hole through the back wall so we can fit through it. But we can't use too much explosive and risk caving the whole place down around our heads."

"Do you still have a formula chart card showing the amount of explosive material used to blow apart certain materials?"

"Yeah, I do. Thank god I never threw it away with a lot of other stuff I never use. Okay, Jimmy, shine your light over here. I can read this pretty good. Okay, I know how much to use to blow a hole three square feet near the far back corner.

"Use some of those large blocks of ice to make a small wall we can lie behind to protect us from most of the blast. I shaped the C-4 to explode out the back, and I hope it works. Here goes—fire in the hole," *kablam.*

With their ears ringing and covered in ice and insulation and burned wood and pieces of metal siding, these two lucky soldiers grabbed the packages of wrapped-up money and slid out the back wall. They were fifteen feet from the Toyota they had stolen earlier.

"We better make tracks out of here," John says just as AK-47 bullets started to bounce off the tarmac and what was left of the back wall of the freezer.

"Holy crap, John, those bullets are meant for us." Jim pulled his big pistol, a .357 Magnum Colt and returned fire toward the way the shots were coming from. After two carefully aimed tries, he hit the guy in the head and hit another shooter in the upper body.

"Good shooting, Jimmy. Get in the truck. I will hand you the goods, and we can get out of here." As soon as he said that, more shots from the same area, only a little closer, started hitting the tailgate of the Toyota. John pulled his 1911 ACP .45 automatic pistol and started taking aim at the truck where the shots were coming from. He got in and started the ignition, put the truck in drive, and let down on the gas pedal. Out in front of them up the street a half a block, another Nissan pickup blocked the street partly on one side.

One guy holding another AK-47 started to take aim at the guys, but Jimmy was way too fast and hit the Malaysian in the left eye, taking the back of his head off. Ahead of the blocked truck, another car was blinking its headlights. "What the hell is that all about?" says John. Right at the same moment, the driver's side door opens, and someone shooting a BAR past the guys truck was devastating the shooters behind John and Jim.

The BAR shooter was motioning with his arm to keep on coming forward. "Keep down as low as you can get," yells John just as a round shatters the rear window and blows the rearview mirror to bits and kept right on going through the windscreen. Three more bullets mow through the back of the cab but are too high to do any damage.

The idea wasn't out of his head, hoping these guys didn't have any rifle grenades, when *whoosh*, an RPG round flew past the right side of the truck and buried itself into the Nissan blocking the way. Jimmy said, "That was so close it burned the hair on my shooting arm." The RPG round blew the Nissan pickup apart along with the driver.

At least it helped clear the way around that truck when John rammed past what was left of it and kept on going up the street toward the shooter with the BAR. The shooter was still waving his arm to keep on coming and, balancing the Browning Automatic Rifle on the car door, was still continuing to put a steady supply of 30.06 rounds with a good supply of twenty-round magazines, where one magazine would empty and be replaced in a matter of seconds; this shooter was very skilled.

John reached the shooter at the car and jumped out, only to be horrified at the person shooting the BAR. "Laura, what the hell are you doing here?"

"I am saving your lucky ass, my darling. You don't have to thank me now, but later you will pay for it. Now put the contraband in my car and let's get the fuck out of here, unless you want to go pick a fight with some other locals? And I am driving, so get your asses in this car so we can get back to the airport. And don't bother me with a lot of stupid questions. I need to focus on trying to lose any body tailing us."

"Laura, just answer me one question—you were flying that Mooney, and who does it belong to?"

"That's two questions. Of course, I was driving that little bitty airplane, and it belongs to the company now. It used to belong to my father, but he sold it to Wild Bill Donovan for use by the company. Now don't piss me off by asking any more questions."

The trio of Americans sped away from the little village of Kaing and in a few minutes were at the Kuala Lumpur Airport. Speeding down the side road leading to the CIA hangar group, Laura says, "Get all your gear and weapons ready and secure. The boys have the Cessna 310 that you bozos flew down here all checked out, fueled, and ready to go."

Once in the air, with John in the pilot's seat, Laura flying copilot, and Jimmy in the back, John felt he could ask Laura a few pertinent questions. He was wrong. She said, "Just keep your eyes on the instruments and get us back to Bangkok. Andy and the general want an idea how much capital was liberated from the cannery."

"How do you know that?" says John.

"Andy filled me in on this op and said we needed to get as much cash under the table as we can. The company has a lot of operations going on that are not on the books. And obviously the funds coming from those leftist bastards in the Congress are leaving us scraping and bowing to our friends all over America who love their country and are willing to save it."

"Okay, sweet cheeks, why don't you take over the piloting of this bus and I will get in the back with Jimmy and count the bills then we can radio Andy and fill him in as to what he can expect. Less our commission, of course."

"You frigging thief, don't pocket a dollar of that contraband—it all belongs to the CIA."

"But, sweetheart, I need some pocket change to get around the states in two more days."

"Don't call me sweetheart. You were going to try and go after Lequesta and tried to pull a fast one with this operation. If I didn't go over the general's head, you assholes would be floating in the bay right now.

"In two days we leave for the States. I will be in Washington and Langley, and you will be separating from the army at Fort Bragg. All of your pay and allowances will be given to you then. At which time, I expect you in CIA headquarters in Langley, Virginia, the next day."

"I have leave coming, and I was hoping to go back to Pennsylvania to see old friends, and I have to get with my uncle Joe to get the company started."

"Listen, buster, you are not going anywhere near northeastern Pennsylvania till you get sworn in as a secret agent/analyst for the CIA. Do you understand me, or do I have to beat your brains into a pile of pig doo-doo?"

"Yes, ma'am!"

"Don't call me ma'am. Don't ever call me ma'am, or you will be missing parts of your body that you hold dear."

John's thinking, *Yeah, you hold those parts dearly also.*

"And I know what you're thinking, so if you want to have coffee and cake later, keep your mind on the job in front of you."

"Yes, Ms. Diskin. Jimmy, let's put the money in stacks of 100s and 500s—that way, it will be easier to tally up." After twenty minutes, the boys had a pretty good idea of how much they stole. John is now whispering to Jim, "Here, shove this pile in my rucksack. They won't miss what they never had."

Jimmy whispers back, "Captain, I don't want to get in any trouble."

"How can you get in a ditch? We were never here, and this airplane never made this trip. Remember, this is a black ops and not on the books. As far as the army is concerned, you are back in your barracks in Thailand sound asleep."

"Okay, sir, I never heard of either of you."

After the Cessna 310 landed in Bangkok, it was driven right into the secret CIA hangar. It was 0600 hours. Colonel Lord and General Wells met the unholy trio as they exited the aircraft. They had questioning looks for John. John held out a large fireman's equipment bag with the bulk of the money. As he handed it to the colonel, he said, "$2.99 million, sir, all in American currency."

"Wonderful, Captain! Well done, John, Laura, and Sergeant Dwyer. Captain Braz, I hope you are not too angry having Ms. Diskin follow you to that seedy little village, but you know how well trained and confident she is."

"Sir! She can have my six anytime. I never saw a broad—I . . . er . . . ah . . . mean lady—handle a BAR with such expertise."

Laura chimed in, "Oh, ah, just a little skirmish at the end, sir. My daddy said I could shoot any gun that was made. So I thought I would take a couple of potshots at the guys that were shooting at the boys.

CHAPTER ELEVEN

0700 hours
First Class Forward section
Lockheed C-121 Constellation
a.k.a. Super Connie Seats D-1 D-2

Somewhere over the Gulf of Thailand, heading south toward Singapore, Ms. Laura Diskin and US Army captain John Michael Braz are discussing the up-and-coming new jobs waiting for them in the States.

John is in a near state of trepidation brought on by his coming separation from the US Army, his home and connection to the CIA for the last sixteen years. Sitting next to Laura only increases the uneasy feeling. He knows his love for her is boundless. This only messes his mind up to the point where he can't think of a way to start a meaningful conversation.

Laura feels his apprehension and asks John, "How are we going to make our situation comfortable so that what we have does not flame out and go to hell?"

John says, "I guess the word is 'compromise'? Before we go on any further with this discussion, I need to iterate that I really love you! More than anyone or anything ever. I think maybe it's a bit early to talk about a wedding? Oh! Shit, I mean . . . er . . . ah . . . cripes, honey, help me out here. I am fumbling around like a duck out of water."

"John! John! Sweetheart, let's just take it one day at a time? What we have was not built up in one night's passion. We have known each other for more than sixteen years. I know during this time we only saw each other infrequently and sometimes every day. It took only a short time before I realized I had a crush on you. And every operation that you took those damn dangerous chances and we heard you dodged most bullets except one or two, I was so afraid for you and pissed off 'cause you think you can't be killed or hurt.

"And another thing, I think you really like the nickname Mad Dog. All you paratroopers have an ego that rivals MacArthur's. He thinks he is a king or something, snubbing Truman like he did years ago on Wake Island.

"I know that you and your uncle want to get started building this company in Pennsylvania. But for now I want you close to me in Langley, Virginia."

"Laura, honey, how do we know the CIA will give me the job?"

"Oh shit, John, we went all over this. As the number-two person, they know I already cleared it with the White House. So just concentrate on the ceremony at Fort Bragg, accept the accolades, the medals, the honorable discharge, the back pay, and do it very graciously and diplomatically. What I am saying is just be the nice person that you really are. Then come to Virginia, and we will square you away in your new job. In a few days, you can go to Pennsylvania and get the company rolling. I know it will take more than a couple of days, so I fixed it so you can take two weeks and an extra week if needed. And oh yes, I love you and can't wait till we get to Tachikawa air force base tonight. The transit housing officer is a college dorm mate of mine, and she will get us a private room."

After fourteen hours in the air, the C-121 Super Constellation landed at the American air force base at Tachikawa, Japan. All of the military people headed toward their assigned areas. Military dependents went another way, and John and Laura were met by an air force housing specialist. First Lieutenant Rose Kowolski and Laura were old friends. Rosey said, "Come on over to the bar and let me by you a drink?"

"Okay, Lieutenant, but we are dog tired and are in need of some sleep. We are on the same plane tomorrow at 0700 hours."

"All right, guys, I won't keep you long. I just haven't seen Laura in such a long time. I thought we might catch up on things? Oh, and congratulations on the appointment. I will bet you will set

Washington back on its ass. Those bastards are always cutting my operating budget and expecting to do more with less resources. I might finish up this hitch and ask you for a job?"

"Great, Rosey! Send me a resume."

After another day and a half traveling, Laura ends up at the White House, and John reports to the commanding officer, Gen. Earl North.

"Sir, why am I here?" as he is led into the general's office.

"Well, Captain, we here at Bragg know your reputation for wanting to do things, shall I say, not the army way but your way." The general was in a good mood, and he wanted to meet the soldier called Mad Dog.

Smiling, General McNabb shook hands with John and said, "Sit down, Captain, and let's you and I have a talk. By the way, Gen. Donald Ward gave you a good report card.

"When the army chief of staff told me to let your separation papers go through, I can't argue with him. He is my boss even that I would really like you to stay in the army. The people on the Joint Chiefs of Staff have read all your theories and political studies for the coming years' military progression, and they do certainly realize the sad state of affairs the current administration, the Congress, and Our socialist State Department is in.

"With a new Republican/Conservative president coming on board, we have a good chance of ending this goddamn war. Your separation ceremony is going to take place in the most hallowed of all places on this base. You're going over to Delta on Smoke Bomb Hill. That's how much the Eighty-Second Airborne Division and Rangers think of you. Not only for the combat and fighting you have done but also for the undercover intel and behind enemy lines gathering secret information. And (wink) flying unauthorized helicopters and airplanes in the line of duty (as you saw it).

"Oh, yes, those two rangers you recommended for the Green Beret are making outstanding contributions to the training schedule. They both say they owe it all to you and to your hard-ass daredevil tactics and endless training."

"Enough of this mushy bullshit. Let's get over to Delta?"

At the White House in the Rose Room, Ms. Laura Diskin is being sworn in as the deputy director of the CIA. After all the photographs, and photographers, well-wishers, and political hacks leave, Laura is ushered to her armored limo and takes off for Virginia and the sanctity of her new office.

"Helen, get me Fort Bragg Eighty-Second Airborne Headquarters," Laura spurts out as she rushes to her inner secure office.

"The CQ dayroom, Eighty-Second Airborne, Sergeant Levetski speaking."

"Sergeant, is Captain Braz available?"

"Yes, he is, ma'am, one moment."

"Captain Braz, I . . . uh . . . mean John Braz here."

"Hey, lover boy, the ceremony is over. Now get your ass on the plane. I expect you in my office no later than 1800 hours."

"Yes, dear, just saying good-bye to some of my old buddies."

"The hell with your over-the-hill friends. There is a shit house load of things we have to get on with. And you have to be sworn in and issued ID, weapons, and all kind of stuff. Do you know how many times you were vetted by the FBI? My higher-ups almost did not let me hire you. So just get up here today, and no fricking excuses. Bye, I love you."

On a twin-engine Piper Comanche privately owned by Laura Diskin's father heading north from North Carolina to Langley, Virginia, private citizen John M. Braz, dressed in a Brooks Brothers blue pinstripe suit, sits back in a plush chair and puts his elbows on the desk in front of him, thinking, *What in the world have I done? First, I fall head over heels in love with a goddess, someone who is so far out of my class. I feel like a thief or an interloper. How could this girl—excuse me, woman!—go for a schmuck like me? It's a mystery. I swore I would never let this happen again after all the time it took to get over Barbara. I guess I'm just a sucker for a beautiful lady. And also she treats me like I am her property. Ah, I can't lie to myself—I love it.*

And there my ego went off the edge again when I wrote those essays and political treaties about how the United States is getting to be a real pussycat in the court of world opinion. And how the eastern Liberal faction seems to steal elections, county and statewide. These stupid, fucking, greedy, power-hungry Liberal/Progressive politicians can't see ten feet in front of their noses. Those papers were only for Andy Lord to see. Either he is tremendously smart and farsighted or he is feathering his own retirement coffers. Why did he pass them up to the CIA analysts and policy makers, who in turn sent them to the Joint Chiefs of Staff? And now I bet they go to the NSA.

Ah!—the lightbulb just went and had an orgasm—*She is bringing me into the CIA so I don't have to go up to the hill and testify before every little power-grabbing Senate or congressional committee who would not understand what the fuck I mean or say in the interest of national security. As my boss, she is the person that would have to go before any committees, and she knows how to tell them people to fuck off because they're too stupid to realize how fucking dumb they are.*

The Willard Hotel
Washington DC
1800 hours

Sitting at the bar where a ton of famous people wheeled and dealed for decades, John felt a little more assured of himself and the way he handled the meeting with Laura and Director Casey. It is Laura who is nonplussed with John. He doesn't think she should be mad with him; after all, she said he could have time off to go to Pennsylvania.

She reneged on the promise and used Casey as the excuse to set John up with a new team. *I guess she figured I would love being back kicking hell out of the bad guys and would forget about Scranton and Uncle Joe for a while. No can do, I have to stick to my dream and get the ball rolling. I know it sounds like patriotic drivel. But somebody has to help this country from becoming another sheeplike Europe, following the mad dash to political correctness and the pure bullshit of the Liberal politicians.*

Every head turned as the deputy director of the CIA walked, or should we say floated, into the bar.

John stood up and greeted Laura with a little wave. She would have none of that; she wanted to make a statement. With a barely audible whisper, "Hello, darling," and wrapped her arms around the startled John. Kissed him as deep as was possible, which signaled to the concierge to get them a table.

She wanted to sit as far away from the crowd as possible. Every two-bit lobbyist and congressional staff member wanted to say hello and kiss-ass, as was the norm in this town. Laura's bodyguards were successful in keeping the hoi polloi away.

Over in the corner with his back to the wall, and Laura facing him, with a forced smile on her face, "What the fuck are you trying to do to me? With this Pennsylvania horseshit, I come out of the blocks running at full speed, and you put roadblocks in my way."

"Laura, darling, I am not trying to screw up yours and your daddy's ambitions, but doesn't my dreams fit in somewhere? For God's sake, I love you more than anything in the world. We have got to come to some understanding. I don't know how I fit in your plans anymore."

John reaches in his suit coat pocket, pulls out a small ring box, opens it, and presents it to her. "Please, Laura Diskin, marry me."

As she takes the very large diamond ring from the box, she is floored and a little bit awed and overcome with emotion. She always knew but realized it now more than before that John is head over heels in love with her. For the first time in a long while, she is at a loss for the correct answer. A few tears welled up but were quickly brushed aside. "Yes, John, I will marry you, but not just yet. We have to let a little water go over this dam and get our personal lives in order first. It's no use going to my daddy and using him to prod me—that would only piss me off. He has no control over me, and hasn't had any since I was eighteen years old. You don't have a room for tonight, so you are staying with me until you leave for Pennsylvania. I have suite at the Hay-Adams till I decide what part of this area I will settle for."

Laura and John ate dinner. A general and old acquaintance of John's managed to get by the bodyguards and said, "Mad Dog, I thought it was you. What are you doing in civvies?"

"General Williams, meet Laura Diskin, the deputy director of the CIA."

"Pleased to meet you, Ms. Diskin. What are you doing with Mad Dog here?"

"Please, sir, not so loud. No one calls me that anymore."

"John, are you retired?"

"Yes, sir."

"Come to my office in the Pentagon. I can use you on my civilian staff."

"Thank you, sir, but I already am spoken for in more ways than one."

"Yes, sir General Williams, John is my fiancé."

"Oh my goodness, that's great, John. Congratulations both of you." The general is a bit tipsy and a lot too loud.

Laura is thinking, *We got to get outta here. Those nosy reporters who are not allowed in this hotel will have it all over the Washington papers by tomorrow morning. Fuck, we never should have come here.*

In the taxi ride from the Willard Hotel to the Hay-Adams Hotel, conversation was very limited. Both parties were pretty much deep in thought. Although Laura had the psychic ability with an amazing amount of ESP to read John's mind, she was not focusing with as clear a thought pattern. She needed to get the upper hand so as to make her intentions believable.

Laura truly was in love with John but had to have things her way—like someone once said, she wanted to have her cake and eat it too.

Tonight, I will make him never wanting to leave me alone for a second. He is in for the best sex ever. I know that is dirty pool, but it's the only weapon in my arsenal. That will clutter his mind and make him beg me for guidance and clarity. The more-experienced females call this pussy power.

This has to be done before he goes to Pennsylvania. He has an addictive persona. Once he gets his teeth into something, he has to finish the job no matter what it is. Good thing he doesn't drink much—he would be an alcoholic.

John is thinking the same thing, but in a different way. He really just wants to make mad passionate love. His thinking is *Once we get back into a regular rhythm, she will cooperate with me more.*

At the Hay-Adams, John exclaims, "Wow, this is a suite fit for a princess. Where is the bathroom? I think I had too many beers."

"The best part of these living conditions is the company is paying for all that you see. Plus I have room service for anything I need, like booze, food, valet, cleaning. And my bodyguards are on the same floor close by in case I need help of any kind. There is a gym, a pool, a steam room, a sauna. My armored SUV is in the garage below. There is only one thing I need most right now. And you guessed correctly, it's you in my bedroom, sans clothing."

"Darling, I hope I can treat you right tonight in lieu of all the mental crap we seemed to have grasped on to.

"Sweetie, don't hand me that line. That is not a screwdriver in your pocket. And you have that lean and mean and hungry look, and I might add horny glaze over your eyes."

"C'mon, let's go to bed and not discuss anything. Let's just do what comes natural?"

Heading toward the bedroom, looking back over her shoulder, Laura smiles. "Unhook the dress and unzip me please. I have a great need to get out of these girly girl clothes. I hate panty hose—the damn things are so hot in the summer and hard to get off in a hurry."

The passion these two lovers had for each other was legendary. Each one filled the other with a lot of energy. It was well past midnight when they finally collapsed into a dreamless sleep.

Saturday, 0650 hours

At Washington National Airport, John was the last passenger boarding the US Air commuter flight to Scranton Wilkes-Barre Avoca Airport. He and Laura both overslept.

Laura checked in at the office and went shopping for some new chic pants suits. She had seen the styles most power dealers (females) wore and justified the spending of her own money as an official expense. She also knew her daddy would want her to look as good or better than the current first lady, even though she was ten times more beautiful than anyone in Washington. She could wear jeans and a sweatshirt and turn more heads than Rita Hayworth ever did.

Chapter Twelve

Now to get the address and phone number of the Romanian lady who supplies us with all that good intel about the Russians and a few satellite countries. What is her name—Madam something or other?

"Hello, madam, this is—"

"I know who you are. You need a reading. You come tonight."

"I don't know if I can do it tonight."

"You listen to Madam Riasa. You will come tonight. It is very important that you be here. The moon is good for tonight only. I feel you don't know this address—it is for you only. Copy it down, memorize it, and burn paper. Eleven o'clock sharp, not one minute after. The man who loves you will be in very much danger if you do not learn the secrets to be had only for you. Now you go and buy your things—you will be safe. I will see you tonight at eleven and bring me a little cash."

"How much, Madam Riasa?"

"Not too much. You will know what to bring, and please leave your bodyguards at home—you will be safe. Now I go, good-bye."

At that Madam Riasa hung up the phone, and Laura felt a chill like she never had in her whole life. *I think I will bring her a few hundred dollars.*

Somewhere on Great Falls Street, near the railroad tracks, *Not too bad an area, just a little neglected by the city of Falls Church.*

At 10:50 p.m., sitting in her armored vehicle talking to her personal bodyguard, she calls Pete and the other one she calls Amy. "Miss Laura, I don't think you should be going in there without us."

"Amy, you and Pete are always so protective of me, and believe me, I feel very grateful. But this is something I have to do in order to stay sane."

"We won't say a word to anyone about this."

"My transponder is in my underwear, so if I get grabbed, you will be able to follow me. If I don't come out by midnight, break the door down and come for me. Be discreet and park where she can't see out any windows. The alley in back is pretty dark, so I think you will be able to hang out and not be seen. Amy, I will take the street side, and you the back entrance. There are only two exits from this building that I can see."

"Miss Laura, do you have a weapon?"

"Of course, Pete, I feel naked if I am not armed. But I would much rather street fight—it's a lot quieter, and I fight very dirty. Plus Johnny Braz gave me a few pointers about using a knife like the one on his forearm."

"Okay, Ms. Diskin, please be careful. We all stand to lose a lot if something bad happens."

"Pete, stop fussin', you sound like a mother hen."

At the front door of Madam Riasa, Laura jumps back a little startled as the madam opens the door. Laura didn't even get a chance to press the door chime. "I am glad to see you are on time, it's very important. Come sit here at my table. This piece of history is over four hundred years old. So be mindful of what you put on it. It was built for my family in Romania. The wood is red and white oak." As Laura lightly touched her hands to the highly-varnished-from-thousands-of-polishings table, a wonderful feeling of peace came over her. She felt as if she had been transported to a tiny Irish village in a time long ago. She wanted to ask Madam Riasa a hundred questions.

"I see by your eyes your mind is open to hear the warnings from the elders. The beautiful man you know as your lover is always on the cusp of danger. Unbeknownst to him, it is the connection of your souls that keeps him well most of the time. He must never be sent back to the war, for he will surely perish. A long time ago, an Irish lass and a Czech soldier of fortune fell madly in love. The family of the maiden abhorred the thought of their daughter marrying a common European soldier. They set the Irish wolfhounds on him if he dared come near the girl. One night when the moon was in the third quarter, he abducted his true love and fled to the sea. Alas, it was not to be. The whole village turned out to capture the star-crossed lovers. He protected her from the angry villagers, but it was him that they wanted to kill. She could not protect him. He was thrown from the highest moor to the sea and the rocks, several hundred feet below. The maiden was with child. Her family shut her away in a lonely cottage. As punishment for the shame brought to them, the child was taken away and raised in a convent. That was the last anyone ever heard of her. The Irish family's surname is Diskin. The surname of the Czech soldier was Brazlovitch, shortened at Ellis Island to Braz.

"The maiden vowed she would keep alive the memory of her lover. And she would be the protector of his soul. And so on the third day of the third month of the three hundredth year on the third quarter of the moon, the vow must be renewed by you, Laura. That date was missed, and now as you must have felt, you are the person responsible for his life. There will always be you, him, and a third person, or third persuasion, involved. This sacred vow taken by the maiden has been passed down from generation to generation. If you truly love this man, you will keep him in your thoughts, for the both of you are soul mates and will be till the demise of one of you.

"Now you go and take heed of the words I spoke. They are not my words—I am only the go between you and the memory from hundreds of years ago. You must never speak of this to anyone, not even him.

"Now you go, and please the three hundred dollars.

CHAPTER THIRTEEN

Ten years earlier
Thanksgiving, the day before
Wednesday, 25 November 1956

Back in the land of the big PX (Scranton, Pennsylvania), the hometown of Lieutenant Braz, the local high school teams were getting ready for the big football classic on Thanksgiving Day.

Three senior girls wearing traditional cheerleader outfits, short skirts, matching short panties, white blouses trimmed in school colors, same-color socks, and woolen gloves, stood offstage with the rest of the cheerleading team, ready to go center stage when the curtain went up. The seniors sat in the first twenty rows of the big auditorium. The senior boys all pumped up from hormones going haywire waited with bated breath to ogle all those bare-legged beauties. This was the weekly pep rally held at most schools in that school district.

The four lovely young ladies who were best friends with John (Bo) Braz, even though he is older, they are the sisters of Bo's buddies, and he being ever pleasant and nice to everybody came to think of these girl as little sisters. The smart one of this henhouse is Katherin McGuinnes, next is Mary Ann Orielly, then Ann Marie Casey, and Mary Beth Yokaitus.

Kathy and Bo were kindred spirits. They were both brilliant and dedicated, which didn't stop them from being friends with everyone else. They would sit for long periods discussing everything in the textbooks and saying how the theories do not jive. Bo at this age had already been through high school and college. Bo realized the brilliance of Kathy and encouraged her to seek everything she could get from her education. Kathy, as everybody called her, thought she would someday go into research and development. Bo prodded her to take as many science courses as she could handle. Thus a lasting friendship tossed in with a little bit of love evolved.

Mary Ann Orielly, the sister of Bo's car guy Buddy, was a real pest at first. When Jimmy and Bo worked on Jimmy's hot rod, she was into everything from the intake manifold to the brakes. It never failed whenever you needed a tool, she had it in her hot little hand or her back pocket. Bo always tolerated her mainly because she was so cute and mostly 'cause she was a girl. Flaming red hair, freckles, tough as nails, swore like a sailor, and followed the boys everywhere. Even at that early age of twelve, she had a crush on Bo. He didn't have a clue about Mary Ann or any other girls' feelings. All he thought about was his education, cars, making money, and when he could get into the army. But he still had a little time to drop by the diner where all the kids hung out. The diner (Ruthy's) was the place everyone, from young teenyboppers to young adults, gathered every day, summer or winter, it didn't matter, because Ruthy's was where everybody caught up on all the latest happenings, gossip, news, love life, and the stuff that was nobody's concern.

Ann Marie Casey, another of the girls in this click, a dark-haired beauty, was a lot more worldly in her outlook, but she was the shy one who would just roll her eyes when Mary Ann started swearing at the guys for not letting them go wherever the boys went. She was tall and had long pretty curls, which her older sister rolled up on toilet paper inserts for her, not as many freckles as the other girls but not a blemish or a zit anywhere, and hazel-colored eyes that just oozed passion and a connotation of sex. Her family had a little more money than the other girls, and she was able to dress somewhat better, but she only kept up with what Mary Ann and Kathy normally wore. Except her older sister made her wear underwear that was much higher quality and costlier, betting on the premise that when Annie got older, her taste in clothing and men would fetch her a husband of means.

Mary Beth Yokaitus, another Catholic girl, was the most beautiful of all, medium height with a stunning figure. Older girls were so jealous they would not even speak to her. She could care less 'cause she had a very good sense of who she was and where she was headed. She filled out her cheerleading sweater so nice that all the boys, men, teachers, everyone stared so much that she didn't notice anymore. She inherited her good looks and body from her mother who had been a Radio City Rockettes dancer with long blonde hair (and not from a bottle). Mary Beth had her eye on a modeling career and had several offers for picture shoots. Her mom watched her very closely when these promoters came around. She was aware of the sex these smut promoters tried to push on young beauties, for she had had the same offers years ago. Mary Beth would never be a Rockette; she did not possess the long legs required. She and the other girls seem to be very happy with their circumstances in life. What else could they want at this early age?

Life in northeastern Pennsylvania was good right after WW II. A lot of work had come to these former coal-mining communities. All of the defense plants went back to their earlier manufacturing specialties. The machine shops that sprung up during the war started getting more and more work from the military. Injected molded plastic manufacturing for the military, the medical field, the burgeoning civilian aviation industry, and new car manufacturing were out of site. The new homes required for the returning soldiers, sailors, airmen, coast guardsmen, and civilians working overseas gave birth to a whole new construction industry of tract homes (i.e., Levittown). Due to the GI Bill, colleges started filling up again. So as a nation, the former OSS (now the CIA) and other intelligence agencies let too many good assets retire, which put the nation in a very delicate position, for this was the start of the Cold War and the belligerence of the Russians. The Red Chinese, Castro, and Che Guevara, Pol Pot in Myanmar, Ho Chi Minh and Juan Peron in Argentina created a need for the American spy agencies, the FBI, and other under the counter-black operations to broaden the scope worldwide for as much intelligence gathering as possible. This is the time the US Army and Navy started playing footsie with the CIA and each other to recruit more officers in to the clandestine service. Young newly minted officers with engineering and science credentials such as Lt. John M. Braz, his lifelong dream was to be an army infantry officer. He didn't realize he got shanghaied into the CIA also.

John Michael Braz come about having money through the good fortune of having a generous amount of common sense. His father's brother, Joseph, adored little Bo, as everybody called him. Joseph had been a B-17 pilot in WW II, and he was a graduate of Columbia School of Law and Finance in which he was a financial genius. Right after the war, Joseph got recruited by a large financial corp. His superiors saw a very good investment counselor in his dealings with their wealthier clients, so he advanced up the company ladder. In less than six years, he was made the manager for all of the northeast states.

John came to Uncle Joseph and asked him for help with the small amount of money he made working on the farm and at the golf course, and picking coal and berries in the summer months. But his dilemma was not a small one. Irene, Bo's mother, took away from him almost all of the money he made. When he was younger, it wasn't such a big deal; but now as he got a little older (he was twelve years old), Bo realized he would never have anything if this continued. *I have to take matters in my own hand, so I'm going to see good ole uncle Joe.* At the investment company offices, Bo went right in as if he owned the joint. "Please, miss, I am John Braz, and I would like very much to see my uncle Joe." Miss Kelly, the receptionist and secretary, was impressed with the wonderful manners this youngster possessed. She directed him to an overstuffed leather chair and said she would get Uncle Joe for him.

"Mr. Braz, you have a visitor. It's your nephew John."

"Thanks, Kelly. Send him in."

"Hi, Bo, what can I do for you?"

"Uncle Joe, I have a real problem with my mother."

"Oh, I think I know what it is."

"No, Uncle Joe, I don't think so. She is drinking more now, and she takes all (well, most of) the money I've been saving for college. She still goes to work every day, she and Gramma, but almost every night she is with her so-called boyfriend Stanley. Ever since my dad died in Korea, she seems to have gone a little nutty. I just can't wait until I can go to college (if I get a scholarship) or join the army."

"John, now you know your mom has mental problems, so you and your sisters have to abide with it and help out as much as you can."

"Yes, I know that, but I can't stand the punishment she gives out for the smallest things I do or *don't do*. She never hits the girls or takes their money, just me. She talks to Olga (the oldest sister). I hear them at night when she gets home, if she's not too drunk, and says that I was an unexpected baby and she hates my father for it."

"Well, Bo, your mom was a mother when she was sixteen years old, and she had you kids one right after another. So when your dad (my brother) died, she was and still is a young woman trying to raise three kids and working fifty to sixty hours a week. She feels that when he died that the best part of her life went with him. And she really resents and feels that he put her in this position. And now you are bearing the brunt of her resentments. Let me relate to you how we (meaning my brothers and sisters) coped with her so-called hatred for our family.

"She thinks we are a bunch of wealthy fancy-pants—that is so far from the truth. Yes, it's true—I, your dad, my brothers and sisters all went to college, but we all worked hard to get into and stay the course. I feel very lucky and blessed that I made it to the long gray line (West Point). Your dad was the smartest one of all of us. He earned his commission the hard way on the battlefields of Europe. Your aunts Lily and Dorathy taught school and retired to running a dairy and cattle farm. My oldest sister became a doctor and runs a school for seriously sick children. The reason I am telling you this is because your mom will never tell you the truth about your father's family. So now that that is over, how will I be able to help you?"

"By investing my little bit of money I stashed away as much of all that I earned last summer. Carl Jones at the hot rod shop by our house lets me use his safe. He likes me and always says I do a good job for him. Nobody knows I drive his old '35 Ford pickup truck down to Sarge's junkyard and auto parts place to pick up parts and coffee and sandwiches and doughnuts and whatever the guys need or want. All the guys let me drive their cars and motorcycles because they say I'm tall enough, so the cops would think I have a driver's license. Carl is going to let me buy that truck when I get a license. My mom would kill us both if she knew that I secretly hid most of my earnings. Uncle Joe, I have some very good ideas about investing money that will really pay off in the near future."

"Okay, Bo, let me tell you some good news. I am going to tell your mother the children's court ordered me be the guardian of a trust fund that my sister Lily set up in the probate of her will. It has been a year now since she passed, and now it's time to distribute what little money she left all of us."

Bo, pointing to himself, says, "Me too?"

"You were her very favorite nephew, and she was very generous to you."

"But what about my mom? Won't she try to get it from us?"

"No, she can't. The law is very clear about children, heirs, and rightful inheritance."

"Uncle Joe, I am sorry I barged right in your offices without asking for an appointment. That was rude of me, but as you see, I am kind of desperate."

"Oh, that's okay, Bo. I had on my agenda to see you and your mom soon. You can always come to me for whatever, so why don't you let me hear your ideas?" Joe not realizing how brilliant John's ideas were.

"Well, Uncle Joe, that old saying, if you don't study history, you are bound to repeat it."

"Yes, Bo, I firmly believe in that old axiom."

"I believe we will be in another war like Korea pretty soon. The French are getting their butts kicked in a place called Dien Bien Phu—it's in Indochina. President Eisenhower has sent troops (Special Forces) soldiers to help the French foreign legionnaires get out of trouble in that hellhole of a jungle. The Geneva Accords Peace Treaty is the only thing that is going to save their butts. That happens this week, July 1953. We are leaving our troops behind—that means this skirmish will escalate till we have full-blown armies in this place called Vietnam. We (meaning us, you and I) can take advantage of the need for all the new munitions, guns, and military hardware, electronics in the way as radios, airplanes, new ship designs, to navigate jungle rivers and streams, helicopters, etc.

"I have a list of companies I've been researching: Raytheon, General Electric, Boeing Aviation, Bell Helicopter, Colt Arms, Hiller Aircraft, American Plastics Inc., North American Aviation, Hughes

Rotary Aircraft, Piasecki Aviation Co. Inc., Sikorsky Aircraft, Kaiser Aluminum."

"Wow, Bo, you have put in some time on this."

"Let me interrupt please, Uncle Joe. I sent away and got prospectives on most of these companies. When you read between the lines, the optimism is compelling and so overwhelming that it would be a crime not to get in on the start with investing this way."

"John Braz, I knew you were smart, but I didn't realize how intense you thought about things like this. If we invest some of your money and it doesn't pay off, it's all gone. You know we can't ask for your money back."

"I know that. Please don't try to persuade me. I can feel in every fiber of my being that we are on the right track. Will you put together a portfolio for me so we can get this thing rolling?"

"Okay, Bo, we will start a file in your name with me as the guardian and overseer of the account. You know the company has to charge this account a fee to make it legal."

"Of course, I did not think otherwise, and if you trust my intuitions, we will make a lot of money in the long and short run of the venture."

John at this time did not think that all the reading of books on economics and the Second World War, the scanning of op eds from all the newspapers he could get his hands on, and the current money and economic magazines would give him such a great insight into the immediate and near future. His uncle Joe was greatly impressed with the professional attitude and passionate plea Bo went about to get his ideas across so this could become a viable venture.

Bo left the downtown offices and drove the old '35 Ford back to Ruthy's Diner. He wanted to share his good fortune with the crew, but mostly he wanted a little friendly companionship with people he grew to really love and cherish. (Little did anyone ever think that because of John, some of them would become wealthy because of his largesse.)

CHAPTER FOURTEEN

Friday, 1300 hours, 3 July
The sidewalk in front of Ruthy's Restaurant
It's summertime; schools and colleges are not in session.

John pulls up to the curb in his beloved '59 Impala. "Hi, guys, what's happening?"

Billy Pearson comes over to the car, admiringly drooling with envy. "Hey, Bo, you want to go to the carnival over in Keyser Valley? Everybody is going. The whole gang is here. Most of the people only had a half day's work. How come you're not at work?"

"Same reason, Billy. I gave most of my people the weekend off. Except the real essential personnel. And yes, it might be fun going to a carnival. I haven't been to one in years."

"Can I ride with you, Bo?"

"Sure, Billy. Let's ask who else needs a ride."

"For damn sure Kathy will want to ride with us. Annie has her Mustang. Mary Beth has her father's DeSoto, and Freado has the old Buick Roadmaster."

"Hi, Bo, were you not going to come over and say hi to us?"

"Yeah, Kathy, and you too, Mary Ann. I just didn't get a chance yet. Billy grabbed me before I could get outta my car."

"We can ride with you, okay, Bo?"

"Of course, you can, and we have room for two more. I'm sorry I've been such a stranger. We got a lot of work since I got back from Washington. And we are shorthanded, so I get to do a lot of the grunt work that normally the analysts do. Believe me, I am not crying the blues—the extra money makes it all worthwhile."

North Keyser Avenue
Keyser Valley, Scranton, Pennsylvania
1330 hours

The heat was in the high eighties. The smell of greasy funnel cakes, popcorn, cotton candy, hot dogs, burgers was in the air. The atmosphere of children laughing, crying, teenage boys and girls holding hands and looking at each other with puppy love in their eyes, and the boys with lust on their minds, the midway, the rides, the music from the merry-go-round, and the barkers urging people to pay a dollar to see the weird freaks of nature made this carnival typical of every carnival in the world.

As the group walks in the carnival grounds, Bo has that nagging feeling of trepidation. *Dammit, what the hell is going on now? I bet Laura has something mental to do with my having fun like a teenager again. The powers that women have are almost supernatural. Or then again maybe my conscience is telling me to be extra vigilant. If we go on some rides, I can loosen up a bit and get rid of the crap spinning in my head.*

Bo and Kathy go on the large flying swings, the kind that twists around a center pylon and swing the riders way out in the air over the heads of the crowd. Kathy is on the outer swing, and Bo the inner, as they fly around about twelve to fifteen feet in the air. Kathy is holding on the chains for dear life; she is shit scared and almost paralyzed with fright. Bo looks over at her, thinking maybe this was a bad idea. Just then Bo gets hit in the right side of the head. *Ping snap.* A link of the left chain holding Kathy's seat broke apart and flew off like a bullet out of a gun. With blood running down his cheek, and Kathy screaming loud as a siren, Bo grabs her seat and pulls it to him. She reaches around his neck and grabs his shirt. "Hold me, hold me, Bo. Don't let me drop." Kathy is as frightened as a girl could be. Bo grabs the loose part of the chain and pulls it to his seat and, one handed, wraps the loose piece still connected to her seat around his thigh.

"Kathy, Kathy, please stop screaming in my ear. I have you. I won't let you get hurt."

Billy and Annie are on the seats right behind Bo and Kathy. Billy starts yelling at the ride operator to stop the ride. The moron is just looking at Kathy and wondering why she is screaming. By now everybody is running over to the control station, yelling at the moron to shut down the ride. He is yelling back, "I can't do it till the ride is over. The boss will kick my ass." Freado runs up on the platform and throws the fucking idiot off the control platform and pulls back the lever controlling the speed of the swings. The swings start slowing down and finally stop.

Bo unwraps the chain from around his leg, unsnaps both safety harness catches, picks Kathy up, and carries her over to the bench. All the time Kathy is crying and in a low almost hoarse voice, "Please, Bo, hold me, hold me, don't let me fall."

"It's okay, Kath, we're on the ground. It's okay, honey, we're gonna be all right." Sitting on the bench with all the kids milling around, Bo has Kathy on his lap, and she still has a death grip on him. "Kath, honey, let my shirt go. Just let your hand rest on my chest." Bo asks Freado, "Where is your flask? Bring it over here please. What's in it, your grampa's homemade wine?"

"Yeah, Bo, it's the wine all right."

"Mary Ann, let me have your cup with the ice cubes please? Freado, pour some of that in here. Kath, honey, take a sip of this. It will help you."

"Bo, what's the matter with her? She is staring off into space. Annie, I am afraid she might be going into shock. That look is the thousand-yard stare acquainted with shell shock that soldiers after a combat experience suffer."

"Then let's get her to the state hospital downtown."

"No, no, that is not an option. Them clowns would put her in a psycho ward. That would screw her up so bad it could take years to get straightened out. What we have to do is get her up and walking. I will get her up and hold her. You and Mary Ann, get on each side, and the three of us will slowly help her to my car. Let's wait a minute and let me put some cold water on my hankie and cool her face and forehead. Keep talking to her. Let her hear some voices. Talk to her like an adult, not like a little kid. She is very brilliant, and we don't want her brain to regress listening to baby talk.

"Oh holy god, Stan, Vito, stand right there. The moron and his boss are back at the ride. I hope the bastard did not get a good look at me. Don't nobody go over there. That son of a bitch is the guy we have been looking for. He is also after me. His name is Lequesta, and he is a psychopathic killer. He is wanted by every agency in the country including Interpol."

"He is looking right at you, Bo."

"Oh shit, my gun is in the car. And I can't leave Kathy."

"Don't worry, Bo, he is running back to the office trailer. I hope he is not going after a gun."

"No, Stan, he is a knife expert. He loves to kill women and girls with a knife. And I don't have my Fairbairn-Sykes on me."

"There he goes, Bo, in that black Mercedes, out the gate and down Keyser Avenue."

"Billy, reach in my pocket, take my keys, and in the trunk under the left wing fender is my satphone. Would you please get it as fast as you can?"

"Sure, Bo, consider it done."

"Thanks, Billy."

Pulling up the short antenna, Bo gets Helen at the office. "Helen, John here. He's here, and I need help."

"Who's here, and where are you?"

"Helen, it's Lequesta, and I am at the carnival in Keyser Valley. He got away before we could do anything. Who is on today? What assets are close?"

"Mickey and Carol are here."

"Good, put Mickey on. Mick, you and Carol get to the airport as fast as your Corvette will go. Lequesta is making a beeline for the airport. He just left going south on Keyser Avenue. The only place I could think of for him to go is the airport. Remember he is a highly trained killer. Take him out if you get a shot. The CIA will cover our ass if need be. Helen, get me Barry Shapinski at ground control at Avoca.

"He's already on the line, John."

"Good girl."

"Barry, did Helen fill you in?"

"Yes, she did, John."

"Good, Barry. Have you noticed any strange private planes come in, in the last few days?"

"Yeah, John, one white and yellow twin King Air, with Florida tail numbers."

"Barry, that is probably his plane. My guys are on the way. I hope they get there in time. Don't try to take this guy yourself. He is a very bad actor. He has killed at least two hundred people or more. He is a professional assassin."

"If he is driving a black Mercedes, he just pulled in the back unlocked gate by the private plane tie-downs. And, John, he is going right to the King Air. Now he is throwing bags in the baggage locker and getting in. He started it up, both props are spinning. He ain't wasting no time. The asshole didn't even check in with flight operations."

"Barry, can you tell him to hold at the taxiway?"

"No way, John. He just turned at the threshold and is moving down the north/south runway. And your guys in the Corvette just drove up to his car."

"Thanks, Barry, and can you keep the King Air on your radar till it fades out so we have an idea which way its heading?"

"Barry, this is Helen. We will keep on the line as long as you can accommodate us, okay?"

"John Mickey and Carol need instructions."

"Tell them to get a tow truck and take the Mercedes back to the office compound. We will do a good forensic cleaning and then let the FBI have it."

"Helen, did you call Laura yet?"

"No need to, John, she called me when I was talking to Barry. I swear to god, John, that woman has uncanny ESP. Here, I put her on your line."

"John, do we know where he is heading?"

"I got a pretty good idea, sweetie. Barry Shapinski says his radar so far tells him the plane is headed north toward Southern Tier, New York State, which makes a lot of sense these carnivals travel from small towns to small towns. North of here is Binghamton, Endicott, Johnson City, etc. all the way to Syracuse and the New York turnpike. Does the company have any assets in or near any of these places I mentioned?"

"I don't know yet. Rosey is working on it. If we have somebody in that part of the country, we will get back to you. John, can't you fly your plane up there with some of your guys as backup?"

"No, not right now. We have had a traumatic little accident, and I can't leave. Nobody here knows how to deal with this kind of situation, and I am hoping my army experience will get us out of a jam."

"Okay, lover boy. Do the best you can for her. I know it's a woman or a girl—my intuition is tingling off the charts right now. Keep me informed of the Lequesta situation? Casey is on my butt to clear up a mess we have."

After all the excitement died down, Kathy was still sitting and shivering on Bo's lap. "Please don't let go of me." She felt they were still on the swings.

Bo was looking into her eyes and thinking, *Holy crap, this girl is in a very traumatic condition. She has the thousand-yard stare like a kid who has just been through a bad battle and seen people getting killed. This death grip on my neck and shoulders is starting to get very uncomfortable. I have to stand up and get her to stand and walk.* "Mary Ann, help me get her feet on the ground please? You and Annie each very gently take a foot and slowly lower it to the deck, and I will slowly let Kathy and me stand up. There, Kathy, see, you are standing with Bo."

"Bo, hold me! Please don't let me fall."

"It's okay, baby, you're doing real great. Move this hand down to mine. Keep your other hand on my waist. Now look at me? See Annie and Mary Ann? They are both alongside of you. Now take baby steps, and we will go to my car, okay? Just look ahead at Keyser Avenue and West Mountain. The sun will be setting in another hour or so, and we can all have supper together. Kay, I am getting a little thirsty."

"But, Bo, I can't go home! Nobody is home! My mom and dad are away on vacation. My brother is on a fishing trip in New York. Please, please let me stay with you?" Kathy is crying again. "I can't bear to be alone tonight."

"Can't Mary Ann or Annie let you stay with one of them?"

"No, no! They have so many kids, brothers, and sisters—there is no room."

"All right then, you will be my guest this weekend, or how long you want to be. Now here, give me a little peck on the cheek to seal the deal." *Smack*, and Bo kissed her right back. His psychology was to keep her spirits up and to try and get her to smile again.

Mary Ann whispers to Annie, "I think his plan is starting to bring her out of the traumatic shock she just had."

"Yeah, I think so," says Annie.

Bo says to everybody, "Supper is on me. Let's all go over to my place? I will order us up a great big feast with drinks and all you can eat."

"But, Bo, we all don't know where you live."

"No sweat, just follow me, enough of you know where my house is. How many are coming? I am going to order us a bunch of food from Tony's. Let's see, there is Kathy, Annie, Mary Ann, Billy, Fritzi, George, Angie, Louise, Norman, and me. That's at least ten of us." Bo leads the way up to the old farm road that takes the caravan to the gate of the army compound, his sentimental name for his small farm. Bo's 1959 white with blue interior Chevy Impala stops at the gate. He aims the remote electric eye at the box controller, and the gates slide back to let the cars in. As the cars start parking next to each other and the people exit them, a loud Klaxon starts blaring. Bo quickly hits a button under the dash of his Chevy, and it becomes quiet again. "Everything is okay. That is just part of the security system." A few steps from the driveway to the first front door, hidden lights activated by motion come on at the eaves of the house. Bo waves to someone at a front window, and the lights go off. "We are going to enter by the side door." Annie says she has been here before. Bo again takes out the remote and points it at the lockset on the door. The door unlocks, and everyone goes into a small anteroom. "Don't be alarmed when you see the size of this guy. He and his wife are my housekeeper and bodyguard."

"Good evening, Captain Braz," says Wanda and Eddie.

"Same to you," says Bo. "We are having some guests for dinner."

At this announcement, Wanda pales. "I am not prepared for a large group, sir," Wanda pleads.

"Not to worry, dearie, I am having it all brought in." A sigh of relief crossed her face. "Eddie, would you please tend to the bar so my guests can get whatever they wish to drink? Thank you, Sergeant

Eddie. There is a beer and soda cooler next to the bar, guys, so don't be shy—dig right in."

All the time from the minute they exited the car, Kathy didn't release her grip on Bo's right arm. She whispers in his ear, "Please don't let me be alone." Again the tears are forming in her eyes. Bo can see that it's going to be a long night. Kathy slowly maneuvers Bo over to a short hallway and again whispers in his ear, "I have to pee very badly. Can you come with me to your private bathroom?"

"Yes, of course, I can. It's down the hall on the right. I will wait right here by the bathroom door till you come out."

"No, no! You have to be in there with me."

Oh lord, thinks John, *what am I gonna do?*

Kathy has him by the arm and is pulling him into the bathroom with her. "Hold my hand. You don't have to look if you don't want to. I can one hand open my jeans and slip my panties down. Don't let go of my hand please, Bo?"

John is thinking, *Boy, I thought I have and seen it all, but this experience beats it by a long shot.*

"Bo, I need help?"

"Okay, sweetie, what can I do?"

"Reach down and take my jeans off."

"Okay, I got them off. What's next?" He almost did not want to know what's next.

"Take my panties and put them in the sink. You can toss them from here. I am a little ashamed, I peed my panties a little at that goddamn park."

"Kathy, I don't have any girl's underwear in the house."

"That's okay. Sometimes I go without panties when I wear jeans."

"You do? I am shocked." He is not really but just kidding around.

"Okay, Bo, please help me get my jeans on. Don't let my hand go."

I guess I will have to wash and rinse out her underwear tonight when she goes off to sleep, I hope.

The two of them go back to the others who are getting a little tipsy and having a good time. Mary Ann comes up to Bo and says, "Is she looking better, or is it me?"

"Yes, Mary Ann, she is very slowly coming around. That is why I didn't want her to go to the state hospital. Those bastards would put her in the psycho ward, and that would fuck her up for the rest of her life. I have seen marginal cases of shell-shocked soldiers. All they needed was rest, a good meal, and understanding, but they were rotated out of a good combat unit and sent to a psych unit and discharged with a 208 discharge, which screwed up the rest of their days, and a lot of good men took their own lives."

CHAPTER FIFTEEN

Bo and Kathy came back in the kitchen and said, "We have to order our food now, or it will be too late for the delivery. Has anybody decided what they would like to eat? If not, I will order for us all?

Bo calls Tony's Restaurant.

"Hello, Tony's," answers Vito.

"Hey, Vito, this Bo Braz."

"Bo, how the hell are you? We read the papers saying you were captured by the Vietcong and you were dead."

"No, Vito, I am as alive as the yeast in your pizza dough. I want to make an order. Put Tony on, okay?"

"Sure, Bo. I am glad you are here back in Scranton."

"Bo! You old Polack, it's about time you called."

"Ah, hell, Tony, my guys have been ordering food all the last three years while my new house and offices were under construction."

"Is that your building project up on the Moosic Mountains? The one over the old mine workings?"

"Yeah, it is. My uncle Joe hired Stanley Robeski to run the project."

"Really? That old grumpy lithwak, he would only let my delivery boys on the job at 10:00 a.m. and 2:00 p.m. and only at noontime on the weekends. Okay, let's cut out the bullshit—what's your order?"

"To start, Tony, I want four big pizzas, two with extra cheese, two Tony specials. Four T-bone steaks, all done medium. An antipasto salad, large. Four calzones, two with sausage, two with meatballs. One dozen cannolis. And, Tony, as a favor to me, I know you don't have an off-sale wine license, but could you hide in the order of two bottles of your homemade Chianti?"

"Bo, what the fuck is going on? Are you having a party or something?"

"No, Tony, we are just celebrating an accident that turned out all right. Tony, tell me the cost, and I will have the cash ready when your guy gets here. Tell him or her to hurry but don't speed. There is a very nice tip in this order. And thanks, Tony. It is very good speaking to you again."

Forty minutes later, the outer gate speaker sounds off to the tune of the Marine Corps hymn from the Halls of Montezuma, etc. "I got it," says Annie, as she hits the button on the security control panel. "Drive up to the front door," she says, "and blow your horn so we can help with the order."

When the panel truck parks in front of the porch, Sergeant Eddie is standing near the corner of the house, completely in the shadows. Cradled in his arms is a German MP 38 Parabellum 9 mm with a thirty-two-round box magazine. Sgt. Eddie Orloski takes his job very seriously. He checks in with Wanda in the secure office. "Everything out here is looking good."

Wanda replies, "Same here. All the monitors surveilling the property 360 degrees are all showing negative. Come back in. The boss invited us to eat with him and the guests. Good 'cause all that food will go to waste the way these kids eat today."

The delivery person is Tony's sister. She forgot to blow the horn and bounds up the sidesteps and presses the door button, and the outside lights go on, and the army fight song starts playing in the house. Again Annie goes to the security panel, shuts down the music, and opens the door to the anteroom. Bo opens the door and says, "Gina! I sure did not expect you? Tony doesn't let you deliver at night, if I recall that old rascal."

"Bo, it is you," as she grabs a hold of Bo's other arm and gives him a kiss on the cheek. The other arm is still locked up by Kathy. "What's happening here? Is Katherin your new love, or maybe I should mind my own business?"

Mary Ann, from across the room, gets Gina's eye and mouths, "No, no, leave it alone." Then she says, "Let's get to the food, I am starving." Ten minutes later, it looks like a herd of hungry bears were eating everything in sight. Bo grabbed a bottle of Chianti, and he and Kathy settled down at a coffee table. Mary Ann and Annie served Bo and Kathy a little bit of everything that Gina brought. Gina sat on the other side of Bo and tried to squeeze him to tell her what was wrong with Kathy.

Bo whispered, "Gina, leave it alone. I will tell you all about what happened at the carnival when I come over to the restaurant later next week."

After everyone was through eating, Angie, Billy, and Louise started cleaning up the leftovers. Bo said, "No, don't bother with the dishes. I will clean up after everybody leaves."

Louise and Billy chimed in and added, "Like hell, you treated us to all of this food. The least we can do is get this mess dealt with." Bo was mentally tired having put up with Kathy all afternoon and evening. He just wanted everybody to go home and leave him and Kathy alone. She was coming out of whatever cloud she was on, and he didn't have to hold her hand or any other part of her body. All the people started saying their good-byes and hoping Kathy felt better in the morning. Hugs and kisses were tossed around like it was Christmas.

Only Mary Ann and Ann Marie hung around. Both of them were as curious as to what the sleeping arrangements would be. Bo already knew what these two best friends wanted to know. "Annie," he said, "Kathy is going to sleep in the guest bedroom. And, Mary Ann, she can lock the door if she thinks it is prudent. I don't have any desires on Kathy's sexuality 'cause I know what is bouncing around your pretty little head."

"Well, you better keep it in your pants, buster. Only a fucking moron would take advantage of her now."

"Yeah! That goes double for me," Mary Ann seconds that motion. "In fact, we may as well stay here all night to make sure our friend stays a good girl."

"No, no, no!" Kathy blurts out, "You guys go home. We're going to be all right by ourselves. Bo is one of our best buddies and has helped me all day. He would not do anything to harm me. He loves me as much as he loves you two. So you two worrywarts go on home, and we will see you in the morning. And besides, Annie, I might be the one to jump his bones."

"Okay, Mary Ann, let's go? When Kathy starts talking like an old slut, I know she's in control."

As the girls are going out the door, Bo sees them to Annie's Mustang. "Girls, thanks for all the help with Kathy. She really had me concerned. When you get to the gate, you might see Sergeant Eddie in the shadows. Don't be alarmed. He is only looking out for my interests."

Back in the house, Kathy is lying on the couch. "Can you make me a wine spritzer with the Chianti that's left—if there is any left?"

"All those guys went through the food like a swarm of locusts. It would do my grandmother's heart good to see everybody chow down like that."

Sitting on the couch with her legs tucked under, Kathy utters in a low throaty voice, "Bo, sit close to me and let's talk like we used to?" *Ring, ring* goes the phone, and the army fight song starts playing.

Bo answers, "Braz here, sir. Hey, Kathy, guess who?"

"Give me the phone please, Bo? Annie, what the hell is with you? You guys just left here not more than a half hour ago. And no, we are not doing anything that we should not be doing. And if we were, it is none of your friggin' business. Now leave us alone already? We need to get some sleep. Bo has a busy day at his office tomorrow."

"Jeez, Kathy, you don't have to be such a grouch. We mean well, you know."

"Bullshit. You and Mary Ann are just being nosy and trying to find out if I am getting laid."

"Why, Kathy, we would never—"

"Bullshit again, Annie. You two are pissing your panties wondering if we are doing it. Now good-bye and good night.

"You know those two are my best friends in the whole world, but they are the two nosiest fucking bitches in all of Scranton. For Christ's sake, I will be answering questions all day tomorrow."

"Kathy, tomorrow morning we get outta dodge early and go shopping for new underwear for you. You can call them when we are on the road, and nobody will know what we are up to."

"But they know all my favorite stores."

"So screw 'em. I know some beautiful women's stores in Wilkes-Barre. It's only twelve miles from south side. We can be done shopping before Cinderella and her maid get their asses out of bed. You know how hard it is for Mary Ann to get started in the morning. And if you feel undressed without panties, you can wear my very tight silk swimming trunks. They will fit you perfect. How about you take your shower now? Then I can shower and hit the hay. In the guest bedroom closet is a real thick and warm long robe, and in the top drawer of the chest are a pair of woman's pajamas, pink with little bunny rabbits, and a pair of fuzzy slippers. So you should be quite comfortable. The bed is a queen size and has 800 thread count sheets. Extra pillows are in the hall linen closet next to the guest bedroom. There are wrapped in plastic new toothbrushes, toothpaste, and fragrant soap bars in the medicine cabinet. I am sorry, but I only have men's bodywash in the shower. The bed and bath store was all out of women's style bodywash."

"Bo, I really should call you John after all these years we have been friends. You didn't have to go to all that spiel about the bathroom and such because we are going to take a shower together. And I am sleeping in your bed with you. After I saw you kissing Gina, I realized I have had a small puppy love crush on you for a long time. And I felt a bit jealous, so I made up my mind that life is too short, and after today, I better get with the program. I am twenty-nine years old and have not had many sexual encounters. Today when I was holding on to you and would not let you out of my sight, I felt your presence, your aroma, your whole manly firmness, and your voice taking charge of everything around us. I have always been around girls and women. I have never felt an experience with a man as I have today. So tonight let the chips fall where they may. I need and want to be with you, and whatever happens, happens."

John Braz was shocked from the top of his head to his toes. *What the hell did I do to deserve or earn the chance to have a lovemaking session with a girl as wonderful as Katherin McGuinnes? I am so far out of my league here. I don't know what to say or do. But I better do something or at least acknowledge the fact that Kathy is a grown woman and do the right thing.*

"Well, darling, you threw a big curve at me, and I swung and missed. I will wash your back and any other parts you let me, and you have to wash my back and any other parts you want to. Sweetheart, we have known each other since we were little kids. I have only seen you in a bathing suit a dozen times and never in a bikini or two-piece suit. We can't count earlier this evening in the bathroom 'cause my eyes were closed the whole time. So we are going to take it slowly. I don't have much experience in sexual matters. And I am not a Casanova-type guy."

"Bo, you have spent a lot of time in the army overseas. Don't tell me you haven't gotten your share of women? Especially in Southeast Asia? Or don't tell me you are gay—are you?"

"No, Kathy, I'm as straight as an arrow. I just never chased women like a lot of soldiers did. It took me a long time to get over Barbara, my very first girlfriend and the only girl I ever kissed when I was sixteen years old. And we never did it. God only knows I wanted to, but I am such a coward and a romantic, I thought it best to wait till I was out of the army.

"When Barbara dropped me like a hot rock, I thought my whole world collapsed, and like a dumb ass, I carried a torch for years and passed up any chances for romance, thinking I was being true to a stupid memory."

"Gee whiz, Bo, if I let all the boys who tried to get in my pants, or even a small part of them, I would be the biggest whore in town. I just never cared about those things. My schoolwork and writings meant more to me than the social life a lot of the kids pursued at those times.

"So what do you say we explore a part of life we never had time for? You have the biggest grin on your face like your were in the Castle Restaurant facing a great big banana split sundae.

"I am going in the bedroom and undress. I will be in the shower facing the wall with the water running. I won't see you, and vice versa. You come in and start washing me then I will do the same to you. By that time, we will have broken the ice, gotten to know each other more intimately, and hopefully all bashfulness will only be a memory."

Going into the shower with breathless anticipation, Bo went straight to Kathy, and she held out the washcloth already soaped with Bo's bodywash. "Hi, beautiful, do you come here a lot?"

Kathy responded, "That sure is an old trite pickup line. But no, this is my first time, and I hope not my last."

Bo started at her neckline and proceeded down her shoulders to her back and at the curvature of her spine and ass, letting the washcloth slip to the floor. He soaped his hands and washed her cheeks and legs bare-handed. He was astounded how beautiful, small, rounded, and tight her derriere is.

Kathy said, "My turn. Please hand me the washcloth, and you up against the wall."

Bo turned to the wall and felt her hands on his neck and back. It was her turn to marvel at Bo's ass. But she used the cloth instead of her bare hands.

"Okay, we're half done now, Time for the front parts to be cleansed." She was dreaming about how he was going to play this scene out when he took her in his steaming wet arms. They kissed with a singular passion, which made the shower hotter than a steam bath. Bo's left hand clutched the back of her head and pulled her in tight to him. As his right hand caressed her soaped cheeks, Kathy pulled away.

"I have to catch my breath, and we aren't finished here yet."

"Give me the cloth?" Bo asked and started to wash her neck, her chest, her breasts, and belly. He was very careful with her nipples. Someone a long time ago said a girl's nipples are very sensitive so be tender if you ever get the chance to touch them. Bo was more than tender; he barely slid his hands ever so near them.

Using the washcloth, he washed the rest of her torso from her belly to her toes, got up off his knees, and said, "Your turn." Of course, he had a smile from ear to ear and an engorged penis that kind of moved Kathy away from him a little.

She had never seen a nude male with an erection before. If she wasn't embarrassed before, she wasn't now either. This young lady was going for all of what this night has to offer. And by everything she deemed sacred, she was going to make it last as long as they both were willing to make as much love as humanly possible. She swore to herself that she would not fall in love. She was only out to prove to herself she could have an affair and enjoy the sex along with the friendship.

In the back of her mind, the nagging conscience along with the Catholic guilt kept telling her most of this is pure lust. She kept telling the angel on one shoulder to fuck off, and the devil on the other shoulder, *Don't mind me. It's my turn to be a bad or good girl, however you want to call it.*

"John, I love calling you by your real name instead of Bo. Is that all right?"

"Of course, it's all right, and by the way, how do you like the music in here?"

"I love it. I never took a bath or shower with piped-in music."

"When I built this shower, I wanted everything I ever dreamed of here."

"John, I never was in a shower this big with all the glass on three sides and tiles on the walls and ceiling. How big is this room?"

"It's five feet wide by seven feet long. Four people can have a party in here. I play my stereo all the time when I am in here. I really like the Beach Boys and Frankie Valli and the Four Seasons. I have tape players in my hot rod and my Impala. And I listen to music when I go to bed. It's turned down low and on a timer so when I fall asleep, it shuts off automatically."

"Kath, reach out your door and grab two towels off the towel warmer rack?"

"Holy cow, John! These towels are the thickest and largest I've ever seen."

"Here, let me dry you off so you can get to the dresser and put on those pajamas I told you about earlier."

"Do you use jammies?"

"No, Kath, I can't stand to wear clothes to bed. I mostly go commando."

"What's commando?"

"Naked, nude, no clothes, no socks. Nothing."

"Well, what's good for the goose is good for the gander. I'm going commando also."

"Okay, turn around. Let me dry your front."

Ring, ring. The phone starts playing the army fight Song. "What the hell—if it's those two again, I am really going to be pissed."

John answers in a very stern voice, "Braz here," as he is trying to wrap a towel around himself.

"Hey, lover boy."

Oh shit, it's Laura.

"What's happening in Pennsylvania? Helen called me and said you spotted Lequesta and there was an accident at the amusement park or someplace? You are not charging after that fucker, are you?"

"No, sweetheart. We have a real bad situation here. It's a medical problem. I have to see this through."

Laura is thinking, *What the hell is John up to now?*

"One of the people was on an amusement ride when the chain broke. This girl thought she was going to be killed. We stopped the ride and got her off. She started going into shock. She has that thousand-yard stare and can hardly talk. Her friends want to take her to the state hospital. I won't let this happen-—they would put her in a psycho ward, and a brilliant girl like that would regress and get really screwed up. I can't let that happen. We will bring her around slowly."

"Okay, lover. I know how compassionate you can be when someone is in trouble. You said you were coming to DC and spend the weekend with me at my home in Maryland? I really need some Johnny time and to get out of the rat race."

"Maryland? I thought you said you lived in Virginia?"

CHAPTER SIXTEEN

"No, sweetie, I only work in Virginia. I can't live where it's too close to work. I need the travel time in the morning to get my head around what I need to focus on, like ex-agents who don't return my calls and official correspondence."

"Where in Maryland do you reside?"

"In a little village called Dunkirk, near the dirty Chesapeake Bay in the county of Calvert. It's about forty miles south of Washington DC. At the time I leave for work, about 5:30 a.m., there is hardly any traffic on Route 4 or the Beltway, so it takes me thirty or so minutes to work. Okay, I feel that you need to get back to whomever you are doing—oops, I am sorry, slip of the tongue—I mean whatever you are doing."

"Listen, Laura, I will talk to you this weekend, and I will be in DC next week. Bye for now, and I still love you." *I hope Kathy didn't hear that.* John hears a faint click as he hangs up the phone. *Son of a bitch.* He thinks somebody was taping that call or listening in another phone. He is wondering if it is Kathy and hopes it is. He doesn't want Laura taping his phone calls. *I know there is no bug on the line 'cause Sergeant Eddie would have found it in a New York minute.* Walking into the bedroom, with his libido at an all-time record-breaking high, shedding the towel, sliding under the covers, and finding the warm soft physique of the virginal Kathy, John cautions himself to go slowly, very slowly. *Remember, Johnny boy, this is her first time, and you want it to be the most wonderful she will ever remember. I just got to get Laura out of my head. The psychic bitch won't let me alone to enjoy myself.*

Kathy moves closer and throws her arm around John's shoulders. Just her aroma puts John in a loving frame of mind. This first kiss in bed drives both of them to a sexual frenzy. Their lovemaking started with John doing his very best to be as gentle as he knew how. Kathy would have none of that. She thrust her hips and thighs up to match John's movements, saying, "Make a woman out of me, and don't hold back anything." With the low music in the background, they both surrendered to each other with a passion that Kathy never knew existed this side of heaven. They made love in every way possible and for as long as possible before a dreamless sleep overcame these neophyte lovers.

The time 0500 hours finds John in the third lap around the compound. "Captain Braz, it is getting ___ on this morning, and I don't think you should overdo your run. You haven't run much in the last week. You don't want to come up lame or worse?"

"All right, Sergeant. Is Wanda going to make breakfast?"

"Yes, sir. She wants to know if she should wash the young lady's clothes?"

"No, Sergeant Eddie, she will wear what she has, for we are going shopping this morning. Before the other two girls get here, we need to fly outta here as soon as possible. Her friends are the nosiest, most inquisitive women on the planet."

John leans over the sleeping beauty and kisses her solid on the lips while slipping his hand under the covers and caresses her breast. "Wake up, Snow White. We have shopping to do. If you need to take a quick shower—if not, splash some cold water on your pretty face. Wanda has breakfast for you made to order. We have to get down the road before your wicked stepsisters interrupt our plans."

"That was a delicious breakfast your housekeeper Wanda made for us. Does she cook for you like that all the time?"

"Only when I'm home and let her or Sergeant Eddie know in advance. Come on, get in this hot rod and let's lay rubber and get on down the road."

"John, I like this old car."

"It's not a car. It's a '35 Ford pickup truck."

"But it cruises like a car."

"Me and your brother and Mary Ann's brother rebuilt this hunk of prewar iron from the frame up. New everything, that's why it runs so nice and rides like a newer car. We are on Route 81 going south. We will be in downtown Wilkes-Barre in about five minutes."

Minutes later in the Shoppe of RoseAnne. "Wow, what a pretty store. I never knew there was such an exclusive woman's store here." Whispering now, Kathy, burying her face in John's shoulder, says, "Bo I don't have the kind of money they get for clothes here."

"Listen, sugar bear, you are not spending one red cent—I am paying for everything. It is no fun having a pocketful of money if you can't spend it on your best friends. I am going to sit over here in the area where the guys sit and make a few phone calls."

"Hi there, welcome to the Shoppe of RoseAnne. My name is Bridgette. Is there anything special you would like me to help you with?"

"Yes, Bridgette. I am John, and this is Miss Kathy. If you would show her around the intimate apparel and casual clothes, It would be very helpful.

"Kath, don't be shy. Get at least two or three of each of the things you need and want.

"You will see that she is not so frugal, and help her in choosing some of the right colors and such, won't you, Bridgette?" The way Bo looked at the salesgirl told her she was in for a generous tip on the side, which is not unusual in a store like this one. After John checked in with the office and found no emergencies, he called Laura, thinking, *I think I am in for an inquisition. My nerves are starting to tingle, and that only means she is putting the juju on me.*

"Hi, sweetheart, are you at home? The sounds in the background are different. It doesn't sound like the noise from the bullpen or very silent like your inner office."

"And good morning to you also, and what the hell are you rambling on about? Are you doing something naughty? Because it sounds like you are harboring a guilty conscience. You once were a man of few words. Now you run off at the mouth like you are trying to hide something. And don't try to lie or story out of it. I always know when your ass is in a crack."

"The situation, Laura Diskin, is your psychic persona reaching into my very soul is driving me to distraction. I still love you like crazy even though you said we have to tone it down 'cause our careers need to be more settled and formalized before our personal lives mess everything up, and till we have our paths on a good direction toward attaining the best goals possible. I love you and miss you, and I need you mentally and physically. I have got to touch you and smell your perfume, and I want you to do the same to me. Darling, we have to settle this distance situation even if I have to turn over the day-to-day operation to my managers."

"No, John, don't do anything so off the cuff that you will regret later. But please do come to Maryland to my house where we can relax and talk about us and do the things we liked so well. And yes, I still love you very much and want to be with you. I really do miss you. Please call me to make time for us this coming weekend at my place?"

"Okay, sweetie, I will call by Thursday morning so you can get your priorities in order. Bye for now."

Strolling across the shop like she owned it, Kathy is wearing a big grin and new duds, a pair of Capri pants, a new lacy blouse, socks, and new white sneakers.

Also carrying two big shopping bags, accompanying her, Bridgette pleaded to John, "She won't let us get her some new shoes to go along with the clothes. Kathy, at least a purse or a handbag or something?"·

"No, no, Bridgette, this is enough. Do you realize how much of John's money I have spent today? Let's see, a pair of Capris, two pairs of slacks, one pair of denim shorts, three sets of matching underwear (bras and panties), three T-tops and three Blouses, and these sneakers I have on."

"Kathy, don't worry about anything. I am very fortunate my company makes a lot of money, and I told you before, I enjoy spending money on my friends who bring a lot of fun and happiness my way. Did you try on everything so it fits okay?"

"John, she is all brand new from the skin out."

"Good. She needed some new things, and she deserves every single thing and more."

"Let's pay the lady and go find something to do, like an early lunch."

"Bridgette, may I ask you a question?"

"Sure, John, I will tell everything but my age."

"Well, you are about the same age as us, so that's not the question. Did you go to GAR High School?"

"Yes, yes, I did. How could you know that?"

"Lucky guess on my part." John is thinking, *Do I want to ask this question or not? It can only open a can of worms, and I am not going fishing—for fish anyway. Oh shit, here goes.* "Bridgette, did you know a girl named Barbara Rozell?" *Oh god, please let her say no.*

"The Barbara Rozell who lived on Meade Street across the street from the GAR High School?"

Bingo. Oh shit, please don't say any more.

"Yeah, I know her. She used to hang around with Thresa Robbins. Everybody called her Terry."

John's thinking, *Please don't say any more. I screwed up. I never should have said anything.*

"Yeah, poor Babs, she had a bad marriage, lost a baby, and the SOB she was married to used to wail on her. They finally got divorced. I see her every now and then at the grocery store. She only lives three houses from our house in a new development out at Harveys Lake. I'll tell her you stopped in."

"No, no, don't do that. Those memories are best left in the sixties."

"Okay, Kath, grab your treasures and let's leave. Bridgette, thank you for all your help and service," as John shakes her hand with a fifty in it.

"Oh, Mr. Braz, you don't have to tip me," Bridgette whispers. "We don't allow our salespeople to accept gratuities."

"Then don't tell anybody, silly, and hide it away for a rainy day." At that point, Bridgette hugged John, gave him a little peck on the cheek, and wished him well, and implored him to come back to the Shoppe again.

As they walked back to the hot rod, Kathy playfully said, "Boy, you will do anything for a hug and a kiss. And why are you so pale? Do you feel all right? You look as if you want to smack somebody. Was talking about your old friend Barbara upsetting you?"

"Please, Kathy, let's not discuss her. I don't want to play those old tapes. They left a real bad taste in me. And besides, we are having a great time, and I don't have a worry in the world right now. What say we find a shoe shop and find you a nice pair of shoes?"

"I don't need shoes. Look, you just bought me these beautiful new white sneakers. Can't we just slowly ride on back to Scranton? Mary Ann and Ann Marie will be trying to call me or you, trying to find out what the hell we are up to. And I left my cell phone back at your house."

There goes the army fight song again. John hits a button on the dash and says, "Braz here." The sound comes through the radio set up by one of John's electronic wizards at the company.

"Captain Braz?"

"Yes, Sergeant Eddie?"

"Sir, the other young ladies have been calling here all morning. They are sitting at the front gate demanding that I let them in. The one who does all the swearing says if I don't let them in, she will call the fucking cops."

"Eddie, let them come up to the house. But don't let them roam around, specifically my office and the bedrooms. We are a half hour away and will be home as fast as this old hot rod will take us, providing I don't get a speeding ticket."

"Hey, sugar, how about I pull over here and let you drive us the rest of the way home? Or wherever you want to go?"

"Oh could I? I haven't driven a stick shift in a while, but I know how."

As Kathy puts the truck in first gear, lets off the clutch with the rear tires squealing and laying rubber, both their bodies are pushed back against the seat. Then she goes through all the gears as smooth as a drag racer. On Route 81, she asks John, "Is it all right if I open it up a bit?"

"Yeah, but keep an eye open for the state troopers. I have several unauthorized and loaded guns under the rear floorboards. So keep it at the speed limit, okay? If we get caught and they find any of my weapons, we both go to jail, and it would take a special favor from the CIA to get us out."

With a happy grin, Kathy kept the truck at about sixty all the way back to Scranton. She pulled up to the first gate; it opened. The second gate opened, and she drove the hot rod right up to the side entrance. Mary Ann and Ann Marie stood on the porch with resentment and a little envy. No one had ever asked them if they would ever like to drive a hot rod.

"Where the fuck have you two been?" Ann Marie yelled at no one in particular. "We have been worried sick, wondering what the shit you guys have been up to—I mean we just wondered if you were all right of if you had a relapse or something. You could have called us and let us in on what's up or whatever."

Wanda appeared in the kitchen. "Captain John, can I make lunch for you and the ladies?"

"Thank you, Wanda, but, no, we have a lot of things to do. But we will be home at dinnertime, if that helps. Just us four for now. I will call if I expect any more guests or stray dogs or cats or what have you.

"Kathy, why don't you take the bags into the guest bedroom?"

"Okay, John, and can I show the bedroom and shower to my nosy buddies here?"

"Sure, knock yourself out," as John and Kathy look at each other with a flutter of eyelashes, meaning no secrets will be dispelled about last night or today's trip down the line.

Annie shouts, "Oh goody, we get to see all the good parts." As the three ladies troop into the bedroom, Kathy leading the way, Annie, leaning over Kathy's shoulder, says, "Kath, you smell just like John."

"Of course, I do. I used his bodywash last night when I took my shower."

"Oh yeah, sounds fishy to me. What do you think, Mary Ann?"

"I don't know? That soap that John uses has a real nice, fresh, and clean smell it goes a long way, and I like it. I always know when Bo is close."

Annie moves over to Mary Ann and kind of whispers, "Don't be so agreeable all the time. Remember we are trying to find out what went on here last night."

"Hey, you two want to see the private bathroom?"

"Wow, look at the size of that shower. I bet ten people can fit in there."

"No," Bo said, "only four people can shower at a time. Of course, I never had four people in it at a time."

"Bo, where was Kathy standing when you were washing her back last night?"

"Nice try, Annie, but Kathy is a big girl and can wash herself."

Annie is a little pissed off at herself; she felt she could catch him off guard.

Kathy had gotten a little blush when Annie ran off with that question. But she recovered quickly, and Bo said, "Wanda looked in after her last night and inquired if she might like some herbal tea or some sleeping meds."

"Oh, I see," said Mary Ann, "and what bed did you guys sleep in?"

"That wasn't even a nice try, Mary Ann—it was pretty bad. I slept in my own big bed, and Kathy slept in the guest room. Case closed. Game over. Now that the fun and games are over, let's get down to business."

"What do you mean by business, Bo?"

"Well, Kathy, you are well on the way to a very lucrative and successful career. I want to talk to Annie, Mary Ann, and Mary Beth about coming to work for my company (Guardian Inc.)"

"Bo, we all have jobs. We don't make a lot of money, but it pays the bills, and we are both saving up for new cars."

"And you all live with your parents. Don't you think it's time to break the apron strings and be on your own?"

"Bo, even in this blue-collar town, living expenses are still a reality."

"Yes, I am very aware of the social/economic situation in this valley. That is why I believe I can help you guys (my very dearest friends). I am willing to offer entry level positions to all of you, including Mary Beth, at three times the salary you pull down now, starting with a $5,000 signing bonus. You can quit your jobs today and come to work on Monday."

Annie is crying now. Mary is all red eyed and close to tears.

"Bo, why are you saying this? Goddammit, you know we don't have a lot of money. We are just as poor as you when you were a little tyke."

"Annie, wait a minute?"

"You know, Bo, talking like this is scaring the fucking hell outta me."

"Mary Ann, I really can do what I say I can do. Stand up, c'mere, hold on to me, let me look you right in your beautiful eyes, and you look in mine. You and I have never been this close before (maybe when we danced). I can see right into your soul. I don't know what my eyes are saying to you. I swear to my one and only true God that I can give you all a chance to work for and be part of one of the most upcoming and dynamic new industries this country needs.

"The fact that it's Saturday, I would like all of us to go to the office and meet some of the people you would be working with. And we can get lunch on the way. Who needs something to drink after that news?" A lot of I dos were heard. "In the meantime, I have to talk to Sergeant Eddie."

CHAPTER SEVENTEEN

Bo knocks on the door to Eddie and Wanda's suite. "Oh, Captain John," Wanda says, "I washed out the lady's panties. They are dried and in her bag from the Shoppe.

"Captain John, I know this is none of my business. I was a mother to a older teenage girl once, and I cared for her till the war took her. So you know I care about you like my own son. This is hard for me to say. Sir, there was blood on the sheets you both slept on last night. I know that girl was a maiden when she came here yesterday afternoon."

"Wanda, she told me everything about her physiology and her intimate cycle information. She is a brilliant woman. If she should be with child, I will do the honorable thing. After all, I am a retired army officer and a gentleman. And above all that, I love her. We have been friends since we were small children, and I have always had a special place in my heart for Katherin McGuinnes. I could think of no one better to be a mother to my child than Kathy. Thank you for your kindness and caring, Wanda. Bye for now. See you at dinner."

"Sergeant Eddie, did you get the oil I asked you last week?"

"Yes, Captain, I did. I changed the oil and filter in the Impala on Thursday. I got two cases of Quaker State 10w-30 and two cases of 10w-40. I also got some STP and fuel injection cleaner and rotated the tires on both the hot rod and the Impala."

"Good, Sergeant Eddie. I am taking the Impala this afternoon. Would you get one of the young lads that works for you to wash the Mustang? It's Annie's car, and she doesn't take as good a care of it as she should. And if you have time, I would like to take that car down to Butches Garage and have him give it a good going-over. I am thinking of buying it for the start of my collection."

The 1959 Chevy Impala was Bo's pride and joy. He loved using it as his daily driver. The girls were a load of questions on the way to the mountaintop office Bo and his uncle Joe created out of the abandoned mine workings and buildings. He asked, "Where do we want to eat lunch?"

"No, Bo, no lunch yet. Let's just go to your office," cried Mary Ann. "You have me so scared and full of trepidation, I need to get to a ladies' room quick." Bo turned onto Route 91 and floored it. The big Chevy held the road like a racing car, with a 427 Corvette engine, fuel injection, 3/4 race cam, and a finely tuned undercarriage. The Impala took the twists and turns up the mountain with an ease that would make a GM engineer proud to be alive.

As they pulled up to the front gate, the sensors on all of the security cameras that were interlocked with the integrated security system set off the low-sounding claxtons and strobe lights in the main work areas. This only happened on weekends and holidays, when there was a small force on duty. Most of the assets, analysts, and computer operators worked a regular forty-hour week. Bo used his handheld remote to open the first gate and announced his arrival. The first gate closed and locked, and the second gate opened and let them proceed to the front of the large one-story building.

"Everybody, follow me through the first set of doors into the anteroom. I have to announce to whomever is on duty that you are all with me, and everything is normal."

"Hello, John, what are you doing here today? We thought you were going to take a few days off."

"Hi, Helen, let me introduce you to some prospective workers for our analyst and computer sections. Helen Raskousas, meet Katherin McGuinnes, Mary Ann Orielly, Ann Marie Casey, and I have another young lady we would like to join us. The problem is she is a model. Her name is Mary Beth Yokaitus. She may not want to pursue this kind of work, but I have not asked her."

"Oh, John, all the bright young talent you can recruit will be welcomed with open arms. We are up to our asses in new clients and the government projects. John, your secretary left you some messages in your secure file. Maybe you want to read them while I show the ladies what it is we do here?

"Mary, Ann, and Kathy, would you please come with me to the map and situation room?"

"Helen, that's okay. I will wait with John. I have a great career, and I am not interested in switching jobs. Thank you for your hospitality. I am sure John depends on you a great deal." Kathy was full of confidence after last night.

After two hours of briefings, movies, questions and answers, even a weapons demonstration in the downstairs shooting range, where the girls got a lesson on weapons safety and learned to shoot several kinds of pistols and automatic assault rifles, Ann Marie and Mary Ann were ecstatic and excited over the way they were treated. Both girls iterated that they were not bright enough to learn all there was to know to be able to do a decent job. Helen assured them they were perfect candidates. They were both fresh and young, in good health, and had not been overtaken by the pure Communist rhetoric and bullshit being thrown at America by the liberal press. Helen told everybody a few short stories about her twenty years in the Central Intelligence Agency. That kind of helped to seal the deal, and both Mary Ann and Ann Marie said they would have to give notice to their present employers.

Ann Marie, who was always hungry, bitched about not getting anything to eat. "We are going to the Raven Inn near lake Sheridan, if that's okay with everybody," John had to shout over the noise coming from the radio. Kathy was driving and enjoying the hell out of it, with the radio blasting an Elvis song. She had the car up to sixty-five and was scaring the piss out of everybody. John reached over, put his hands on the key, and yelled, "Slow the fuck down before you kill us all. Did you not have enough excitement yesterday? Or was a sleeping giant awoken in you? I know you love to drive my car and truck, but a person can't beat the hell out of a vehicle and expect it to last long and perform well. And don't start crying 'cause I am ragging on you. I want all of us to be alive when the Bobbsey Twins start their new careers. The both of them are sitting back there scared to death. They will make a beeline for the ladies' room as soon as we get to the restaurant. They're ready to pee their pants now."

"John, now that we can hear again, what kind of food does the place have?"

"Mary, they have all kinds of an American menu. But the specialties are Polish food like what my grandmother used to feed me. Potato pancakes stuffed cabbage, pierogis, halupki, etc. I don't come here often, or I would be fat as a pig.

"Which reminds me, you guys have to get in as good a shape as you can. Sometime in your early training, we will send you to the secret training base known as the farm in Virginia. There you will learn self-defense, weapons use, some martial arts, spy craft of sorts, map reading, living off the land. It is just like being in the military, but not as tough."

"Oh shit, John! Helen didn't tell us that part. I only went camping with my brother twice. I don't know a fucking thing about the outdoors."

"And that goes double for me," squealed Mary Ann.

"That's why we send you to school there so you get a better understanding what the field agents are up against 90 percent of the time. It only helps you to get a grip on what the hell we are all about. Don't worry, you will love it. Most of the people going through the course are big, brawny, and cute soldiers. Be prepared to give out your phone numbers a hundred times a day."

"Don't fucking sugarcoat it, John. My brothers went through basic training. I know what the hell it's going to be like."

Saturday afternoon at the Raven Inn, the foursome was led to a booth and ordered drinks all around. The waitress, a nice elderly Polish lady, came back with the drinks and chided Bo for being a stranger. Kathy spoke up in Bo's defense. "He is too busy rescuing fair maidens in distress."

"Yah, I don't think so, miss. There is only one thing he wants to do with maidens."

Bo's face blushed red as a fire engine, and Annie elbowed Mary Ann. "See, I told you so."

"What? What did you tell her so?" retorted Kathy.

"Oh, nothing, just a little private joke. Maybe someday I can tell you, but not right now."

"Hey, what the hell, Annie? We are all friends here, and we don't keep secrets from each other."

"Okay, forget what I said, didn't mean to hurt anybody or start a fight."

"Holy cow, look at all the food she is bringing us. Guess we will have doggie bags going back home." Both Mary Ann and Ann Marie started laughing and would not look at Kathy.

Bo finally realized the innuendo of the situation. "Hey, you two gooney birds, knock off the insinuations and eat your lunch, or I will make you walk home."

Back at the house, Ann Marie saw her car all washed and cleaned. She was flabbergasted, and here comes the tears again. "Bo, who did this? It looks like a brand-new car."

"Sergeant Eddie had some of his boys give it a good going-over. If I am going to buy this Mustang, I want to know what's good and bad about it."

"I never said I would for sure sell it till I talked to my dad and brother."

"Bullshit, you told me I had first rights of refusal."

"What the hell does that mean?"

"It means I have the first crack at offering to buy it. In most jurisdictions, it is a verbal agreement that would stand up in a court of law."

"You mean you would sue me?"

"Of course not, you dingbat. I love you too much to even think of such a thing. But I would take it out of your hide, and Helen would give you all the shitty jobs at work. And besides, you both are going to get company cars, vans really."

"Bo, you know I will sell it to you. We don't have to get all wacky over a stupid car."

"She calls a classic Ford a stupid car. Good if her brother doesn't interfere. I might get a nice deal. I am going to put at least twenty grand in it to bring it up to collector car status."

"Thank you very much for the work on my car, Bo. Come on. Mary Ann, we don't want to be late for confession. You too, Kathy, get your stuff, and we can drop you off at your house."

CHAPTER EIGHTEEN

Office of the Deputy Director, CIA

"John, I am so glad you're here. You remember Rose Kowolski from the air force at the base in Japan? She is my personal secretary, since you stole Helen Raskousas from me."

"Laura, sweetie, she was tired of the DC area and wanted a quieter environment."

"Well, I don't believe that, but that's not why I asked you to come here ASAP. My good friend over at NSA has a serious problem. And you're the only person smart enough to handle this delicate situation."

"Oh, oh, you need a big favor. Who is your friend and what does he need?"

"My friend is a she, and her problem is of the life-or-death kind. Rosey, please bring me Carol Wilson's file and Jakes 201 file please?"

After browsing quickly through both files, John still was in a quandary as to what Laura needed him to do. He had a good idea, but he needed a lot more intel and current data to fabricate a plan and an end result answer to help Carol.

Sitting in the secure inner office, John recalled a rogue agent named Jake that was tossed out of the CIA a few years back. The file he just read was the same asshole. Laura came in and sat down in the chair next to John with her knees touching John's legs, all the while thinking and plotting, *If I come on a little strong, he can't turn us down.*

John knew exactly what she was doing. He had already made up his mind to take this job and run with it.

Rosey buzzed Laura. "Your party is here, Ms. Diskin."

"Send her in please, Rosey."

"Hi there, this is my friend—" as Laura put her finger to her lips and said, "No names please. It's better if you all don't know any names—that way, everybody has deniability and no one can get in trouble. He has read Jake's file and knows he worked here. Now you can tell him all the dirty little facts as to why we are all here."

Carol is visibly shaken and nervous as a kitten. "Laura, do you have anything strong to drink? As you can see, I am a freaking mess and scared to death. I took two taxis and a bus to get here in case he followed me."

"Don't worry, he can't get on this campus, or we would have him locked him up already. And I am sending you home with two of my agents, a man-and-wife team. They will spend 24/7 with you until this is resolved."

"Oh, thank you. I knew I could count on you."

"Okay, tell my friend what's going on."

"What shall I call you? I know, I will call you babe if that's okay?"

"I worked for the company when we were in the old building. Jake worked as an outside agent until they found out he is a lying bag of crap. He accused me of lying to the higher-ups here, and that's what got him fired. Of course, it's not true. He was selling dope the company took off the people we busted. And he was caught up in a sting operation. They let him off too easy. He didn't even do any jail time.

"I was in my eighth month of pregnancy. That's when he started beating me up, and he was drunk a lot. I came home from the doctor's one day and found him with a professional hooker in my bed.

"I lost the baby, a girl. I filed for a divorce in Maryland. You have to wait a year before the divorce is final, and he had to move out of the house. I lost that too. I could not keep up the mortgage payments.

"He has been following me and waving his gun at me. I find notes in my mailbox saying I will die before the year is over. He can't get on the property at NSA, or I would already be dead." Carol starts weeping, "I can't eat, I can't sleep, I lost twenty pounds in two weeks, and my supervisor at work is covering for me because I have trouble concentrating."

"What about the police, the FBI, the Maryland State Police?"

"They won't do anything. They all say until I get assaulted, it's out of their hands. The CIA can't go after an American citizen in the continental US—it's the law."

"Where does he hang out?"

"Over in PG County where the titty bars are—that's where he sells his dope and anything else he can fence for the sleazy bastards."

"Does he go by any other name or nickname? And what kind of car does he drive?"

"No other name that I know of. He mostly drives a white Lexus, two-door, with a sunroof, Maryland tags. And he usually has some bimbo with him. I don't know where he lives now either."

"All right, I know what to do. Try to calm down and listen to the agents that Miss Laura is providing you with. Don't go and get all supergirl on him. He is a trained killer and a psychopath. He would kill you and not blink an eye."

"Mr. Babe and Laura, I don't know how I am going to pay you back. I have only about ten thousand in my savings and a 401(k)."

"No, Carol, there is no paybacks here. Me and my friend Mr. Babe"—as Laura starts to giggle over the Mr. Babe remark—"are helping you from a friend's vantage point. Don't ever worry about paybacks. Remember, you were never here and you never saw Mr. Babe and he never saw you."

Carol left with the team that will be her constant companions for the duration of this little operation.

"John, I am so glad you agreed to help. Whatever you need, you have it. I want you to have some backup in case you get your butt in a crack."

"No, no, that would be the first thing this sleazy bastard would see. I can do this job in my sleep. Please don't put a tail on me. It will only screw things up. What I do need is a beat-up old car that runs well and one a person could expect to see in those parts of PG and Fairfax Counties. An older model Toyota or Subaru dark colored would be a perfect vehicle for an undercover op like this. And I need some more, possibly two more IDs, a confiscated weapon, preferably a 9 mm autoloader, and a call to a thrift store where I can get some old used clothing."

"All right, sugar lips. Will I see you in the morning?"

"No, you're going to see me this evening at 2100 hours. I still have a suite at the Hay-Adams. We will have a late dinner and dessert. So go get your kit in order. The car is in the lower garage, you know where, and see the properties agent. He will fix you up with any weaponry you may want. And don't be late, 2100 hours, you know the floor and the suite."

The bar stunk of smoke, stale beer, body odor, and a miasma of grease-fried foods, the daily menu of people who lived a day-to-day existence.

John, dressed as a customer who normally would be a habitual frequent in this environment, shuffling to an empty bar stool but moving his eyes and noticing everything and everybody in the joint, came to a conclusion that his man was not there at the moment.

The bartender, a short skinny Hispanic fella, asked, "What can I get for you?"

"A bottle of Bud, buddy, and maybe some directions."

"The Bud is $3.50, information is more."

"Boy, sir, that is a steep price for beer?"

"We have Bud on tap for only $1.50 a glass, a big glass like this, the one I am holding."

"Nah, that's okay. I usually only drink bottled beer or water when I am in a new place."

"Want something to eat? I got burgers, fries, wings, hot or mild, tacos, and crab cakes. The crabs came in last night, so they are really fresh."

"No thanks, sir, I believe that your food is great, but I don't have much to spend on food these days, since I got laid off from my last job. Anyway, I was looking for a guy named Jake."

"If it's Jake Wilson, you're much too early. What do you want with Jake? You do know he is a real badass? You got to be real careful with him. He will kick a person's ass in a New York minute."

John's thinking, *He doesn't know me and that when I get done with him, even the maggots won't bother to crawl in his ears.* "Sir, I don't know him. I never met him. I heard he has some tools for sale. I need new tools in order to get the job I applied for. I don't even know what he looks like."

"Well, mister, you got a name?"

"Everybody calls me Babe—I got that moniker from my army days."

"Mr. Babe, can you come back about nine o'clock? Jake will probably be coming in around that time. Or if you have a number, give it to me and I will pass it on to Jake."

Reaching into his beat-up old windbreaker, the throwaway Walmart one-time user cell phone number came up on the little screen. John passed it on to the bartender. "If this Jake guy comes in, please have him call me. I can get the money for tools in a hurry. Thank you very much, sir."

Holy crap, that was too much of a coincidence to have lucked out the first bar I tried. I've got to be a little more skeptical and outthink this bastard before he realizes I am after his sorry butt. Now I got to change into my good clothes, or they won't let me into the hotel. And she will claw me a new one, and I really don't care to disappoint her, or mostly Carol. From what I know now, this Jake guy is out to kill Carol the first chance he can get. And he doesn't care what bimbo is with him, he will kill the bimbo too just to cover his ass.

"Midnight, be at the same place. Somebody will contact you and lead you to the goods. You pay her first before you leave the bar. I will be eyeballing you, and if I see any cops, you're a dead man. And no guns—you will be frisked by two girls who know where all the right places are."

"How will you know it's me?"

"Don't be such a jerk. You will be eyeballed before ya get to the front door. See ya at the place, and remember, all cash, sucker."

"John, you can't go there tonight. You know it's an ambush. They will take the money and kill you."

"Yes, I know how these amateurs operate, but I always beat them at their own game."

"John, I have to go with you. Together we can get this jerk and put him away forever."

"No, Laura, we can't risk you being out on the street. If the damn press found out, this administration would be screwed every which way from Sunday."

"Yes, we can, Johnny. I will wear a wig and my old slutty cloths, a .357 in my purse. There isn't a bimbo out here that can take me. Don't forget I am a master four times black belt in Israeli jujitsu. And don't forget also my bodyguards follow me around like little puppy dogs."

"Yah, but one little .22 automatic trumps any martial arts expert. And he will have several thugs waiting for me to make the wrong move—wrong for him, right for me."

"Sweetheart, I know you are correct about this, but I would die if something happened to you. And also this little caper is not a sanctioned CIA op. It's off the books, and if one of them dies, we spend a long time in the Baltimore jail."

Going through John's mind, *One of them, mainly Jake, is going to die tonight, and I have to plan this a little more carefully.*

"Leave your satphone on please? If I need the cavalry, you will hear my bugle. It's only 10:00 p.m. now. Those lazy bastards, if there are as many as he says, won't be near the place till eleven thirty or so. I am going to park the car in the historic Indian Queen Tavern lot on the back side where all the shadows favor my plan. That's the good thing about government license plates—you can park anywhere you please. And the olive drab old army color is a perfect disguise for any snooping PG County cops."

At 11:00 p.m., old route, one on the right side of the one-way street coming from the Peace Cross. *I wonder if Jake's bimbo is in the joint yet. This thousand-dollar wad of bills is making my pocket bulge out like I was excited at seeing a nude female. If I can see it, so can everybody else in that tavern. I took the extra two bills because these kinds of people only know how to shake somebody down. And the poor guy or girl is so happy to get the goods they are all over themselves thanking the crook for screwing them. And happy they weren't killed in the process.*

Let me duck in this alley behind the dumpster. It's nice and dark, and I can watch the front door and the alley leading to the back kitchen door.

And here comes the white Lexus. Shit, tinted dark windows, I can't see inside. No problem, it's parking in a handicapped spot right in front. What balls this jerk has. The fine is real stiff in this socialist people's commonwealth of Maryland for parking in a restricted zone. Oh shit, looky, there he has handicapped tags, the rotten skunk.

Both are going in. That's good. Let me wait at least another forty-five minutes out here. There does not seem to be anybody else out and about that might be part of his party. I am going to walk through these shadows in this alley and sneak past the kitchen door. I know it's open, I can hear the Hispanic cook bitching about something.

On the other side of the parking lot, it's just as dark. Jake or one of his cohorts put out all the parking lot lights for their convenience. One or more of Jake's girls can do business in the backseat of a car or truck in a darkened parking lot.

I will just walk in the front door from this side of the building. If someone is watching, it is to my advantage.

Oh crap, my satphone is buzzing. "I am in the parking lot just about ready to go inside."

"I was getting anxious, my senses are tingling. Okay, go do your thing. I love you."

Jake and his girl are sitting in a back booth across the dance floor. John's thinking, *This bimbo is a sight to look at once and erase from your memory forever—fat rolls dumping over the sides of a pair of yellow pedal pushers, big boobs, 44Ds, bulging from the V split multicolored T-shirt, bright green socks peeking over the tops of high-top basketball sneakers, and smoking a panatela woman's cigar.*

Here she comes, Milly the Whale.

"Are yow the asshole they call Babe?"

"Yes, ma'am, I sure am."

"Show me the money?" John counts out the eight hundred and hands it to the bimbo. She leans over his arm and is trying to look at the rest of the money as expected. "Hey, how much more you got there? You ain't holding out on me? You might get a reamed out, asshole, if I come up short, ya know."

John quickly grabs the money back from her. "Okay, you don't trust me? We will count it out together. I need those tools and don't want to be jerked around anymore. You got that, sister?"

Sitting back at the booth, Jake was getting a kick out of all this play acting and posturing. He decides to go over and end this bullshit before any kind of authority person walks in. As he comes across the dance floor, he starts to realize how big and fit John is. *Well, if he was a cop, they would be all over the place by now putting that thought out of mind.*

"Hello, Mr. Babe! I see you are a man of his word. Give me that money, Tilley. Can I buy you a drink or would you like to get the merchandise and go to work?"

"I would like to get the tools and be on my way please, sir?"

"Where are you parked?"

"Oh, I parked across the street in the tavern's lot. There were no cars there, and it seemed a good place to park."

"You dumb shit, that's a federal park—the park police will tow your car."

"It's okay. It's my girlfriend's car, and she works for the Census Bureau, and it has government plates on it. Where are you parked?"

"Out front. Let me drive to the back lot. You follow, and we can transfer everything, and nobody can witness a damn thing. Tilley, you stay here. I will be right back, and tonight I can buy you that little trinket you want so bad."

"Okay, honey, you be careful? Bye, Mr. Babe."

John backs up the Chevy alongside the Lexus and opens the trunk. The trunk of the Lexus is open, and Jake starts putting tools in John's car. Slowly and deliberately, John eases the Beretta .45 out of the belt holster in the small of his back. As Jake puts a bag with small tools in the Chevy, it's one of the last things he will ever remember. With his left hand, he grabs Jake's right wrist and twists it so hard you can hear the ulna and radius crack like a small gunshot; the eight carpal bones are mangled severely. As John pushes up on the elbow and using his weight against Jake's right side, the shoulder dislocates and Jake faints.

Just for insurance, John cracks Jake across the side of his head to keep him unconscious for the trip to southern Maryland. John duct-tapes Jake's mouth, wrists, legs at the knee joint, and around his shoulders, tosses him in the trunk, and flies up Route 450 to 202 and down to south on Route 5 and in a gravel and dirt road that leads to the great Zekiah Swamp.

The great Zekiah Swamp was the same place John Wilkes Booth ran to and barely made it out the night he shot Abraham Lincoln. Many people have gone in but never came out. Crossing over a small wooden bridge, John found what he was looking for—a small pirogue-type boat almost barely usable. Aiming his small LED flashlight, "Okay now, Jake, you are going to pay for all your transgressions. You no-good bastard, you killed yours and Carol's baby from all the beatings you put on that poor girl. You turned traitor and treasonist when you were in the CIA. You no-good bastard, you screwed over my country, now you have to pay. I am going to take the tape off your mouth now. You can scream as loud as you want. Nobody can hear you—we are miles from civilization.

"I bet you wish you had some of that dope you sold to kids, children at best, ruining the lives of not only the kids but their parents and families as well. You're a lucky guy I am not going to let you drown tonight. The crabs, raccoons, skunks, fish, and even a bear or two might get to feast on your rotten flesh. This knife strapped to my wrist is a wonderful tool for getting revenge from a worthless piece of human garbage," as John cuts away the duct tape, the clothing, and takes Jake's shoes. The Fairbairn-Sykes makes a few more cuts and slices all over Jake's body. Wearing a pair of rubber gloves and a pair of black leather army gloves over the top, he says, "These tools you stole will help weigh you down. I am glad you put some pliers and tie wire to attach the saws, drills, hammers, etc. to your carcass. I said I won't let you drown, but I have to make sure you are dead. The point of this knife driven with hardly any strength into the base of your skull into the medulla oblongata kills instantly. Now let me paddle out a little further. Boy, I am sure glad there is no moon tonight. Here we go. The water is about eight or ten feet deep here, and with all the crabs and fish and snakes, there will be no meat on Jake in a few days. Case closed."

Man, I just made it back to dry land before this old pirogue started falling apart. That's good, less evidence that someone was here. Although I never heard of people fishing or hunting here since that illegal body of socialists, the EPA, outlawed this swamp for recreation.

I better call in. She probably has a troop of Boy Scouts looking for me. I wonder why she hasn't called me. Oh, oh shit turds, my phone was turned off. I am in for an ass-whipping now. "Hello, I'm sorry, my phone was turned off. I turned it off when I went in the bar. I could not let it ring and blow my cover."

"How is it going? And are you all right?"

"I am fine. It's all done. The subject will never bother a living soul ever again."

"Can I call Carol and tell her the good news?"

"Maybe it would be better to let her sleep and you tell your team. Have them call you in the morning when she wakes up, and you can tell her yourself."

"That's a better idea. If her intuition is like mine, she is getting some well-deserved sleep right now."

"So tell me something, darling, there is a new comic book character, Mister Spider or Spider Guy or something like that. His spider sense starts tingling like yours when he senses danger. Is yours tingling now?"

"No Mr. Smart Ass. Just get your butt back here. We have a few hours before wake-up time. And where the hell are you anyway?"

"I really don't know. All I know is I am heading north toward the beltway and your loving arms."

"We will see about that when you get here. You are going to spend some time in the shower. And yes, I will wash your back and front and whatever. Hurry home. I love you. Bye." Turning off Route 5 north and onto Route 301 north, the worst off all luck happens. The large doe deer wasn't fast enough to escape getting nailed by a car traveling south in the other lane. She was knocked into John's car, even though he pulled hard to the right. He knocked the doe off the side of the road and slammed on the brakes. The other guy was not so lucky. The front of his Toyota was crushed in. The guy flew into the windshield just as the air bag went off. He was dead when John got back to check on him.

Poor bastard. Maybe it's better he cashed in. This car smells like a bunch of teenagers were having a pot party. I guess I better call in and call 911.

"Yes, dear, the other fella coming south hit the deer first. I am okay, and the car is drivable. I can't leave till the state or county cops get here. I see red, blue, and white lights. Now I hear the sirens. Listen, I got to make up a story why I am here so late. I will call as soon as I am on the road again."

I lucked out again tonight. The trooper did not even notice the mud on the tires and wheel wells. If he was sharp, as they are supposed to be, my ass might be in a crack. Jake's muddy and bloody clothes are still in the trunk along with any tools that did not get tossed. The best place for me to get rid of all this evidence is the burned building at Langley. That will mean it will be too late for a date with the boss. The things I do for that woman—who the fuck am I kidding? I love every minute of it.

CHAPTER NINETEEN

In John's office in Pennsylvania, Ann Marie asks Helen, "When is John coming back from DC?

"Well. Annie, on Wednesday of this week, he did a small thing for the NSA as a favor to Laura."

"Is he still tied up with that bitch? She really has his mind all messed up. I feel sympathy for him. I know he proposed to her. He bought a big diamond ring and everything."

"Ann Marie, don't get all upset about Laura. She has a very important position with the federal government. John is a big boy and knows what he was doing. And besides it takes two to tango. Is it something I can help you with? I mean, if it's not too personal."

"No, since my dad passed last month and my mom is in a nursing home, I like to talk to John. We have been friends since we were in diapers, and he helps me and Mary Ann with a lot of stuff. He always said his door was open if we had problems. I kind of miss him when he is not around. The whole room lights up when he is in it."

Aboard US Airways commuter flight to Avoca Airport, "I hope the young lady driving this bird does a better job landing than she did last week. The wheels touched down and gave off a little burned rubber as the lady pilot went through the procedures to slow the plane."

"Thanks for coming for me, Annie."

"It's okay, Bo, I really wanted a chance to talk with you."

"I see you have something on your mind, and I am all ears."

"Well, I am kind of nervous, so I better get to it. This is very personal, so don't get too upset with me, okay? You know how you always say you love me and Mary Ann And Beth and the whole gang? Just how far do you mean it?"

"I think I see what you are getting at, Annie. We go back a long way, since we were kids in school and beyond. I used to think of you as my little sister. I watched you grow into a beautiful woman. Now we see a lot of each other. I depend upon you at the office and marveled at how you took to this kind of service. Just like all my brother soldiers out there, I need you to watch my six as I watch yours. Our kind of love comes from dependency on each other and the friendship of over twenty-nine years. The fact that you are yourself the lady I call Ann Marie, one with a big heart, a soul mate, and somebody who cares about me and her best friends, ours is a kind of relationship money can't buy. It is built up in bits and pieces through all kinds of experiences, and that is a wonderful feeling.

"There are lots of different kinds of love. One is the sublime emotion—that unexplainable phenomenon that sends an electric charge through the heart, brain, stomach, and various other body parts. This is what I feel when I see you guys after being away for a time. For I know that I am here where I am the most comfortable and wanted. One other kind is the earned type of being with your guys in a stressful and maybe a combat situation. That could be a living or dying experience because we never left a guy behind. That is a basic creed of the Airborne Rangers. That is another kind you can't buy. I've been doing all the talking. It's your turn."

"Bo. everything you said, I can relate to, and I am jealous of Kathy. Don't try to bullshit me or lie to me. I know you and Kathy did it that Friday night and Saturday also. And you are going to make love to me the same way you and Kathy did it."

"Annie, we did no such thing. We slept in different rooms."

"I said, Bo, no lying. There is too much evidence proving you and Kathy did the between-the-sheets cha-cha. She also denies it, but she can't hide the emotional change in her face when Mary Ann and I hit her with the evidence. She was never a very good liar either.

"Kathy said she had an epiphany after the swing incident. She said she had been missing out on a lot of things life has to offer. She said she felt renewed energy, things were clearer, and maybe she needed more love in her life. There is no other explanation for this new behavior—Kathy got laid, and she loved it.

"Now I need the same kind of loving, and I won't give up till you give me what you do best. The sooner the better. Because I have never been this horny and this jealous in my whole life."

John was thunderstruck. He had nothing to rebut Annie's claim, since it was the truth. "Annie, sweetheart, I have been on airplanes all day. The first flight to Scranton was full, and the second flight was an hour late, and it was routed through Pittsburgh and Allentown, which made for a long day. Please take me to the office so I can get my car, and you can go home—it's close to closing time anyway."

"Ann Marie, you know I am your boss and office romances are a no-no in any business."

"John, I am not asking to be your girlfriend. And I am not trying to blackmail you. I just want you to be my first, just like Kathy. Any other guy would be salivating at my front door for the opportunity that I want us to share."

"Darling, you make a convincing and persuasive argument— that's why Helen was glad I hired you and Mary Ann. Sergeant Eddie and Wanda are in New Jersey all this week, so I have the house all to myself. If you want to come over later, we can discuss this further? No promises, no strings attached, tomorrow morning I will still be your boss, and you will still be my wunderkind whiz kid. If you would like, I can meet you at Preno's in about an hour or so and we can have dinner. Would you like to have dinner with me?"

"Yes, if you don't try to talk me out of my dreams for later."

"Okay, I promise."

Preno's, a busy Sicilian restaurant on south Washington Avenue, in downtown Scranton, a hub for business executives, politicians, and would-be wise guys, served some of the best Italian food this side of the Bronx, New York.

Marian Shumacher. waitress for twenty-five years, in typical waitress uniform, comes over to their table. John and Annie were seated in a small private kind of dining area. The walls, covered with scenes of Sicily, the bay at Palermo and Messina, contributed to a relaxing and congenial atmosphere. "Oh, Bo, I was never in this part of the restaurant before. It's so nice."

"Hey, look who's here. Johnny, long time no see. What are you, robbing the cradle these days?"

"Hi, Marian, how's the mister?"

"Funny you should ask, the fat bastard kicked the bucket six months ago."

"Oh, I am sorry to hear that."

"No, don't be sorry. The rat died with a smile on his face. He was in his girlfriend's bed when the coroner picked him up."

"I hope he left you something?"

"If he did, I wouldn't be working in this joint. These mob guys only tip good when they get something back."

Marian brings their drinks and delicious fresh hot Italian bread. "I will be back to take your order in a few minutes." John scans the room and the back corridor where the rear exits are. He always takes that little extra caution. It has saved his butt several times. He relates this to Ann Marie, saying it is a life lesson well heeded.

"Annie, if you have another drink, will you be able to drive okay?"

"Yes, Daddy. Please don't treat me like a teenager? You do have a bunch of booze at your house, so I can get a glow on sitting on that great big divan of yours. I don't need any more to drink right now, thank you. And you didn't even notice what I am wearing tonight. And I am not fishing for compliments."

"Annie, that little black dress, with the single strand of pearls, is so chic and sexy. I apologize for not saying something earlier. This evening I need to soak in every bit of you slowly. So when and if we come together in an intimate way, it will be a wonderful threshold we pass through. And tonight after seeing you so beautiful, I can only wonder why someone hasn't proposed to you?"

"Oh, I have been proposed to a few times, but I could not see spending my life cooking, cleaning, and raising a brood of kids, while the husband goes off with the boys, hunting fishing, drinking in the local bars, chasing pussy, and watching football. People may say what they want about women's lib. I am all for it, and so are Mary Ann and Kathy. I am so thankful to you and Helen for the position I now have. And I hope there is some more travel coming up for Mary Ann and me? With the better salary, I can now afford clothes that are up to my sister's standards. She is always on my case to dress better than I did."

"Okay, sugar, let's get moving. We have an interesting evening ahead of us. Now follow me to the house and pull up in front of the garage. Remember, don't get out of your vehicle till I open the garage doors and we pull in. Sergeant Eddie and Wanda are out of town, and I don't have complete faith in those younger bodyguards he is training." Just then. John's phone rang. *I was wondering what time she would call. Her intuition must be in high gear now.* "Good evening, dear. How are you?"

"No, Braz, where are you? You were going to come to Maryland this weekend, and we were going to have a nice romantic sojourn through the Virginia back country."

"I am so sorry, Laura. I had to get back home. So much work came in these last two weeks. Even your boss is on my ass to help you guys out. With the new terrorist threat in the Canal Zone, Potus is shitting bricks. The OPEC people are scared their oil can't get through the canal."

"John, don't hand me that horseshit. You can't work for Potus before I set it up and clear the way. Remember, this is a new president, and you are not the fair-haired boy like you were with the last guy."

"Well then, darling, why does his chief of staff call my office five times a day?"

"John, you SOB, you went around me and over Casey's head to secure those under the table and not on the book's contracts."

"Darling, as much as I love you and everything, that is pretty common even for you."

"Now I really need you to get your ass to Langley. We gotta get to an understanding about which work is yours, what work is the agency's, and what work is yours, mine, and ours. I am not threatening you, but if the FBI gets wind of hacking into secure computers, we all could be in Leavenworth for the rest of our lives. So, darling, please be careful. And goddammit, stop stealing from my recruiting teams."

"Darling, I am very tired, and I will go in the office tomorrow, so sleep tight. I love you."

Pulling into the garage, John remotes the door closed. Through the garage and through the laundry room, John checks every monitor. Everything checks out, and both would-be lovers start to relax. John says to Annie, "You can call me Bo now if you want to. I am really not hung up on formalities." Right then he sweeps Annie into his arms, and they kiss very deeply. Bo slides his right arm and hand to the small

of her back and over the curve of her butt. A slight caressing motion
with his hand gives Annie a warm feeling from her knees to her navel.
Face-to-face, only an inch apart, they rub noses, and Bo says, "Let me
make you the best dry martini you ever had." It was all Annie could
do to shake her head up and down. She could not utter a word.

"Can we sit on the couch for a minute, Bo? I am a little shaky
in the knees."

"Okay, sweetie. The remote is right there on the coffee table. We
can listen to music or watch TV."

"Do you have any Dean Martin or Jerry Vale or Frank Sinatra?"

"Oh sure, I have all those guys. Just scroll through the remote
and find anything you like. I love all that kind of music." Annie is
sitting about midway on the couch and resting on a big pillow. Her
legs are under her body, and she seems as content as a girl could be.
Bo sits on the other side of the pillow and hands Annie a very dry
martini made with Barclay's gin. He has a brandy snifter with a shot
of VSQ warming in his hands. They just sit and listen to the softly
playing music, with their hand touching across the pillow. After a
short while, Bo asks Annie, "Being that it's Saturday, how about I
take you shopping where Kathy and I went in the summer?"

"Oh my goodness, Bo, why would you do that for me?"

"Because you are you and my wonderful friend, Ann Marie."

"Why don't you make me go in to work tomorrow? I know we
have a ton of things to do, and Helen is stretched pretty thin."

"Don't be concerned about Helen. She thrives on this stuff, and
she would not have it any other way. She does not want you and
Mary Ann taking on too much responsibility yet. It could lead to
disastrous conclusions. She is very happy with your progress and
wants you to keep moving along at this speed till you know more of
the political ramifications associated with our intel."

Now it was Annie's turn. She finished the Martini, set the glass
on the table, crawled over the pillow, took hold of Bo's face, and
kissed him so deep she had to come up for air. She moved the rest
of her torso over the pillow, and as her dress rode up to her hips
and over the hips, she sat on Bo's lap and started taking his tie off.
Unbuttoning his shirt, her hands were all over the muscular six-pack
he used for a chest, all the while gurgling with as much excitement
and sexuality as had ever entered this girl's mind. While Annie was

exploring a world she never had been to, Bo had his hand on her beautiful thighs and derriere, caressing every square inch he could reach and at the same time wondering why she didn't have panties on; she was wearing a thong her sister brought her back from New York. She stood up and didn't even try to even out her dress, which was up to her waist by this time. Grabbing Bo's hand, "Come on, let's get to your bedroom, or somebody's bedroom." She was thinking and praying, *Please don't let me have a premature orgasm and ruin one of my fantasies. Hurry up, Bo, I am ready to explode,* as her dress and slip and stockings were being thrown about. Her thong and little black bra were hung on the first passing doorknob. They both reached the king-size bed, and the covers disappeared in a flash. Annie and John spent the rest of the night discovering each other many times over. By three o'clock in the morning, the two lovers intertwined and, with just a single sheet covering them, slept the sleep known only to those who have traveled a path fulfilled with a caring love for each other.

On Saturday, 0500 hours, Bo unwound himself from Annie. He put the covers over her nude body so she would not wake up and be cold. Dressing in his running shorts, a T-shirt, socks, and a good pair of running shoes, Bo puts his cell phone in a pocket and a small .38 automatic in his ankle holster and quietly slips out the side door. Doing his morning run of at least five to six miles gets the adrenalin pulsing through his body and brain, waking up his thinking and using the gray matter to his best advantage, and it brings him back to the training regimens that have kept him so healthy. In the shower, Bo has the water as hot as he can stand it, even though he was sweating. With the radio softly playing, the shower running, Annie sneaks up behind, grabs the washcloth from his hand, and says, "Let me wash your back and the parts you can't reach. Then you can reciprocate, okay?"

"Good morning, sweetie. I thought you were still sleeping."

"Bo, when you finish and dry off, would you be a dear and get my bag from the backseat of the van? I have a change of clothes and sneakers. I could not go out this morning wearing a sexy party dress now, could I?"

"No, you couldn't, and good thinking about clean clothes. When we are finished here, we will get some breakfast at the Mid Valley Diner and head toward Route 81 and Wilkes-Barre."

With breakfast over, the happy couple, captivated by the events of last evening, pull into the parking lot at the Shoppe of RoseAnne. As they enter, Bridgette, the salesperson, greets them warmly. "Mister John, how nice to see you again."

"Bridgette, meet another of my employees, and a very dear friend. Ann Marie Casey, meet Bridgette, a most professional woman in the clothing industry."

"Thank you for that introduction, John. Miss Ann Marie, may I start off in the intimate apparel area? Then we can move over to our new fall and winter togs. John, are we still doing the same amounts you had specified in the summer?"

"No, Bridgette, we are going for at least three or four of whatever Annie wants. She needs to project a professional image in my company. Her sister in New York City is quite the connoisseur of fashion, and we want Ann Marie to be proud when she sees her older sibling. So please go for broke—the costs are not even to be discussed. Something very stylish that she can walk in the snow with. Also some gloves and scarfs, and nice leather gloves for driving."

"John, enough is enough. I can buy my own clothes. I don't need you to outfit me with a whole wardrobe."

"Ann Marie, be quiet and enjoy the moment. You deserve every bit of this. Bridgette, take her by the arm and show her all the goodies. She will give you a hard time, but she knows this is an important step in her career. And I am having a grand time."

"Okay, John. Come on, Ann Marie, this going to be fun. I know you have a good sense of fashion. I saw you fingering the material and matching up and coordinating tops and slacks. Ask any question about what you don't see. We can always get it or have it made in any color, pattern, material, etc."

In the meantime, as John was relaxing in a big old overstuffed chair, drinking coffee, the army fight song goes off in John's pocket. It's Vito from last night at the restaurant. "Hey, Johnny boy, when can we get together and discuss my situation?"

"Hello, Vee. Right now, I am down the line in Wilkes-Barre. I plan to be here till at least noontime. We will probably be in the office at two o'clock. I can see you then."

"Good, Johnny, that's real good, two o'clock is just fine."

"Vee, come alone, no one else, *capisce?*"

"Yeah, John, just me and nobody else."

"And, Vee, when you pull up to the first gate, follow the instructions and don't deviate from the roadway. The dogs and the guards take their work seriously."

"Okay, John. Arrivederci."

After nearly two and a half hours, three trips to the Impala, and Bridgette and Ann Marie carrying bulging shopping bags, John, with a smile from ear to ear, says, "Do we have to come back next week, or are we good to go for a while? Well, I guess I better pay the lady so we can get back on the highway." Ann Marie sits in one of the big chairs. She has a look on her face like she is ready to cry. No one has ever treated her with such generosity and caring.

Bridgette senses Annie's feelings and says, "Come here, give me a hug." She whispers in Annie's ear, "This is no time for tears. Mr. John really enjoys being the philanthropist. He cares for you and the other lady Kathy. After the first shopping spree, he called Ms. RoseAnne, the owner here, and said a lot of nice things about me, and Ms. Rosey, as we call her, gave me a bonus. He told her he has several ladies working for him that he will bring to us. I guess you are one of those ladies, so enjoy everything and wear the new things. He may not compliment you on the days you dress in the new clothes, but be rest assured he notices everything. It's all part of his highly skillful training. And I imagine that we will be seeing you before Christmas."

CHAPTER TWENTY

Saturday morning, eleven o'clock

"Are you hungry? Of course, you are. Choosing new clothes and shoes makes a lady hungry. What say we eat at Denny's? The food is good and the service is fast, and we have a two o'clock at the office with the guy you met last night."

"Oh, John, I don't like the looks of that crook. You have to be extra careful around those mob guys."

"You're right, Annie, but we have to look at every bit of possible work that comes our way and from where it comes. Your intuition is right on—I smell a rat. Vee is only a small-time player in the Jersey Mob. His importance of himself is way overblown. That is why I would like you and Mary Ann to sit in on this sit-down. Call Helen and see if Mary Ann came in today or if she can get her to the office by one thirty. My phone is buzzing like crazy—it's Laura, I know. Good morning. How's the weather in Virginia?"

"It's about time you answered. Where are you? If you're driving, look around real good. My ESP has been going bat shit since last night. For whatever this means, stay away from Italian food, specially calzone with three kinds of cheeses. And another thing, the ocean is not your friend for the near future. I wish we could get together. I miss you and need to talk about Casey wanting you to lead a mission of ex-rangers to Nicaragua. The money is real good, and the risk is small."

"Darling, I can't set foot in that country. If you remember I was declared persona non grata by the dictator after we grabbed the Russian nuke expert and whisked him off to Guantanamo where he mysteriously died of a heart attack. But we did the right thing—we gave his body back to the Russians so they could bury him in Mother Russia."

"John, don't worry about being not welcome in Managua or anyplace else in Nicaragua. Casey has set it up so you can travel anywhere down there. The rebels are playing footsie with Castro and being supplied by the Chicoms and Russia. They are trying to get Noriega from Panama to screw with the canal operations. It would hurt the economy of the United States big time with a lot of Commies running around Central America and fucking up the day-to-day workings of the canal. Please try to get here to Langley? Casey and some of the other bigwigs around here think you have gotten too old and have lost your nerve and your fighting spirit."

"Darling, the old Mad Dog has not lost his love for America. Tell Casey I would like to talk to him and make operational plans on my functionality and direction only. I will be in my secure office at 1450 hours today and all day on Sunday. I will be in Washington on Tuesday for the FBI auction. They have a nice new Sabreliner taken from some drug dealers. The FBI owes me a favor, and I think I can get this airplane for a good price. I may ask your father to pony up some quick cash as a deposit till I get my uncle to release some of my money for the sale."

"John, my dad will do anything for you, you know that. He wants you to marry me so bad, he would probably buy the friggin' plane for you."

"Or he could keep raising the bid so I don't get the damn aircraft."

"No, sweetie, he would not do that 'cause that would piss me off so bad he would be on my shit list for a long goddamn time. And he could not live with that situation. John, I got to go. I have three phones ringing. When you get to DC, call me, and we will get together for drinks. Bye now. I love you."

"Oh, Bo, sometimes I hate that woman. I wonder if she really has great psychic powers or an overabundance of women's intuition. If it keeps you out of trouble, great, but she strings you along and always says I love you, I love you—it must really fuck your mind up. Oh shit, I am so jealous of her."

"Annie, just roll with the punches. I doubt if anything will ever become of our relationship. Laura and I have been coworkers for a long time. And the power business in the Washington area means a lot to her, and I just happen to be in her loop far longer than anybody else she is close with. Right now, you, I, and Mary Ann are developing a close and very personal and professional team. And I see us going a long way forward before it ends. That is why I want you and Mary Ann with me today."

"I am staying with you tonight, aren't I?"

"Of course, you are. I would like to see you model some of your new outfits, if that's okay with you."

"Yes, yes. I feel like a princess or a queen or a spoiled child the way you have treated me today. I know that Mary Ann is going to be green with envy when she finds out all—that I was the benefactor of your sweet generosity today."

"No, Ann Marie, I think that she is not the least bit envious of other people's good fortune. Anyway, her turn is coming. And Helen also. This way we can keep a harmonious working environment and nobody feels left out. The better we all labor together, our end product results in happier clients and lots more projects, and we all make more money. Our future gets better and better all the time. When you look at the big picture, the more money I throw back into the company and its employees, the more professional we become, and that makes us look good to current and prospective customers."

"Bo? This is more on a personal level. Last night was the greatest night of my life. And not having a lot of experience in sexual matters does what you did and the way I reacted to the different kinds of lovemaking the normal way that say married people do it."

"I know what you are referring to, and the answer is yes. We did what normal people, married or not, enjoy as a normal way of making love. There was nothing kinky or unusual about what we did. And I sincerely hope it was as wonderful for you as it was for me. Whoever gets to be your husband is going to be one lucky SOB. We can talk about this further. We're here at the office, and I want you and Mary Ann to step right in and kind of take charge. Ask a lot of questions and don't let Vee bully you. Get in his face if you have to. Let him know you can't be pushed around because you're a female."

Saturday, 1400 hours, John's secure office

"Hi, Mary Ann, did Annie fill you in on this meeting?"

"Yes, John, and she is glowing all over about her new clothes. Now this mob guy—is he really an asshole like Annie said?"

"Yeah, sweetie, so don't you take no shit from him or it could blow the whole deal, okay?"

"I get the picture. These self-important types try to project the image of the bigger dick syndrome—'my joint is bigger than yours.' I know how to treat these idiots. Let's bring him in here so we can get started on him. My claws are real sharp, and I need a good jackass to bury them in."

"Ciao, John and ladies. It's okay to talk with these ladies in the room?"

"Vito Bevalaqua, meet Mary Ann, another of my very trusted operators and a member of my team. You already met Ann Marie."

"What, John, these ladies ain't got no last names?"

"Vito, you don't have a need to know. Just let us have the facts of your problem."

"Fer God's sake, John, yer all business from the get-go."

"We can't afford to waste time. Come on spill it or go somewhere else. I got a lotta irons in the fire, and time is money. Hold on a sec. Helen, would you get one of our computer girls to bring in a big pot of coffee and four cups please? Thank you."

"John, this the problem. Over in the Jersey Pines Area, there are three middle schools in an eight- to twelve-mile circle, and a towel head is selling drugs to the kids at one of these schools every other day. We can never catch the bastard. He has lookouts at strategic points and is warned as soon as one of my guys shows up. You know my first cousin Aldo is the head of that family, and he is pissed off that we can't get to this stunade. I told him about you and why they call you Mad Dog. He said to hire your outfit and bring him this Arab, and that there will be five hundred thousand in it for you."

"Vee, why can't you just get a good shooter and whack this guy?"

"Because, John, it would look too much like a mob hit, and the feds would be on our ass in a New York minute. These areas where the schools are located are in very upscale urban settings. A lotta rich people with a good amount of juice in the right ears, and we all get a vacation in Sing Sing. So this caper has to be pulled off by the best-trained people in the country, capisce?"

"Mr. Bevalaqua, do you"—Mary Ann is visibly pissed off—"think we all just fell off the turnip truck? First of all, capturing a foreign national in the United States is a huge federal offense. And for a measly half a mil? I know for a fact that your cousin Aldo is not a cheap bastard. You fucking amateur were going to try to screw us out of the real price of one million. We do not deal with second-rate assholes like you. We only would talk to Aldo and negotiate a sensible commission for a very risky and dangerous operation like this."

Ann Marie joins the conversation, "Your story is full of holes and sounds very fishy to me. If we were even thinking about taking on this project, we would need good-quality pictures or even video of the action. Plus we need to do our own surveillance and get familiar with all the schools involved. We need to know the habits and procedures of the local and state police, where they eat lunch, and at what times, and the normal shift changes. We have to be provided with throwaway weapons. Where is the closest small airport? Preferably one with no tower and does not have a lot of traffic. If your people are serious and want a professional squad like we are to do this job, have your cousin Aldo DiAngelo call me, and we will talk serious business."

"Call you? A woman? He would laugh in my face and kick me in the ass if I ever said that to him. John, is she for real? We don't even let our wives talk to us like that."

"Vito, wake up and smell the espresso. Ann Marie is one of the best strategists I have ever had the pleasure of working with. She will know everything about the towel head that even his own family doesn't. And Mary Ann is one of the best shooters to ever shoulder a weapon. She can knock the balls off a bullfrog at two hundred yards with a .30-30 using iron sights, no scope. If I had these women with me on my CIA team in Vietnam, we could have waxed Ho Chi Minh in his own bedroom."

CHAPTER TWENTY-ONE

Tuesday, 0700 hours, Washington DC National Airport

A tall and military-looking young man, holding a sign that says "Captain Braz," is watching for John coming off the US Air commuter from Scranton, Pennsylvania. John was going to take a taxi to the FBI building where the auction takes place at 0900 hours. Laura sent a car and driver to fetch him to her office, where breakfast is waiting. John hopes maybe dessert is on the menu this morning also. Captain Braz, US Army, retired, is ushered to the top floor where the executive offices are. Ms. Kowolski, Laura's private secretary, eyes John and swoons a bit. "Put your eyeballs back in you noggin, Rosey. This guy is private property," as Laura kisses John and flirts like a teenage schoolgirl. "When you get through with the auction, your driver will take you back here, and we can have a meeting with Director Casey."

"Sure, sweetie, that is okay with me, but I don't know what time the Sabreliner is scheduled to go on the dock. Your father is going to be at the auction also. He said they have a Cessna Citation up for bid, and he really would like to have it—for the right price, of course. That particular airplane is worth at least $17 million. He hopes to get it for about half the cost."

With breakfast over, John's driver takes him downtown to the Hoover Building. There he meets Mr. Thomas Francis Diskin, Laura's father. "Johnny, my lad, how are ya? I hear your are up to purchasing a used airplane. Not the same one I am bidding on, I hope?"

"No, sir, that Cessna is too rich for my blood right now. If the logbooks and records are as good as the people who have the Sabreliner in their possession say it is, then it might be a good buy."

As the prospective buyers were led into the auditorium, and their credentials and IDs were verified, the selling staff called the room to attention. The bidding started out on the low side, and quite a few buyers went away very satisfied with planes they bought. But not John. The Sabrejet turned out to have too many hours on the current engines. In less than 150 hours each, both engines would have to be completely overhauled or replaced at a cost of $3 million. John would have to look elsewhere for the type of small private jet for his needs.

Later that day, back at CIA headquarters in Casey's conference room, John went tete-a-tete with Casey, Laura, and several military field specialists. "Gentlemen and Lady, I will take the mission on the conditions that I, and I alone, plan and pick the operatives who will be going with me on this run-and-gun exercise. We need at least three weeks at the farm to set up a similar-type village to train every single maneuver. I will go down there myself and surveil the area, just like we did in North Vietnam. We will use the same techniques. I will HALO in (high altitude low opening) at night from at least ten miles out, get what intel I can, and walk back to the infiltration point. There you can extract me, and we will better be able to make a plan that will work and be relatively certain to cut our casualties or deaths to the bare minimum."

"Colonel Briggs and Colonel Tyson, sirs, there are two Green Beret sergeants—I even think they may be Delta by now—that I would like you to use your juice to secure for TDY to train the team and even accompany us as part of the team. These two soldiers are the very best the army has in clandestine operations. If you called on me to make this work, then you know I work with only the bravest and most loyal soldiers the army can produce. Give me two weeks, and I will be ready to parachute into Nicaragua, and I would like partial payment up front. You can wire it to our bank in Scranton, Pennsylvania. Call my office, and Helen will get you to the correct person at the bank."

"Captain Braz, Colonel Tyson and myself admire the confidence in your professional attitude, but as you can ascertain the international repercussions if something, anything, goes wrong, the CIA, the army, the White House will be vilified to no end by the goddamn media and every Communist country in the world, not to mention the liberal bastards in this country."

"Colonel, sir, I am not a captain anymore, just a private citizen who loves this country almost more than anything"—as he winks at Laura, letting her know he loves her more—"and I can and will execute this exercise to the very highest standards of the United States military. If knowing my reputation and the words I spoke here still does not convince this august body of professionals, then you better start looking for somebody else. Thank you all for the opportunity to serve my country. Can I be dismissed now, sirs?"

Casey looks over at Braz and says, "John, I like the way you handle a problem by getting all the intel you can beg, borrow, or steal. You put yourself in the worst possible situation, so your team suffers the least. But all this bravado is for younger guys to do. And yes, I do know your reputation and some of the illegal things you have eked out to barely save your ass and your men's lives on. Your conclusions and demands here today border on total insubordination and arrogance against the army and the CIA. And I wouldn't have it any other way. You shall have everything you need, including the two Special Forces troopers. Keep in daily touch with Laura, and we will expect to see you in two weeks."

On the way out of the office, Laura taps John on the butt. "In my office right now. Why the fuck do you have to jump into the damn country? Can't you let one of the younger guys get what you need? Or do you have to have all the goddamn glory all the frigging time?"

"No one else can size up the territory and read the situation as I need it to be. I don't want my guys walking into a bucket of bat shit. We have to capture this Commie bastard before he turns over all of Central America to Castro. Not even to mention the terrorist bombs they have been using against the civilian population. When we get this Marxist rat, it will deflate their big red balloon and stop the rebels from being so overt in their dealings with Russia."

"Darling, I know you have to run the operation, but I don't like the parachute part. Johnny Braz, I know you love this country, and I know you love me. Please be on your game as you never were before. No more screwups like that time in Thailand in the fish freezer." Tears were starting well up in her eyes as she grabbed John and kissed him with a passion both had not seen in a while. "Now get the hell outta here and come back a few days earlier than the two weeks so we can spend some much-needed time for ourselves."

Back at his office in Scranton, John is in conference with Helen. "Tell me, do you think Annie and Mary Ann are ready to come and do some surveillance on the job in Jersey? I don't know, John, they still are a bit green, but they will do anything to get out in the field."

"No, we only got the still pictures of the dope dealer. And Aldo did not answer any of our calls, but that sleazy Vito came by with part of the money, only 250 grand. That scummy jerk tried to put the make on me. I was ready to pull out my pistol and plug the son of a bitch."

"No kidding, he really tried that in this office?"

"Yeah, and Mary Ann was laughing so hard she dropped her Beretta. She took it out as soon as she saw who it was and before we let him through the secure doors.

"Carol, Annie, and Mary Ann took their lunch break down in the target range. They said a guy like that makes them want to be better shooters, and Mary Ann put in a request for a Glock 17 9 mm Parabellum with the seventeen-round magazine and two extra magazines. She said she liked Carol's Glock so much because of the success at keeping the rounds in a tighter circle. I told her, yes, I will order several so we can get a discount for more units."

CHAPTER TWENTY-TWO

Lower Central New Jersey, the Pine Barrens
0900 hours, in a medium-priced motel room, Motel 6

"Mary Ann, you take the van over near the first middle school, park about two blocks away so as not to grab any attention from the lookouts, go into the office, and use the story we made up. If you see the guy or anything unusual, call us. And, sweetie, be careful. Annie, you go with her, and she will drop you off near the second school. Same story, okay? And I will take the third school. We all meet back here in two hours, and, Mary Ann, don't forget to pick up Annie where you let her off. Everybody check your watches—it's ten after nine now. See you all at eleven o'clock, and good luck."

Mary Ann drops Annie off and drives to her designated area, parks near a mom-and-pop grocery store, and immediately spots a young guy hanging near the parking lot, looking under the hood of a Chevy Camaro, pretending to be working on the motor. Mary Ann is looking out the window of the store and notices the guy looking up out of the hood and scoping the surrounding area. She asks the older woman clerk if she knows the boy working on the car.

"No, can't say who he is, but it's mighty strange that for the past several weeks, at least twice a week, he is under the hood of that car, tinkering and talking on his cell phone. I've never seen him before, but he parks in the same place every time." Mary Ann buys some bagels, cream cheese, and canned soda, and asks the lady for some plastic utensils and goes back to her van.

"John, I spotted a lookout near the store by the school. I am coming for you and Annie right now. Annie, do you copy?"

"Yes, I will be waiting right where you left me."

As the van stops for Annie, she says, "Shit, you picked up a tail."

"John, we are being followed. Should we shoot it out with this guy or try to capture him?"

"Negative. Just get back here, and we will decide what action to take. And don't be heroic by trying to lose him. Let him come to us."

The van stops and picks up John, and they drive away doing only the speed limit. In the meantime, the tail takes another route to the Motel 6.

"Looks like he didn't want to get involved with us or he is setting something up. Let's go back to where you saw the lookout. Maybe we can find the towel head still plying his trade."

After driving around to all three schools, they had no luck in finding the dope dealer or any lookouts. "Back to the motel, Mary Ann. Let's pick up our other gear and kits, and we will go down to Atlantic City—it's not too far from here. There we can get some nice rooms in a decent hotel and some good food."

When the threesome enters the room, Annie yells, "The dirty bastards busted in here and all the gear and clothes are scattered on the beds and the floor. Lucky for us we all had our guns. I want to catch those guys and shoot them. I hate anybody going through my stuff."

"Calm down, Annie. This is one of those things you don't plan for, but it still happens, and it pisses me off that I did not think to come back earlier instead of chasing shadows. Right now, we're going to the manager's office and talk to him in a nice way for only a minute, then I am going to beat the hell out of him until he tells us what we need to know."

As John opens the door, chips of brick busting off the door frame hit him in the right side of his face from a high-powered rifle bullet. A second shot grazes his left arm high on the shoulder. He slams the door quick and hits the floor. Annie and Mary Ann are kneeling behind the bed with their guns drawn and ready to start blasting away. John's face is bleeding from the sharp shards of brick, and his upper arm is starting to hurt a little where the round cut some of the flesh away. It also was bleeding, but not as much as his face. "Stay down on the floor," he says. "If these people mean business, they will start shootin' through the window. There is no other way out of this room, and I can't get to the van to secure the rifles inside the gun locker."

"John, you are bleeding pretty badly. Let me gather up all the first aid equipment and get you bandaged up."

"Okay, Annie, but stay on your stomach. I have to upset this bed and push it up against the window, with the box spring and mattress, in case these bastards have grenades to throw through the window." Needless to say, both girls helped John secure the mattresses and bed frames, blocking the window from flying glass and any IEDs. "Now listen carefully, I am going to open the door and try to locate where the shooters are. If they are close enough, we might get a couple of shots at them and scramble to the van." As the door opens, a volley of bullets slammed into the door, the opening, and the night table, and ricocheted off the floor into the ceiling.

"That idea wasn't so good, and that was plan B. We can't get out through the back wall—it's the same construction as the front, reinforced concrete block and brick veneer."

"John, I am a little frightened, and I don't want to die here. Could we use the mattress as a shield and work our way to the van?"

"No, Annie, those high-powered shells would shred the mattress to bits before we got past the sidewalk. The sidewalk is eight feet wide, and the van is parked two spaces away from the door. We are not going to die here, please believe me. I have my satphone and lots of battery life left."

John slowly pushes the short antenna through a broken-out piece of window glass in the corner of the frame. Another two shots smash through the glass, but too far away to hit the antenna. "Helen, this is John. We got our ass in a crack here in Jersey and need help. We are pinned down in a motel room with shooters in the buildings across the parking lot. Go in my bottom desk drawer and look in my old address book for the number for Carmine Joey Bonadero, goes by the nickname Joey Bondi. It will be a Pennsylvania prefix. Thanks, Helen. Yes, the girls are fine. They are real stand-up troopers, and I am proud of them. I will call you as soon as I get this shit worked out."

"Please, miss, may I speak with Carmine Bonadero? Yes, miss, I know he doesn't take personal calls, but this is a very serious matter.

Please tell him it's Johnny Bo Braz. Hello, yes, Joey, this is Bo Braz. I know it's been a few years, but, Joey, I am in a real fix here in Jersey. That rat bastard Vito Bevalaqua set me and my team up for an assassination. He lied to your cousin Aldo DiAngelo so he could make a half a mil off of a contract we were going to do for Aldo. Aldo's shooters have us pinned down in a motel room in the Jersey Pine Barrens. Could you please call your cousin and get these guys off my back? It's Vito that screwed Aldo, not me."

"Sure, Johnny, I'm gonna call right now. You hold out for fifteen minutes, and everything will be copacetic. Give the girl your number. Yes, that is my daughter. The last time you saw her she was a young teenager. Now she is getting ready to graduate from college."

Ten minutes later, John's phone is buzzing. "Hello, this is John."

"Johnny, my cousin in Old Forge tells me that no-good rat Vito set all this bad stuff in motion. Don't worry no more, the guys are going. There won't be any more gun play. I am so glad you have sense enough not to call the cops. It would be bad for all of us—the feds would be involved, and we could kiss our ass good-bye."

"Aldo, thank you very much. I would like to know where you got the suppressors your guys have on those weapons."

"John, I can't tell you that, but they didn't come from this country. Maybe if you talk to Moises Silverstein in New York City, he might know a guy who knows a guy."

John and the girls move all their gear into the van. "Mary Ann, you and Annie bring the van down to the motel office. We have to talk to the manager. Damn it, guys, nobody's here. The little weasel took off as soon as he saw Aldo's guys."

"Okay, we're going back where Mary Ann saw the lookout."

"Let me off here. It's about a block to the school play yard. Annie, you go around the store from the back and strut your stuff as you walk up to the lookout. Make up a story about needing help. He's a guy—he can't help himself when his eyes are glazed over with lust. Clock him real good and knock him out. Mary Ann, sneak up to the dope dealer's car. It's the dirty blue Ford Taurus. Duck down in front of the car. I am going right for the bastard. My weapon has the suppressor on, so make sure both your guns are silenced. I am going to try and wound the guy in the legs if possible. Mary Ann, don't let him get too close to you. Take careful aim and shoot him anywhere you can get a good sight picture. Keep shooting him if he won't fall on the first shot. The lookouts are probably just local thugs. Shoot him also if he won't cooperate. Let's let this scene play out as it will. We need to capture the dope guy. If the other lookout gets in the way, wax him also."

Coming around the school yard from the parking lot and sneaking from car to car, John spots the dealer and says into his headband mike, "Okay, guys, I have a good eye on him. He is partially hidden by a large maple tree near the bike racks. The schoolteachers can't see him from any windows—the dirty rat. Everybody, get ready. I am only thirty feet away, and he hasn't spotted me yet. Annie, give me a report if you can talk."

"I am five by five, John. This asshole had his head under the hood of the Camaro, and when I bent over to say hi, his eyeballs went right down my shirt. I asked him to loan me a wrench, and when he bent over in the trunk, I hit him so hard I thought at first I killed him. I have him all wrapped up with duct tape and construction wire. He ain't going nowhere. I locked him in the trunk."

John is thinking, *I am only twenty feet away from this idiot. I know he must have spotted me by now. Maybe he figures I am no threat, so he is playing it nonchalant. Or is he carrying and is waiting to get the drop on me? This big gum tree shields me, so let me get a shot at him. Shit, I waited too long. He is running right for the Ford.* "Mary Ann, can you see him coming?"

"What the hell, why wait? I got a good bead on the large body mass." John squeezes of three rounds, and the doper goes ass over tin cups. Mary Ann is crouched right by the front tire of the Ford as she fires two shots, both hitting him in the chest and stomach. "John, I saw blood squirting from him when I shot, and I know you hit him also. I am going to get the van so we can get out of here before the cops come."

Annie already is in motion and driving the van right up to John and the bullet-riddled doper. The guy is still alive and bitching. None of the wounds are life threatening yet, but they need to get him to some emergency treatment. With the van loaded, they pull up to the Camaro and yank the lookout from the trunk and secure him in the van.

"Hello, miss, this is Bo Braz again. May I please speak to Aldo?"

"Hello, Bo, how is it going?"

"Good, Aldo. We got the dope dealer, but he is a little shot up. Do you have a friendly doctor we can take him to? Someone in your family maybe?"

"Sure, Bo, you got pencil and paper? Here is the number and address. You sure he will live that long? The place is in Trenton. I will call the doc and tell him you are on the way. And, John, thanks a million. I will wire the rest of the fee to your bank. Give me the phone number of your office. Arrivederci."

After interrogating the scared-to-death lookout, John got a wealth of information out of him. The name of the dope dealer is Mohammed Bin Aziz, a Saudi of the Royal House of Saud who was banished from the kingdom of Saudi Arabia for multiple crimes. John said, "I know now who put Vito up to this caper. And I know how to deal with it." They let the kid out of the van near Browns Mills, New Jersey, with a warning if they ever saw him again, the DiAngelo family would want to talk to him.

After getting the towel head medical attention, the team headed back to Pennsylvania. John wanted to stop and get a nice dinner in Trenton and stay in a hotel for the night and go back to Pennsylvania in the morning. The girls vetoed that suggestion; they wanted to sleep in their own beds. They had enough of motels for the time being. So they stopped at a fast-food place; hamburgers, french fries, milkshakes to go.

From Trenton, New Jersey, to the Delaware Water Gap, the rest of the trip to Pennsylvania was uneventful. John had to relinquish the driving to Mary Ann. The antibiotics the doctor gave him were sedating, and his attention to driving was going south.

Annie nudges John. "Wake up. Helen's on the phone."

"Yes, Helen, everybody is okay, and we will be in Scranton in about an hour. So tell me how many times has the queen of DC called? I have five or six messages on my satphone. She is probably in a snit about now. Her uncanny ESP is just about driving her bat shit. You didn't tell her I was winged, I hope. Good girl. She always knows when I am in the crap."

"Did the doctor give you some meds?"

"Yeah, and a tetanus shot also."

"Are you coming to the office? Or are you just going to drop the Amazing Amazons home?"

"They're going home. They had enough training for a while. And I am coming back to the office."

"You are home, aren't you? John, you need rest and for your own doctor to look at your wounds."

"Don't be a mother hen. You go back to sleep, and I will see you in the morning. I have to take care of the towel head and get him secured in our own little hotel. And I have to make some phone calls. Good night, sweetie. See you in the morning. Thanks for being at your post when we needed you."

John let the girls off at their respective homes, went to the office, and met with the assets on duty. "Mickey and Carol, I am glad you're here. Mick, I need your help. I have to drive the van down to the lower level, and I want you to open the door to the secure holding room. We have a guest for a day or two. He needs to be held in maximum security. This guy is a hired assassin. We shot him up a bit. We got him to a doctor in Trenton. He is on antibiotics and is still pretty well sedated. I have to get him out of here by tomorrow evening at the latest."

"What are you going to do with him?"

"As soon as I make some phone calls, I will formulate my plans for this asshole."

"Hello, Mr. Diskin."

"Johnny, me lad, top o' the evening to ye, son. What brings you to call at this late hour? And, John, please call me Tom or Francis— don't be so formal. You need a favor or something?"

"Yes, sir, I do. Do you still have that de Havilland Beaver you traded that Canadian bush pilot for?"

"Yes, of course. That is a great plane for how old it is. My guys keep it in tip-top condition. I won't sell it to you, but you can borrow it if need be."

"Well, Tommy, I would like to trade airplanes for two or three days. I need to fly a guy to a grass landing strip somewhere in Florida, and it has to be in the next twenty-four hours. I would let you have my Twin Beech King Air, and I could borrow the Beaver because it has the wide track landing gear, which gives it great stability and STOL performance. I have to get in and out of this strip in record time before anyone knows it's me and my guys. And I would like to have it tomorrow in the early morning?"

"It's yours, Johnny. Shall I have my pilot fly to Scranton? His name is Joe Naylor, and he can fly anything with wings."

"No, Tommy, have him (better get something to write on) file a flight plan to Harrisburg International Airport. From there to Richmond, Virginia, and on to Charlotte, North Carolina, then to Columbus, Georgia, and last Ocala, Florida. Then we reverse the plan for the return trip. But here is where it gets interesting—there is a little airstrip near Honesdale, Pennsylvania. Called the Cherry Ridge Airport. It is not even on a lot of aeronautical charts. It is a private strip owned by a farmer friend of our family. It has no VOR, no tower, no fixed base operator, and no lights. When Joe is ready to leave Chicago, he can call me, and I will give him the coordinates. I will be there with the King Air, all fueled and ready to go back to Chicago, or wherever you send him. Then I will leave and continue on to Harrisburg and fulfill the rest of the flight plan. That way everything is legit, and I don't have to sneak in under the radar at any of the airports."

CHAPTER TWENTY-THREE

John got up from the couch in his office and changed to a pair of running shorts and an old army T-shirt. He only had a few hours' sleep, but his discipline and paranoia about keeping fit help his internal clock to awake him and get on with the morning five- or six-mile run. After a hot shower and some breakfast, he is on the computer to aviation weather and the normal info for private aircraft flying to certain destinations.

"Good morning, Mick. Ready to get our guest and take his ass to the sunshine state?"

"Yeah, boss, I am ready to move scum like him out of the country. Carol is a little pissed off. She thought she was coming on this project in lieu of the fact you took two rookies on a dangerous job in Jersey."

At 0700 hours, the Cherry Ridge Airport, Wayne County, Pennsylvania. "Mick, there is hardly any wind moving the sock around. Can you see which direction, if any, it is blowing?"

"Yeah, it's moving about ten degrees off the north/south axis."

"Good, Mick. Take her out a mile or so in the downwind leg, turn left, and we slip on to the base leg in one more minute, another left, and you got her on final. She's all yours from here. Line up your glide slope with those red panels and put the wheels on the ground.

"Great landing, Mickey. Park over by that old C-45. That's our old Civil Air Patrol plane," John says with a lot of pride, "and she is still air worthy."

"Hi, Joe, we are here at Cherry Ridge. Where are you? I am north and east of Harrisburg about twenty minutes from the coordinates you gave us."

"Who's 'us'?"

"Mr. Diskin is with me this morning. John, he wanted to say hello in person. He has a present for you."

"A present for me? I hope it's not what I think it might be?"

"Johnny, me lad, this is Tom. No, set your mind at ease—Laura is not with us. She pestered me last night to let her join up with you lads at the Richmond, Virginia, airport. I am sorry, but I gave her your flight plan to get her off me back."

"Oh shit, sir, I wish that didn't happen."

"No sweat, Tom. I can change the flight plan in Harrisburg. That will piss her off, but she is too damn quick on the trigger, sometimes I think she thinks she is Wonder Woman. She loves that BAR and is a good shot with it. You know she shoots every day at the CIA shooting range in the basement?"

"Johnny, she is bugging me to buy her a Barrett .50 cal sniper rifle."

"Joey, I see you. You're about at our seven on the north/south axis."

"Yeah, John, I got the runway in sight. What are the ground winds? I can't see the sock."

"No wind, Joey. The sock is as limp as you know what."

"Okay, John. See you on the ground."

"Good morning, Tom, and good to meet you also, Joey. Tommy said you can fly anything with wings. The Twin Beech is an easy plane to fly. It has a ton of navaids plus a new radar altimeter digital readout glide slope, which is great for getting in small landing fields."

"Anything we should know about the Beaver that is unusual? And how does she do on fuel?"

"She is so-so on the fuel consumption, and is a bit sluggish above angels 12. But she will get you into any small field that is fairly level."

"That's wonderful, guys. Now let me and Mickey get our Arab friend in the aft portion and secured. Why don't you and Tom get in the Twin Beech and familiarize yourselves with the controls, while Mickey and I do our job. I would prefer you don't see what is taking place. That way you have plausible deniability if something should go wrong. If you don't see anything, the feds can't use a polygraph to squeeze information from your memory that you don't possess."

Tom takes a wrapped package from his briefcase and hands it to John. "Happy birthday, Merry Christmas, Happy Hanukkah, and so forth, Johnny."

As John opens the package, a polished box holding a Colt M1911A1 pistol was in his hands. "My god, Tommy, this is a magnificent gift. It is exactly like the one issued to me at Fort Bragg years ago. Thank you very, very much. I will treasure this forever."

"Ah, Johnny, you're welcome. I still hope that someday you will make an honest woman of Laura. Since her angel of a mother passed on, I always hoped I could play with some grandchildren. But that dream is pushed way back on the burner. The power of her job is foremost in all of her being. Washington DC can corrupt the best this country has to offer. The search and rise to power has even my darling daughter hearing that siren song. Now it's time for us to leave, and you also have to get in the air and on your way to Florida."

0745 hours, Harrisburg International Airport, Harrisburg, Pennsylvania
Private Aircraft Operations

Mickey and John wait their turn at the operations desk. "We are the DHC-2 Beaver Charlie Bravo Delta. We are a little late in getting here, and we would like to change our original flight plan. We started in Chicago and are heading for Florida. Also we would like to top off the tanks while we are parked at the fuel depot. I would also like to get some coffee to go."

"Mickey, how do you like this old-time steering yoke? I am going to recommend Tommy change the whole steering system to a hydraulic one. It will change the dynamics of the flight characteristics and make a better airplane out of this bird. And at higher altitudes, it will not be so sluggish."

"You know, boss, I like this old bird. Mr. Diskin outfitted the instrument panel with these new computer aided navigation systems. It sure makes navigation a lot easier here on the East Coast with all the traffic around the larger cities. It's time to call Atlanta Approach Control for landing instructions."

Leaving Atlanta and heading on a south-southeast bearing, John was checking on their passenger. "Uh-oh, Mick, I think our Arab friend is about an hour from checking into paradise. He has almost no pulse, and the color of his ugly face is like putty. About how long till we put wheels on the grass?"

"I can put us on a better course if I can get by the Tampa radar. Then we just head directly for the strip north of Lake Okeechobee."

"Okay, call Tampa and ask for permission to pass over or around their airspace, and that will put us in the clear till we land at the carnival grounds, Winter Quarters."

"I make it about thirty minutes to touchdown."

"Good, Mick. We will do everything as was rehearsed. Check your weapon. Lock and load with the safety off just in case the local boys decide to get frisky."

East of the carnival grounds airstrip at two thousand feet and slowly descending on final approach, the de Havilland Beaver was rock solid in a glide slope. Mickey held the airplane on a very level attitude, which enabled them both to see in a 360-degree pattern. They flew right over the main building and touched down near the start of the runway. The plane continued on to the far west end of the runway, and Mickey stood on the right brake and brought the Beaver around ready for takeoff. John jumped out the side door and pulled the dead body of Mohammed Bin Aziz out of the plane. He unceremoniously dumped the assassin in the ditch alongside the runway. Jumping back in the plane, he asked Mick, "Do you see anybody that wants to give us a problem?"

"No, boss. The way back east up the runway is all clear so far." Pushing the throttle forward, the Beaver lurches ahead and starts its takeoff roll.

"We're rotating," says John. "A little higher, and we clear the main building."

Ping whiz, a .30-caliber bullet ricochets off the right strut. Another comes up through the floor in back of the pilot's seat. "Shit, Mick, there is a shooter on the roof of the building, and I see red and blue flashing lights about two miles off to the southeast. That's not all the crap we have to contend with. A round must have hit a hydraulic line in the floor. We only have 25 percent rudder. We're going to have to depend on the flaps, ailerons, throttle, and skidding and slipping to turn this plane. Mickey, I have an idea. If you or I can land this bird, which I know we can, will you be able to fix the line without too much of a problem?"

"Sure, boss, I can fix anything, provided I have some tools. But where are we going to set down without the cops on our butt?"

"I got a friend who knows a friend, and we will be able to land in their own backyard."

John pulls out his satphone and gets Langley. "Rosey, hi, this is John Braz."

"Hi, Mr. Braz, she isn't here right now."

"Oh, Rosey, did she tell you to say that?"

"No, sir, she really is not here."

"Oh crap, Rosey, we have us a little thing going on, and we need her influence. Rosey, has Ms. Diskin given you any juice?"

"Juice? I don't understand, Mr. John."

"Rosey, 'juice' in military parlance means 'power.' Has she given you power to order people and things to do as she needs?"

"Yes, Mr. John, she makes me do that sort of stuff all the time. She even has me tell people in the White House what to do."

"Good girl, sweetie. Here's what we need you to do. Call MacDill Air Force Base Ground Operations and let them know we have an emergency and have to land there. It's a matter of national security. We are flying a DHC-2 Beaver, call letters BDC9. We are in their airspace right now. Call me right back after you talk to the operations officer of the day."

"John, he says to call him with your emergency, and approach control will assign you a landing slot."

"Thanks, Rosey. We owe you a big favor. Think up something, a dinner or a show or whatever, and next week, I will pay you back. Ms. Diskin doesn't have to know what happened today, does she?"

"Mr. John, you know Ms. Diskin knows every single thing that happens in this office. I would not try to cover up or lie about anything you do—she would have me for breakfast."

"Yeah, Rosey, you're right. Thanks again."

"MacDill Air Force Base, this is CIA Beaver BDC Niner requesting landing privileges at your facility. We are declaring an emergency. We have, to the best of our knowledge, a broken hydraulic line. It has rendered our rudder to only 25 percent steering ability.

We can make it to your main north/south 90 Runway without too many emergency maneuvers."

"CIA Beaver, we have you on radar. You are next to land. We have you lined up on final on above-mentioned north/south 90 Runway. Turn on your glide slope. Your decent is too fast. Throttle back to 10 percent above minimum stall speed. A follow-me truck will direct you to the CIA hangar complex."

"Thank you, MacDill. Your instructions are clear. We are on final 90 N/S Runway. Glide slope is activated. Follow-me truck will direct us."

"CIA Beaver, pay strict attention to follow-me vehicle. Armored vehicles will also escort you to CIA complex. Do not, I repeat, do not get out of your aircraft till the officer of the day releases you to the custody of your superior."

"MacDill, this is CIA Beaver. We have wheels on the ground. I acknowledge your last transmission and will stay in stay in our aircraft until released by MacDill officer of the day.

Mickey turns off the radios in the Beaver. "Now they can't hear us, boss."

"Mick, we are lucky to be so close to Tampa and this base. Now I got to think up a story why the bullet holes are in this bird. Look out your side window. See those quad fifties on the back of those pickup trucks? These guys mean business. All them boys are in battle dress uniforms. Here comes the OD in this Ford Crown Vic. The driver is pointing toward that hangar second on your left. Pull over there and shut her down."

The air force officer, a lieutenant colonel, with his driver holding an M-16, comes over to the Beaver. Opening the right side door, John welcomes the colonel. John stays in the plane until asked to stand on the ground, and Mickey does also. The OD comes up to John. John automatically stands at attention and throws the best paratrooper salute, even though he is not in uniform and not required as he is fully retired from the army. This impresses the heck out of the colonel. He returns the salute and asks, "Are you army captain John M. Braz?"

"Yes, sir, I am John Braz, civilian now."

"Were you the one called Mad Dog?"

"Again, yes, sir. But that was years ago in Vietnam."

"Well, John, I am very glad to meet you and say heartfelt thanks from myself and my family. My uncle, my father's brother, was the air force officer you rescued from the Vietcong."

"That's quite a coincidence, sir. I was just doing my job as any ranger would. And I am glad it turned out good for your uncle."

"Will you both accompany me to the officers' club for some lunch? I feel like I owe you a great debt. My uncle was my inspiration to pursue a military career. The air force won't let him fly fighters anymore, so he retired and is flying for American Airlines."

"Sir, we have to get the Beaver fixed and vamoose outta here. We are on a tight schedule."

"Don't worry about the plane. My mechanics will fix those hydraulic lines, and you will be on your way in an hour or so."

"Sir, I have to get to the Beaver and secure some things in the locker. It's for eyes only of the deputy director CIA in Langley, Virginia, national security and a need-to-know type equipment. I am sure your mechanics don't have high enough security clearances to eyeball these things. So may I go and do this, and I will be right with you? Lunch sounds wonderful, since Mickey and I haven't eaten since 0450 hours this morning."

After lunch, John signed the work orders and the requisition for fuel.

John took over the left seat in the Beaver and ran the engines up; all systems were functioning five by five, including the hydraulics. Mick called the tower, and permission to taxi was granted. At the threshold of N/S Runway 90, the Beaver sped down the concrete strip and was airborne. Not too much was said on the way back to Pennsylvania. Then John's satphone rang. "Well, Mick, I was wondering how long it would take for her to catch up with us"

"John Braz here."

"And where is here, Mr. Going-behind-my-back-and-having-my-secretary-get-your-butt-out-of-a-crack?"

"Hi, sweetheart, we had to make a private delivery to a friend of the Saudi's."

"I know what you did,"—Laura is really mad—"goddammit, John. This fiasco is not two hours old, and the Royal House of Saud is on Casey's ass already."

"They will be thanking him before the day is over. The exiled Saudi was banished from their family, the country, and is, or was, wanted by Interpol.

"Is that the truth?"

"Yes, my love, it is. Talk to the State Department. Ask for Janine Bailey. She has the file on this Arab. She will tell you Mohammed Bin Aziz is a rapist, murderer, and he pulled a Ponzi scheme in Yemen until they found him out. He left the Middle East in a hurry. Now he works, or did work, for, of all people, my friend and yours, Charro Lequesta. I interrogated the bastard, but he was shot up so bad I could only get a few words from him. His lookout guy told me everything about this Aziz. I let the kid go so I can go back and question him again if need be. I didn't shoot the rounds that did the guy in. It was Mary Ann. She is getting to be almost as good a markswoman as you."

"No freaking way, sugar bear. She will have to come a long way before she can stand on the same range as me."

Now Laura is getting steamed again. "What the fuck are you doing taking rookies on a shoot? You must have something going on with those broads. If I find out you have been doing the naughty tango with any of your employees, I will be in Pennsylvania in a heartbeat. Don't forget, Helen is my very good friend and confidant."

"Darling, why do you have to jump to conclusions when you have no facts to base your intuition on? I have been as celibate as Monsignor Flynn and Mother Superior Ignatius."

"Yeah, Johnny Boy, you were always the shy one. She is wondering if that was only an act until you discovered that certain parts were not hung on you only for decoration or bodily functions."

"Darling, let's leave this conversation for another time please? We are nearing Harrisburg and have to get this bird on the ground. Fuel is starting to get low."

"Don't you dare dent my daddy's airplane."

Harrisburg International Airport, Harrisburg, Pennsylvania, 1600 hours

"Boss, when we finalize out this secondary flight plan, are we going back to Scranton?"

"Yeah, Mick, we are. Mr. Diskin will want his airplane back tomorrow. We have to fix all the bullet holes and repair the strut that was winged and hope we can match the paint color. We are going to tell him the whole story as it happened—truthfully 'cause Laura told him her version of what she thinks happened. I need to stay on that man's good list. Ms. Laura does not make it easy to be in good stead with her daddy."

On the way to Scranton, a late summer thunderstorm tossed the little DH Beaver around, crossing the north end of the Blue Ridge Mountains and entering the west portion of the Pocono resort area. The Beaver was made for bush country, and it handled beautifully in the wind and rain.

"Mickey, this is a dream to fly in crappy weather. You take over the controls and get us in to Wilkes-Barre Scranton Airport at Avoca, Pennsylvania."

"Okay, boss. I like this plane better than the Apache for flying over these mountains in this storm."

John gets on his satphone. "Helen, it's me. Are the two mechanics still at our hangar at Avoca? I need them to work on Mr. Diskin's plane. We are about twenty minutes out of Avoca. They need to work on the aircraft first thing tomorrow."

"John, Mary Ann would like to talk to you."

"Okay, put her on."

"Hi, John, are you guys all right? It's all over the TV about the shooting at your plane. Ms. Laura called here three times. She is really pissed. She wanted to know why you turned your satphone off. That bitch is more worried about her daddy's plane than about you."

"Thank you, Mary Ann. Ms. Laura is just being herself. In her subconscious, she is concerned about me and all of us. She has a hard time admitting she cares for people more than she knows. Don't be too hard on her. She has pulled my chestnuts out of the fire more than I could ever repay her. As a client and a go between us and the government, her power is invaluable."

"Thanks for hearing me vent—oh, and do you need a ride from Avoca to here?"

"Yes, we do, sweetie, and also did anyone get Mickey's car back from Cherry Ridge?"

CHAPTER TWENTY-FOUR

1000 hours, Dulles International Airport
Loudoun County, Virginia, 23 September 1985

A tall clean-looking man with a buzz cut and holding a sign "Captain Braz" was standing in the US Air concourse, scanning the passengers coming off of flight 1245 from Pittsburgh. Another man was in a short coat wearing a Jackie Stewart racing hat and sporting a mustache, pretending to be reading *Car and Driver* magazine and leaning against the wall by the concession stand, only two feet away from the man with the sign. "If you're looking for Captain Braz, he won't be exiting from that Jetway. What are, or were, you—marines, army, air force, SEALs? No, you couldn't be a SEAL. A SEAL would not stand for this demeaning bullshit. Keep holding the sign and get a look of frustration on your face. Don't look at him directly, but at your ten o'clock, the swarthy guy with the rags on his noggin. Over to our right in the red chairs next to the window is the other hit man. Both are Islamist professional assassins—they want me."

"How do I know it's you, Captain Braz?"

Thinking to himself, *Now I know this guy is a marine.* "Sonny, you better hope the towel head looking straight at you can't read lips. Or you and I are going to be ducking bullets in a minute."

"I still don't know who you are."

"Casually look at my left hand right at the sleeve. Anybody you know carries one of these?"

The marine courier hides his mouth with his hand and whispers, "Holy crap, it is you, Mad Dog."

"Please don't call me Mad Dog. I left that name back in Vietnam. They recognized me. We only have a short time to get out of here alive. Are you carrying?"

"Yes, sir. Ms. Laura made sure of that."

John turns around and goes in the concession stand and jumps the counter, yelling at the young lady cashier, "Call security. Two guys out there have guns." The marine jumps the counter, and he and John run into the service corridor. The towel head sitting in the red chair pushes people left and right, runs up to the counter, and starts shooting through the doorway. The marine drops to one knee, aims, and puts two bullets in the forehead of the second assassin. John gets on the security wall phone, ID's himself, and describes the first guy and which way he was headed. The first guy knows the building layout, as he once worked in the maintenance crews. When he realized he was made, he used an old key card to get in the service corridor. He spotted the marine and John. Carrying a Tokarev TT-33 7.62 mm with an eight-round magazine, the towel head blasted off two shots, narrowly missing John and hitting a soda cooler. John and the marine both fired at the same time. The shots were snap shots, and both missed. There was an adjoining corridor 90 percent to the service corridor. John moved around the corner, and the marine got behind the soda cooler. The assassin moved up to another 90 percent adjoining hallway. As he peeked around the corner, John, with perfect timing and a good aim, hit the guy dead center in his left eye, blowing the back of his head into a pink spray from the ears back.

By this time, the building was crawling with security, FBI, Loudoun County cops, and anyone else with a badge. The marine and John were taken to the security office. They were questioned and released after a visit from the director of the CIA, Mr. Casey.

On the way to Langley, "Director Casey, I believe there is a mole in your organization, or your office is bugged. Are there any new people whom one might be suspect?"

"John, maybe there is a mole, but the office is not bugged. It is swept at least four times in a twenty-four-hour period. Also Laura's office is swept five times a day—she is paranoid about security."

"This morning when we left Pennsylvania, I sent one of my people on the US Air flight We played switch-the-driver's-license at the counter. Only because we are both armed. I flew my Apache here, and my guy is flying it back."

"How did you know there would be an ambush?"

"My intuition was tingling like crazy. I also called Ms. Diskin, and she was quite upset. Once, she had warned me about Italian food and went nutso when I told her the food service truck was rented and had a picture of calzone and lasagna and meatballs on it. The truck was the same one servicing the US Air flight 1245 that I was ticketed to be on. Only ten passengers got on in Scranton. I stood back in the lobby and waited till my guy parked the car. Then we made the switcheroo, and I flew here myself. My guy will fly the Apache back to Pennsylvania. Please excuse me for a minute." On his satphone, John calls his office, "Helen, I was right on the money. They were waiting to ambush me at Dulles."

"This call is encrypted, so no one else can understand us, right? Okay then, we might have a mole in our organization or my office is bugged."

"See what you can do, and I will check in later today."

Riding up in the elevator to the executive offices in CIA headquarters, John puts his index finger to his lips, turns away from the surveillance camera, and whispers in Casey's ear, "This car may be compromised. We better have it checked on a more regular basis." Casey nods in agreement.

Exiting the elevator, Laura spies John and Casey. She comes over and lays a nice ladylike kiss on John's cheek.

"It's about time you got back here to Virginia." Addressing Casey, Laura asks, "Will John and you be in strategy meetings all day and night? I would like to have him for a few hours this evening for dinner?"

"No problem, Ms. Diskin. The bulk of strategic planning and selecting will start in two days. Captain Braz has the rest of today and tomorrow for his own research and coordinating. Oh, and by the way, your two Green Beret friends are in town. I suggest you don't get in touch till tomorrow. I believe a lot of your time will be spent in our research center on the fifth floor. You also have to return a call to the Royal House of Saud. Prince Abdulla Bin Aziz wants to congratulate you on the success of that last escapade that helped the

Saudis save face around the Arab world. He would like you to visit him in Riyadh and to bring your lovely fiancée.

"That ain't going to happen anytime soon. The last time I spent in a tent in the desert, I was being shot at with AK-47s and RPGs. The wall of a tent does not deflect bullets very good."

That evening at a seafood house in Calvert County, after feasting on fresh cod flown in from Nova Scotia, clams, local oysters, and a bottle of local pinot noir, the sated couple relaxed and let the business end of their work fade away. "You know, Johnny, I am taking you to my house on the bay."

"That's fine, sweetie. I had not thought where I was going to sleep tonight. I hoped I knew where I was going to find romance."

On the western side of the Chesapeake Bay, halfway between Solomons Island and the town of Prince Frederick was a little no-named village consisting of a dozen or so homes. It was a Cape Cod–style sided clapboard with an enormous brick fireplace house, very well crafted by a family of carpenters and boat builders, and overlooking the bay about a hundred feet above the high water mark. The view was spectacular in a dramatic sense. One has to traverse a graveled long private winding road to reach the secluded area. It's a ten-mile trek back to the only link to connect the south county to the northern portion of Calvert County, and that road is Route 4/2. No one can reach the house by boat. The cliff the house resides on is so steep that only Alpinists could climb it.

This suited Laura very well. The house was well protected with every new electronic surveillance and detecting device the military has to offer. In the smaller but very similar in architecture carriage house, two round-the-clock guards and their dogs resided. The grounds were patrolled every two hours at staggered intervals.

The temperature in Laura's swimming pool was about eighty-five degrees. The air temperature was ninety degrees, and about to get hotter. John was slowly treading water, sitting on a pair of plastic noodles. He watched as she approached the pool, wearing the most daring French bikini ever made.

"I hope you only wear that suit at home and not to pool parties. If you will notice, the water around me is starting to boil."

"No, darling. This suit I bought just for you. I hope you like it."

Then she dove in the deep end and swam underwater to John. He bent down and kissed her. She grabbed his neck and pulled him under. There they proceeded to kiss and roll around in the water till both needed to come up for air. An hour later after showering together, they ended up in Laura's huge king-size bed. They both were a little bit starved for a close encounter of the intimate sort. The same passion they shared the first time was renewed and lasted past midnight. It seemed Laura could not get enough of John, and he of her. As she started to fall off to sleep, she whispered, "We have tomorrow and the next night to do this all over again and again."

Laura's bay home
0530 hours, 24 September 1985

John was wondering, as he kept the steady jogging pace, *Why is it so warm for September?* Then it came to him—*I am in Southern Maryland, not Pennsylvania.* The sweat pouring from his forehead was salty and kept him from seeing clearly, saying to himself, *There is a lot of fishing boats on the water this morning.* Then he stopped and wiped the water from his face. *Why is that boat anchored about two hundred yards offshore when all the other boats are trolling for stripers? There is no bottom fishing this early.* Then he saw the glint of sun reflecting off the glass. The glint was being refracted from the side of a piece of stainless steel commercial fish box. John sprinted for the house. "Laura, get up. We may have a situation here. Where is your telescope?"

"What's going on? The big scope is in the locker on the porch. What's out there that has your antenna vibrating?"

"Look there, about one o'clock, the blue-and-white commercial crab boat? Here, take a peek through the scope. See the guy standing next to the wheelhouse by the blonde in the red pants? He has a telescope and was aiming it right up here."

"Johnny, yes, he is looking right at the porch. But he can't see us. The screens make everything look black, and we are still in shadow on this screened porch." Laura calls the carriage house, "Tim, we may have a serious situation here."

"Yes, Ms. Diskin, we have been keeping watch on that fishing boat. It's been there since before daylight. I sent the bow registration numbers to the marine police. The boat is registered to a fish house in North Carolina. But the owners are C. L. Brothers Amusements LLC in Florida. Shall we call the Coast Guard or the Department of Natural Resources Police?"

"No, Tim. We need to be discreet in the way we handle this. Keep a good lookout on this craft. We will have a meeting at the house at 1000 hours. In the meantime, try to round up two fast boats. We can berth them at the Town Center Marina in Deale, Maryland. The owners are good friends of Captain Braz."

"I have to get ready for work. You can handle this. You will have to do it at night. You might catch Lequesta if he's personally out there."

"No, sweetie, I don't think he knows these waters well enough to risk getting caught. I will take you to work. The bad guys might have an ambush waiting for you. And don't try to sneak out by yourself. I have all the keys to all the vehicles."

Fort McNair, Southwest, Washington DC
0800 hours, office of the transient NCO personnel

Captain Braz enters the office. Captain Braz identifies himself. "Sergeant, is the OD available?"

"Yes, he is, sir. I will call him right now, sir."

"First Lieutenant Evens, sir. How may I help you?"

'Lieutenant, you have in your custody two Green Beret sergeants, one is named Hansl Von Stead and the other snake eater is Dean Young."

"Yes, sir, we do. I expect you have authorization to collect these men now. Their orders state them to be released to you tomorrow."

"No, Lieutenant, I don't have orders for today, but I need them now."

"Then I am sorry, sir, but I can't release them without proper authorization."

"I understand your position, Lieutenant. Please may I use your phone?"

"Of course, sir, be my guest."

"The Pentagon please, Sergeant."

"Yes, sir, what number, sir?"

"Gen. Donald Ward's office."

"Sir, he is the chairman of the Joint Chiefs of Staff?"

"I know who he is, Sergeant. Just get me his office please?"

"Chairman's Office, may I say who is calling?"

"Colonel, this is ex-US Army captain John Braz. May I please speak with the general?"

"Good morning. General Ward here."

"Hi, General, John Braz here."

"Johnny, hello there. What can I do for you? And, boy, am I sorry I let your separation papers go through. Casey over at CIA, General Desmond, Gen. Shorty Wells, and a host of other commanders wanted your sorry butt to stay in my army. They all cried the blues when you walked out of Bragg that day. I keep hearing good things about you and your company. So, Johnny, what kind of scrape did you get into that you need my help?"

"Sir, I have two snake eaters assigned to me and Casey at CIA for TDY for about six weeks. The duty officer at Fort McNair won't release them till tomorrow. Their orders are for tomorrow, but I need them today. Can you intervene on my behalf?"

"Johnny, anything for you. Are you at McNair now?"

"Yes, sir. I am standing right next to 1st Lt. Edward Evans, the duty and OD. I will put him on, sir."

"Lieutenant Evans here. Good morning, General."

"Evans, you accommodate Mr. Braz in every way possible. Release the two men to him. And if he needs anything else, you provide it. Do we understand each other, Lieutenant?"

"Yes, sir, loud and clear. I understand your instructions and orders and will obey the general."

"Thank you, Lieutenant. Put John back on."

"Thank you, sir. The lieutenant is getting my guys now."

"John, when this operation is over, and you can tell me the story, I want you to come up to the house for dinner and drinks, and bring your Ms. Diskin along with you. So long, Johnny, and good luck."

Fort McNair, Southwest, Washington DC
0900 hours, office of the transient NCO personnel

Senior Master Sergeant Hansel Von Stead and Sergeant Major Dean Young, both Special Forces and Army Delta Operatives, enter the room, come to attention, and salute not the uniformed lieutenant but John Braz civilian. This is highly unusual, but the comradeship among these three former rangers is like a woven mass of genes as if they all had the same mother. Nothing was said as the friends hugged each other like no brothers ever did. They all relived in that moment, the bad times, the battles, the dangerous moments, and the good times.

After an awkward and emotional silence, they all tried to speak at once. Hansl (Hun), wiping a small tear from his face, said, "I was wondering how long it was gonna take before you commandeered us to bail your ass out of a crack."

Yorkie (Dean) retorted with "Yeah, Captain Braz, you know you can't get a decent operation completed if me and Hun ain't got your flanks. I hope this is going to be a worthwhile gig and we get to shoot some bad guys."

"That goes twice for me," says Hun. "My trigger finger is starting to lose its callus. Is it all right if I call you by your Vietnam name, or will you kick my ass, Mad Dog?"

"Hun, you, of all people, know that moniker was left in the jungle. So don't be a wiseass and bring up old wounds. Unless you're ready for me to open a can of whoopass on you? All screwing around is over. Get your duffel and your special kits. We're going to the farm."

"You hear that, Yorkie? We're going to the farm. This must really be a big boy's operation."

"Button it up, Hun. The captain is as serious as I have ever seen him."

1000 hours, Route 50, Northern Virginia
On the way to the farm

"Captain, can you tell us what we're getting into?"

"No, guys. Just talk small talk—this car may be bugged. I screened it for bugs and searched it for transponders before I left Langley earlier. We think somebody very clever has gotten into an office or a computer or a phone line at CIA headquarters or in my office in Pennsylvania. We should have the leak found by today."

"Captain, if you find out it's a mole, can Yorkie and me deal with him? We can wring any and all intel out of him or her before it's just a bag of bones."

"No, Hun, you guys are going to be pretty busy building things and training people."

"Captain, tell us, how are you and Laura doing? I don't see a gold ring, so I guess you didn't make an honest woman of her? Sir, don't take this the wrong way, but every time I was near her, I could not even think straight. She the most beautiful woman I ever had the pleasure to speak with. The general at Delta is so happy with her. She, through her power and influence, got Delta a substantial raise in its budget."

CHAPTER TWENTY-FIVE

Meanwhile on the Chesapeake Bay near Buoy 6
About three hundred yards east of Willow Beach Colony

Ramon Sanchez and Sergio Guadera, two old out-of-work ex-Cuban soldiers leftover from Castro's days in the Sierra Madre Mountains in Cuba, were sitting in the cabin of the wooden bay-built fishing and crabbing boat, waiting for sundown to make their way north to the point off the cliffs where Laura's summer home was. Little did they know that danger lurks in these waters this night.

Three weeks ago, when landscapers were working on the lawn and garden facing the bay, Jamie Guadera, the son of Sergio, while working on the rearmost part of the lawn near the very thick brush, pounded a one-twelfth-inch steel rod in the ground hidden by the brush. He rolled a spool of heavy-duty fishing line down the cliff, tied a couple of two-pound fishing sinkers to the other end with a loop, and then let that part of the line work its way down to the waterline. That night under darkness (there was no moon), Jamie and Sergio Senior tied a mountaineer's scaling rope to the end of the fishing string and pulled up the rope so it wound around the steel rod and came back down to the waterline. Another Cuban climbed the rope and installed hidden in the brush a powerful parabolic listening device pointed toward the house. From a boat a couple of hundred yards away, anyone with the compatible instruments could listen to anything being said in the yard or house.

Town Point Marina, Deale, Maryland
2200 hours

Mickey, Carol, Mary Ann, and Ann Marie are divided in two pairs, Mickey and Mary Ann, and Carol and Ann Marie; one boat, a Boston Whaler with twin 75 hp Mercury motors, and one boat a Glastron Streak with a 300 hp inboard/outboard motor. Everyone is dressed in black jeans, black long-sleeved shirts, black gloves, and ski masks; overhead coming up the bay from the confluence of the Potomac River and the Chesapeake Bay, flying as low as he dares in a CIA black Little Bird helicopter John calls the number-one fast boat. "Mickey, give me a shot on your strobe light so I know where you are. You too, Carol. There is a lot of fishing boats out this evening. Be sure to stay out of the big cargo boat channel. If they can't see you, they will run right over you."

Coming out of the Rockhold Creek Channel into the Bay Proper, "Mary Ann, do you want to take over the helm while I check the guns and other gear one more time? Keep your speed down. We don't need a visit from marine police. Reading the compass and the radar scope like I showed you earlier will get us to the location in about forty-five minutes."

"Mickey, this is fun. I never was on a boat this big. I was glad when John asked Annie and me to come to Maryland."

"Mary Ann, turn right in this inlet. We are picking up two friends of Captain Braz. This cove is Herrington Harbor South. We get one guy, and Carol gets the other. Their names are Hun and Yorkie."

"Boat 1 to Boat 2, hey, Annie, I am piloting the boat. Pull alongside so the new guy can get aboard."

"So am I. Carol is a good teacher. Her father had a boat on the Delaware River when she was a kid, and he taught her about boats. She is checking the guns and the rest of the gear again."

"Boat 2, this is Cloud Cover. Keep up with number 1 boat. We don't want you getting lost. It's a big body of water. I will let you know when you're getting close to the fishing boat. Remember, all we want to do is apprehend these guys and take whatever equipment and guns they have. Please don't shoot to kill. I need every shred of intel we could wring out of this group. Once we have them incapacitated, we will let the Coast Guard know the boat is unmanned and drifting. Make sure all the syringes are loaded up with the go-to-sleep juice so you don't have too much trouble. I assume all your watches are synchronized? It is now ten thirty-five and counting. Twenty minutes till boarding."

Mickey and Carol filled in Hun and Yorkie on the priorities of the mission. Both Special Forces troopers gave a little lecture on the safety aspects on handling of the weapons. Yorkie wanted to disarm the women. After seeing the fire in Annie's eyes, he quit that idea.

"Boats 1 and 2, five, I repeat, five minutes till engagement, lock and load. Cleat tying lines at the ready. Large 500 watt searchlights ready. Good luck down there."

The tide was incoming at about four knots. The wooden boat was anchored with a bow anchor on the prow facing south, also with a sea anchor facing north, putting the length of the craft on a north/south axis, the starboard gunwale facing the land. The tide stretched the bowline taut.

Sergio and Jamie Guadera were sitting on the deck with their backs up against the port gunwale, holding the listening device, pointing up at the house. The top of their heads were below the gunwale, so they could not see the fast boat creep up alongside, nor could they hear it. The two other Cubans were in the wheelhouse sitting on the deck. Holding a laptop computer connected to the sophisticated listening device, all they could hear from Laura's house was the television and the radio. The all-world band radio was tuned to a Russian channel. Both devices had the sound turned up very high. Then one of the guards would turn the sound low. This made all four Cubans intently focused on their eavesdropping and very lax in what was happening around them. All four were wearing ear-hearing devices.

Fast boat 2 came upon the fishing boat from the south. Ann Marie slowly and quietly tied a small line to a cleat on the Cuban boat. Mary Ann did the same on the other gunwale. Hun and Yorkie each tossed a flashbang grenade in the wheelhouse and closed their eyes to prevent temporary blindness from the tremendously bright light. Mickey, Carol, and the girls jumped over the sides with their MP3s pointed at the Cubans. Hun and Yorkie, each with a syringe in hand, stuck the Cubans one by one with the go-to-sleep juice. Very quickly, Annie and Carol tossed two Cubans over the gunwales into boat 1. Mickey and Mary Ann did the same with the other two. Everybody started grabbing anything that looked like military or electronic hardware, put all the contraband in two duffel bags, and tossed them in the fast boats. The radios were taken from the mounts and put in the bags also. All the locker doors were knocked off the hinges, and lockers looted. The Cuban boat was started up, and the winch holding the bow anchor was pulled in. The sea anchor was pulled aboard. One running light was turned on. Both fast boats were quickly unfastened from the cleats, started up, and moved on upriver.

At seven hundred feet altitude (they dared not go higher; they are right in the pattern for BWI Airport) in the cloud cover halo, John came on the air, "Fast boat 1, report."

Yorkie reported, "Mission accomplished, sir. All troops in good shape, no casualties. Picked up four passengers, will deliver them to evacuation point."

At the evac point (the Town Point Marina), all the equipment and stolen contraband were loaded in the black Chevy Tahoe. The fast boats were returned to their owners. The two teams from Scranton drove to a motel near Baltimore-Washington Airport. They had an early flight back to Scranton by way of Pittsburgh.

Hun and Yorkie drove the Tahoe to Langley. At the CIA headquarters, the Cubans were taken to the secure area to be interrogated. The senior master sergeant Von Stead wanted to interrogate the Cubans, torture them, and kill them. He hates the Cuban Commies. He was at the fouled-up Bay of Pigs Invasion and is still carrying shrapnel from several wounds. Instead, John, Yorkie, and Hun questioned the four surly prisoners. Getting nothing from them, they were turned over to the professional physiological types, who, in a matter of hours, had them telling everything about themselves—the Cuban army, who hired them, how they got into the States, and where the equipment came from. These guys were shit scared they would be sent back to Cuba. They would rather spend time in an American prison. Castro would torture them and kill them if they were sent back.

It came out during the interrogation that Charro Lequesta, through one of his dope dealing Cuban army commanders, hired the ill-fated four to gather as much information on Laura as possible. It was also found out the mole in the CIA was a so-called ex-patriot from San Salvador. He had a secret computer hidden in a janitor's closet in the Progressive Insurance building in Crystal City. When it was discovered, the mole tried to get away on his motorcycle. One of Casey's inner circle of go-to guys ran the cyclist off the road somewhere in the Shenandoah Valley. The drop from the roadway to the stream below was well over a hundred feet. He died instantly of a broken neck.

CHAPTER TWENTY-SIX

The CIA farm, somewhere in Southwest Virginia

John Braz and Sergeants Hansel Von Stead and Dean Young reported to the base operations commander, known only as the commander for obvious reasons.

The sergeants were assigned to a billet with an office, computer facilities, encrypted phone service, a small dayroom, and a very large library with a map room. There they would spend a week to ten days interviewing prospective operatives for the upcoming raid in Nicaragua. They had personal records, files, pictures, letters of recommendation, and private one-on-one talks with each of the former and present Green Berets, Navy SEALs, Recon Marines, Air Force Service Troops, and British SAS personnel.

All the applicants would go through an extremely tough physical training course over a period of a week. Then when the teams were selected, the simulated village where the people to be captured was shown to the selectees. "Until John comes back with the lay of the land, the main buildings where the Commies are constructing a dirty bomb, and who we are dealing with, we can only rely on past experiences and similar operations to put together workable plans. John will be the overall commander and expediter of the op."

Meanwhile, leaving the airspace of Costa Rica at thirty-three thousand feet, 0400 hours

85 deg.10min.3Sec.E Longitude 11deg.-15min.-6sec. Latitude

In a converted Lockheed Martin C-130 Hercules painted in the colors of the Costa Rican Air Force, a lone parachutist wearing a special skydiving rig exits the aircraft and is flying across the sky on a north-northeast direction attempting to land fourteen minutes later in the Nicaraguan state of Chontales near the mountain town of Acoyapa. Wearing night-vision goggles and armed with only his .45 automatic, the Fairbairn-Sykes, his homemade crossbow, and a lot of confidence, John hopes to land to the east of the town, on the west side of a mountain canyon. There he can scout the area and the village and not attract any undue attention.

Luck is with the former ranger this morning. He lands in a dry wadi with only thick brush and small trees. Being able to see in the darkness, he quickly buries the canopy of his chute. He retains the suspension lines and harness. It might be the only way for his evacuation in three days. He climbs higher on the canyon wall, settles in a scree of large broken boulders, checks all his equipment, takes a drink of water, and, fairly confident he is well hidden, dozes off till the warm sun wakes him. Hearing the dull brass sound of cowbells tells him a farmer is moving his cows to a pasture nearby.

Taking the covers off the binoculars, switching from infrared to daylight. The village of Acoyapa is starting the same morning routine that has been going on for centuries, except for the presence of rebel Communist sympathizers. The area to the southeast has six buildings, mostly made of concrete block with metal roofing. Two of the buildings are made of adobe; these are long and narrow, probably the living quarters for the rebels. There are several Toyota pickup trucks, one with a heavy machine gun mount, a four-door Mercedes sedan, a Volkswagen bus, and an old Harley-Davidson motorcycle.

The largest building is a Spanish-style church. The bell is ringing, calling the devout to mass across the courtyard, which doubles as a marketplace, which is the cantina.

The area with the six buildings has a small probably four-foot-high adobe wall, making that place a compound and off limits to the local populace.

John's powers of observation honed from thousands of hours doing surveillance has that fine quality of situational awareness one can only get from experience. The taller building in the compound has an antenna farm on the roof, making it the logical place to conduct covert business, also the shop for making explosive devices and/or dirty bombs.

Taking a lot of notes and hundreds of pictures of the buildings, vehicles, people, and the animals used in the villagers and farmers daily lives proved invaluable. The sketches he made using a small six-inch architectural scale helped to determine heights of the buildings, using shadows and angles of shadows as reference at various times during the day. Distances between buildings are very important when an attacking force has to run and gun from building to building. At any time the CIA's satellites were in sync, John could upload the pictures back to Langley—that way, the analysts could start identifying the players going in and out of the main building. Then they could let John know who he is dealing with.

The two main scientists identified were Bruno Brecht and his son Otto Brecht. The elder Brecht, eighty-five years old, was a nuclear physicist working with Robert Oppenheimer, and Gen. Leslie Groves Brecht was fired by Oppenheimer soon after the start of the Manhattan Project. He offered his services to any country who would have him. No one wanted him; his arrogance and terrible temper preceded him. He took a teaching job at a college in India. His maniac grudge against the United States stayed with him for the last sixty years. Now it was his turn to claim revenge on the United States in the form of a dirty bomb exploded in a populated city. His son harbored his father's feelings. Otto was accepted at the University of Cairo, where he studied physics. He was barely a C student. He ran around with a bunch of Marxists whose main reason for existing was to protest everything and anything to do with the United States.

John could have easily taken both Brechts out with a well-placed bullet. But the mission was to capture them and anyone else knowledgeable in the nuclear studies. The compound was to be destroyed with all its equipment, tools, vehicles, and any armed combatments. All computers, electronic gear, radios, iPads, written notebooks, personal communication in the form of letters, etc. were to be packed up and taken back to the farm and eventually to CIA headquarters, and maybe if Laura is in a generous mood, some of the intel would go to the FBI or NSA.

As the sun set over the horizon, in the Pacific Ocean, John stashed his gear. He took the crossbow, the camera, his pistol, the small camera, and one thermite grenade. Over the low adobe wall, he scrambled up to the main building. Lying low next to the back wall, he waited fourteen or fifteen minutes, listening for any unusual sounds or people moving about. It was completely black, which was to his advantage.

He got to get close to the big garage door to get a peek inside. Moving on all fours and quiet as could be, he made it to the opening. Lying on the ground, John slowly looks inside the shop area of the building. *Looks like a government office on Friday at four o'clock. Not a thing moving.*

Well, I better go inside and case the joint. They have some nice metal and woodworking machines. From the writing on the manufacturer's ID plates, these all look like Italian toolmakers, lathes, and such. The computers that run the design configurations are all British. Using his LED penlight, John spies a cabinet with a large keyed lock. *I bet I can open this with my picks.* After five minutes using his lock picks, John gets in the metal cabinet.

Oh yes, just as I hoped, this looks like the outer casing for a load of chemicals and some explosive material. And here is about four pounds of plastic explosive C-4 or Semtex. I don't see any wiring or computer-aided sending units. No blasting caps or mining blasters either. Oh crap, I hear someone or two someones walking around upstairs. There's a light at the door on the balcony, and now it's opening. I better hide among the machine tools. There're two sets of feet coming down the steel stairs. I hope it's the both Brechts going out to the cantina. If they give me fifteen minutes, I might be able to get in that upstairs office and bedroom. It will contain irrefutable evidence about illegal nuclear possession, about weapons, and whom they are going to use them on.

The two people who came down the iron stairs were the Brechts Bruno and Otto. You could pick them out of a crowd. They dressed like the euro trash they are. Their clothes looked like they were picked out of the goodwill bin. Speaking French, the Brechts let it be known they were on the way to the cantina for supper and drinks. This gave John the opening he needed.

Slowly making his way up the stairs, John stepped very lightly. *I hope there are no loose treads or railings to make noise. I don't think anybody is still here, but no use taking chances. I better put a dart in this crossbow.* At the top of the landing, a corridor led all the way to the other end of the building. Slowly opening the first door, John saw a filthy bedroom, no doubt it was Otto's—full ash trays were everywhere and empty beer cans were strewn about. John took a zip drive from his pocket and inserted it in the only computer in the room. The next room was Bruno's. John repeated putting zip drives in both a laptop and full-size computer.

The bathroom connecting both bedrooms was also a pigpen. He checked in the toilet tank and behind the tank for any contraband and for hidden weapons. There is no ceiling, only the exposed steel-framed rafters and metal roof; no place to hide anything. The last two rooms contained a cache of AK-47 rifles and boxes of ammo, some mortar tubes and bases, two wooden crates full of RPGs, and at least a hundred 80 mm mortar rounds. John made a quick sketch of the upstairs layout, noting where the ammo is stored. *I got to leave now. Those Belgians will be back here shortly. Good the zip drives are all loaded and ready for me to send to Langley.* Going down the stairs, he hears talking on the outside near the side wall. *I got just enough time to hide in the tool room, I hope.* With seconds to spare, John hides behind a large turret lathe. The lights come on, and there is an argument between Bruno and the commander. The commander is yelling at Bruno to work faster and make the weapon serviceable.

"I can't work any faster with the trash computers you make me work on. Get me some of the computers the American military has, and I can show you real progress."

"We don't have that kind of money to buy that sophisticated equipment. I think you don't really know what you two are up against here. This equipment is top of the line."

"Yes, maybe ten years ago. This junk is too slow for the millions of calculations we are asking it to perform."

"Monsieur Brecht, you better have the system up and running in three weeks, or my brother Charro Lequesta will kill you himself, and I can assure you it will be a most painful death."

"I am not afraid of you or your brother. My work as a nuclear physicist is the very best you could find in a short notice. I don't respond to idle threats, so leave us be so we can continue doing the devil's work."

The commander leaves Bruno's bedroom and runs down the stairway. He doesn't want the senorita at the cantina to wait too long, or she will leave with somebody else.

John sees the commander run out the door. He waits ten more minutes to see if anybody is coming back to also threaten the Belgian's welfare. At the door looking both ways, John scoots back over the adobe wall and heads over to where he left his kit. He checks his watch and the satphone for the alignment of the three satellites so he can upload the intel from the computers.

After the intel has been sent to Langley, Laura is on the line. Talking in a very low tone, she acknowledges the material stored on the one laptop and one computer is invaluable. John hurries up and destroys the zip drives. He uploads all the pictures taken these last three days and erases everything from the camera. If he should ever be caught and taken prisoner, the satphone has a self-destruct feature. John gives Laura the coordinates for his extraction and the time agreed on beforehand. He has eight hours to get to the extraction point.

John makes a rig from the parachute harness and suspension lines. Using bamboo poles and cross braces, the extraction frame is set up and ready for the C-130 Hercules rescue aircraft to fly low and snag the suspension line rig and lift him upward. With his headset on and tuned to the frequency of the Herky Bird, John calls the airplane, and in a matter of minutes, he is being jerked up, and the aircraft crew is hauling him inside the plane. The mission is over; the C-130 is on its way back to Lackland Air Force Base in Texas. There John will catch a ride in a CIA Gulfstream back to Langley, Virginia.

CHAPTER TWENTY-SEVEN

CIA headquarters, Langley, Virginia

In a secure conference room, Laura, Mr. Casey, John, and the team picked by Sergeants Hun and Yorkie start planning the mission to Nicaragua. The more artistically talented members of the team built a sand table. It showed all the features of the compound, the buildings, the river, and the surrounding town. With the info from all the pictures and scouting reports sent by satphone from John, the team is able to get a good feel of the very ground they will walk on in a few days. The team will consist of twenty-four members, each man a veteran in his own specialty. Then John, Yorkie, and Hun left for the farm, somewhere in Virginia, with the sand table, where they connected up with the rest of the team.

CIA farm, Virginia, USA

John divided the team into six squads, each led by the most experienced troopers. They will fly into Costa Rica, an hour's march north of the compound they will attack. There is a small dirt and grass airstrip that used to be a CIA staging point. This will be the infiltration and extraction area. John let the squad leaders alone with their men so they could pick each other's brains and get to know where their strengths lie. This is SOP with counterterrorism groups. John excused himself and went in another room to sit at a desk and write a letter. The letter was to be sent by FedEx to a friend of his in Pennsylvania.

Hi Jerry,

I will bet you never expected to hear from your old hot rod buddy. I have a great favor to ask of you and Margie. I realize she is the talented one in the family, but your fabricating genius is what it is going to take to make this project work. Enclosed is a check for 20K, that should cover labor and materials and shipping costs. If you need more money, call my office, and Helen will take care of you. I need you to make an insulated shipping container. The inside dimensions need to be able to hold a basketball-sized object. The thickness of the double- or triple-walled box has to contain enough dry ice to last for at least three days in subtropical climate. You do the calculations. The material should be high-strength aluminum sheeting, all welded construction. The top cover will be a lid connected with a continuous stainless steel hinge, two hasps for locks, and a leak-proof weather seal connecting both pieces. Paint the box with the colors of the International Red Cross. The wording needs to say "Rush. Do not delay. Human organs for transplant." Send it to me at Deputy Director, Central Intelligence Agency, Langley, Virginia. Send it counter to counter US Airways from Avoca Airport. Jerry, I need this as fast as you can fabricate it.

Getting back to the skull session with the team, John had some salient points for the team to consider. "If the squad with the SEAL team members want to come in from the river side, I think it's a good idea. They are in their element and might be a better way to cover the rear of the compound. We need to capture two or three pickup trucks right away. We will need them to transport all of the computers, files, laptops, and anything else that looks interesting. All that equipment will go back to Langley. The only truck we need to destroy fast is the one with the .50 cal machine gun mount. From our pictures and my surveillance, the peons that were taking the bullets apart were saving the gunpowder in one bucket, and the lead was being melted down. They are making lead shields to transport the radioactive material, probably spent uranium rods for the dirty bomb. They have to make the shields themselves so as not to alert anyone to what is going down. Remember, the only guys to go near that last little shack by the river are the two men wearing the proper suits, boots, hats, and goggles.

"Another thing about these troops—they are not a ragtag bunch of peons. They are highly trained Cuban mercenaries. Most of them wear BDUs during the day. They are armed with an assortment of assault rifles, Russian AKs, Israeli Uzis, Belgium Nagants. They all carry sidearms, mostly machine pistols and knives. By the way, they were moving around in and around the compound, I suspect there are no mines or antipersonnel weapons, a.k.a. claymores. Everyone whose job is not to go in the big building, stay away from the second floor northwest corner—that room is loaded with explosives. We're going to blow it on our way out to the extraction point.

"Everybody's headset is tuned to the same channel. Don't change it. As soon as the fight starts, the plan all goes to hell—you all know that, you are all combat veterans. As the scenario changes, you squad leaders will change with it. Remember, we have the advantage. They don't suspect anybody knows about their dirty little secret. Kill every Cuban you see, except if you see Lequesta—only wound him. I need him alive. But if it's a life-or-death situation, kill him. Don't let him get you. Also me and the two French-speaking snake eaters will get the Brechts. They want him back at Langley. He has a lot of Russian secrets we need to exploit. The son can be wasted. He is an alcoholic and doper with a dead brain. He is of no use to anybody.

"Once more, we will go over the plan. If anyone has a better way of doing something, anything at all, speak up—it could save somebody a lot of pain or their life. The townspeople are not combatants. For the most part, they hate the Commies. Unless one is armed and pointing a weapon at you, hold your fire. We will be surrounding the compound at no later than 0630 hours. All of the Cubans will be in the buildings working at whatever they do. The three designated snipers will pick off anyone coming through the doors or windows. This will help the rest of the squads perform their tasks. Myself and the two SF troopers will make a beeline for the back door and climb the stairs to the second floor where we hope to capture Bruno and the commander, maybe Lequesta too.

"Yesterday's photo overflight spotted Lequesta's oceangoing yacht. It's a sixty-seven-foot all white, with a pale blue stripe docked at the river pier in the rear of the compound. He probably has at least six armed sailors on board. The squad with the SEALs will breach the yacht. If the Corsican is aboard, capture him or kill him only if necessary. Kill everybody on board and blow up the boat. Remember, I need his body in one piece, dead or alive. Everybody tasked with destroying the machines will carry extra thermite grenades to ruin every single woodworking, metalworking machines and all the presses. The small hand tools we can give to the village people. Tomorrow we make another run through the whole operation, except for the SEALs—they have to go down to Little River, Virginia, to practice taking the yacht out of commission, as we have no river close by."

CIA farm, somewhere in Virginia

The phone in John's office rang its usual ring, but John knew who was on the line. The old and persistent nagging feeling was back. "Hello, Laura, is everybody at headquarters up to speed for this new operation?"

"How did you know it is me?"

"Sweetheart, when it gets this close to moving-out time, your ESP and mine are on the same wavelength."

"Yes, sir baby, I am like a long-tailed cat in a room full of rocking chairs. I had the same old dream about Italian food again last night."

"Holy crap, the guys are talking about going to Lasardo's pizza joint tonight. We are giving a send-off to the two rangers that Central Army Command stole from me after all the special training we put those guys through. Now I have to dig up two new qualified warriors and crash-course them."

"No, you don't. Casey and I are sending you two SEALs to fill out your team. You can thank me when you get back. And be sure to come back in one piece with all your parts in working order. When you go to the pizza joint tonight, only eat pizza and stay away from the rest of the goodies. My gypsy lady has been trying to get in touch with me all day. I know what she wants—she is trying to tell me to warn you of all the bad juju down there. Is there any way you can grab an airplane and come up to see me tonight? I really miss you and need a whole bunch of you."

"I miss you a bucketful also, but I can't get away this evening. I have to redo the battle order to fit in the two SEALs in the squad coming in from the river. And we also have a crypted call from the mayor of the town near the compound. This mayor was the CIA's contact when we used the airstrip during the Contra screwup. He promised to call me at 2200 hours for a last-minute okay on the status of the area. Okay, sugar, I have to go now. We will talk again in the morning. I love you. Bye."

Two days later, 0330 hours, dark time

The big and powerful C-130 Hercules lined up with the grass and dirt airstrip. The pilot, an old hand at landing large cargo planes on short runways, greased the turbo prop in between the lights made of fifty-five-gallon trash barrels burning everything from old used oil to discarded rubber tires. The team of twenty-four men plus John unloaded the bird as fast as humanly possible. Twenty minutes later, it was wheels up, and the Herky Bird was back over the Gulf of Mexico on its way home to Virginia. The local men who were helping the mayor extinguished the fires in the barrels and took off for their homes.

John and his squad leaders got the men organized and suited up for the hour-long trek to the site of the upcoming raid. They left the airstrip at 0430 hours. At 0530 hours, all the team was in place.

The main body of the team had surrounded the compound and was waiting for a signal from John or to hear if the SEALs had captured the yacht. The navy SEAL team split off from the rest of the squads. They carried their inflatable boat with an small quiet outboard motor to the river. With the motor covered with some old blankets to muffle any sound, the team got as close to the yacht as possible. They beached the inflatable and slowly swam to the big boat. Two guys went over the transom, met no resistance, and ran across the deck to the ladder for the pilot's cabin. Both doors were unlocked. At a signal, both guys threw open the doors. There was no need for stealth; the only sentry was unconscious from the bottle of Cuban rum lying on the deck. The first SEAL sent him to his paradise with a quick piano wire garrote around his neck. Two of the other team members climbed up grappling hook rope ladders amidships. The last two came up over the bow by way of the anchor chains. The leader said, "I don't like this. There should be more people out on the deck, unless everybody got drunk from last night's party?" The team, in their usual breaking-and-entering mode, lined up behind the leader. The door to the main cabin and sleeping quarters was locked. A set of lock picks in the hand of the chief petty officer made short work of the locked door. The chief slowly pushed the door open, and all six guys went into the main salon. A corridor at the far end of the salon revealed six more doors to the various sleeping rooms of the heads and the owners private suite.

All the men, using hand signals, only crept along the corridor, listening at each door for sounds of breathing, snoring, bathroom sounds, etc. The second CPO slid a small TV cable under the last door on the left, viewing the screen on the monitor. He was only able to see clothes, women's dresses, underwear, shoes, and several empty rum and whiskey bottles. This TV unit has an audio feature so they can hear the sleeping sounds of at least two people. This door was locked also; the first chief picked that lock. The first two shooters were entering the bedroom when the woman awoke and started screaming; she was blown away instantly. Both SEALs were right on Lequesta with their MP3s stuck in his face. A third SEAL came right up and stuck a syringe full of sleeping meds in the bulging neck artery. Lequesta was knocked out in five seconds. Meanwhile, the three men in the corridor had busted down the doors to the other rooms and tossed in flashbang grenades. The first SEAL going in the room was met by three very disoriented Cubans. He mowed down two guys in their underwear, but the third Cuban got his AK-47 up just in time to send a round to the spot where the bulletproof vest connects the front and back. The SEAL was hit in the lower chest. He staggered a little but still put a full magazine into the face of the Cuban shooter. The other two SEALs tossed fragmentation grenades in two of the bedrooms. The Cubans still alive started spraying bullets through the thin paneled walls. The guys were ready for this. They all dropped to the deck and returned the fire. The bad guys were not finished yet. Two more men came around from the door leading to the engine room. They were lugging a heavy machine gun. As they got to the deck right outside the salon, the older chief shot one guy through the head. The other Cuban was trying to feed the ammunition belt into the receiver. The SEAL who got shot used his pistol and shot the Cuban three times in the chest.

Two of the men were dragging the unconscious Lequesta from the bedroom. They heard a lot of shouting coming from below decks. The leader of the SEAL team sent one guy to get the inflatable boat and get everybody off the yacht. The shouting from below decks was getting louder as the rest of the Cuban crew started coming onto the main deck.

The bad guys formed two groups and started circulating around the main cabin and salon. The air was thick with bullets flying everywhere. The crew didn't know what they were shooting at; they just started firing into the main cabin. The master chief, with hand signals, ordered the men to lob frag grenades out the shot-out windows. The grenades gave the SEALs time to get in better firing positions, and in a few minutes' time, most of the bad guys were dead or dying. The last four jumped or dove off the boat and were swimming for the shore. They were picked off one by one and became food for the caimans, crabs, and turtles. These employees of Lequesta's were not trained soldiers, only out-of-work seamen and pier bums he picked up in the Malay Peninsula. The SEAL came back with the rubber boat, and everybody got on board, but not before the demo guys placed the explosive charges to blow the big yacht in a million pieces.

While all this was happening, the Cuban mercenaries, all trained soldiers, were coming out of the smaller buildings and running down to the river. Most of them were shot as they ran across the open ground. The Special Forces troops, along with the rangers and snipers, killed most of the Cubans. The first squad of troopers captured the Toyota with the .50 cal machine gun and were using it against the bad guys. They soon ran out of ammunition and destroyed the big gun with thermite grenades. The other squad dispatched to get as many vehicles as possible and drove the rest of the pickup trucks and the two Mercedes out of the compound. They parked them behind the church. The mayor and his men hid all the vehicles till John's guys could retrieve them for the extraction. John, Yorkie, and another Green Beret got to the rear of the main building. Slowly the entered the stairway and worked their way up to the second floor. There was nobody in sight along the corridor. Trying the doorknob to Otto's room, it was locked. Two shots rang out, and John was hit in the chest; the bulletproof vest took the 9 mm rounds and saved his life. Yorkie kicked the door in and sprayed Otto with the MP3. He tried not to hit any of the computers or laptops. All three troopers standing in the corridor kept watch down the stairs and along the corridor. Alex, the third man, peeked around the corner of the open door to Bruno's room and saw no one. John feared the worst; he thought that the commander killed Bruno. John entered the room, while Yorkie and Alex stood watch. Sitting in an easy chair and drinking wine, Bruno said, "What kept you people? I expected you long before now. Would you join me in a glass of good French wine? It is so much better than the swill these Cuban pigs drink."

"Hurry up, Bruno, drink your wine and stand up. You are going on a plane ride back to the land of the big PX. Where's the commander?" John asked. Bruno pointed to the next room, the one with all the explosives and guns. John nodded to Alex, and Alex set a ring of C-4 around the lockset and along the hinges of the heavy steel door. The door was blown in the room with a mighty blast and a lot of smoke. Alex and Yorkie lay on their stomachs and looked for the commander; if he was shooting, it would be in thin air. The commander was standing by the only window in the room, trying to catch his breath. He was not armed as far as the men could see. They took no chances and in a split second were on him and tossing him to the floor. The blast and concussion made him so disoriented, he was useless. Quickly Alex had the cuffs on him and was searching him for weapons, phones, iPads, etc.

Meanwhile, downstairs, the battle raged with the mercenaries and the rangers. The rangers and Special Forces troopers were slowly wrapping the Cubans up. The rangers had all the exits blocked, and the Cubans could only fight to the death or surrender. They would not surrender because they knew they would be handed over to the townspeople. They would be tortured and then killed in a very painful ritual.

All of the small buildings were captured and were being emptied of all that seemed useful to the CIA. After another twenty minutes, the battle was over. Lequesta, Bruno Brecht, and the commander were tied up, their mouths taped with duct tape, and tossed in the back of one of the pickup trucks. All the small buildings were leveled with explosives taken from the main building.

The building with the radioactive material was waiting to being searched by the group of technicians from the facilities at Oak Ridge Tennessee. They were in a C-45 circulating the area, waiting for the word from the team to land and get to the compound. They wore all the gear, suits, helmets, gloves, and boots needed to resist the poison in the uranium bars. They would stay until a team from the Atomic Energy Commission decided what to do with the spent uranium bars. They would probably be used as weapons material.

John got on the radio back to Langley. He had to make a preliminary report to the director and his deputy. His report stated six wounded, non-life-threatening, no KIAs, all enemy combatants killed. Two hostages, two and a half tons of electronics, manuals, radios, and personal records captured. Mission accomplished. Townspeople happy.

The C-130 Hercules airplane was loaded and ready to get back to the CIA farm in Virginia. As the Herky Bird was wheels up, a Grumman G-55C was landing at the same airstrip. John and Yorkie met Hun coming off the airplane with a cooler box labeled "International Red Cross, Do Not Delay. Human Remains." John was not going to relish what he was about to do, but a promise is a promise.

The pilot of the G-55C is an ex-Air Commando, part of the British SAS. He stepped off the aircraft right behind Hansl Von Stead, a.k.a. Hun. He introduced himself as Lional Pepperedge, "but you mates can call me Pep, everybody does. That's my call sign also. So then, Captain Braz, where are we off to? Someplace with cold gin and warm ladies?"

Braz had watched as the pilot slipped the G-55 on to the runway and said to himself, *This air jockey has been around jungle airstrips, which is a good thing, as we might need another savvy pilot on this trip.*

John asked Pep a few salient questions concerning torture and death. "I have no problems with those things. I rather enjoy sending the bad guys to the hell in which they were born, mate."

"Okay. We better get this show on the road."

"I am going to the town mayor's house. Be back in an hour or so. Keep a real close watch on the prisoner. I don't want to lose him again. Senor Mayor, I need to ask you a favor, *por favor*, do you know if any of your farmer friends has a cow or horse or a water buffalo that is sick and dying? I will pay him and you a good deal of money if I can buy it from him. He won't get the animal back, as I plan to destroy it in a humane way," thinking, *I can shoot the animal, but the human animal is in for a very bad time.*

Years ago in a little Taverna on a Greek Isle, John struck up a conversation with an old priest. It was this man of God who told John a way that the ancient Persians tortured a captive. This priest made a life study about the horrible things ancient peoples did to one another. John planned this adventure after his old Montagnard's family was senselessly killed by Lequesta.

The mayor took John to a farm where there was a very sick milk cow. The poor animal was skin and bones; cancer had ruined her. The farmer was very eager to sell the cow to John. He gave the man $500 cash. He also gave the mayor $1,000 for work to be done later. *Now the fun begins,* thought John. Transporting the animal back to the airstrip, John asked the mayor to hire as many men as needed to take all the dead bodies of the Cubans and bury them. "I will pay each man in cash American money if they could do the job today."

John had the cow in the back of one of the Toyotas. He picked up all the guys and their gear and headed for the river. It was sweltering hot and humid at only ten o'clock in the morning; it was 115 degrees. The humid coastal lowlands backed up to the tropical rain forest and gave no relief from the insects, snakes, gators, caiman, and other forms of life that could kill you with a very painful and slow death. John was counting on this climate to help with his plan.

"Now that we are at the river, help me unload the cow and Lequesta."

Hun and Yorkie are full of questions. "What are we doing with the animal?" asked Hun.

"You will see in a minute," says John, as he takes the pistol and shoots the cow in the head; she died in a second. "Yorkie, get us the long plastic gloves the vet doctor gave us back in Virginia." John took a kbar and slit open the cow from the neck to the anus. "Put those gloves on and start taking out all the guts. Yeah, I know it stinks, but remember this is the guy that was taking both of you to the VC to be executed the next day.

"Now we take all the clothes off Lequesta. Retie his hands and feet and keep the duct tape on his mouth." Pep was watching all this and holding off vomiting. He didn't want the rangers to think he was not tough enough to be there. The captive was still out from the injections. The guys lifted him and put him in the cavity of the cow, with his head only sticking out. John proceeded to sew up the cavity with large needles and heavy monofilament fishing line, letting only his head sticking out. By the time he was finished, there were a million flies all over the carcass. Dung beetles started to crawl into the cavity and feed on the putrid flesh. They also were chewing on the naked body of Lequesta. Several turkey buzzards landed only ten feet away from the cow. They didn't seem to be at all concerned with the people.

Lequesta came to, and he was screaming. No one could hear him with the tape on his mouth. His eyes were as big as silver dollars. John came over to him and ripped the tape from his mouth. "You, Braz, I was the one that was to kill you."

"Tough shit, you no-good piece of human trash, I get to kill you first. It took a long time, but you lose. And you are going to suffer as no human has since the fifth century."

"Please, please, I will make you a billionaire. I have money in banks all over the world."

"No, Charro, the CIA has taken just about all of your money. We even got the gold you stole from the South Africans. Now the beetles and flies will eat you alive. The buzzards are waiting to pluck the eyes from your skull. The alligators will come on shore and pull you into the water and make fast work of your filthy flesh."

Lequesta was almost out of his mind. His head was tossing and turning trying to get out of the bindings. He kept begging and pleading. That's when John took out the Fairbairn from his wrist. "Lequesta, I am going to take great pleasure in severing your head from your body. First, you need to suffer more for all the innocent people you killed."

"Please shoot me, Braz, please, for the mother of god shoot me?"

"No, no, and no. You will die like the scum that is feeding on you." That's when John took the scalpel sharp knife and sliced through the neck like he was cutting a cantaloupe. "There, that's done. Let me set this head on the ground so more blood can drain away."

"What happens now, Mad Dog?" asked Yorkie.

He got a look from John that could freeze lava. Then John did something unusual; he started laughing and said, "I told you never to call me that again." All three guys knew John was all right again. "Pep, please hand me that box so I can save this head for later."

Pep asked, "What are we going to do with it?"

"We are going to grill it, of course, and eat it later." Pep lost his cookies and looked at John like he was a vampire or something. John and the guys each grabbed a leg of the cow and dragged it halfway in the water.

Yorkie laughed and said, "The gators will clean up that mess in a matter of minutes."

With the pickup loaded, the four soldiers made their way back to the airstrip and the mayor's house. Pep and the boys started the preflight check of the G-55. The oil and fuel were sufficient for the upcoming leg of the flight. John was at the mayor's house. "My friend, Senor Mayor, how is the burial detail doing?"

"Oh, Mr. John, my men have most of the graves dug and covered over. We will cover over the area with brush so it looks undisturbed."

"Good job, Juan."

"And who may this be?"

"Captain John, meet Father Sebastian. He is kind enough to come by and say some words over the site when my men are finished."

"That's okay, Juan. I suspect these men were Catholics, and maybe their souls may be saved."

"Here is more money for the upkeep of the airstrip. We probably will be calling on you in the future. And, Father, some money for your church and for all you do for the people of this town."

"May God bless you all. I have to get going. Adios."

1300 hours, the airstrip in Nicaragua

"Pep, you take the right-hand seat. I am going to fly this bird outta here. Righto, mate. What do I set the course for?"

"We have a change in plans—we're not going to Managua. We're going south to San Jose in Costa Rica—it is a lot safer. There the CIA station chief will set us up at a safe house. We can have the G-55 gone over for any problems, like transponders, bugs, booby traps, remotely controlled or otherwise. We can get some good chow, a shower, change of clothes, and eight or ten hours' sleep. I can check in with the head shed and let Laura plot a new course over the Pacific for us. We can't get any weather info here, and Managua was out of the question. Too many people know Yorkie, Hun, and myself."

1400 hours, CIA safe house in San Jose, Costa Rica

John's satphone starts buzzing. John looked at the monitor and said to himself, *I was wondering when she would call.* "Hey there, blue eyes, did you forget I am in the loop?"

"No, sweetie, we have been very busy, and we don't ever have to worry about Charro Lequesta again."

"Why? What did you do to him?—as if I didn't know. You weren't supposed to kill him, I wanted him back here so we could get as much intel from him as possible."

"He would not talk. He could be tortured till the cows come home. And you would have to kill him anyway."

"I guess you are correct, but why are you in Costa Rica?"

"Managua was out of the question—too many people would recognize us."

"When do you get back to Langley?"

"In three days, if the weather cooperates. Take this down please. We leave here for Hawaii then Guam then Manila, and finally Bangkok."

"Bangkok? Are you seeing Andy Lord?"

"Maybe or maybe not. I have a delivery for my old friend, Meong Hua, the Montagnard soldier whose family was butchered by Lequesta."

"What kind of delivery?"

"Don't ask. In time, I will tell you the whole story. Please set up landings and departures for the G-55C at those places. Do it all under the auspices of the CIA so we don't have to clear customs. It could be quite messy if we run into some self-important customs officer. Thank you so much, and I can't wait to get back to Langley, and you, I really missed you this time."

"Well, you get your ass back here as soon as you can. Delta Force wants their two sergeants back at Bragg."

"I will call Col. Charlie Beckwith, the commander of Delta Force, and get him off your back. Charlie is one of the very best soldiers in the US Army."

"Okay. Bye. I love you."

After the guys got settled in the safe house, shaved, showered, and had eaten at the mess hall, the three troops, sans John, wanted to go to a local bar and have a couple of beers. "Hey, Pep, let those guys drink all they want. You limit yourself to two beers. We are flying at first light, and I need your navigation expertise. A hangover will be a pain in the ass for all of us. Remember, American cold beer is a lot stronger than that warm horse piss you Brits drink."

CHAPTER TWENTY-EIGHT

0600 hours, Santa Rosa, Costa Rica Airport

The nose of the G-55C jet was moving down Runway 92 west. John knew in his butt "We are rotating and wheels are off the ground. Okay, Pep, we are on a heading straight for Honolulu. If we don't hit too much of a headwind, we can be there in about eleven hours. I am going to let the boys get some copilot time. They both have been taking a lot of instrument classes lately. That way, we can keep going, with you or me as pilot and one of them as copilot. We will rotate sleeping and pilot duty. Make sure everybody's logbook gets signed. These Delta troopers need as much airtime as they can get. Colonel Beckwith is a real hard-ass and expects his men to be able to do as much as possible at any given time."

1300 hours, Bangkok, Thailand

Two generals come to meet the CIA G-55C jet. As the airplane pulls up to the CIA hangar, John peers out the pilot's window. "Gentlemen, we have a greeting party of some high brass, so square yourselves away and try to look like soldiers." Hun opens the door and lowers the steps. Gen. Shorty Wells and former colonel now brigadier general Andrew Lord enter the plane. Everybody stands at attention and salutes the generals, even though this is not protocol. Andy Shorty and John grab each other in a big bear hug, and everyone starts talking at the same time. "Congratulations, Andy. Now you are going to find out how much more politics will you have on your everyday life. The Senate, the Congress, and the Oval Office will take a piece of your ass anytime they think it's good for the country."

"Thanks for the warning, John. General Wells already gave me the facts of life on being a general officer. Did Laura make reservations for you all? Or are you looking for a hotel?"

"Well, gentleman, we were hoping to treat you to dinner, and we need to get the G-55C in a CIA hangar for maintenance. We flew nonstop from Central America to Honolulu and would like to get some bed rest, some food, and a few cold beers. I would like to rent one of your Little birds tomorrow and fly up to see my Montagnard brothers and honor a promise I made years ago to Meong Hua, the leader of the ranger company we trained in 1967."

"John, you don't have to rent the helo. Just bring it back in one piece and in flyable condition."

"Thanks, Andy. I can still call you by your first name out here in the field, can't I?"

"Of course, you can, Mad Dog. I knew that was coming. Old habits like old call signs are hard to resist."

"I am forgetting my manners. Sirs, this is Sgt. Lional Pepperedge, loaned to us from British SAS. He is a damn good pilot for bush flying, lots of experience in Angola and Western Africa. And of course, you know Sergeants Hansl Von Stead and Dean Young, on loan to us from Delta Force."

"Yes, John. Col. Charlie Becker called me and asked if I had any influence over you and to kindly return his men to North Carolina. I said I didn't know what he was talking about. He just laughed and said he is friends with the army chief of staff. So I told him as soon as you show up, I will put his men on a flight back to the States."

"Well, General, as soon as we leave the yard village, we will be wheels up for the States no later than 1500 hours tomorrow."

The team checked in at the Hilton Bangkok, ate dinner with the generals, and went to the bar. John only allowed the men two beers each. "At 0600 hours, come early, guys, and we are flying in some dangerous hill country. I want everybody on their game tomorrow." At 0430 hours, John was dressed in his running shoes, shorts, and an old Army T-shirt. He wore a small fanny pack to carry his radio, a small Browning HP-35 and a plastic water bottle. He did six easy miles in under an hour and ran hard back to the hotel. The men were all up and dressed in BDUs. John took a shower and dressed the same. Gen. Andy Lord was kind enough to provide them with a car and driver to get them to the airport and the waiting Little Bird helo.

The Little Bird landed in the clearing of the Montagnard village of Sui Thong, Meong's home village. When Meong saw John get out of the helo, he started to shed a few tears. John also was overcome with a little of emotion. The two old friends grasped each other in a hug and held on for a good two minutes before letting go. Meong could hardly talk; he was so overwhelmed. "Lieutenant John, you came back. You said you would, and I knew this day would arrive."

"Meong, I am here to keep the promise I gave to you so long ago." Yorkie brought the cooler box to John. John opened the cooler and showed Meong the contents.

"John, that is the head of Lequesta?"

"Yes, my brother, now you can avenge the deaths of your beloved family." John and the guys knew it was time to get out of the village and back to Bangkok. The rituals involved with avenging the family deaths were not for outsiders to see. They made their good-byes and were wheels up and on the way out of the mountains.

The G-55C got permission to land at Pope Air Force Base, next to Fort Bragg. Because of the clandestine missions and secret clearances everybody had, they were allowed to go up to the old stockade, now the home of Delta Force. Hun and Yorkie were welcomed back into the compound. John and Pep were met outside the wire by the deputy commander of the highly secretive unit. The commander colonel Charlie Becker was in Washington on official army duty. The light colonel met the guys and took them to lunch at the officers club. There they unofficially talked about the mission/ nonmission they were just on. All the intel and actions taken were of substantive quality as a learning tool the deputy commander could pass on to the instructors. No word would ever be spoken of this off-the-cuff skull session. It was time to get back to Langley, Virginia. Within a half hour, the G-55C was wheels up and in Northern Virginia at 1350 hours.

Landing at the CIA airstrip on the farm, Pep drove the Gulfstream to its allotted hangar, where a concerned crew chief was happy to see the bird in one piece. John checked in with air operations and said "so long" to Pep. An armored SUV was waiting for to take John to

Langley. In Laura's outer office, John was buzzed in and welcomed by Rosey Kowolski, Laura's personal secretary. "Captain Braz, it's so nice to see you, she has been like a hen on eggs since you left."

"Okay, Rosey, get your ass back to work. Captain Braz is not going to entertain us with any war stories. Rosey, hold all my calls for at least thirty minutes. I don't care if it's the Oval Office—they can wait. Now, my love, get your sorry buns in my office. I read all the after-action reports from the squad leaders. Nothing new there. We're waiting for the first reports from the interrogation people. Now get over here and kiss me before I explode." After a few passionate kisses and caressing, Laura pushed away and said, "No more, not now. We have the whole night and tomorrow night to catch up on all the romance."

"Yes, dear, but I can hardly hold my hormones from pulling my brain apart. And besides I have to get back to Scranton. I have a company that needs my direction."

"Screw you and that damn company of yours. You are mine for the next two days. If I have to get a squad of Green Berets to tie you up and sit you down at my house. Don't piss me off, or I will shove this ring where the sun don't shine. You got that, buster?"

"Darling, I need you as much as you need me. I will be right where you want me for the next few days." For two nights and the whole weekend, Laura and John hardly left Laura's bedroom, only to eat, use the facilities, and run on the beach each morning and evening.

Reagan International Airport Washington DC, 0700 hours US Air flight 1241

The short flight over the mountains to Scranton Wilkes-Barre Avoca Airport takes only an hour and ten minutes. Meeting John in the Yukon Denali armored truck was Helen, his office manager. "Oh, John, it's so good to see you in person. We were all worried sick that the mission failed and you were killed or, worse, captured."

"No, sweetie, everybody made it. No one was killed, and only a few wounded."

"When we didn't hear from Laura or the NSA, we assumed the worse."

"I am sorry I am remiss—I should have called. But the commo traffic out of Nicaragua is monitored by the Commies. And they would have sent jets after us, then our asses would really be in a crack. How is everybody at the office? Any new work?"

"Yes, Prince Abdulla Bin Aziz has called and needs our services in Riyadh and Paris."

"Have we sent anyone there?"

"No, not yet. He wants you to come see him. Our regular staff meeting is on for this morning, okay? Oh and one more thing, all the new girls have been asking for the latest models of assault rifles and pistols. I told everybody that as soon as they qualify with the guns we have, we can start proficiency tests on the latest Berretta and HK models. Also Mary Ann has been acting a little strange lately, like she misses you more than normal."

"Oh crap, Helen, I think I know what that's all about. It's time Ms Mary Ann and I had a little gab fest."

"Don't get her all upset now. She, Annie, and some of the other new people are coming along great. Their professionalism grows every day. Well, here we are. I will let you off in front, and I will park in the underground garage."

Upon clearing the security systems and entering the main office, John is swamped with "welcome back," "good to see you," "thank god you're home," and a great big kiss from Ann Marie and Mary Ann. When things settled down a bit, John tackled the pile of telephone messages, most of them he tossed. "Mary Ann, get me Prince Bin Ryaza on my encrypted line please?"

"Salaam alaikum, my prince, how nice to hear your voice." With all the traditional niceties aside, John and the prince got down to business.

"Johnny, I need your help. Please come to Riyadh at your earliest convenience?"

"My brother, I just got back from a mission, and I need at least ten days at home. But I will call you and set a time for my visit."

"Thank you, my brother. Allah will smile on you."

"Helen, round 'em up for the staff meeting."

"Good morning, troops, and welcome aboard the new people. I will get around to meet you as time permits. I am sure you are getting to realize what we do here. If Helen Raskousas hired you, you must be on top of your game. Also again I submit to all of us here—what happens in Vegas stays in Vegas. The freedoms of the whole world sometimes depend solely on our ability to do our job, and to do it so nobody ever knew we did it—except the people whom we help and who help us.

"I am a very lucky person. I knew from the time I was a little guy I knew where I was headed and what I wanted to do. Every one of you is a patriot who loves this country. A lot of you are ex-military, and the civilians here know that the undercover and not sanctioned jobs and missions we do for the US government and private individuals are mostly adhered to our Constitution, the Bill of Rights, and common sense. We don't go out and waste human life for the thrill of it. Some of you did not know what mission I was just on. There is a reason for that. You don't need to know, as they say in the military. My pay grade is too low for me to know certain things. So if you're wondering what just happened, if you have a need to know, you will be told. Otherwise, keep your pie hole shut.

"There are plenty of ways to be creative, so don't think you are being held back from using the talents you possess and the ones you will acquire. If you have an idea (and there are no bad ideas), present them to somebody. A little idea surely has saved someone's tail at one time or another. Many times in a combat situation, a trooper with a little bit of ingenuity has pulled my ass out of the fire. When I was fed up with the liberal horse shit coming down from the Senate and Congress to the army is when I got out and started this firm. I only wanted bona fide patriots and people loyal to the Constitution to be on this team. I told my backers I will pay the best salaries to all my team members—that way, we are ensured of getting the best, brightest, intelligent, loyal, and creative people this country has to offer.

"I know that some of you who have been here since the beginning have heard these words before. It can only reinforce your beliefs in why we do what we do. This idea of a below-the-radar counterterrorism group is not new. There are a few groups like ours, and they do a world of good for the United States and the rest of the free world. George Washington, John Adams, and like-minded individuals were doing this before the American Revolution took place. They risked a hell of a lot more than us. They used their own money and resources. We are a lot better off than they were. We have more at our disposal to work with. So I am asking you—no, I am pleading with you. Use every bit of God-given talent you possess to make our mission here a happy one. We are a happy and generous collection of brilliant deep thinkers, I know this, for I have watched many of you struggle with problems, and when you find the answers, bingo, it's like a firecracker going off in your mind. This is why the terrorists will never win. Our dedication is based on humanity and love of people who want to be free, in spite of the idiots in our government, who are only in office for a paycheck. Thank you all for letting me give my monthly pep talk. Now if you check in with Helen, she will give you a time to talk to me about anything. You can contribute to making your projects get off the drawing board.

"Mary Ann and Ann Marie, I want to talk to both of you in my office in ten minutes, let's say about 0930 hours?"

"Hi guys, I missed you. How is everything going? Also what's up with wanting new assault rifles and pistols?"

"John, we have been reading the latest gun magazines, and it seems our stuff is kind of out of date for this century."

"Annie, you, of all people, know that the weapon in your hand is only as good as the person using it. I know that both of you are really good shooters. But can you shoot with both hands and hit what you are aiming at? I know you can't be that good yet. But with a lot of practice, both of you will be proficient with both hands and several different types of weapons. Now, Annie, you scoot along, I need to see what's on Mary Ann's mind. Thank you.

"You know something, darling? I always have a hard time trying not to call you Red? I have always been a sucker for red hair on a beautiful girl."

"John, stop the bullshit. Flattery will get you everything."

"Okay, sweetie, spit it out. You look as if the tears are ready to start. Please don't cry. You know how nutso I get when one of you ladies turns on the waterworks."

Mary Ann is weeping already. "John, I have a problem. The people who own the building my apartment is in are going to remodel the whole building, including redoing my suite. I have to find a place to live in less than two days."

"Mary Ann, they can't do that. They have to give you ample time to find another place."

"Their lawyer said he sent notices out two months ago. I either misplaced it, or I never got it. My landlord's wife is a mean old shrew, and she said to get my stuff out by tomorrow evening, or they will take it out and bill me."

"Don't you worry—if they do that, I will blow that fucking place to smithereens."

"So, John, can I rent one of your bedrooms till this is over or until I can find another place?"

"You can't rent a damn thing. The bedroom and the whole house is yours for as long as you need it. Now dry those baby blues and take the rest of the day off. Do you have help in moving your stuff?"

"Yes, yes, I do. My brother and a couple of his buddies are going to put my furniture in storage at his garage. My clothes and day-to-day articles, Annie will help me with. Can I move them in tonight?"

"Of course, and take Annie with you now. Helen, tell Annie she is to go with Mary Ann, and I will see to their dinner for tonight."

John's office, 1100 hours

"Carol and Mickey, we have a new project that may or may not take us overseas. Rob Gaudio and Jim Corbetta, meet Carol Devers and Mickey Jorden. You four along with Mary Ann Orielly and Ann Marie Casey will be going to Philadelphia for three days of training (actually four days, a refresher course) in tailing a subject, being the subject, and surveillance of a subject. You are to plan a capture of said subject using every known procedure at our disposal. The reason Philadelphia is being chosen is because it's the largest city close to us with normal high-rise structures, wide and narrow streets, lots of storefronts with acres of glass, and loads of people moving about day and night. Helen will billet you in a nice hotel in the downtown part of the city. Mickey, you will fly the team in the Piper Apache to the North Philly Airport. You need to rent two cars and a van. When we get the intel from the CIA or FBI, we will know what city the bad guy is in. Then we can make more specific plans. You will leave day after tomorrow. In the meantime, I will be going to Riyadh, Saudi Arabia. The prince is going to give me the goods on the person we need to capture and return to Ar Rub' al Khali (the Empty Quarter). It's in the southern part of Saudi Arabia and is the homeland of the prince. Remember, speak to no one of this—your lives may depend on it. Helen, please come in to the conference room. Now, dearie, what is on your mind?"

"Well, John, you know I worked for the CIA for over twenty years and with your company almost ten years now."

"Okay, sweetie, if you need a raise, you got it."

"No, no, John, that is not what this is all about. I want to retire and spend some time with my husband and his grandchildren."

"What? Are you kidding me? What will I do without you? I will really be in a jam if you're not here to run this outfit. Oh crap, Helen, I need you."

"John, I am giving you a year's notice. I have someone picked out to replace me. She starts in two days. I will train her like she was me but a little younger. She is very bright and pleasant with a good brain. Nothing rattles her, and she knows how to use a gun. She worked for the FBI for several years until she realized what a bunch of ass-kissing morons they are. She is a local lady born and raised here in the Scranton area. When I told her about the job opening, she said yes in a heartbeat.

"Her name is Marie Vallela, Italian heritage, of course. And what a great cook. She is not married, no kids, and nothing to tie her up socially. She told me, in the strictest confidence, she wants to sink her teeth into something substantial, something she can put her heart and soul into a meaningful and beneficial job where her opinion counts and her ideas have worth. When you come back from Riyadh, you will meet her. I know she will make you realize that we can't do without her—I hope so anyway. I think I've said enough for now. I have to get back to work. Oh yeah, which disguise are you using this trip? We have to get all your creds and passports ready to match whomever you are to be."

Charleston, South Carolina, Charleston International Airport, 2030 hours
Aboard Delta Airlines flight 607, Charleston, South Carolina, USA, to Lisbon, Portugal

John, posing as Dr. Hans Fenstermacher, PhD, soils engineer/geologist, has just settled in first-class section seat F-1 window. The airplane has only six rows of first-class seating, and John, for reasons of security, will only sit in the last row where he can watch every first-class passenger. His paranoia about airplane hijackings has made him a very cautious and alert traveler. After scanning the passengers and noting little things that made each one of them unique, he finally relaxed and assured himself this leg of the journey would be a piece of cake. The cabin attendant brought him some twelve-year-old Grey Goose Scotch. After three of these, he went off to sleep and didn't awaken till the change in pitch and sound of the engines told him they were getting close to Portugal. The pilots were Americans, most likely trained in either the navy or air force. John has a lot of confidence in military-trained pilots, albeit he is mostly self-trained. The large 747 was at the gate. Almost all of the passengers had off-loaded. John liked to get off last so he could scrutinize the swarm of people in the waiting area. He had a fear of being discovered by the customs people. But Dr. Fenstermacher sailed right through. Next up was if someone held a hand-lettered sign with his name on it. If that happened, he knew he was being set up for something nasty. In front of the Royal Saudi Airlines ticket counter, John discovered he had prepaid first-class tickets to Riyadh, Saudi Arabia. He glanced around, looking for anything or anyone that shouldn't be there. Again he came up empty. *My paranoia is starting to make me more than cautious. It's ageing me too much too fast. I better get to the bar and have a couple of soothing drinks. You can't buy an alcoholic drink on a Saudi airplane, and I sure don't want to take any pills. I need to be as alert as I can be. First, I got to find out who paid for the ride to the big sandbox.* "Yes, ma'am, you're sure it was Prince Abdulla Bin Aziz? Thank you." *I feel better now I know who secured these tickets for Dr. Fenstermacher. Helen and the prince get to be as thick as thieves when it comes to my concerns. God bless 'em both.*

After crossing the international dateline, it is 8:30 a.m., Lisbon time.

"Yes, operator, the number I dialed person-to-person, Mrs. Helen Raskousas, Scranton, Pennsylvania, USA. Hi, sugar, I know I probably woke you up. It is nighttime in Pennsylvania, isn't it?"

"Hi, John, what's up? Are you in trouble or something?"

"No, I am fine, and thank you for arranging with the prince the free ride to his country. No one else knows my identity, do they?"

"No, of course not, and stop being so paranoid—goddammit calling me at 3:00 a.m. Everything is going okay, and don't be checking in with me. You know your rules—just get in and get out. The prince is expecting you in Riyadh sometime today, your time. So don't go pulling a fast one and book a flight on another airline as you have been known to do."

"No, sweetheart, the good doctor is all right with the situation. Good-bye. Tell everybody I love 'em and will be home soon."

The customs waiting room, Riyadh International Airport, Saudi Arabia

"There he is," said Prince Riyaza. "Dr. Fenstermacher, I am so glad to see you again." The prince clasped John around both shoulders and, as was his custom, kissed John on both cheeks. John really hated this old Arabic and European custom, but he has to endure the theatrics in able to make the scene seem as palpable as it could be. "Come, Doctor, my helicopter awaits."

Once aboard the chopper, John started to relax. "So, my prince, tell me your troubles so I may help you."

"First, Johnny, while no one is looking, a toast to your health and a prayer to Allah for sending you to me. Johnny, we don't talk business." The prince was looking at the overhead and pointing in all directions. John caught the drift of the prince's gyrations and said very quietly, "You think your personal helo is bugged?" The prince nodded very vigorously with a sad–sack expression."

"Yes, Johnny, my enemies are everywhere. So we just relax and enjoy each other's company till we get to Al Ubaylah, my home in Ar Rub' al Khali, in the Empty Quarter. There we can talk in relative safety. You know the old saying, keep your friends close and your enemies closer. Nowhere in the world is that more relevant than here in the Middle East."

Ar Rub' al Khali, the Empty Quarter, Saudi Arabia

The multimillion dollar French Airbus helicopter made in Marignane, France, created a cloud of dust and sand as it landed near the main abode of the prince and his family. They are Bedouins and have lived the nomadic lifestyle, as their forefathers had for ages uncountable. This prince has homes in Riyadh, Lucerne, Paris, and Argentina. To say he and his family were very rich would be an understatement. He is more at home and more comfortable in the desert than anywhere in the world.

As John and the prince alight from the chopper, a servant leads the way to the large tent. They are met by another servant holding a tray with cold fruit drinks and finger food. As they recline on large pillows and eat, John finally says, "My friend, I need to know what it is you wish for me to do."

"Okay, Johnny, we can discuss my very great problem. And, my brother, nothing we say or do ever leaves this humble abode. The problem is with my oldest son, Fariq. He has taken up with the rebels who would destroy our world. He gambles away his money and spends it on whores. He also gives money to the worst terrorist organizations in the world. And he has been seen drunk in some of the finest hotels in the whole of Europe and America. He only talks to me to give him more money when his allowance is used up. Johnny, you are the only person who can stop him and bring him here to me. My brother, I tell you this with a sad heart. If you can't bring him here to me, kill him and any of his friends that you can. Then bring or send his body to me. He is a disgrace to Royal House of Saud and our family. If my brother, the king knew, of this behavior, he would make me kill Fariq. So, Johnny, none of this can be told to the CIA, not even your lover, the one with the red hair. She is too close to the American press."

"Prince, my brother, please tell me all of the story. I have known you too long, and I can see the torment in your soul. Don't hold out on me now. It could be very dangerous for my people and anyone connected to the terrorist groups, whether they know it or not. I give you my solemn promise I will deal with this problem as most professionally as possible. I know you are torn between the love for your firstborn and the innocent lives that could be lost because of his misguided religious fanaticism. There is more you want to tell me, so please place your trust in me. No harm or shame will come to your family or the Royal House of Saud. I will make this an undercover, off-the-books, even my books, operation so nobody will ever be the wiser, not my government or yours.

"Where is Fariq? And how many people does he have with him?"

"I don't know how many people he is using. One of my trusted bodyguards is on his staff. This man has been with me since we were children. I fear for his safety because Najib—that is his name—thinks that Fariq is onto him for passing on information about the Holy Crescent, which is the name of these religious fanatics. If this group finds out that Najib is an informer, they will kill him."

"My prince, where is he and his band of murderers?"

"Johnny, I am sorry to say they are in your country in the town of Las Vegas."

"Well, that makes sense. He can do a lot of harm in that part of the world. My prince, I am very tired. It was a long plane ride. May I please take advantage of a bed? We will talk more in the morning. And please don't worry so much. My people and I will do the will of Allah."

The International Airport, Riyadh, Saudi Arabia

Professor Fenstermacher, a.k.a. John Braz in disguise, is one of the last of the first-class passengers to board the flight returning to Lisbon, Portugal. John is beside himself because he can't notify the CIA as to what may be a very serious attempt to kill innocent Americans. The flight back to Portugal was short—thanks to a tailwind coming from the African continent.

John grabs the first taxi available and shouts to the driver. "The American consulate please." The driver was only too happy to appease John. The trip to the consulate was longer than any fare the driver had in two days. "Get there as fast as you dare, and there is one hundred extra euros for you." That was all this crazy taxi driver needed to hear. The beat-up old Mercedes took every turn on two wheels. Even John was a little uncomfortable, rolling around in the rear seat. At the front gate to the consulate, john paid the driver and gave him the extra euros and another fifty in American money. Bounding up the steps to the entrance, the marine guards held their rifles at the ready.

"Halt, senor, and stay right where you are," the lance corporal shouted in Spanish.

John knew better than to proceed any further. "I am an American, and I can identify myself," he shouted to the guards. "Please get a member of the military attache's office to speak with me. It is a very serious matter regarding national security."

"Okay, mister, drop the suitcase and open it using one hand and the other hand high above your head. Fingers spread open. Now approach the guard kiosk with your hands held high."

"Sergeant, did you not hear me? Call upstairs and tell whoever is in the desk that Mad Dog Braz is here on serious business."

"Mister, I don't know what kind of bullshit you are trying to pull. Just face the wall and put your hands on the surface. Spread your legs and shut the hell up, or I will be forced to kick your ass." John almost laughed in the marine's face. *This tough marine sergeant hasn't a clue who he is dealing with. But for now, I better do as they say. No use messing up this guy's face and career over a little pissing match. Good, here comes somebody now, wearin' a suit, so I guess he is important. Or thinks he is. Oh, oh, he pulled a .45 from a shoulder holster, and now he is cocking it. I better watch what I say to this asshole, or I might be going home in an aluminum coffin.*

With the pistol in his left hand and pointed at John, the suit speaks into a cell phone. "Now, mister, very slowly take out your ID and passport. Make one false move and you're dead." John knew an asshole when he saw one, and this idiot has first-class anal all over him. Slowly, John lowered his left arm and with his fingers only and opened his suit coat to reveal the pocket with his phony passport. Then with the right hand he very methodically pulled the passport out, handed it to the marine guard, and backed up to the wall of the guard kiosk. The suit grabbed the passport from the hand of the marine, looked at the picture of John, and got pissed off. The picture and other info all seemed to be in order. He got on the phone and started yelling at whomever he was connected to. "Yes, sir, it looks legit, and the picture matches the guy we have at gunpoint. Now, Mr. Braz, or whomever you claim to be, what are you doing here?"

"That's none of your business, and you don't have a high-enough salary to know what I am doing here. So you can go screw yourself till someone from the CIA gets here. If you think you are scaring me with that pistol, think again, because in a second, I can have that weapon shoved so far up your ass it will stick out your ear. Now get somebody from the station chief's office down here pronto. Sergeant, you look like a marine who knows what's happening here. Please call upstairs and tell the lady on the desk that Captain Braz, US Army, retired, is needing some assistance."

John is thinking, *Why is it when I am in a hurry, there is always some frigging idiot in the way? Ah, here comes somebody I recognize.*

"Captain Braz, Captain Braz," this person was saying as he was running toward the group. "Captain Braz, it's me, Major Evans. We have been looking for you for two days now. I am so glad you showed up here. The deputy director is on my butt day and night."

"Major Evans, good to see there is somebody with brains at this little piece of America. When I saw you last, you were a first lieutenant. You must be on the good side of the promotion board."

"Aw, no, sir, I just worked harder than the rest of the guys."

"Let me say something to the marine guards first before we go inside. Sergeant and Corporal, of course, you didn't know who or what I was. But I am impressed with the way you followed protocol and your orders. Your superiors will surely hear about this incident from the right side of the tracks. Keep up the good work, and Semper Fi."

"John, that was very nice of you to commend those marines. They work very hard trying to keep us safe here in spite of the assholes from the State Department. Let's get to my office on the double. Ms. Diskin must know you are here by now. This command has more leaks than a sieve, and I mean the state side, not the military side."

On the phone with Laura, "Yes, dear, I know, dear, but give me a minute and I will explain everything." John holds the phone in one hand and covers the mike with the other hand. "Damn, she is really pissed off at me this time. Laura, please let me talk. What I have to say is of the utmost importance. We have a national security situation brewing in the state of Nevada."

"Oh, as if I didn't know you aren't the only one with friends, Jack."

"Darling, you know how I hate it when you call me that. You know I hated that president."

"Listen to me, sugar, you get your ass back to Langley as fast as you can. The director, the president, the secretary of defense, and little ole me need to hear what the prince whispered in your hot little ear. Now do it and don't dawdle. And no side trips to Pennsylvania either. I sent the G-55 to Lisbon to fetch you. You have to be wheels up and out over the Atlantic in two hours. Oh, and PS, I love you."

"Well, Major Evans—it's Jerry, am I correct?"

"Yes, Captain Braz, I was with the 114th down in the Delta when you borrowed the Russian helo. Then they sent me to SF Camp 105 at Lai Khe. Soon after, that senator was found dead. They closed that camp down and destroyed the whole side of the mountain so the Cong could not use it. We booby trapped everything for a hundred yards around that piece of real estate. I guess the Charlies got a good surprise when we left."

"Jerry, how did you end up in the CIA?"

"I was wounded at the battle of Hue, and they said I could never be a paratrooper again. So I requested an interview with the company, and here I am. I know you're probably sick of flying, having been on airplanes nonstop for four days, but the G-55 is here and being readied and refueled for the trip back over the Atlantic. How about an early dinner and some delicious Portuguese wine? Then you can sleep all the way back to the land of the big PX."

"I want to give Ms. Diskin a case of this wine. She hinted it was some of the best in the world. And I could use the brownie points also."

Washington Dulles International Airport

Alighting from the CIA's Gulfstream jet, John is met by none other than Ms. Laura Diskin and her driver and her bodyguards. "Boy, darling, you really meant it when you asked me to be here as quickly as possible." After a quick kiss and embrace, "Okay, tell me what you know in a nutshell before we get in the car."

"Do you think your car is bugged?"

"I know it is. I had it bugged. I have to know every single thing that goes down in and out of the secure offices and elsewhere."

"We may have a national security crisis on our hands."

"So please tell me all you can in the next few minutes."

"Okay, sugar, but you got to let me in on your info also.

"It goes like this: the son of Prince Abdulla Bin Riyaza is tied in with a terrorist organization called the Holy Crescent. He wants me and my people to capture the son. His name is Fariq Bin Riyaza, and this little bastard wants to start a war all by himself. The prince, through his informers, knows the son is in Las Vegas. This formidable group is made up of ex-military men from all over the Middle East. They hate Americans. Their holy mission is to cause as much pain and suffering to as many people as possible. They can't get their hands on nuclear weapons, so they are trying to bring into the United States dangerous biological pathogens. I don't know what form or shape they are being transported to the States? All I know is the system for getting this bunch of garbage to here will be coming through Canada."

"Okay, John, that makes sense. We have been picking up a lot of commo from somewhere in Nevada and Nova Scotia. Now we just have to find out where in Nova Scotia the sleeper cell is holed up."

Waiting at the CIA building in Langley, Virginia, was Mr. Casey. He was not a happy camper today. In fact he was pissed off knowing that Laura pumped the secret information out of John before he could be in on the knowledge coming out of the Middle East. In a very nice but demanding sort of way, Mr. Casey wanted to know what the hell is going on in Canada and Nevada. Laura brought him up to date on the project and said, "We better get some real-time answers as to why the Royal Canadian Mounted Police, special police, have not conferred with the CIA in this matter."

"Because they are too goddamned liberal and can't find their ass in the dark. I have to get back to my office. Myself and my staff have to go and find this little princeling bastard and shake the friggin information from him."

"I will help you guys with whatever info I find. Maybe we can find out what these people are trying to accomplish."

CHAPTER TWENTY-NINE

"Wait, John, you can't go yet. We have a fair amount of talking to do. We can't do it in my office—too many ears."

"Okay, darling, what do you suggest?"

"I am taking the day as a personal day. We are going to my home in Calvert County."

"That's fine with me, but you have to get me back to BWI to catch a flight to Pennsylvania."

"That's all right, John. We have so much to discuss about us and my position, which by the way, the president wants me to be the next director."

"I knew that was going to happen, as did everyone in Washington DC. What's next, the White House? Darling, I do believe the power in this town has gotten to you as it has every other person in a responsible position."

"Yes, sweetheart, maybe it has, but I can do a lot better for the American people than some of the past directors. I have charming pussy power nobody else had."

"Yes, you do, my love, yes, you do. Darling, use your charms and intellect for the whole good. God knows you don't need money. We have enough between us to last three lifetimes. So, Laura, I mean this now with all sincerity, please marry me today? Let's not waste another ten years without each other. You know I love you more than life itself. Let's go to a judge or a justice of the peace or a rabbi or even a priest if we could find one. Just let's do it and put all my trepidations and worries behind us."

"Johnny Braz, you know I love you, but right now, I can't deal with marriage and a career, especially a long-distance marriage, with you in Scranton or around the world somewhere. I need to have you where I know where you are and what you are doing 24/7. I can't keep my mind on the job and be wondering what and whom you are doing something with. Notably because of the nature of our work puts us all at one time or another in harm's way. Now you want to go after the son of a Saudi prince. That in itself could be a very dangerous undertaking. What we know of these people is they are killers and terrorists. So be careful where you go after these guys. As Muslims, this life is not the one that counts—their life in paradise is what the stupid assholes aim for any way they can reach it. And please don't take those young girls along on another mission. I don't care how well trained you think they are. Helen says they aren't ready for prime time, and you should respect her judgment. She has been around this game a long time, and no one is a better judge of character than Helen Raskousas. And I am still pissed off that you took her from me."

"Yes, baby, but you have someone just as good in Rosalee Kowolski. And for your information only, Helen gave me her retirement notice. We are training a new lady for her position."

The ride to Southern Maryland, Laura's house, was brief. Laura and John had a long talk about their future lives together and apart. At the house overlooking the Chesapeake Bay, the lovers settled on the upholstered rattan couch, each with a scotch on the rocks and in a relaxed atmosphere, created by getting out the long suppressed feelings and ideas each had about the other. John's thoughts coming to life are articulated by his somewhat disappointed realizations that he and Laura would not make her daddy a very happy Irishman by letting him plan the biggest wedding Chicago had ever see. John was happy, though; he knew she wasn't ready to get married, but someday it would happen, he knew, when she was over the power-snatching phase. He was shaken from his reverie by the ringing of his phone. "Hello, John here" he answered. "Hi, Helen, I was just thinking I better make arrangements to get back to Scranton. I'm so glad you called. If anything is important, I will address it tomorrow, unless you think I should know now. Good, everything is okay for now. Helen, send the Piper Apache to BWI in the morning to pick me up at ten o'clock. Thank you. And how is Marie coming along? Tell the staff there will be a briefing in my secure office at 1100 hours, okay, and I want everybody there on time."

After a long nap and a swim in the pool, Laura and John went to Skipper's Pier in Deale, Maryland, for supper courtesy of Captain Cindy, one of the fishing charter boat captains. Cindy's old bay-built wooden boat, circa 1935, was well maintained and breezed through the water like a million-dollar yacht. It was after 10:00 p.m. when they got back to the house. They showered together, and John shaved. Their lovemaking was at a sexual peak, so high, Laura's guards moved to another part of the house. It was 3:00 a.m. before both lovers crept into the arms of Morpheus and enjoyed the sleep of the innocent.

Laura and several of her bodyguards left the house late the next morning. The temptation of an early morning lovemaking was too good to pass up. One of the bodyguards drove John to the airport at Baltimore. There waiting for him in the Apache was, of all people, Ann Marie. John was completely blown away. He knew she was taking flying lessons. It had not occurred to him that she was so far advanced in getting a commercial ticket that she could fly passengers. She sat there in the left seat with her chest stuck out with pride, the earphones tipped up on her baseball hat, and the biggest grin on her beautiful face. Of course, she had to say something smart, like "Hey, buddy, can I fly you somewhere?" John quickly ran around the plane, got on the wing near the passenger door, opened it, threw his kit in the rear seats, and sat down. John's eyes were as big as silver dollar as he reached over, grabbed Annie by her shoulders, and kissed her right on those full pink lips. It was a full thirty seconds' kiss.

"My goodness, baby, I am so freaking proud of you. Let me see your logbook and your license. This calls for a party one weekend when we have the time."

"Oh, John, thank you. I was worried you would insist I not fly home until you made me fly a check ride with you."

"Baby, cut the crap, turn this buggy on, turn into the wind, and get us back to the Lackawanna Valley. I am not going to say a word till the wheels are on the ground at Avoca Airport. Oh, and by the way, you look very pretty today."

"Thank you, John. I was wondering if you realized I was a female—barring that one time, of course." John did not want to go there. That statement by Annie was a field full of land mines. "By the way, John, I did a preflight check just before you got here. I thought you might want to do another with me?"

"No, Annie, if you said it's done, that's good enough for me. I always knew I could trust you for anything."

"Okay then, I'll start her up and let's do it. Baltimore Ground Control, this is Apache Niner, Aztec, three, victor, asking for takeoff permission."

"Apache NA-3V, proceed to taxiway 2 south. Hold behind US Air commuter. You are third for departure." After planes one and two had taken off, Apache NA-3V, hold at the threshold, one inbound Gulfstream, then wait for the green light. There's the green light, Apache. Turn onto Runway 92, and it's your turn. The wind is at your twelve, gusting at eight knots. Take off and climb to angels five and make a right turn. Continue climbing to ten thousand feet and set your course. Good-bye, and come see us again."

"Thank you, Baltimore. My course is set for Avoca Port, Wilkes-Barre, Scranton."

1120 hours, the secure office of the Guardian Security Co. Inc.

"Good morning, everybody. First things first. Annie, stand up. Everybody, this is our newest pilot, and I personally am so darn proud of her. Let's give her a great big hand, for she did in half the time what takes more experienced guys the time to learn to fly and ground school included to do. There will be a catered lunch here today in honor of Ms. Ann Marie Casey and party at a later date at my house. Now, everybody, the pictures in front of you and the images on the screen are of Prince Fariq Bin Riyaza, the son of one of the best clients we have and a good friend of the United States of America. This prince Fariq is a no-good rotten bastard. We will just leave it at that for now. He and his band of terrorists are preparing a nasty surprise for the people of Nevada. We have to apprehend this little shit and take him back to his father or kill him and as many of his boys as possible. They call themselves the Holy Crescent, and true to form, they are religious fanatics and very dangerous.

"I am putting together a team to go with me to Vegas and do only, and I mean only, surveillance work. We have to find the little prince before his plans are implemented. His father has a mole in the Holy Crescent infrastructure. We need to find him. He can give me the info to take down the whole rotten bunch. This I will work on by myself. The rest of you will do the surveillance work. The team will consist of Mickey and Carol, Ann Marie and Mary Ann, Jim Corbetta and Rob Gaudio. You will work in pairs, boy and a girl acting like husband and wife. It will take some good acting to get by the Arabs with a lot of street smarts. Most of these guys have paramilitary training, so they are good.

"Our good friends in Las Vegas are setting us up on the second floor of a five-star hotel, including meals, valet service, the use of all the facilities including the pool, the gym, the casino floor, etc. We obviously don't use valet service. Some could be sending us a bomb. Laura and company are setting us up with a clearing team to sweep the suite's four times a day for hidden cameras, bugs, or anything that could harm us or the mission. The three suites we will occupy are conjoined, and the windows are soundproofed, so someone with a parabolic microphone can't hear what we say inside. We are taking two planes, both with people and equipment that we need to pull this off. We will need some extra volunteers to come out after we are established to work the computers and other equipment. Every hand in the room shot up. That's what I love about this group—everyone is a patriot and willing to go in harm's way. We are taking the Apache and the Beech Queen Air. Mickey, you're pilot 1 on the Queen Air. Ann Marie, you are pilot 1 on the Apache. We leave tomorrow morning at 0700 hours. Remember, it is very hot in Vegas this time of year, so dress to fit the time day or night."

McCarran International Airport, 1300 hours

The Howard W. Cannon Aviation Museum. In order to maintain the general theme of typical Americans on vacation, the group tours the aviation museum in order to get in character. They can rehearse their respective roles to get comfortable with each other. After the drill was complete and a once-over by John, the teams got into the limos provided by the CIA. Only four people in that group were ever in this city before, so it would not be hard to look the part of tourists. Out Tropicana Avenue to Las Vegas Boulevard north to the hotel up near Circus-Circus, the limos pulled under the porte-cochere and unloaded the luggage and passengers. Then the limos pulled around back and in the underground garage, unloaded all the weapons, electronic gear, computers, etc. The private service elevator whisked everything up to the second floor. Conventional wisdom dictates that they be on a high a floor as possible. John wanted to be as close to the ground as possible to be able to respond to a situation ASAP. Besides, the CIA has used this hotel on previous occasions, and a hidden shaft is prewired to connect the gear to hidden antenna on the roof. The concierge is an ex-NSA operative on the payroll of the CIA. As the bellhops wheeled the luggage carts to the elevator bank, a swarthy Arabic type dropped a fifty on the floor behind John. Mary Ann noticed and reached in her bag, coming out with a Beretta 9 mm cocked and ready to shoot, all the while shouting a heads-up to John. "I am so sorry, sir, I mean no harm. I believe you dropped this and wanted to return it to you."

"Mary Ann, put that away, and good thinking. We are all right now." John got in the lift with the luggage cart, slowly unfolded the fifty-dollar bill, and extracted the note inside, only after checking the ceiling and four ceiling corners for hidden cameras. The note had written on it "Najib Mahood" and a cell number. John eyeballed the bellhop and smiled, for he at last had a lead. John took out the key card and handed it to Najib to open the door to the suite. Once inside, they went into the bathroom. John turned on all the water faucets in order to make as much noise as possible. He also turned up the volume dial for the piped-in music. Getting as close to Najib as possible, John whispered, "Do you have any news for me?"

"Yes, kind sir, I can tell you when the prince comes into town and where his whereabouts will be at a certain time."

"Very good, Najib," as John handed him back his fifty and another fifty with it. "Where is the prince now?" John asked.

"He is at the safe house."

"Where is that, Najib? I need to know, and I need to know right now."

"They won't let me know. The prince knows I am a spy for his father, and he keeps me in town all the time. He says I am too valuable to be away from the casino for any length of time. I keep him informed of the high rollers at the gaming tables. I do know the house is in a place called Sunrise Manor on the street called Lake Mead Boulevard. I do not know the number. The house is a rental property, and I don't know the owners."

"That's okay, Najib. You told us enough to give me a good idea where to look for that unholy alliance. Now what is it they are transporting from Canada that is so dangerous?"

"Oh, Mr. John, that is only a decoy—how you call a red herring—to throw anybody off the trail of the real dangerous cargo."

"Great, Najib. You did a good job. Now you better get back to your regular duties before somebody misses you—then you might be in real deep trouble."

Everybody was squared away in their suites when John called them together. "Gang, we have a good lead on the safe house. I am going to see if I can find it. In the meantime, you guys get your teams on the Strip and make like tourists. I'll be back about 1700 hours. If anybody comes up with something, don't try to be a hero. We will plan a way to snatch the prince when we have more info. When Gen. Omar Bradley helped win the war in Europe, he did so with careful and thoughtful planning, and keeping Generals Patten, Truscott, and White from getting too far ahead of their supply lines and being outflanked by the Nazis. We have to play it cool also. We can't tip our hand before we know the quarry can be caught. Now go out there and have fun, but not too much fun."

Chapter Thirty

Lake Mead Boulevard, Las Vegas, 1430 hours

I think I am on the wrong street. This boulevard is a major artery. I need to go up or down a block where I can see the houses are a little closer together. Let me turn right down Lamb Street and a left on E. Bonanza Road. Ah, that's more like it. This looks more likely a neighborhood to hole up in if you were trying not to bring any undue attention on oneself. This looks promising. Up ahead two houses, a guy is taking trash to the curb. Must be pickup day? Let me swing by and talk to this fella. He has the Middle Eastern complexion. "Hello, sir, can you tell me how to get back to the interstate?"

Mustafa is thinking, *These stupid Americans. This is their country, they live here, yet they don't know how to get from place to place.* He answers John, "Turn around and go back seven blocks. You will be right on it."

"Thanks, buddy, I'll do that."

I am not your buddy, you infidel. "Allah be praised."

Again, John is thinking, *I am one lucky son of a bitch. We just hit the jackpot. How many Arabs can be in this kind of a neighborhood? We have to come back after dark and properly surveil this house. Too many eyes in the daylight, and we don't want the local cops on our ass.*

About 3:30 a.m. John, Rob, and Mickey parked in the lot of the Desert Pines Golf Clubhouse and hiked the two blocks back to the house on East Bonanza Road. There are no streetlights, so this place in the desert was pitch-black—all the more easier to try to get a peek in the windows. "No such luck, this place has every shade and blind drawn tighter than a drunk on payday. Okay, so now we take the garbage bags we brought and empty the garbage cans into them and lam it outta here. Back at our hotel, we will be able to tell how many and what kind of people we might be dealing with." At the hotel, going through the trash from East Bonanza Road, they found enough evidence to convince everybody that they had the correct safe house. Since there were no cars in the driveway and no lights on in that house, also no noise of any kind, John was certain the group was downtown on the Strip. Everybody got dressed in the appropriate clothes. The same teams went into different casinos, looking for the bad guys with orders not to try to apprehend the prince. John's idea was to break in the safe house and set up an ambush to either capture or kill the prince. John went to the personnel door of the garage; he knew he could get in the house that way. Using a set of lock picks, the garage door was a breeze. He waited just a second in a low crouch to hear if there were dogs. *No dogs, good,* he said to himself, but there was a Mercedes with the keys in the ignition. He took the keys and opened the trunk; this was an expensive car, so there are side panels made of leather covering the wheel wells. Just the right place to hide a bug and a transponder. When that job was finished, he went in through the kitchen—again no alarms, so with the small penlight, he found his way to the bedrooms and the room with computers he assumed was an office. He planted one hearing and one microscopic TV camera in the ceiling light. In the bedrooms, he just planted regular bugs. The place was very neat, meaning these terrorists have a cleaning service; they would not stoop to doing women's work. They are wrapped up in their own self-importance. John wondered how often the cleaning service stops by. If they find the surveillance devices, these people will move to a new location. The house looked very neat and clean; no dishes in the sink or on the counter, no papers lying around, no bottles or cans in the trash. *Which leads me to conclude, the cleaning was done today, which gives me a window to formulate my plan.* John made his way back to through the garage, slipped out the same way he came in, and started to go the two blocks over to his car. When two sets of car lights lit up the street, he dove for cover next to some bushes separating the house next door. He waited till all the occupants were in the house before he got up and, sticking to the shadows, made his way back to his car. He is thankful this is a new development and the streetlights were not operable yet.

At the hotel, 0430 hours

Everybody had a story to relate. Mary Ann and Rob stood next to several of the bodyguards as the prince rolled dice. Ann Marie an Jim watched the prince and his head man argue about a prostitute the prince wanted to take back to the safe house. That did not happen. Good thing for the girl; she would have been killed and her body dumped in the desert. Mickey and Carol engaged in a conversation with a dealer, the pit boss, and the two remaining bodyguards. The dealer and pit boss were both Saudis, and Mickey speaks Urdu, Farsi, Paki, and several dialects of Saudi Arabic.

There will be no sleep for this crew tonight. In fact, the sun will be up in a few hours anyway. Mickey was listening to the conversations of the bad guys. "John," he said with a lot of concern in his voice, "we got to act fast. They keep talking about the trucks meeting up at the intersection of Las Vegas Boulevard and Flamingo Road."

"Holy crap," said Rob, "that's on the Strip. There are four major casinos at that intersection the Bellagio, Bally's, Caesars Palace, and the Flamingo at any time, day or night. There could be hundreds, if not thousands, of people in the streets and in the casinos."

"Well," said Mary Ann, "we know where and maybe we know something is going to be blown up or people gunned down, or worse. John, I think we better have another talk with Najib, and real soon?"

"I agree, Mary Ann. The rest of you, keep monitoring the computers and the one with the camera. Annie, I know you don't like her, but get on the phone with Laura. Let her know what we know and get any info she will give you. Please do it as a favor to me."

"Boss, you don't have to ask me like that. I can handle that bitch—I mean, woman with all the finesse in the world."

Down in the basement of the hotel where Najib lives, John and Mary Ann make their way to his apartment. With guns drawn and the safeties off, Mary Ann knocks on the door. "Najib, hello, are you there?" No answer. She knocks again and tries the lock.

John says, "Let me use this." He has a master key card. They enter and go from the living room to the bedroom—no luck. The kitchen is next, same thing. Upon entering the bathroom, they find Najib lying in the tub with his tongue cut from his mouth, his throat sliced from ear to ear. "Ah, crap, Mary Ann. I figured they had made us and knew Najib was the rat. That is their warning to people—they cut out their tongue as a retaliation. The poor bastard, he got to his paradise earlier than expected."

"Oh, John, I am so sorry. What do we do now?"

"We let the hotel manager handle this. Remember, this operation is undercover and off the books. The CIA will clean up this mess. They will ship his body back to Saudi Arabia, and no one will be the wiser." Back on the second-floor suites, Annie had news from Laura about the trucks. It seems that the truck sent from Nova Scotia was a red Herring. The Holy Crescent group bought two tanker trucks that look like milk transporters from a dealer that is going out of business in a place called Dolan Springs, Arizona. None of the trucks have the HMR identifiers (hazardous materials regulations), NRC, or OSHA certification papers. So we know that these vehicles will only travel at night. Okay, guys, let's put our heads together and figure out what is in those tankers."

After an hour of looking at every kind of liquid, from rancid milk to molasses, Annie comes up with "I remember from high school chem. class that if you mix chlorine with ammonia, you get a deadly toxic and poisonous substance that will kill you in a matter of seconds. It will peel the paint off of cars and burn a person so bad it's as bad or worse than nuclear radiation."

"Annie. Annie, baby, I think you got it. When I worked on fishing boats in west Texas near Corpus Christi, I remember that in that part of the world was a lot of chemical plants. It would not take much to ship tanker trucks west on Route 10 to Phoenix, Arizona, to the north to Las Vegas. Great thinking, Annie, and, Jim, I'll call the National Institute of Health and talk to one of the scientific eggheads to see what has to occur to create a disaster of the magnitude that will kill a lot of people. In the meantime, get to the state police of Texas, Arizona, and Nevada to alert them of uncertified tankers traveling through their respective states, but not to apprehend at this time. We can't let the Holy Crescent know we have their plan. They could push up their time table and do the deed somewhere else. And we have to find those tankers and get a transponder on each one so we can stop this madness before a disaster occurs."

When the teams were posing as married couples, they were indiscreetly photographing the individual members of the Holy Crescent group. The pictures were sent electronically to the CIA lab at Langley, Virginia. All the men were in the crime base data system of the FBI. Laura sent the identified photos back to the team's computer. The men are identified as Mustafa Haleed and Hassan Farhla from Yemen; Mohamed Halibi, Hussien Narid, and Ali Bin Kalhid from Saudi Arabia; and Narid Al Mahood, an Iranian. All are wanted for crimes in their respective countries and wanted by Interpol.

John had sent Mickey and Carol back to the neighborhood where the safe house is. They rented a used pickup truck and went to the far east end of Bonanza Street, posing as construction workers. One of the almost completed houses has windows facing the safe house, where Mickey set up a heavy-duty parabolic microphone and a tripod mounted surveying theodolite machine that was rebuilt as a camera. He hired a couple of workers to pretend to survey the last few new homes at the end of the street. The purpose was to keep watch on the comings and goings of the bad guys. It paid off handsomely, for the bad guys crew was down to only four bodyguards plus the prince.

Back at the hotel, the two missing guys were ID'd as the two Yemenis. Both were experienced truck drivers and heavy equipment operators. Rob and Mary Ann drove south to Dolan Springs to try and interview the people who sold the tankers to the bad guys. They were told some Arab guys found out the trucks were up for sale before the bank could reclaim them. It was on the Internet that the tankers were to be sold at auction. The seller said a big Mercedes with the Arabs came by and handed him a wad of cash more than he asked for and drove off with the trucks. He said he didn't care who bought them; he was glad to be out from under the debt. He said they went south toward Phoenix. They asked about how far it was to a motel and restaurant. Rob showed the dealer some phony FBI ID and said to keep this under his hat, as he slipped him a hundred-dollar bill. The man was only too happy to agree. "Mary Ann, we have got to find those trucks and somehow put a transponder on each of them. I know it won't be easy, but we can do it." Traveling southeast on

Interstate 10, near the small town of Benson, they spotted the tankers partially hidden behind a rundown motel.

"I see them," Mary Ann said.

"Yeah, I spotted them too. Now we have to park somewhere in back of that motel and wait till it's dark before we can make a move." At about 10:00 p.m., they crept over to the trucks, and each one crawled up the ladder on the side of the tank, peeled off the plastic coating to expose the sticky surface of the bug, and stuck it in a place under the ladder where no one would look for it. Most of the bugs were magnetic and could adhere to almost any place on the rig. But the tankers were almost all aluminum, and the magnets would not adhere to the nonferrous metal. The sticky adhesive invented by the army served this purpose very well. Rob called John back in Vegas. John reported the bug was activated and was working well. John told Rob and Mary Ann to get back to Las Vegas and not proceed any further south because he surmised the Arabs paid off the dealer to let them know if anybody was on their trail. "At least with the bugs on the trucks, we will know exactly where the tankers are at all times."

John reported to Laura the situation as he knew it. He figured the tankers were headed to Texas and some illegal chemical storage facility. Traveling at night only, it would take a day and a half to get there and three or four days to get back to Las Vegas. That left five or six days at the most to apprehend the bad guys and prevent a disaster. In the meantime, John was going to nab the prince and keep his promise to the father. This sounds easy enough, but the prince is never too far away from his bodyguards. John thinks he will have to catch him with a prostitute, when his guard is let down and his bodyguards aren't close enough to help. John will need his whole crew to pull this one off.

Three nights later, 11:30 p.m., on Interstate 10 west

"Mustafa, my brother, can we pull off at the next truck stop? I am so very hungry."

"Hassan, I told you no unnecessary chatter on this CB channel. Pull over if you wish. Hussien is going to be angry with us." At the truck stop restaurant, Mustafa never let off of Hassan. In Arabic, he chided him for not asking Allah for the strength to go further faster.

Hassan was afraid the police would get them for traffic violations, and if they found out about the illegal cargo, they would spend a lot of years in a southern jail—worse yet, they would not get to martyr themselves and kill hundreds of the American devils.

"This has got to be the night," Jim Corbetta says to the team. "The prince has gone for quite a while without getting laid. I'll bet he goes after a hooker tonight."

"I tend to agree with you, jimmy, but we have to be 100 percent certain that we get the bodyguards first. We could have an international incident if this doesn't go right. Do we know which casino he is at?"

"Yes," Annie says, "he is right under our feet."

"What a stroke of bad luck. The feds know that this place is a CIA hangout. We are doubly screwed if some liberal reporter finds out what we are up to. Okay, everybody, get your teams together. Let's play this one like we know what end is up."

The casino and the bars were doing a lively business as the three teams and John strode around the floor. John's earpiece crackled with Mary Ann saying the prince is chatting up a cute little hooker at the Mayfair Bar in the small gaming room at the rear of the building. John spoke for everybody to concentrate on the bodyguard assigned to each team. He would take the fourth guy out. The prince and the cutie left the bar and went to the elevator corridor, got on, and went up to the third floor. The bodyguards left, and one went to the left staircase, two got on another elevator, and the fourth guy went to his demise in the left staircase. John was ready for him and, with his suppressed HK P9, shot the guy in the forehead. He dragged the body to the basement, left word with the manager's office that more cadavers are on the way, then ran up three flights of stairs only to encounter one towel head holding his chest and watching the blood pouring from the small hole Annie just put there with her 9 mm Beretta. Mickey and Carol had the last two bad guys at gunpoint in the elevator. John, Mary Ann, and Rob made the Arabs lie in the floor, while John disabled the elevator car so no one could use it. With flex cuffs on, the Arabs were taken to the basement and held in the secure room the CIA used as a staging area. The other two dead guys were also deposited in this room, and all four were held until Langley decided what to do with them.

The team got on another elevator and went back up to the third floor. By this time, Jim knew what room the prince and the cute little hooker were using. The whole team split up alongside each side of the door. John used his master key card to break in. He shoved the door to the inside, but the chain lock was secured, and the door would only open two inches. "Shit," he said, backing up and throwing his shoulder and all his weight against the door, tearing the key chain lock from the jamb. The cute little hooker was totally engaged in her profession. The prince was halfway snockered and reeling from the way the girl was treating him. Both of them together could not have prevented John from entering the room, except the prince had his PPK 9 mm pistol pointed at John. He cocked it and got off a round, which went wild and missed John by a foot. That was his last mistake, for John drilled two holes through the heart in less than one second.

The girl wasn't even fazed by these events, as if this was a normal thing that happened all the time. She grabbed her dress so no blood would soil it and put her underwear on and then put the dress on. She then asked John if he could reach in the prince's pants pocket and pay her the thousand he promised her. John obliged her and gave her all the cash in the pocket of the pants. He took out the fake FBI identification and showed the girl. He said, "Forget everything you saw here tonight, or you could be in big trouble. Do you understand?" She nodded yes, and John let her go. She got on the elevator and was not seen again.

John called the manager. He came right up together with his special employees who were all on the payroll of the CIA. The prince's body was taken to a mortuary in a funeral home out in the desert. John called Laura and played out the scene as it almost happened. She was relieved to know it worked out so well. No publicity surrounded this incident, and that was and always is a major concern when the CIA is involved in an incident in the continental United States. Now the team has to deal with the tanker trucks. The leadership of the bad guys is dead, and John knows these guys can't make a decision to save their ass, so he knows they will follow the last order and crash these trucks—only they will try to crash into each other at the intersection of Las Vegas Boulevard and Flamingo Road. John has to take out these trucks before they get near any large population.

John has to monitor the exact location of the tankers and find someone who has an intimate knowledge of the roads these guys will be using to get into the Las Vegas Strip. That next morning, he pays a visit to the largest over-the-road trucking company in this part of Nevada. John explains in a roundabout way the situation that is engulfing the whole region. He needs to talk to an experienced driver who knows the two main roads, Interstate 95/93 and 515. He needs to know this so he can set up an ambush to take out these deadly cargo carriers. The owner of this trucking outfit was a military veteran, and he was more than willing to help out because he knew these roads better than any of his drivers; he was born and raised in this part of the country. Within the hour, they were wheels up and flying south-southeast of Las Vegas and Boulder City.

John was on the radio conversing with the team back at the hotel, keeping tabs on the location and assumed headings of the trucks. The sniper teams had all their gear set up and ready to fly to wherever John decided was the best place to ambush the tankers. For now it was still daylight and too risky to move the tankers. The two drivers were parked in the back of the same place they bought the rigs from. Both drivers had been praying to Allah all day and were fasting and praying again. They knew tonight was the last night they would spend on this earth alive. Mustafa was concerned why they could not get in touch with the others. Hassan assured him it was so they would not be distracted from their holy jihad. Both drivers were giddy with anticipation of becoming martyrs and entering paradise and being welcomed by the seventy-two virgins.

Annie talked to John in the helo and told him the tankers were at Dolan Springs, and she didn't expect them to move for at least five to six hours. Mr. Madison, the trucking company owner, said he knew exactly where they could set up a roadblock and ambush. "Annie, get us another helo and bring the whole team and all my gear to these coordinates as soon as possible."

"John, I can't fly a helo yet."

"Yes, I know. Mickey will do the honors. Just get to these coordinates as soon as you can."

"Roger, John, I read you loud and clear. See you soon." She wanted to say "I love you," but she wasn't ready to commit to that yet.

She was pleased with herself and yelled, "Yahoo." Mickey sent a steady stream of bullets into the engine and the cab. As John had assumed, Hassan tried to bail out the passenger door. He was shot twice before he hit the ground. The first-in-line truck received the same treatment from Annie's machine gun. As the rounds hit the engine compartment, the fiberglass hood, and fenders just shredded and dropped off the cab. Annie could see the silhouette of Mustafa Haleed in the cab, and she raked the cab with just enough rounds to kill him instantly. John ordered all to stop firing. The trucks never got up enough momentum to gain some speed, so they just ground to a halt. John ordered everyone to secure all weapons and return the same to the choppers. He and Jim along with Rob checked the bodies and inspected the tankers for any stray penetrating rounds. Both drivers had gone to their Islamic paradise, and the tankers were in good shape. Carol, who had been sitting in the one helo, monitoring the chatter on the headsets, brought over to John two body bags. She knew John would bring the dead Saudis bodies back to the prince Abdulla Bin Riyaza for burial in the Saudi Arabian desert.

Mr. Madison was all worked up. "I have not been this alive since I was a teenager." He was talking to anybody who would listen. "John, I can see what you do is vitally important to the people of America. I can get these trucks out of here tonight. If you want me to, I'll just call my office and have my guys bring over a couple of wreckers and cabs. When the FBI comes snooping around, there won't be anything to see except a lot of empty shell casings. I can have my grandsons pick up the brass and sell it to the junk dealer also."

"Okay, Mr. Madison, but we will have to clear it with the CIA first. They will want to find out what to do with the chemicals."

The teams returned to the North Las Vegas Private Airport. All the equipment, including the weapons, were loaded back on the Apache and the Beech Queen Air. John sent all the team members back to Pennsylvania. He stayed behind to clean up a few things. He first went out to the safe house in Sunrise Manor. With two assets from the hotel staff, they went through the residence from stem to stern, gathering up any monies, computers, laptops, and personal properties of the late Holy Crescent group. Everything including the cash was given to the CIA. The eggheads, back east at Langley, would put to good use any intel on those computers. John returned to

The whole team arrived at the coordinates John gave them in less than an hour. John explained the order of battle, so to speak. The two tanker trucks will be coming down the one-way road out of the defunct dealer's parking area. They will be traveling less than twenty miles per hour, for the road is a gravel-paved secondary tributary. The ambush points are to be set up a hundred yards apart. Both points have a heavy machine gun position. One ambush setting, the first one has the Barrett .50 cal automatic rifle. This weapon can destroy a truck or car motor in a second. The ambush points are to be on the same side of the road so no one gets hit by friendly fire. Except a sniper with a Browning .303 rifle equipped with a night vision scope will be on the opposite side in case the driver decides to bail out the passenger side of the cab. He can be immediately dispatched by the sniper. The heavy machine guns John brought from their headquarters in Pennsylvania will tear up a truck motor, stopping the vehicle within a few yards. The idea is to not harm the tank part holding the chemicals. The first truck to be shot will be the second truck in the line, if the first truck was disabled. The second truck could run into it and cause the accident, which John is trying to prevent. So the second truck will be the first victim. As soon as the firing starts, the second ambush team waits five seconds and starts tearing up the cab in the first tanker. The shooting is to be precise so as not to penetrate the chemical tanks. Rob, an ex-marine sniper, will be on the .303 rifle, Mickey will be the machine gun shooter, and Mary Ann will operate the .50 cal automatic weapon. The second team farther down the road will have Ann Marie as the machine gun operator, Jim Corbetta, another ex-marine, across the road in a hidden position with a .303 sniper rifle, and John on the phones directing the operation. Mr. Madison, a veteran of the Korean War, will help Annie with the ammo belts feeding the heavy machine gun.

Precisely at 10:00 p.m., the trucks started to come out of the parking area and onto the gravel road. John's voice came on over the headsets everyone was wearing. "This is it, boys and girls. On my command, first team commence firing. Good luck and good shooting." The first truck passed the first ambush point. The second truck came up to the point, and all hell broke loose. Mary Ann shot first and put a round through left front fender into the engine block.

hands with some guy (who later turned out to be her husband), I thought someone hit me square in the face with a baseball bat. The disappointment of that night was so overwhelming that I got sick to my stomach. I couldn't eat or drink or sleep for days. I got drunk every day for at least a week. I ruined my class A uniform. I got back to Fort Bragg with two hours to spare and five dollars to my name. I carried her picture with me for sixteen years. Yes, I am a first-class asshole. It seems every girl who showed me any kind of caring I fantasized about. This self-searching is all about Laura. I know in my heart we will never get married. This is a time of enlightenment for me. The siren song of the Washington DC power structure has gotten to Laura. I believe she will someday be president. I am not the kind of person who is comfortable with politics, politicians, and the facade one has to present to the people who have elected you.

    I feel a great calmness and inner peace settling over me now. The demons of indecision, worry, and fright have left me. It is not so much a formidable task for my people to respond when we have only days or minutes to prepare for a mission. We have chosen our people well. I am proud to say that I have the honor to work with the best patriots in all of America.

the hotel, shaved, showered, and got dressed up in clean clothes. He was to meet Prince Abdul Bin Riyaza at McCarran Airport. He had made arrangements for the bodies of the slain Saudis to be delivered to the Airbus 300 private airliner of Prince Riyaza, including the body of Najib, Prince Abdul's childhood friend.

When the customs agents were done with their part of regulations, only then was John permitted to board the aircraft. Walking onto that plane was like going into a five-star hotel. The prince greeted John in the usual manner then they got on with the business at hand. My prince, I am so sorry it all had to end this way."

"Do not fret, John, it is Allah's doing. The men and my son are with him in his paradise—they will harm no one ever again. My brother, the king, is pleased this did not turn into bad news that could harm relations with our two countries. Inshallah (God willing)."

"My teams were up to their usual professional class, and we also had help from your informant and the CIA."

"John, my brother, I know how well you train your people. The young ladies on your teams show bravery—that is not known in my world. So if you would please give these small tokens of appreciation to the four ladies involved, it would please me greatly." The four leather-bound boxes held identical strings of very expensive pearls strung on very delicate strands of gold cable with a single carat diamond set in the clasp.

"My prince, this is not necessary. My girls get paid very generously for the work they perform. All of them understand the risks they take. And it is all voluntary."

"John, please do this for me. It is a sad and joyous time for me and the mother of Fariq. This small token is her way of thanking the ladies for his early martyrdom to paradise."

John can only think, *These people have an unusual way of thanking someone who may have killed their eldest son. It is what it is, and who am I to judge a way of thinking that goes back thousands of years to the time of Abraham and King Saul?*

On the plane ride back to Pennsylvania from Nevada, John has an epiphany. *For years I carried a torch for Barbara Rozell. Everybody told me it was just puppy love. I never laid a glove on that girl. We went to a million dances and movies. We roller-skated till our feet hurt. The night I came to Wilkes-Barre to see her, and she was sitting on their front porch swing, holding*